MAR 09

Basketball Jones

Basketball ⭐ Jones

E. Lynn Harris

Doubleday

New York London Toronto Sydney Auckland

DD

DOUBLEDAY

Published in the United States by Doubleday,
an imprint of The Doubleday Publishing Group,
a division of Random House, Inc., New York.
www.doubleday.com

DOUBLEDAY and the DD colophon are registered trademarks
of Random House, Inc.

Library of Congress Cataloging-in-Publication Data
Harris, E. Lynn.
    Basketball Jones / E. Lynn Harris. — 1st ed.
        p. cm.
    1. African-American gays—Fiction. 2. African-American
bisexuals—Fiction. 3. Basketball players—Fiction.
4. Basketball stories. I. Title.
PS3558.A64438B37 2009
813'.54—dc22

                                        2008028383

ISBN 978-0-7679-2627-0

PRINTED IN THE UNITED STATES OF AMERICA

10 9 8 7 6 5 4 3 2 1

First Edition

Dedicated to
Friends for life

Anthony Q. Bell
Carlton A. Brown
Kenneth Hatten
Christopher Martin

Thanks for always being there even when you're not

Acknowledgments

Like the words from one of my favorite hymns, I'm truly blessed and duly grateful to publish another novel.

I'm blessed to have a God who provides my every need and stories I can share.

I'm grateful for my family (all of them), especially my mother, Etta W. Harris, my aunt Jessie Phillips, my son, Brandon, and godson, Sean. Also my nieces Bria, Whitney, and Jasmine, and my nephew Bryson for helping me to keep a young spirit.

I'm blessed with wonderful friends. Among them, Vanessa Gilmore, Sean James, Anthony Bell, Carlton Brown, Lencola Sullivan, Cindy and Steven Barnes, Robin Walters, Pamela Fraizer, Derrick and Sonya Gragg, Pam and Donnie Simpson, Sybil Wilkes, Yolanda Sparks, Ken Hatten, Reggie Van Lee, Tony and Brenda Van Putten, Blanche Richardson, Christopher Martin, Proteus Spann, Debra Martin-Chase, Kim and Will Roby, Victoria Christopher Murray, Troy Danato, Kevin Edwards, Tracy and David Huntley, Roy Johnson, Janet Hill, R. M. Johnson, and Dyanna Williams.

I'm grateful for my family at the University of Arkansas-Fayetteville. Especially Jean Nail, David and Jane Gearheart, and the U. of A. Spirit Squads.

I'm blessed with the best publisher and people in the business. They include: Stephen Rubin, Stacy Creamer, Alison Rich, Andrea Dunlop, Meredith McGinnis, Michael Palgon, Bill Thomas, Pauline James, Gerry Triano, Dorothy Boyajy, John Fontana, Christian Nwachukwu Jr., Laura Swerdloff, and Travers Johnson. Special mention to my former editor Janet Hill, who started with me on this novel and is truly missed.

I'm grateful for my necessary support team. Agents, John Hawkins and Moses Cardona. Lawyer, Amy Goldson. Accountants Bob Braunschweig, Barbara Sussman, and Richard Goldenberg. Outside editors Don Weise and Chandra Sparks Taylor, who help me mold the book into shape. My assistants, Celia Anderson and Addis (AJ) Huyler, who try their best to keep my life in order. A special thanks to Trina and Jeff Winn, who are like members of my family.

Finally I'm thankful for bookstores, booksellers, book clubs, my students, radio stations, and all the readers who have supported me with love and prayers my entire career. Thank you from the bottom of my grateful and blessed heart.

Basketball Jones

Prologue

Can you keep a secret? Well, I, Aldridge James Richardson (AJ on the short), can. I've been doing it for so long it's become second nature. I'm not a secretive person either. That came in time. Seven years to be exact. That's how long I've been with Dray Jones. It's for him—for us, really—that I keep all the secrets that allow us to stay a couple. I don't mean ordinary secrets like "Where were you last night?" "Working late," you say, when in reality you're out with the bois. No, I'm talking career-destroying secrets that can make or break a guy and destroy a family. Stuff that, if word got out, your life is basically over—or in my case "our" life would be over, because Dray and I are in this together. Not that we're in any real danger of having our secrets exposed. We're extremely careful to make certain that never happens. Dray knows I love him with all my heart and that I'll keep quiet as long as he needs me to.

But this hasn't been a cakewalk for me. Truth be told, there are times I think I'll burst from holding so much inside. Watching his back and mine is full-time work—a job made no easier by having to keep everything to myself. If there were just one person I could confide in, then some of the weight would be taken off my shoulders. Only I don't dare breathe a word of our business to anyone, not even my best friend or my mother. Instead I spend my life dancing around the truth with the grace of a prima ballerina. The things we do in the name of love!

I don't want to mislead you: I wouldn't have it any other way. I'll do whatever it takes—and have *done* whatever it takes—to be with my first and only true love. That probably sounds romantic and sentimental, like the kind of melodrama that plays out only in tearjerkers. But I really do think of us that way. At the same time, I hope that with all the secrets and the truths not getting told I'm not kidding myself. I sometimes wonder if I've created this romantic image of our relationship to endure the demands our life together requires. It's been so long since we first met that I can't say for sure.

Dray, or Drayton, as his parents named him, wasn't always a big basketball star hiding out from his adoring fans, and I wasn't the boyfriend in the background who pretended to be the star's buddy for their benefit. I fell in love with him in college, back when he didn't have a pot to piss in or a window to throw it out. That's real talk, people. I'd never before been involved with a DLB—otherwise known as a "down low brother"—but knew enough to guess that this probably spelled trouble. At first I wasn't so willing to compromise myself. I've known I was gay my whole life and didn't go out of my way to hide it. That meant I wasn't prepared to help someone else hide his sexuality. But Dray didn't see it like that. He wasn't gay, he assured me. He pointed out the obviously gay men on campus, and would say, "See? That's gay. I'm not like that." Never mind that I was gay and I wasn't like that either. When it came to discussing who or what Dray was, you didn't ask and he didn't tell. In time it made less of a difference to me what he called himself or what people might make of our relationship if they ever found out about it.

We met when I was a senior at Clemson University. I was just a year away from getting my degree in architectural design and Dray was a five-star freshman point guard from Vicksburg, Mississippi, struggling with college algebra. I was hired by the athletic department to tutor him. For a semester our relationship was strictly business. Three nights a week I taught Dray math like he was learning it for the first time. He was an attentive student, but he was more interested in learning what he needed to know about managing his money once he went professional—and there was no doubt in his mind that he would—after a year of college basketball.

Let me say right here that Dray was drop-dead gorgeous. I don't mean run-of-the-mill handsome, but a real knockout for a man. With graham-cracker skin, bow lips, and thick lashes that curled at the ends, he had me ready to lie down at his feet from the word go. The only thing that stood in the way—apart from his being straight and off-limits—was that Dray thought he was slick. He believed there was no one he could not charm or any situation he could not talk himself out of, and at first that ego turned me off. I discovered just how smooth he thought he was when he used a little innocent flirting to try to persuade me to sign in and take a test for him. You know I fought like hell not to fall for his come-on. Although he had no way of knowing it, he had me in his grip so badly that I'd have done backflips over a bed of rocks if he'd asked. But I came to my senses and told him flat-out that there was no way I was going to be part of his scheme, adding that he'd better not try talking some silly girl into taking the test for him, because if he did I'd turn them both in. I took the honor code seriously.

It took my threat to cut through that slick veneer. For the first time, Dray understood that I wasn't just another hustle but someone who took pride in his work. I could see that he was surprised and flattered that his passing the course actually mattered to me. Well, he jumped into his studies with the determination of a star athlete. He not only blocked out time on weekends to devote to algebra, he took the additional step of buying flash cards to improve his retention. He couldn't wait to impress me with the latest lesson he'd learned. Naturally I had no trouble lavishing him with attention, which he ate up as if he'd never been praised for his intellect. This new spirit touched me, and I found it harder than ever not to fall for him. I had a history of falling for straight guys, especially athletes, so I reminded myself that these feelings led nowhere but heartache. Besides, with final exams nearing, it was only a matter of days before my job with him was over and we'd part for good. In the meantime I immersed myself in my own studies to put him out of my head.

As it happened, things weren't that simple. Once classes let out for Christmas break, I flew home to North Carolina to visit my family—and to forget about Dray. I managed to do that for the most part, spending my days shopping with my little sister and enjoying my mother's incredible home cooking. But I couldn't leave him behind entirely. A television character in a syndicated sitcom that ran nightly looked a lot like Dray, and I was reminded of him every time the actor appeared. His character's signature line was "Do yo thang, playa," and each time this was said, he looked into the camera as if speaking directly to me. I grabbed a book and spent the rest of the week avoiding TV during that particular half hour.

My first night back in my studio apartment, there was a knock at the door. The clock said it was half past ten, so I thought it had to be the crabby engineering student next door who sometimes complained when my music was a bit loud. There wasn't any music playing, however, so I couldn't imagine what his problem was this time. I opened the door and, if it had been my own father, I wouldn't have been more surprised. There stood Dray, holding out a slip of paper in one hand and a paper bag in the other. He wore a very sexy gap-toothed grin that practically made me melt right there in the doorway.

Startled to see him so unexpectedly and thrilled to find him at my apartment, I asked with a laugh of disbelief what he was doing there.

He handed me the slip and with a playful slap on my shoulder said, "Take a look, boi." It was his grade card, with a big letter B circled in blue ink.

"Dray, you passed!"

"I didn't just pass, I got a B, dude!" He laughed. "Can you believe it? I've never gotten anything higher than a C in my life, least of all in math. Come on, this calls for a celebration."

"Why do we need to celebrate? You're the one who worked his ass off."

"Because I couldn't have done it without you, dude. But it's not just the grade I'm so excited about. Seriously, if I hadn't passed, I might not be playin' this semester. That would hurt the team and my chances to be a first-round pick for the NBA." As if suddenly remembering he was holding a bag, he said, "Hey, I brought you something." He reached in and pulled out a six-pack of Coronas. "Aren't you going to ask me in?"

I wondered what I might be getting myself into by inviting him in. Was this visit all about college algebra, or had Dray been doing some personal math in his head while I was away? Straight guys don't just show up at a gay man's place late at night with a six-pack of beer. You didn't have to be a genius to know two and two makes four. But that wasn't my only concern. Being conscientious of boundaries, I also asked myself if fraternizing with a student broke any rules set up by the athletic program. Dray wasn't in my charge any longer, so technically we were cool. I thought, "What the fuck," and let him in.

Fast-forward a couple of hours. After Dray's third beer and my second, we stretched out on the Pottery Barn jute rug and fell asleep. Actually, he dropped off first, and I, lulled by the alcohol and the sound of Dray snoring, soon followed. About a half hour later, I opened my eyes and found myself staring into his childlike face. His mouth hung wide open with a tiny trickle of saliva drooling down his chin. Here at last was the slick ballplayer with his guard down. A handsome man-child. But even in that condition—or perhaps because of it—he looked so damned adorable.

I moved in nearer and lay down right beside him, just a breath's distance from his face. I couldn't resist the opportunity to admire his beauty more closely than I'd ever been allowed to see it. I lay there alone in my own private world, watching Dray's peaceful body sleep for the next twenty minutes.

When he woke up, he turned his head toward me. I stared straight into his eyes, not knowing what was about to happen. My heart quickened in anticipation.

"How long have I been asleep?"

"About an hour."

Dray smiled. "And how long have you been staring at me like that?"

I was at a loss but he wasn't waiting for an answer. He slowly reached for my hand as if it were the most natural thing to do and pulled me into him. I curled up beside him, and without another word Dray held my hand tight in his for the rest of the night. Obviously mathematics wasn't the only thing he was struggling with.

At first our relationship was based on the hottest sex of my young life. I mean we put it down! I'd had boyfriends over the years but the guys I met didn't last. When they weren't lying to me, they were coming up short in the bedroom. Not Dray. The boy could pound my ass into next week. In fact he was so skilled in this department that I would have sworn he'd been doing it his whole life. When asked pointedly if he had, Dray confessed to just one—and only one, he emphasized—drunken night with a basketball-playing buddy. Otherwise, he dated girls exclusively. I don't know why this admission comforted me, but knowing that he slept with women somehow put my mind at ease. I guess I felt they were somehow less competition than another guy.

But our sex life was not without its complications. After our first time together, I could see how guilty he felt the moment sex was over. He shut down suddenly, as if someone had thrown a switch. No longer the sweet-talking, smooth-as-silk man between the sheets, he turned dead serious, and in a tone more forceful than the situation called for, Dray made me promise to keep what we'd done a secret. He was especially terrified of his father finding out, believing the family would disown him. I thought this scenario a bit unlikely and said so. How would his father even hear about it, I asked. Rather than reassure him, my comment only inflamed his paranoia. Dray sat straight up and told me in no uncertain terms that if I so much as hinted to anyone that we'd gone to bed, he'd kick my ass. Not exactly my idea of pillow talk, but in that moment I saw that Dray was hurting more deeply than he was letting on. His threat felt overdone, a tough-guy pose meant to frighten me, when in reality the bewildered look on his face was all it would have taken for me to stand by his side. I stroked Dray's arm gently, vowing to keep his secret—now our secret. Nobody would ever find out, I promised, ever. All I asked in return was to continue seeing him.

Visibly relieved, Dray smiled his little-boy smile, then leaned over and kissed me gently on the lips. It was our first kiss. Although he didn't have to say it, I knew he would love me like I'd never been loved before.

The summer after his first year of college, Dray was picked by the Atlanta Hawks in the NBA draft, just as he and his dad had expected. This had been Dray's dream, and I was ecstatic over the news. Of course, I didn't know where the sudden shift left me. Our relationship had blossomed into a deep and loving one, and as much as I couldn't see Dray walking away from it, I couldn't see where I fit into his new life. While there had to be gay ballplayers, none of them were out of the closet. Dray wasn't about to become the first. Between the millions of dollars being thrown at him and the glow of celebrity that would accompany his career, our relationship would be scrutinized like never before. Something was going to have to give, and I feared it was going to be me.

I was therefore bowled over when Dray announced that I was moving to Atlanta with him. I asked how he planned to pull off our relationship right under the noses of the NBA brass, coaches, and agent. Apart from the NBA, I pointed out, there was also the media and all the fans. And let's not even get started with Dray's close-knit Southern family; surely he didn't think he could fool everyone. Dray smiled and told me not to worry. He had it all figured out, he said. I was hardly convinced, but I set aside my reservations. I was so grateful to be joining him after all that I didn't ask questions. Instead I threw my arms around his big shoulders and fought back tears of joy. It looked like the Hawks were getting two for the price of one.

One

Although I have two degrees, including an MBA from Georgia State University, I haven't worked a nine-to-five since I met Dray. When we first moved to Atlanta, I was kept busy furnishing his new condo and my town house, which were about ten minutes apart. Even though we spent a lot of time together, Dray thought it best that we have separate living quarters. I understood that. I even picked up a few clients for interior design work and then pursued my MBA at night but didn't tell Dray about it, because he made it clear he wanted me to be able to travel at a moment's notice to attend his road games.

Being Dray's love at times was like having a full-time job. I was responsible for purchasing most of his NBA wardrobe, which meant his suits, shirts, underwear, and ties. He bought his own jeans and sneakers. I set up his computer and iPod and made sure he had the latest electronic gadget. Life was easy and good. I had season tickets to the Hawks: I didn't miss one home game and attended as many road games as I could get to. I wouldn't call myself a huge basketball fan, but I loved going to the games to see what the wives, girlfriends, and groupies were wearing. At first I was envious that they got to show their love and support publicly, but later I felt sorry for many of them when Dray reminded me how much their husbands and boyfriends cheated on them when away on road games.

The first three years in Atlanta were like heaven.

Then she came along and everything changed.

The straight club scene in Atlanta bored me and the gay one didn't do much for me either. So I didn't mind when Dray went to the clubs and strip bars with his teammates. To me it was part of his job. But when one of his teammates suggested that I might be more than his interior designer/stylist, Dray went on a tear to find women. And trust me, the ladies were waiting.

At first he dated a couple of ghetto-fabulous sisters and some plain ghetto girls but got tired of them easily. I knew there was something different when he told me he'd met this young lady at a club in Miami after a road game there. He talked about how smart and beautiful she was and how much she knew about sports. Judi Ledbetter gave Dray the appearance of a socialite but sounded to me like a shrewd gold digger who gave good head, for a female, that is. I guess everybody is good at something.

I imagined her being like the ladies I sometimes saw in tony restaurants enjoying liquid lunches, and having flings with their well-built trainers. I had no proof this was the case with Judi, but it was my secret wish.

Before I knew it, she was doing some of the things Dray had depended on me to do for him, like buying his clothes, planning his vacations, and advising him on what products he should endorse. The difference between her advice and mine was that she did it with a feminine flair, whereas I always pre-

sented my advice as one of his bois telling him what was cool. I
hadn't grown up in the lifestyle Dray and I were now living, but
I'd done my homework to keep my head above water. I pored
over style magazines like *GQ* and *Esquire*. I watched the Fine
Living channel daily. I was constantly reading *InStyle* and
Architectural Digest. My design background came in handy when
I talked with the builders of Dray's condo about crown mold-
ing, marble, and built-in bookshelves. When he built his first
house it was I who suggested the indoor pool and the basketball
and tennis courts.

As far as I was concerned, nothing seemed to change between Dray and me after he met Judi. I still saw him four to five
times a week. But, unbeknownst to me, Dray had other plans
that would cause things to change a bit. I showed no reaction
when he announced that he was marrying Judi in what was to be
one of the biggest weddings Miami's Star Island had ever seen.
I'd seen it coming and told myself that I'd hold it together when
he broke the news. I wanted to show him I could take care of
myself. Needless to say, I didn't attend. Instead I spent the entire month of June touring Europe on Dray's dime so I didn't
have to endure all the press attention their nuptials captured.

When he bought a mansion in Country Club Hills, my design input went unsolicited. Dray had to know my feelings were
hurt, so he moved me out of my town house into a bigger house
with a pool in Brookhaven and bought me a new Porsche. This
didn't make me feel much better but I took his gifts anyway. If
buying me a house and car made Dray happy, then that made
me happy. Judi was none the wiser. I understood that Dray
needed to be married or have a steady girlfriend to enhance his
career with the Hawks and endorsers like Nike, Sean John, and
Gatorade. I didn't like it but I understood. During his third year

in the league, Dray was right behind Shaq, Kobe, and LeBron when it came to product endorsements. In his fourth year he was still a popular pitch man.

There was also the matter of his family, who had been pressuring him to marry. Dray came from a big family with three brothers and three sisters, who were now living in a slew of mansions Dray had built between Vicksburg and Jackson, Mississippi. His father, Henry, had quit his job as a construction worker and came to almost as many games as I attended, but I was never introduced to him or any of Dray's family. From what Dray told me, they were a close-knit bunch, but very country and conservative when it came to certain things. I translated that to mean that they wouldn't be too happy about our relationship.

My family, on the other hand, was a lot different. I'd been raised by a single mom in the small town of Burlington, North Carolina. My biological father left when I was six years old and I don't remember that much about him. Mama eventually started dating a guy who I called "Mr. Danny." I liked him, but he made Mama cry a lot and disappeared when he got Mama pregnant, and she found out he hadn't divorced his first wife. I loved Mama and would do anything in the world for her, because she made sure we always had food on the table and a roof over our heads.

As Dray made life more and more comfortable for me, I could take care of Mama and my fifteen-year-old sister, the beautiful Bella Lynn. With Dray's money I bought them a house in a nice neighborhood right outside Raleigh and paid the tuition for Bella, who was a budding ballet dancer at the North Carolina School of Ballet. I was already planning a sweet-sixteen party for her, which I hoped would rival some of the parties Bella and I watched on MTV.

My mother didn't know about Dray or where all the money

came from, and just figured I was doing well with my career. I assumed she knew I was gay because Mama never asked me about girls or who I was dating, only stating one day very casually, "I just want you to be happy, baby. With whomever you choose."

★ About three months ago Dray said casually, after an evening of food, wine, and great sex, that I was moving to New Orleans. Just like that. He told me he'd found me a gorgeous two-story town house with a wrought-iron fence and a luscious garden and I was closing on it soon. When I asked why, he told me he asked the Atlanta Hawks for a trade because Judi didn't think pretty white girls were appreciated in Atlanta. She wanted to go to Denver or Los Angeles, but the Hawks got the last laugh by trading him to the New Orleans Hornets. Now Dray was on a team that, after Hurricane Katrina, didn't have a place to call home and spent two seasons in Oklahoma City.

So without further discussion I moved to New Orleans. A couple of days after Dray was traded, two burly Mexican guys showed up at my home to pack my belongings. Things were happening so fast, I almost let the movers pack my personal journals, which I protected like the Kentucky Fried Chicken recipe.

After a week in the New Orleans Ritz-Carlton, I moved into a refurbished town house in the middle of the famed French Quarter, now a resident of the rebuilding Crescent City.

I was getting ready to go out and explore my new neighborhood when the cell phone beeped, indicating I had a text message. It was the phone that only Dray called me on. "Got some free time. C u in 3o."

I took off the jeans and polo shirt I was wearing and jumped in the shower for the second time that day. There were a few things I knew Dray liked without his ever telling me. He was a neat freak and personal hygiene was paramount. Dray always smelled good and kept his nails clipped and manicured. I knew he expected the same from me.

When I wore something he liked seeing me in, Dray would say, "You look nice in those jeans, AJ." I would make a mental note and buy several more.

After I got out of the shower, I covered my body with cocoa butter, then applied capsules of pure vitamin E to the few blemishes on my face. I looked at my abs and realized that they weren't as tight as they had been when I lived in Atlanta and worked out with a trainer four times a week. The one thing that I loved about New Orleans—the food—was already showing up on my lean but muscular five-foot-eight, 162-pound body with a booty like two soccer balls tied together. When I hired an assistant, the first task would be to have him find me a trainer so I could get back to the size I was when I competed in college gymnastics. I really didn't need a full-time assistant, but I'd heard a lot of young black men and kids in general were left unemployed in New Orleans after Katrina, so I made up my mind to hire someone who could help me adjust to the city and run errands for me. This would allow me to volunteer for one of the several organizations trying to bring the city back to its former self. I was really interested in Brad Pitt's Make It Right Foundation, which was building low-cost housing in the historic Ninth Ward.

Instead of putting my jeans back on, I threw on a pair of gray warm-ups that I knew Dray liked (without underwear) and a pink T-shirt. Now, it wasn't like Dray and I made love every time we saw each other; it had been two weeks since we'd put it down. I'd missed his smell and big hands caressing my head and ass.

I was still upstairs in my bedroom looking for a pair of

sneakers when I heard the security bell. I looked at the alarm panel in the bedroom, which told me the back door had been opened. Dray had arrived. And not a moment too soon, I thought, as I quickly removed the greasy vitamin E from my face and replaced it with moisturizer.

★"I needed that." Dray sighed as he playfully pushed me off him.

I caught my breath and said, "You? I needed it more."

For a few moments, we lay in the bed in silence. I always loved these moments when the two of us would lie in bed in absolute solitude.

"What are you going to do with the rest of your day?" Dray asked.

"I'm going to meet a lady who heads up Brad Pitt's foundation here. I think they might be able to use some of my skills with the houses they are building."

"That's cool. AJ, you're a smart man. You'd be a big help to them."

"I hope so."

"So you like this place?" he asked, looking around my master suite.

"It's okay. There are still a few things I need to do."

"Like what?"

"I don't know if I like the color in this room. The yellow might be too pale," I said.

"It's calming," Dray said, snuggling closer to me, his arms tightening around my waist.

I quickly tried to pull back, hoping he hadn't noticed I'd picked up a few pounds.

"Don't do that," I said.

"What? Hold you? Or don't you think I noticed you put on a little weight?" He laughed. "AJ, I notice everything. But it's going to all the right places. And that's real talk, ba-bee."

"I'm going to hire a trainer," I said decisively. Even though we never talked about it, I knew Dray wanted me in top shape. I wanted to be in top shape too. It was one of those funny things about our relationship; we seldom said, "I need you to look good" or even "I love you," which I was sure he told Judi every day. Girls needed to hear that, but I told myself I didn't. All that mattered was that I knew Dray loved me, whether he actually told me or not. I just wish he kissed me more often.

"That's what's up," Dray continued. "I got a cousin who lives down here that used to train me. Mainly we just shot hoops. If you want I'll ask around and find you someone good."

"Don't worry about it, I'll find somebody. I know you're busy getting settled in your new house." Judi sprang to mind and I was hit by a wave of jealousy, but I didn't let Dray know. "How is it coming?"

"It's fine. Judi's like you, she's great at all that shit. When she's finished and goes back to Atlanta to close up the old house, I'll take you out to see the new one," he said. Dray's phone rang and he looked at it, then answered. I was lying so close to him that I knew from the look on his face that it was most likely his wife.

"What's up, babe? You miss me? Of course I miss you, J-Love." He smiled at me and winked, and then I heard him say, "If that's what you want, Judi, then get it. You know I'm not worried about how much it costs. Love you too, J-Love." J-Love? So that's what he called her. Dray may have thought it was cute, but it made me want to throw up.

He clicked off his phone and then looked at me and asked what we were saying before his phone interrupted our conversation.

I felt slighted but didn't want Dray to know, so I replied offhandedly, "I was just saying, you know, I'm here if you need me."

"I know you're here for me always. I 'preciate that, Aldridge Richardson," Dray said.

"I know," I answered softly, suddenly wishing I could hold back my tears and hear that every day of my life.

★ With Dray's birthday less than a week away, I still hadn't bought him anything and knew it was time to get busy. I'd thought that by coming to the Canal Place mall on a late Tuesday afternoon I'd practically have the place to myself. Even though I'd been in New Orleans for only a short time, I knew better than to try this place on weekends. Anyone who says the city won't ever be the same after Katrina hasn't been to Canal Place on Saturday. I made that mistake my first weekend there. It was as jammed as Times Square on New Year's Eve. Still, weekdays also brought their fair share of shoppers, I discovered as I circled the parking garage for a space.

I'd seen an ad for Saks in the Sunday paper mentioning a special line of skin-care products for men that I used on Dray when we lived in Atlanta, and I figured that would be one of the gifts I could get him quickly and get back home in time to catch the Tyra Banks show.

I sometimes wondered what Dray would do if I weren't around—who'd buy him the hippest fashions and all the other odds and ends that kept him looking like a male model. Well, I guess Judi would look after him. She already did, from what I could see from the new shirts he'd been showing up in. More Ralph Lauren Purple Label and less Sean John. They weren't entirely his style and were usually the wrong colors for the time of year, but then I didn't expect she'd ever know him or his clothes the way I did. When I casually commented on the new shirts, Dray became self-conscious and tried to play it down. He told me he'd had them awhile, just hadn't worn them out before. I just smiled to myself and went along.

For a big pro basketball player who towered over any room he walked into, Dray sure could act the part of the little boy when it came to his birthday. I chalked this up to having parents who, despite their meager means, never tired of finding new ways to spoil their children. He loved surprises, loved me coming up with them. Didn't matter what. Dray liked not only expensive items like clothes or the latest gadgets, but silly stuff like the basketball-attired teddy bear I ordered from a company in Vermont. It wasn't about the price tag but the gesture. I will never forget the first time I bought the skin-care products and then set up the bathroom like it was a spa. I led him into the bathroom, sat him down, and gave him his first facial ever. He loved it.

Like most people who soak up attention, he wasn't always big on returning it. I don't mean I ever doubted his feelings for me; just the opposite—I always knew he loved me even if it was seldom expressed in so many words. Apart from the mind-blowing sex, there was Dray's romantic streak, which admittedly leaned toward the obvious and unimaginative, like store-bought flowers once on my birthday.

I have to say there were moments in the beginning where his need to be adored exhausted me. I thought, "Damn, how about throwing a bone my way. Make me feel special for a change." But most of the time I got a charge out of our dynamic. I loved taking care of him. I guess that came from my mom, who loved my sister and me more than anything in the world and made sure we knew it. A lifetime of unconditional love had to have rubbed off. I suppose this helps explain why I put up with Dray in departments that frustrated the hell out of me and would have sent any sane person bouncing out the door.

Opening the heavy double-glass doors of Saks Fifth Avenue, I stepped into the silver light of the fragrance department. The elegant room with its soft music, floor-to-ceiling mirrors, and smartly made-up women and men behind brightly lit sales counters looked like every other fragrance department I'd ever seen, but I felt an immediate sensation of well-being.

I'll admit it: I'm shameless when it comes to grooming. I could spend all day sampling colognes and lotions, testing one after another until the clerk finally would have to ask me to buy something or leave. Fortunately it never came to that. I'd promised myself that for once I wasn't going to get caught up. I was there to shop for Dray, and as soon as I had his gift I was done.

Passing the John Varvatos display of facial scrubs and skin cleansers, I was reminded how much Dray loved the Varvatos shirts I'd given him for Christmas. A tall, slim man wearing wire glasses greeted me as I approached the sales counter. There was no question the guy was gay, but the pink handkerchief tucked into his navy suit pocket was a classy touch that set him apart from the other queens working the floor. I asked to sample the aftershave lotion, which he opened for me. I dabbed a little onto the back of my palm and then lifted my hand to my nose, surprised by the pleasantly clean scent. The clerk insisted I try the matching fragrance. I took another sniff and for a moment was lost in thought at the picture of Dray curling up in bed with me while wearing his new cologne.

"Very nice," I said. "It's for a friend," I added, but wasn't sure why.

"Sure it is." The clerk grinned knowingly, then turned to his left to show me a gift box set that included the complete line of Varvatos skin-care products and scents.

I looked at him and wondered if he was trying to read me and if I was going to have to put him in his place.

Just as he handed me the box for inspection, two well-tailored women appeared directly in front of me on the other side of the counter. One was a blonde in an orange print blouse. She wore her hair up and was talking avidly to a younger woman, who I could tell right away was a less-polished carbon copy. The woman seemed to be listening so intently she might as well have been taking dictation. Right away they reminded me of the wives of ballplayers. In fact I only noticed the pair because the first blonde mentioned the Hornets in a voice so loud you could have heard her across a football field. I was used to that. Ballplayers' wives often dropped their husband's name as if it were a solid gold bar, which for them it almost was.

I was curious to know if she was connected to the Hornets, so I decided to listen to as much of their conversation as possible and bought time with the clerk by asking him to bring me other gift boxes of skin-care products. I handed him back the package, which he set on the glass shelf behind him. I pretended to browse the showcase.

As if on cue, the older blonde summoned the clerk. "Listen," she began in a manner so confrontational I couldn't tell whether she was about to ask a question or pimp-slap him in the face.

"Look, honey, it's my husband's birthday. Now he's not big on this stuff," she said with a sweep of her hand, "but he plays for the Hornets and I'm trying to teach him the importance of proper grooming. What would you suggest?"

The clerk graciously indicated the array of products in front of her, taking care to distinguish one from another. She was only half paying attention, however, as she brought her jeweled cell phone to her ear. As the clerk presented item after item, she kept talking on the phone.

"I won't know until he's home. They're in Philadelphia today, but he'll be back tomorrow. Next week is his birthday and I know he'll want to do something special. I might even have to give him some special sex. He can be such a chore." She shook her head impatiently at the last comment, though it could have just as easily been in response to the products being shown to her.

Then it hit me. I knew who she was. The floor might as well have opened from under me. How did I not put two and two together? Of course, who else could she be but Judi? I stood there dumbfounded, trying to decide my next move. Although there was no way she knew what I looked like—much less that I even existed—standing only a few feet from her so suddenly was like waking up with a cool puddle of water in your bed. Was it better to leave immediately or wait her out calmly and purchase my gift as if everything were normal?

I looked at her from the corner of my eye. She was not what I expected. She wasn't pretty or plain. Like many women she had learned that with money she could create the illusion of some sort of sorority-girl-pretty look with the right makeup or hairstyle. I guess the best way to describe her was as a slightly younger version of the lady who played Edie on *Desperate*

Housewives. Thank God I wasn't competing with the character played by Eva Longoria, although with Tony Parker as the prize I might give it a shot.

Dray had dropped bits and pieces about Judi during pillow talk. I knew that Judi's father was loaded after selling his hedge fund for close to a billion dollars. A divorce from Judi's mother had taken care of half of that and Dray told me Judi's father had cut her off when she started dating Dray. He wasn't crazy about his only daughter shacking up with a black guy and told her she was now on her own. I knew she liked to shop and often left town for shopping sprees.

"How long is this going to take to gift wrap? I need to go to the jewelry counter and look at some rings. Maybe I'll use Drayton's credit card and buy you something, Amber. Just because I'm nice," Judi said, flashing a smile as phony as her hair color.

"And because you got a rich husband," the other woman said.

"So true. How lucky can a girl get? Rich daddy leaves, rich hubby appears magically out of thin air."

"I thought you said you met him at some black club in Miami."

"I did. Where else was I going to meet him, at the country club? I don't think so. Daddy's club was so sixties, Amber."

Finally I couldn't bear the pressure any longer, and as casually as I could, so as not to let Judi know how closely I was studying her, I stepped away from the counter. I made my way slowly for the door with my heart beating faster than my footsteps the whole way.

It looked like Dray would get his favorite skin-care products for his birthday, even though they wouldn't be from me.

Two

One of my three cell phones rang with an Atlanta number I didn't recognize, but I answered it anyway. "Hello."

"What's up, bitch?" It was my good friend Maurice Wells, who lived in Jonesboro, Georgia, but had been raised in Selma, Alabama.

"Mo, what's good, boi?"

"Child, I still can't believe you upped and moved away from me. Now who am I gonna shop and gossip with? You know I don't trust these Atlanta sissies. Can't shit be going on in New Orleans."

"New Orleans is going to be all right," I said, as much to reassure myself as assure Maurice.

"You moved out of here so quick it was like the FBI came and moved you into the witness protection plan. Are you still hanging with old boi?"

"Yeah, we still hanging in there," I said.

Maurice was my closest gay male friend and one of the first people I had met when I'd moved to Atlanta. Still, he didn't know who "old boi" was. Maurice didn't know that Dray was one of the NBA's biggest superstars. It wasn't that I felt I couldn't trust Maurice. It was that I'd given Drayton my word that I would never tell anyone about our relationship.

I did share with Maurice that the man I was seeing was in the public eye, but I led him to believe that he was somebody in the music business. Maurice was always trying to guess Dray's identity and once he almost caught us when he showed up at my house a few minutes before Dray was expected to arrive. I panicked and went off, yelling at Maurice about how dare he come to my house unannounced. Maurice is no shrinking violet, and so he started cussing me back, asking me who in the fuck did I think I was.

Maurice left in a huff and it took several calls and a few gifts before the friendship was back on track. At least I never again had to worry about Maurice dropping in. We both learned our lesson after that incident.

Maurice and I met years ago at a B. Smith seminar at the Ritz-Carlton in Buckhead. He came up to me during the break and acted like he had known me for years. By the end of the seminar he was calling me "girl" and "bitch," two words I don't like, but I quickly realized he meant no harm. It was just the way he used them with his dramatic hand gestures when he talked.

He was also an interior decorator and event planner with a growing business. When I told him I did all my work for charity, he realized I wasn't a threat to him and seemed relieved. I never talked about him to Dray because Dray was always warning me about trusting people, especially gay men. But that didn't stop Maurice from quizzing me for clues about Dray.

There were times when I felt like I could trust Maurice because he shared so much of his personal life with me. He told me that when he was younger he was a crafty bitch with more scams than the Mafia. One day Maurice also told me, "I'd just as soon cut a sissy than speak to him. And I didn't do shit unless it was going to put some money in my purse or benefit me in some way. I leave the charity work for the white ladies."

I wouldn't have ever guessed that he was a recovering crack addict until he told me by saying, "I was the kind of functional drug addict that would wake up some days with my draws under the seat of my car."

"What would you do when that happened?"

"I'd ball them up and put them in the glove compartment of my car and go on to my meeting."

I looked at him to make sure he was serious and then both of us just burst out laughing. I adored him and knew I could trust him with my life. And he knew the same was true of me. With Maurice I could be myself, and felt like I did when I was writing in my journals as a young man trying to make sense of life.

"So did that phantom boyfriend move to New Orleans too?"

"Maybe."

"Are you sure he's not a drug dealer? Maybe he's a member of the Black Mafia."

"I wouldn't date a drug dealer," I snapped.

"So when are you coming back to Atlanta?"

"I don't know. I'm trying to get things settled here."

"Do I need to come down there and see what's up? I bet you could get trade down there for a Popeye's two-piece dinner. Extra spicy, of course." Maurice laughed.

"I'm scared of the bois down here. They are desperate and without much hope. What's going on in Atlanta?"

"Besides trying to run my potential new husband out of town?"

"Who's that?"

"Child, you know who I told you I was going to marry if I could ever meet him."

"I forgot." Maurice had crushes on all types of Atlanta men, popular and not. They always had one thing in common, besides being dark and masculine. They were all straight, or what were known as gay-for-pay guys.

"Mike Vick, bitch. They are trying to run that fine man out of town."

"Yeah, I heard that. Looks like he's in a lot of trouble, but we all know they going after him because he's a big name. I hope that shit's not true," I said. For a second I wondered what would happen to Dray if word ever got out about us but quickly realized that wasn't going to happen, because my lips were sealed and so were Dray's.

"I tell you what, bitch. If he goes to jail then I'm gonna throw a brick through a police station or smack a rich white lady so I can end up in the cell next to him."

"You think he's gonna get any time if he's convicted?"

"Oh, hell yeah. And I know you think I'm playing, but if I have to go to prison to meet Mike Vick, then it's going to be skip to my Lou, my darling. I could also spruce the place up while I'm there like my girl Martha did when she was in the pen. I ain't scared of no jail."

"Did you send me the last of those boxes I left in your garage?" I asked.

"Oh, shit, I knew I'd forgotten something. I'll get them out tomorrow," Maurice said.

"That's cool. It's not stuff I can't live without, just personal papers I like to have close by." Maurice had saved the day by holding on to my belongings that I couldn't risk leaving unat-tended on a moving truck.

"Those boxes heavy as dried-up shit, but I'll get one of my bois to help me take them up to UPS or FedEx," Maurice said.

"Cool, and don't forget to let me know how much it costs."

I looked at the time and realized that it was almost three o'clock. One of the candidates interviewing for the position of my assistant was due any minute, so I told Maurice I needed to run.

"Okay, bitch. Now don't let me have to track your ass down again because it won't be pretty. You hear me?"

"I hear you, Mo. Take care of yourself."

"You do the same thang, baby."

Three

There was a knock at my door and I figured it was my deli order of a bacon, egg, and cheese bagel along with some black coffee. When I opened the door, a humid August breeze slapped my face and there stood a young man with a wide grin. He was wearing a warm-up suit with a gym bag slung over his shoulders, but he didn't seem to have my breakfast.

"What's good?" he asked, walking into my home like the place had his name on the deed.

Stunned, I asked, "May I help you?"

"Are you . . ." He stopped and pulled a piece of paper from his pocket. He looked down at the slip, then up at me. "You Aldridge Richardson?"

"Yeah, that's me, but you still didn't answer my question."

"Cisco is my name. I'm your new trainer. I understand you have your own gym here. Where is it, upstairs?" he asked, looking toward the staircase.

"Who hired you?"

"I do some freelance work for the Saints and I got a call

from somebody in their office telling me that I was your new trainer. Got paid three months in advance and I thought to myself, 'Shit, I love these kinds of gigs.' You know, dealing with big ballers again." Cisco pulled the gym bag off his shoulder and laid it on the table where I kept my mail.

"You sure I'm the right person? I didn't ask anyone to call a trainer," I said, thinking I'd been called a lot of things, but never a big baller.

"This is the address they gave me. I was told to come straight over. Your name is the one I was given, so I guess you're my new client." Cisco smiled.

I hadn't yet had my breakfast so I figured this was as good a time as any to get started.

"Okay. I was waiting for some coffee but that'll have to wait. Would you like some water?" I asked. I figured Dray had tried to be helpful and hired me a trainer. It wasn't unlike him to do things like this without telling me, so I guessed I could trust this guy. I hadn't heard from Dray in about four days but this was typical of the ways he let me know he was thinking about me. He also did stuff like this to show that he was in charge, even though I was three years older.

"You know that caffeine shit ain't any good for you. And thanks, but I carry my own water with me."

I was getting ready to tell him that was cool when there was another knock at the door. Breakfast was here. I pulled a ten-dollar bill out of my wallet, opened the door, and paid a small Asian man the money. He handed me a brown paper bag that was warm from the coffee.

Cisco gave me the disapproving look that trainers seem to wear permanently as I placed the bag on the counter.

"That smells greasy," he said.

"I sure hope it is."

"You gonna eat that?" Cisco asked.

"Sure am."

"You know, you might not want to do that."

"Stop tripping. You don't even know what it is."

"I can smell the coffee and the bagel."

"Okay, let's get this over with," I said, pointing to the stairs. My bagel and coffee would have to wait.

"Lead the way."

When we reached the second floor, I gestured to the room at the end of the hall and told Cisco I would meet him there after I'd changed into some workout clothes.

I went into my dressing area and pulled out some black sweats, along with a white V-neck T-shirt. I put on some white ankle socks and my bright red Converse throwback sneakers. I walked down to the room I'd converted into a gym to find Cisco looking out the window. I noticed he'd removed his jacket. He was built like a football player, muscular and compact at about five-nine. He was wearing a white tank that hugged his upper body like spandex, and some baggy black warm-ups. His hair was done in little twists the length of Cheetos.

He pulled out one of the blue mats lying against the wall, placed it on the floor, and instructed me to lie on my back.

"I'm going to stretch you out real good," Cisco said, with what sounded like a double meaning.

I lay down and Cisco took my right leg and pushed it back into my chest until I grimaced in pain.

"That's you?" he asked.

I nodded my head to let him know he had indeed reached my pain threshold.

"How often do you work out?"

"I used to work out at least four times a week. I've been slacking off since I moved down here."

"Where you moved from?"

"Atlanta."

"You ever play sports?"

"A little tennis, and I used to be a gymnast."

"That's what's up. I can tell you're real limber."

"Not like I used to be."

"What do you do? If you don't mind my asking," Cisco said. He moved behind me, pulling my arms behind my neck.

"I'm an interior designer," I said.

"Must be money in that because this joint is hooked up like a baller's pad. This looks like one of them houses on *MTV Cribs*. You seen that show?" I could feel his warm breath on the back of my neck with each of his words. I wanted to tell him if he thought this was something, he should have seen my house in Atlanta. Now that was something special.

"Yeah, I've seen it once or twice."

After a couple of sets of ab work, we moved to the weights. Within minutes sweat poured into my eyes as I lay on the bench. Cisco gave me a small white towel to dry my face.

As we went from station to station, Cisco was so close to me I noticed the faint smell of his soap-scented deodorant. We finished the workout with Cisco throwing a twelve-pound medicine ball to me over a hundred times. After all that I was so tired I thought I was going to tumble down the stairs. I needed some water and food. I suddenly remembered my cold breakfast bagel and hoped it would be the answer to my hunger.

"You all right with the water?" I asked.

"I'm straight."

While I was removing the cap from the bottle and taking

several swigs, Cisco hit me with a barrage of questions: "You live here by yourself?" "You got a female?" "You think Mike Vick going to jail?"

"What do you think?" I asked, wondering which question he wanted me to answer first.

"About what?"

"Mike Vick. You think he's going to jail?"

"Shit, that would be some foul shit if he did. Kobe didn't do any time. And we talkin' 'bout some dogs. This ain't no white girl shit. Maybe if he had some white girls mud wrestling naked and him pissing on them he might have to give the man some time, but he ain't done no shit like that as far as I know." Cisco took a gulp of water from the clear gallon jug he was carrying with him.

"So what days are we going to work out?" I asked.

"It's on you, playa. Tell me and I'm here."

"I like to start early in the morning. Is that a problem?"

"Like I said, my dude, it's on you. Say the time and I'm here."

"Is this all you do?"

"What do you mean?" he asked, slightly defensively.

"Is training your only job?"

"For right now. I was hoping to get into somebody's training camp before the season starts, but nobody has called yet."

"You play football?"

"I played at Southern down in Baton Rouge. A couple years ago I got invited to the Saints camp, but I got cut right at the end. I thought at least I'd make the practice squad. I played in the Arena League but that shit is lame. You have to play two positions and they don't pay shit. It's like peewee football for grown-ass men."

"What position do you play?"

"Safety. What is your favorite team?"

"The Dolphins," I said.

"What do you think about what they did to Culpepper?"

"I haven't been following them lately. What happened?"

"They waived that mofo's big ass. Most likely he's happy as shit now that he's playing ball in a black town."

"Where is he playing now?"

"Oakland."

"I have to check that out. So let's work out Monday, Tuesday. Take Wednesday off and then pick it back up on Thursday and Friday. How does that sound?"

"I'm down. You want to start at seven? That way you can be my first client and we can just knock that shit out."

"Cool. What's your number?"

"Give me your cell phone and I'll punch it in."

I handed Cisco my phone and he entered his number, then threw the phone back to me. He grabbed his gym bag, gave me some ball-fisted dap, and was out the door.

Interesting guy, I thought, taking note of his round ass poking out from the warm-ups.

Yes, sir, that was definitely the body of a football player—or a male stripper.

Four

I was enjoying the first sip of my café au lait at the popular New Orleans spot Café Du Monde when I heard a woman's voice calling in my direction.

"Are you going to use all that sugar?"

"No, not using it all," I said, passing her the light blue dish that held sugar and several kinds of artificial sweeteners.

"Thank you. I thought this was supposed to be a classy joint, and they can't even put sugar on every table."

I took another sip and nodded politely. I was just getting ready to taste my first bite of my beignet when she called out again.

"Why are you sitting over there by yourself?"

"I'm waiting for someone," I said, hoping this girl wasn't trying to hit on me so early in the morning. I was waiting to interview a candidate for the position of my assistant.

"Why don't I join you before he or she gets here?" she offered. Before I could respond she had picked up her coffee and roll and plopped down in the chair facing me.

I was struck first by her boldness, then by how pretty she

was, with her overdeveloped breasts bursting from her silky tank top. She had a soft face with dark sparkling eyes that radiated warmth and confidence.

"I'm Jade. Jade Galloway," she said, extending her hand.

"Nice to meet you, Jade. I'm Aldridge."

"That's a nice name. You got a last name?"

"Yeah, it's Richardson. Most people call me AJ," I said.

"That goes together and I like AJ," she said, blowing on her coffee with her full lips. I admired the way she was wearing her hair down, with a slight part amid an abundance of wavy black hair that looked part real, part weave. She didn't seem to be wearing any makeup on her smooth, tea-colored face, but she was so pretty it didn't matter.

"I'm glad you approve." I smiled.

"Are you from New Orleans?"

"No, I just moved here."

"Me too," she squealed with delight.

"Where are you from?" I felt obliged to ask out of courtesy. I looked at my watch and realized my appointment was running late. That wasn't a good sign for someone who intended to be my right hand.

"I moved here from Los Angeles, but I'm originally from St. Paul, Minnesota," Jade said.

"There aren't a lot of black people up there."

"You got that right. That's why I hauled ass right after I graduated from high school." She looked me directly in the eyes like she was sizing me up, and I couldn't tell if she was flirting with me.

"Did you go to college in Los Angeles?"

"No, I'm not the college type. I took a few acting classes and gave modeling a try like everyone else there." Jade moved her chair back a few inches from the table and crossed her slender legs. She was wearing a cute plaid, pleated skirt with a slight split that revealed her thigh. I thought to myself, if I was into girls this would be the type for me. She was pretty and I could tell that she had a wicked sense of humor.

"Have you been in any movies, or did you meet anybody famous when you were in Los Angeles?"

"I did a lot of extra work, and once Denzel Washington and his wife came in the restaurant where I was a hostess. I used to see a lot of rappers and hip-hoppers when I went to the clubs."

"I would think Los Angeles would be nice for a pretty girl like you. What brought you to New Orleans?"

"I got bigger fish to fry, and I need to catch my fish before everybody comes back here," she said with a grin.

"I heard that. Sounds like you got a plan."

"Miss Jade's always workin' on a plan."

"You think people will?" I asked.

"Will what?"

"Come back to New Orleans."

"I think so, but not until after the white folks buy all the real estate so they can sell and rent it back to poor black people for more than it's worth."

For someone who had only completed high school, Jade sounded like she had a good head on her shoulders, even if she looked like the sports groupies who hung outside the locker room after games or in hotel lobbies.

"Have you found a job here?" I asked.

"No. You got one for me?" she said, laughing.

"I don't think so." I finally took a bite of my sweet, doughy breakfast treat covered with powdered sugar.

"You found a job yet?"

"Who said I was looking for a job?" I asked.

"If you don't have a job, why are you sitting in this café at ten o'clock in the morning? Are you independently wealthy? That must be nice," she said.

"I don't have it like that," I said, fibbing a bit.

"What do you do?"

I wiped the powdered sugar from my mouth. "I'm an interior designer." The truth was that I was a kept man who did a little charity work on the side, but that would take too much explaining. Besides, I didn't like the term "kept." I knew that I could take care of myself if I had to.

"That sounds like fun."

"I enjoy it," I said.

"Where do you live?"

"I have a place in the Quarter."

"You must be a big baller, staying in the Quarter. I'm living in an SRO hotel but I'm going to get me a place once I get a job and a car."

"You got any leads?"

"Yeah, I do. I'm on my way for a second interview as a cocktail waitress at the casino. I heard that you make good tips and I figure it will do until I get the job I came here for. I got some other skills." Jade smiled mischievously.

"You mind sharing with me?" I smiled back. Right as she was getting ready to respond, my cell phone rang and I asked Jade to excuse me.

"Hello?"

"Mr. Richardson, this is Doyle Johnson. I was going to meet you at ten A.M."

"Yeah, Doyle. I'm waiting for you," I said, looking at my watch. It was now close to 10:30.

"Sorry, but I've been waiting for the bus for over an hour. These assholes haven't showed up yet."

"You don't have a car? What about a cab?"

"I don't have a car and I can't afford a cab even if I could get one to come to my neighborhood."

"Would you like to reschedule?" I asked politely. In my mind I knew that Doyle had just lost his chance to be my assistant, but I didn't want to tell him that now. I really didn't need an assistant anyway, and it would just be another person for Dray to worry about finding out about the two of us.

"Sure."

"Okay, I'll call you when I have some more time. Have a nice day." I clicked off my phone and returned my attention to Jade. "Now where were we?"

"I was going to tell you about the job I really came here to get, and my special skills."

"Oh, yeah. What job and skills?"

"You're going to laugh," Jade warned.

"No, I won't." I pulled a small piece from my beignet and popped it in my mouth.

"You might think I'm crazy," Jade said, looking bashful all of a sudden.

"I promise I won't," I assured her.

"Okay, you have a nice face and I think I can trust you."

I leaned in closer to her and gave her an "Okay, tell me" look.

"Which do you want to know first?"

"Tell me about your special skills."

"Oh, that's easy. I'm psychic, and I'm pretty sure we're meeting for a reason."

"You think so?"

"Yeah, I'm pretty sure I'm gonna have something to do with your love life."

"Who said I have a love life?"

"You do."

"So how are you going to do that?"

"I don't know yet."

"Okay, I can live with that. So tell me about this big job you came here for."

She took a deep breath before releasing her big announcement. "I came here to be Mrs. Reggie Bush."

"You mean the football star?"

"Yep, that would be him."

"Do you know him?"

"Not yet," Jade said, intimating that it was only a matter of time.

"Isn't he dating that Kardashian girl?"

"That big-booty gold digger," Jade said, waving her hand in a dismissive gesture. "Baby, please."

"Do you have a plan?" I asked, intrigued by my new friend. I'd heard of girls moving to a city to meet local celebrities, especially football and basketball players, but I'd never actually met one. Dray called them jock sniffers or cleat chasers.

"I do, but I'm keeping that to myself. Oh, shit," she said, with a glance at the huge clock on the wall. "If I don't leave now, I'm going to be late for my interview." Jade grabbed her fake Louis Vuitton bag, rose from the table, and took a final swig of her coffee.

"You gonna leave me hanging?"

"We'll see each other again," she said, and just like that she darted out of the café and into the steamy New Orleans morning.

.   .   .

★ In spite of the heat, I took a leisurely stroll through the Quarter. By the time I got home, I was soaking wet from the humidity. I cooled down with a shower, and when I got out I could hear one of my cell phones ringing.

"Hello?"

"Hey, baby."

"Mama, where are you calling me from? The number came up as private."

"I'm at the department store. I was looking for a dress for Bella's sweet-sixteen party and I wanted to know if I had a limit," Mama asked. I could tell she was clearly hoping there wasn't one.

"No, you don't have a limit," I said. This was one of the more enjoyable fringe benefits of having a rich boyfriend, being able to take care of my mother and little sister. But even if I didn't have Dray, I still would be able to make a decent living on my own. Thank God for my degrees.

"Okay, because I see this cute black lace dress with a pink underlining and they have them in both Bella's and my size."

"Does she still wear a zero?" I asked playfully.

"Yes, that dancing keeps that girl rail thin."

"I was thinking about surprising her in the next couple of days. They have a little more work to do on my place and so I was thinking about getting out of this hot city."

"It's hot up here in Raleigh too, baby. I think it's hot everywhere."

"Thank God for central air," I said.

"But come on. We'd love to see you and get to hug that neck of yours." Just as I was getting ready to tell her I was coming up soon, the phone that Dray called me on rang.

"Hold on a second, Mama."

"Okay, baby."

I picked up the other phone and clicked it on. "Hello?"

"What's up, AJ?"

"Hey, Dray. What up?"

"Check the flights to Los Angeles and get the first thing you can."

"What?"

"I'm in Los Angeles working a camp with some of the Lakers players. They hooked me up with a nice suite in Beverly Hills." Then, in the low sexy voice he used when he wanted me, Dray said, "It will give me some time to give you da business." I'd not heard from Dray all week and the thought of a few days alone with him got me excited just thinking about it. "Give me da business" was the term Dray used for really putting it down in the bedroom.

"When?"

"Today."

"Oh, I don't know if I can do that," I said.

"Why not?"

"I was thinking about going to see my family."

"You see them all the time. Now do what I said, Mr. Richardson, and get that fine ass of yours on a plane ASAP."

"But, Dray, I also have my second meeting with the foundation this afternoon. They were excited to hear from me and think that I can help them."

"That's all well and good, AJ, but I'm sure you can reschedule the meeting for after you get back. I really need to see you. Don't you know what tomorrow is?"

"What?"

"My birthday, silly. Even though you already gave me one of my birthday presents, I know you got something else cooking."

"You think so?" I asked. I had somehow forgotten tomorrow was his birthday, even though I had spent days buying gifts for him, including the new iPhone I knew he wanted. It wasn't like he couldn't afford one on his own; he just liked it when I bought it for him. It didn't matter that it was his money to start with.

"Okay," I said, feeling I was about to let down my mother and my sister too. "Let me get on the computer and check the airlines." I resigned myself to the fact that I was on my way to Los Angeles, and it really didn't matter to Dray how much I wanted to see my family.

"Call me before you take off."

"Will do."

I clicked off the phone and put the other one with my mother to my ear.

"Sorry, Mama."

"Is everything all right?"

"Sure. But it looks like I won't be able to make it this weekend."

"Why?" she asked, the disappointment clear in her voice.

"One of my clients needs me to fly to Los Angeles to check on some furniture. Duty calls," I said, hating that I was lying to my mother.

"Well, maybe next week. I'll tape Bella's performance. AJ, Bella is really getting good with this dancing. She is thinking about running in that teen pageant, and if she does you can't miss that," Mama said. "She'll never forgive you if you don't show up for that."

"I will. Got to run, Mama. I love you."

"Love you too, baby. Don't work too hard."

Five

A little after two A.M. I arrived at LAX. I hadn't checked my luggage, so I went straight to the limo section and saw a big, buff blond guy with sunglasses holding up a sign with my last name on it. When I walked up to him and told him I was Mr. Richardson, he looked startled. As if he doubted I was his real passenger, he asked me where I was going.

"To the Peninsula Hotel in Beverly Hills," I said with irritation.

"Then you got the right guy," he answered, sounding slightly friendlier than before.

I could tell he was the talkative type, so when we got into the car I wanted to say I was tired and didn't feel like talking. He could go back to being his snotty self. But I didn't.

"Where you from?"

"North Carolina."

"Is that where you came from today?"

"No," I said, hoping he would get the clue from my short answers.

"Where did you start your day?"

"New Orleans."

"How is it there now?"

"Better."

"Do you think it will ever be the same?"

"I hope so."

"How long have you lived there?"

"Not long."

"Do you come to Los Angeles much?"

"No."

"You here on business or pleasure?"

"Both."

"The hotel you're staying at is real nice. A lot of celebrities and ball players stay there. Do you play ball?"

"No," I answered. I wanted to respond, Do I look like a ball player at five-foot-eight?

"What type of business you in?"

"Interior design."

"Okay. I'll let you rest. You must be tired."

Finally, I thought, as I repositioned myself in the back of the limo. Just as I got comfortable and was about to kick off my shoes, I heard his voice again.

"Well, here we are. I'm going to give you my card in case you need a driver while you're out here. Do you need help with your luggage?"

"Thanks, but I don't have much. Just one bag. I can make it."

"I guess you won't be out here long."

"No, not long," I said, stepping out into the cool morning air. Thank God it wasn't as hot as it had been in New Orleans.

The opulent hotel lobby was empty and quiet. I walked up to

the marble front desk where the night clerk looked busy on the computer.

"Excuse me," I said.

"Yes, sir, how can I help you?" She smiled.

"Are you holding a key for an Aldridge Richardson?"

"Let me check."

After a few minutes she said, "Yes, here we go. Your party is in villa eight. All you need to do is go out the double doors around the corner. There will be signs. Do you need help with your luggage?"

"No, thanks, I'm fine."

She handed me the pass key and I nodded thank you.

I walked around the corner and through the double doors and followed the sign that led to villas 7 to 12. I got excited at the thought of sleeping next to Dray. We didn't get many chances to do that since he'd gotten married. When I reached number 8 I slowly climbed the stairs and opened the door.

The living room was decorated with traditional furnishing and a fireplace was roaring while soft music played, but there was no sign of Dray. I noticed a half-finished bottle of champagne and some chocolate-covered strawberries on the bar. I walked over and saw a "welcome to the hotel" note addressed to Dray and poured myself some champagne. It was sweet and not flat, leading me to guess it hadn't been open long.

I grabbed my products bag from my suitcase, went into the bathroom, and brushed my teeth and took off my clothes, leaving my T-shirt and underwear on the floor. Then I walked into the large master bedroom. There I found Dray sprawled out on the bed, his back turned toward me. He was sound asleep. I crawled into the king-sized bed as quietly as I could and began to look for the remote so that I could turn off the television.

Just as I settled into my spot in bed, I felt Dray's huge hands wrap around my waist and pull me close to him in the spoon position. Since he wasn't usually a cuddler, I was going to enjoy this.

"You made it," he said, kissing me on my ears and neck. Dray wasn't wearing underwear and the warmth of his body soothed me. "I'm so glad you're here, AJ. You're not mad at me, are you?"

"For what?" I asked.

"Making you cancel your meeting and your trip to see your family."

"No, I'm cool. I called the foundation and they said I could come in when I get back. I'll see Mama and Bella another weekend."

"Cool, boi."

"Oh, I forgot. Happy birthday, Dray."

He looked at the clock and then back at me and said, "Yeah, it is my birthday. Where are my gifts?" He smiled expectantly.

"Why don't we wait until tomorrow?"

"That's cool. I already know I'm getting an iPhone."

"You do? How do you know that?"

"Because I know you and I know you know I love gadgets."

"Maybe your wife will get you one," I said, half teasingly.

"No, she already gave me my gifts before I came out here. She bought me a watch, some shirts, and that skin-care stuff you give me facials with."

I'd debated whether to tell Dray I'd run into Judi. I didn't want to trip him out but at the same time I wanted him to know. Since he brought it up, I went ahead.

"I know," I said quietly.

"How do you know that?"

"I saw her buy it."

"You did?" Suddenly he was wide awake.

"Yeah, she was with some other lady and I was in the store getting ready to buy you that skin-care package. But Judi beat me to the punch. I felt kinda silly."

"Why, baby boi?"

"I don't know. I just did. But don't worry. I didn't say anything to her and avoided eye contact."

"AJ, you could have gotten it for me and just kept it at your house. Do you think she saw you?"

"She didn't even look in my direction."

"I'm surprised she didn't remember you from the party," Dray said.

"What party?"

"Remember the one the Hawks owner gave and you came? She was there. I know you saw her."

"Oh yeah, but remember you didn't introduce us," I teased.

"I didn't think you wanted to meet her."

"That was cool. So how was camp today?"

"It was cool, but they are working my ass off. Still need to get that free-throw mojo working again."

"It will happen, babe. You'll get it back," I said, stroking his chest.

"You ready for da business?"

"Yes, babe."

"So when do I get my birthday kiss?"

"Now, and as many as you want." I kissed Dray deeply and he held me tightly. This was going to be a great couple of days, I thought, suddenly very happy Dray had made me cancel my trip home.

Then he nudged his head into my neck and the next thing I heard was Dray's snoring. Da business would have to wait for another night.

★ When I woke up, Dray had already left for camp. There was a note in the bathroom telling me he'd be back around six and to get ready for a special night. In anticipation I did the Hollywood wives thing, big time.

The weather in Beverly Hills was magazine-cover perfect, with a warm breeze. I had breakfast on the terrace by the pool and was going to call the chatty limo driver to take me shopping, but the hotel concierge offered me their driver. I was taken to Rodeo Drive, where I went into several trendy shops, including my favorite, Gucci. After a couple of hours, I purchased a pair of sheer black briefs with a matching undershirt that I knew would blow some blood to Dray's dick later that evening. I bought Dray five Italian shirts we couldn't get in New Orleans and a couple of knit shirts to wear with jeans. I even found a couple of pairs of size-thirteen sneakers I knew he didn't own. I loved buying clothes for him, even though technically I was spending his money. It made me feel even closer to him.

After a late lunch with two glasses of wine at a steakhouse on Robertson Boulevard, I called the driver to come and take me back to the hotel. I had to get ready for my special evening with Dray.

When I got back to the hotel, the bellman took my shopping bags and promised to send them to the villa. I walked through the lobby empty-handed, noticing several women, both black and white, enjoying high tea in front of a huge fireplace.

I reached the villa and was a little surprised to find the DO

NOT DISTURB light on, but figured it was a mistake. I placed my key in the slot but instead of the green light going off, a faint yellow light in the middle flashed. I double-checked to make sure that I was at villa 8 and then I tried it again, but got the same result.

Maybe one of my credit cards had demagnetized the card key when I put it in my wallet. I went back to the lobby to get another key.

A petite desk clerk with brunette hair wound into a tight bun smiled from behind the front desk.

"Something is wrong with my key," I said, handing her the card.

"Sorry about that, sir. What's your room number?"

"I'm in villa eight."

"May I see some form of identification?"

"Sure." I pulled out my driver's license.

She looked at it and then punched in a few keys on her computer. Something was wrong. She looked puzzled and said, "Sorry, sir, but are you sure you're in villa eight?"

"Yes, I am sure," I answered with confidence.

"Then there must be some mistake. This villa is in the name of Mr. and Mrs. Drayton Jones. I know that's right—I checked in Mr. Jones yesterday and gave a key to his wife a few hours ago. I remember him because he was so tall."

"His wife? Are you sure?"

"Absolutely. We chatted about the huge pink diamond she was wearing. She told me it was a gift from her husband and that they were out here celebrating some big news and her husband's birthday. She was so happy and excited."

I was at a loss for words and for a moment just stood there in silence. At first I was embarrassed. I must have looked like a fool trying to get in a room I obviously now didn't belong in. Then I got mad wondering what Judi's ass was doing out here. How could Dray do this to me?

Did he know about this? And if so, what kind of sick game was he playing with me? I was beginning to wonder just how long I could play this secret-lover bullshit now that Judi was in the picture. It was okay when I was the only one and we were just keeping our secret from his teammates.

Just as I was about to ask if there were any vacancies, I noticed the bellman out of the side of my eye. He had placed my packages on a cart and was getting ready to take them to the villa.

"Excuse me. Are those going to villa eight?"

He looked at the claim tags and said, "Yes, sir. These are for Mr. Richardson."

"I'm Mr. Richardson. I might be changing rooms. Can you just hold them for a second?"

"Yes, sir."

I asked the desk clerk for a new room, but after tapping on her computer for what seemed like an eternity, she looked up and said flatly, "I'm sorry, Mr. Richardson, but we're completely sold out."

"Are you serious?"

"Yes, sir. We are completely full. If you like I can check some other hotels. The Beverly Hilton right nearby might have rooms available. Would you like me to check?"

I wanted to strangle Dray for sticking me in this mess. Here I was, miles from home, looking like a country fool.

"Give me a few minutes." I went into the dimly lit bar off the lobby and pulled out my phone. I didn't have any new messages. Dray hadn't called so I dialed his number. It went straight to voice mail, which meant he was either on the line or it was shut off. I bet he had shut it off the minute Judi arrived. So I sent him a text, telling him to call me immediately. I sat down at the bar and ordered a club soda while I waited.

Thirty minutes later, only my thirst had been quenched, so I called again. No answer. I sent another text. Minutes passed and still nothing. What was I going to do? Heading to the villa wasn't an option. Making a scene wasn't the way I rolled and Dray knew that. I would never serve up a confrontation in front of his wife. I didn't ever let on when I was jealous of Judi. I knew I couldn't beat her if I did the same dumb things Dray told me Judi sometimes did to get his attention, like crying or throwing a tactless tantrum.

The bartender approached. "Would you like another club soda or maybe something stronger? You look stressed."

"What?" I was so lost in my thoughts I hadn't noticed him.

"Would you like another drink?"

"No, I'm fine."

"Okay, just let me know."

"I will. Thanks."

I sat there feeling completely alone, knowing no one and not having a clue what to do next. What had Dray done with the few items of clothing I'd brought for the trip? Would I wait for Dray's call or just take my ass back to New Orleans?

Just as I walked out of the bar, my cell phone rang. Maybe this was Dray and if it was, I was ready to let him have it.

"Hello," I said, more as a challenge than a greeting.

"Dude, I'm sorry 'bout this. I had no idea she was coming," Dray whispered in a low and serious voice.

"What the fuck is going on?"

"It ain't happening. You need to go back to New Orleans."

"What?" I yelled. An elderly white couple turned in my

direction, but I didn't give a damn who heard me. "Like that I'm supposed to turn around and leave just because your wife shows up?"

"Look, AJ, stop trippin' and do like I said. I'll make this up to you. I gotta run. She's just turned off the shower."

Click.

What the fuck?

Three hours later I boarded a flight to New Orleans, having cleared standby with a coach seat at the last minute. No first-class ticket and no magical night with Dray. I was pissed as fuck and was going to let Dray know when I saw him next.

The plane was packed with passengers, including what looked like fifty high school cheerleaders returning from some sort of competition. When I finally reached my row toward the back of the plane, I realized I had a middle seat. Sitting by the window was a young black guy shaking his head with an iPod in his hand. He didn't pay any attention as I sat down.

Just as the plane was beginning to taxi, a white girl who sorta favored Dray's wife sat down right next to me. She smiled with teeth so white she could have lit up a lighthouse. After she had placed her bags in the overhead compartment and under the seat, she let out a loud sigh. "Looks like we got a full flight."

I didn't respond.

"So how was your day?" she asked with the concern of a for-mer high school cheerleader.

Wrong question, lady.

"Bitch, don't ask me shit," I snapped, and I placed the airline-issued earphones into my ears, slipped on my dark shades, and closed my eyes.

Six

Sometimes I don't know if I chose the life I lead or if it chose me. No, I don't mean the age-old question about whether or not one picks one's sexual orientation (I know I was born this way), because I've always been comfortable with the skin I'm in. I'm talking about the situation I'm in with Dray. Why couldn't I have picked someone who wanted only to be with me? Why didn't I meet a man who was man enough to admit who he really was? Could I really be ashamed of being gay but telling myself otherwise?

Thoughts like these have been running through my head lately. I've been back in New Orleans four days and still no word from Dray. Nothing. No calls, texts, or e-mails. When he doesn't reach out to me like this, I don't stalk him down, no matter how mad he makes me. Besides knowing that I'll keep my word about maintaining our secrecy, he needs to know he's not the center of my world. I'm so used to my situation that I can't get mad anymore. If I really didn't like it, I would do something about it. But here's what I do like: a healthy bank account and a partner who can lay the pipe down. Now that's real talk. Who was I kidding? I would be with Dray if he drove a bus or collected trash. I loved this man and it was going to take more than a wife for me to give him up completely.

At times like this, I wish that Dray and I were still back in college when we could be together whenever we wanted. I longed for the days when I had the upper hand and Dray needed me more than I needed him. Back then the two of us didn't have two nickels to rub together, but we were happy. At least I thought we were.

Dray used to tell me all the time about the wonderful places we would live and the cities we would visit once he made it to the pros, but I didn't really believe him. I figured the moment he got that first check from his agent it would be "See you, Aldridge." But I kept my word and never said anything about our relationship to anyone. Dray greatly valued that I was so loyal to him and so he kept his promises—at least he did back then.

Tomorrow I have my second workout with Cisco and I'm looking forward to it. Anything to get my mind off Dray. I've been lazy the last couple of days, feeling sorry for myself and eating a lot of comfort food like fried chicken and pasta.

But I've got to get over myself quickly. Who is going to feel sorry for me if I've got a fat ass? I know the difference between *phat* and *fat*.

★ "Come on, Aldridge, you can do this," Cisco said, pushing me to complete the last set of arm curls. I was sweating like a fat man in a plastic suit.

"How many more?" I asked, almost breathless.

"Last five. Come on. Five . . . four . . . three . . . two . . .

one. Okay, I'll take it," Cisco said, taking the fifteen-pound
weights from my hands. "Good job."

"Man, you trying to kill me." I looked around the room for
the bottle of water.

"Just doing my job." Cisco smiled.

I located the tall bottle and drank until it was empty. The
flat-screen television hanging from the wall showed Michael
Vick dressed in a nice blue suit entering a courtroom surrounded by reporters.

"I think he's going to jail." When I lived in Atlanta, what a
big fan I was of that handsome quarterback until I met Warrick
Dunn, another Falcons player who was really doing something
in the community. Every year Warrick built brand-new homes
for single moms in the Atlanta area. I was so impressed with his
charity that I called his foundation and offered my services
gratis. I'm sure Vick had a foundation as well, even though I'd
never heard of it. After some persuading I had convinced Dray
to start two foundations, one to give back to the community he
played for and the other in his hometown in Mississippi. It
didn't take much to make Dray realize the importance of a positive community image for a highly paid athlete, especially one
with a secret boyfriend on the side.

"Who, Vick? They gonna make an example out of that idiot," Cisco said.

"I heard he's got a great lawyer."

"Ain't gonna make a bit of difference 'cause when the man
wants to get a brotha, they get it done."

"You think he'll play again?" I asked as I positioned myself
on the mat to begin a series of situps.

"Yeah, he'll play, but I bet it won't be for the Falcons.

They're going to drop his ass. I can't believe he messed up his chance to be the shit of the league over some fucking pit bulls," Cisco said as we finished the set.

"Are you going to try out again for the NFL?"

"It ain't up to me, because if it was, I sure as hell wouldn't have my ass back in this shit of a city trying to get a steady gig," Cisco said with disgust. He pulled a plastic water bottle from his green gym bag.

"I thought you liked New Orleans."

"What's to like? I was born here. I just knew playing football was going to be my way out of this mutherfucker. Niggas like me would do anything to play in the league and the ones who have the chance to play are fuckin' it up for everybody else. If they would let me in the league I'd be a model citizen. They would never have to worry 'bout me doing some dumb shit."

"Where would you want to live?"

"Miami or the ATL."

"Atlanta's nice," I said.

"Is that where you were raised?"

"No, I grew up in North Carolina."

"What was that like?"

"It was cool," I said. I heard one of my cell phones on the table ring. I looked at the screen and saw that it was Dray calling. I didn't answer because I was still pissed off at what had happened in Los Angeles. Now that he'd finally decided to call, he'd have to wait for me to get back to him.

"Are there a lot of black folks in North Carolina?"

"Some," I said. Then I heard my other cell phone ring. I looked down and there was Dray's name flashing on the screen. I guess he must be missing me bad right about now. I wasn't going to play it slow and easy.

"Looks like someone is really trying to reach you," he said, nodding to the phone.

"Just a friend."

"Well, AJ, I'm gonna bounce. You did well today. We'll step it up a little bit tomorrow."

"We working out tomorrow?"

"Yeah, like you said, two days on, take off a day to let your body heal, and then we hit two days in a row. That's the schedule I try to keep all my clients on."

"Cool. I'll see you tomorrow," I said as I gave Cisco some dap and watched him walk out of the room to the sound of my phone ringing again.

It felt good to be needed.

A flash of lightning and a clap of thunder that sounded like a slap against naked skin woke me early the next morning. I sat up in bed, allowing my eyes to adjust to the darkness, when I heard a voice.

"Do I have to come all the way over here to talk to you? So why haven't you returned my calls, Aldridge?" Dray was standing a few feet from my bed, removing his V-neck T-shirt. His presence damn near gave me a heart attack. He caught me completely off guard, so much so that for a second I forgot how angry at him I was.

"I got the messages too late," I lied. "I was going to call you first thing in the morning."

"Did you miss me?" He sat on the edge of my bed and removed his sneakers and socks. Then he stood up and dropped his warm-ups to the floor. Down came his boxers, which he kicked across the room.

"Of course I missed you." The rage I felt in the Los Angeles hotel suddenly felt like a lifetime ago.

"I'm sorry about spoiling our trip, AJ. I really am. I didn't know she was coming. I had no idea Judi was going to show up. I wanted to spend my birthday with you."

"I know."

"So you forgive me?"

"You know I do."

Dray walked over to my music system and turned on the iPod. Suddenly Ne-Yo's voice filled the bedroom. Dray was breathtaking to look at walking around the room, nude with his ten and a half inches of Mississippi pride dangling. I couldn't take my eyes off his muscled thighs, narrow hips, and plump, muscular ass.

He crawled into the bed and began kissing me. Dray's kisses were sometimes so deep it felt like he was plowing into me. I remember when we first started messing around he wouldn't kiss my lips, only my forehead and sometimes my neck. Boy, how things had changed. He climbed on top of me and began to grind his pelvis against mine. The pleasure I felt from his kissing only intensified.

As Dray removed my underwear, I noticed a dreamy smile softening his face.

"I want you so bad, boi. You know that?"

"I want you too."

"Show me."

"How?"

"You know what I like."

"You like my sex, huh."

"That's not all I like."

"Really? What else do you like about me?"

"That you're handsome. Smart. And I know you really care about me," Dray said as I stared into his soulful eyes.

"How much do you care about me?"

"Come on, AJ, you know how I feel about you."

"Tell me."

Dray looked away for a moment and then smiled at me and said, "I love you, boi."

"You really mean that?"

"You know I do. I don't know how I could make it without you."

"You'd survive," I said.

"Barely. But why are we talking about serious shit? I thought I was handling da business," Dray said as he got back on top of me.

I playfully pushed him off me, and reversed positions so that I was now on top of him, kissing his chest. I moved my tongue down his body until I reached his groin area and then buried my face into his lap, taking in every inch of Dray's Mississippi pride.

★ When I woke up later that morning, a huge smile crossed my face. Dray was still lying in my bed, staring at me and gently rubbing his huge hands across my forehead. I had just assumed he would go home after I went to sleep. I needed to call Cisco and change my training session.

"So sleepyhead finally wakes up," Dray said.

"What are you doing here?" I said, sitting up in the bed.

"What, you expecting your other boyfriend?" Dray teased.

"Now, you know he comes during the day when we know you're at practice."

"Just don't let me catch you with that nigga."

"Who said he was black?" I said as I got ready to leave the bed, only to be pulled back by Dray grabbing the bottom of my white T-shirt.

"Come on, Dray, let me go. I got to pee," I pleaded.

"Not until you give me a kiss."

I turned around and quickly gave him a peck on the lips and then raced to the bathroom. I tried to call Cisco but got his voice mail, so I left a message. When I came back some ten minutes later, after making sure I'd brushed and flossed my teeth, combed my hair, washed my face, and moisturized my body, Dray wasn't there. I called out his name but he didn't answer. I went down the stairs and when I got halfway down I could smell food. Wonderful food.

I walked into the kitchen and there was Dray in his boxers and T-shirt, managing three different pots and pans on the stove top.

"I hope you're hungry, baby, because I sure am."

"What are you doing?"

"What does it look like I'm doing? I'm cooking us breakfast."

"Don't you have to get to practice? Or go home? Is Judi going to be looking for you?"

"I got that covered, babe. No practice this morning and Judi is down in Miami doing some furniture shopping. You got me all day."

"When is the last time you cooked for me?" I asked. It had been so long that I'd forgotten what a great cook he was. When we started dating in college, he used to make hamburgers and homemade potato chips and then pour blue cheese over them. I loved the fattening snack. I thought for a quick moment about

Judi being down in Miami spending Dray's money, but I wasn't
going to let something I couldn't control ruin my day.

"It's been a while. That's why I'm making your breakfast favorites." Gesturing from one pan to the next, he said, "We got
scrambled eggs with onions and cheddar cheese, grits, honey-
glazed bacon, and some store-bought biscuits. It looks like
you're out of blueberry jam but I found some strawberry."

"It smells great."

"What would you like to drink?"

"Some coffee."

"That's not good for you, baby. How about some cranberry
juice?"

"So I can't have coffee?"

"Cranberry juice."

"Why?"

"Because it's better for you."

"So you know what's best for me," I teased.

"I think I do. Hey, I been thinking that maybe we ought to
change our password," Dray said.

"Why?" Ever since Dray had gotten married, we had a password that only the two of us knew. If I got a text or e-mail that
seemed strange or didn't sound like Dray, I would ask for the
password, and he did the same with me. We changed them
every now and then so as not to get caught with some of the sexy
messages we sometimes left for each other.

"Just makes sense. I know women and I know Judi. She
usually does her best snooping when she's been away. I erase
all my texts and e-mails but you never know. I still have two cell
phones she doesn't know about."

Our current password, which we've had since we've been
together, is "speed bike." Dray thought of it when he came up

with the bright idea in Atlanta to buy us matching speed bikes that we kept at my house. Now it would be my time to come up with a new password.

"So what's it going to be?" Dray asked.

I thought for a minute and then said, "Basketball Jones."

"I like that. What does it mean?"

"Basketball Jones . . . I got a basketball jones for you," I sang.

"So you got love for me . . . huh?"

"Yeah, I got a jones for you, Mr. Drayton Jones. I love you."

"That's what's up, AJ," Dray said, placing a spoonful of fluffy yellow eggs onto my plate.

Seven

A couple of days after Dray's homecoming, I walked into Café Du Monde for a cup of my favorite caffeine. It seemed like everybody who lived in New Orleans came here, along with crowds of tourists, so the place was always packed, especially early in the morning when the house specialties, beignets and chicory coffee, were served.

I paid for my coffee and decided it was cool enough outside to sit on one of the benches across the street at Jackson Square. Just as I reached to open the door, someone called out, "Where are you going? I've been looking for you."

I turned around and there at a corner table was Jade, waving and motioning for me to join her. She was dressed nicely in a crisp white shirt and a black pencil skirt, and her hair was pulled back in a ponytail.

"Jade, how are you doing?"

"Doing well. Why don't you cop a squat?"

"Okay, I think I will. I was going to sit in the park," I said as I took a seat.

"Too many crazies over there for me. You know what I'm

saying? Where have you been? I've been coming in here every day hoping I'd run into you."

"I had to go out of town. How have you been?" I asked, thinking if she was so psychic, Jade should have known that.

"Did you go someplace exciting?"

"I went to your old stomping grounds, Los Angeles, even though I was staying in Beverly Hills."

"I bet you stayed at the Peninsula."

"How did you know that?" I asked, slightly alarmed.

"It's the best hotel in the city. I used to work there part-time in their spa. And you know I'm psychic."

"It is a nice hotel."

"How is that bitch of a city doing?"

I took a long sip of coffee. "I wasn't there long. How is the job search going?"

"Oh, I got the job as a cocktail waitress, but I didn't get any of the evening shifts yet. I'm making decent tips at least."

"How about that other job?" I teased.

"You mean giving facials and massages?"

"No, the one you came here for." I smiled.

She smiled back. "I haven't met my potential husband. I heard they're not even in New Orleans right now. They're in some place called training camp and won't be here until the end of August. But I can wait," she said with a wink.

"Does Reggie Bush live in New Orleans?"

"I don't know. But I'll find out. I plan to FedEx one of my pictures to him at the Saints office. I know it's not a fresh idea, but it's a start and will get the ball rolling. If that doesn't do the trick, I'll find out the name of the club where the players hang. I might have to go out with one of his teammates first, but trust me when I tell you I will meet him, you know what I'm saying?"

she said, raising her cup. "But in the meantime I need to make some money so I can get the right outfit. That way I'm ready to dress like money when that time comes. Real ballers aren't attracted to broke bitches. And I'm not attracted to broke brothas with good dick."

"You strike me as the kind of young lady who gets what she wants," I said, grinning.

Jade smiled back and took a sip of her coffee and then had a surprise question for me.

"So who are you dating?"

"I don't talk about my personal life," I said a little too fast.

"Oh, baby, I heard that. But you're gay, aren't you?"

I didn't mind answering that question. Plus I didn't want any advances from Jade in case she didn't land Reggie, so I nodded and smiled.

"I knew that, and believe me, Aldridge, it doesn't matter to me what box you check. But I appreciate your being so honest with me. You hear what I'm saying? I meet a lot of these down-low brothers and they make me sick with their lying asses."

"I hear you."

"Just tell me what side you butter your toast on so neither of us wastes any time." She leaned in and said, "Don't mean we can't still be friends, right? You never have enough friends, especially when we both new to the city. But you a nice-lookin' man so you probably got a lot of boyfriends or whatever you call them. I had lots of gay friends when I lived in Los Angeles. I used to have coffee with some of them every morning at the Starbucks in West Hollywood."

"I'm very happy," I said. An image of Dray lying in bed popped into my mind.

Jade pulled her cell phone from her purse to check the time

and practically jumped up. "I gotta run. I'm meeting somebody about some big money." She finished off the last of her coffee and folded her newspaper, then stuck it in her bag.

Before she put her cell phone in the bag she handed it to me and told me to punch my number in. I did and gave it back.

"Now give me your phone so I can put my number in it. Maybe we can meet for lunch or dinner sometime soon. That way I can keep you posted on my job search and you can make up lies about who you dating and who you not. But I bet you are like me and like jocks."

"You might be psychic, but I know you're crazy, Jade," I said, laughing. I pressed my number into her cell. I was growing fond of her. She was almost the only friend I had in town.

"That's why I like you. It didn't take you long to figure that out." Jade threw me an air kiss and headed out the door.

Later that evening I was in my office looking over sketches for some designs I wanted to show the people at Brad Pitt's organization, when my phone rang. It was Jade. She was crying and asked me if I could meet her at the bar at the Ritz-Carlton, which was one of the hotels that was running full tilt. I'd been to the hotel a couple of times since it was only about three blocks from my house.

When I walked into the bar, I saw Jade nursing a glass of white wine.

"Jade, is everything okay?" I asked.

"Thanks for coming."

"No problem. Are you okay?"

She gave me a peck on the cheek and said, "I'm okay, AJ. I just needed someone to talk to. I had a date with this guy who stood me up. I guess dudes down here are just like they are in Los Angeles. Plus my landlord is on me for my rent, and not without letting me know that if I give him a little pussy we could work things out."

"Are you serious?" I hoped Jade didn't call me down to borrow some money. I didn't know her well enough to be writing checks for her rent.

"Should I report his ass or just look for another place to stay?"

"You need some money for a deposit if you move," I said. The bartender came over to us and asked me if I wanted something to drink. I ordered a glass of merlot.

Jade continued to tell me how tough it was being single and low on money and how something was going to have to give. She looked so vulnerable at that moment that she reminded me a little of my sister, Bella, only grown up. I told her everything was going to be all right, but wasn't really sure that it would. After all, I hardly knew Jade.

When the bartender brought back my glass of wine my phone buzzed, telling me I had a text. I looked at it and realized it was from Dray. "Who is that girl with you?" I looked up and noticed the restaurant connected to the bar. Dray was facing me with a frown. There was Judi sitting with her back to me, and I wondered if she knew her husband was texting me. I texted him back and told him Jade was just a friend. He texted back, "Make sure you're telling the truth. Also cut your little date short. We just finished our salads and I don't want to chance us coming face to face with you."

I texted back a simple "K" and suggested to Jade that we go around the corner for dessert. I was relieved when she quickly agreed.

Eight

By noon Maurice had left three messages, which had me worried. Normally he wasn't the type to chase after anyone. You either got in touch with him or he kept a cool distance until you did. This was something about Mo's personality that I never completely understood. It was as if he kept score, almost waiting for your misstep, which he inevitably would bring up later and throw in your face during the heat of an argument, long after you'd forgotten about the so-called misstep—if you were even aware of it in the first place! I endured the highs and lows of this often labor-intensive friendship simply because after all these years I had an inexplicable fondness for him. Maurice ran hot and cold like a faucet but beneath all the bluster was a basically good guy who suffered from low self-regard. If I had ever had the courage to broach this delicate subject, I'd have told him that his expectations for himself were set so high that no one could live up to them. Instead I listened patiently over and over, while he ranted about one perceived slight or another, the daily injustices that he alone faced, and sooner or later, a quick rundown

of my own personal failings as a friend. Fortunately, I understood Maurice well enough to know not to take his jabs too personally—just as important, I knew also how to smooth the
situation over before it got out of hand. However, there were
times when I asked myself whether our friendship was worth
all the extra effort. Weren't buddies supposed to grant one another the space to screw up now and then? Lord knows I cut
him massive slack in that department. I guess we take our
friends for who they are, all the messes along with the blessings. Maurice talked a good I-don't-care game, but I knew better. There was something sensitive and hopelessly romantic
about Maurice.

I remember one miserable rainy evening during the last
days of autumn when I got a call from Maurice. From his question "Do you think black gay men will ever learn to treat each
other right?" I knew something was wrong. I asked him to repeat his question to make sure I had heard him correctly and he
broke down in tears that wouldn't stop. When I showed up at
his apartment a short while later, he was still crying.

During the Memorial Day Black Gay Pride festivities in
Washington, D.C., Maurice had met Cullen J. Hartwell, one of
D.C.'s resident pretty boys, at the big closing party. He was tall
and broad shouldered, and a dangerously handsome man with
hazel eyes. Cullen was the kind of guy who when he walked into
a room—any room—people took notice. It didn't matter if they
were gay, straight, or suddenly confused. Maurice had charmed
Cullen with his quick wit, but I sensed from the beginning that
Maurice thought he was stepping out of his league by pursuing
Cullen. He went to D.C. every chance he got, taking rooms in
the best hotels since Cullen told him he still lived with his parents and couldn't have overnight visits. Sometimes when I was

supposed to pick him up at the airport I would get a call from him telling me he'd decided to stay another night. When I asked Mo how Cullen was in bed, he told me they were waiting until they made a commitment before engaging in sex. Without asking I knew this was Cullen's decision and not Maurice's. He always told me that he had to check out the sex before he would allow himself to become emotionally involved with any man.

In late August, Cullen surprised Maurice by showing up at his town house, suitcases in tow, and confessing his love for my friend. I had never seen Maurice happier and for the first month I believed Cullen was in love with Maurice. I kept on believing that until one evening when I was invited to the house for a cookout. Maurice was tending to the grill when Cullen made a pass at me. Something I never shared with Mo.

So I wasn't totally surprised when I found Maurice sitting in a dark house at his dining room table, candles flickering, drink in hand, distraught because after spending all day preparing a two-month anniversary dinner Maurice discovered that all Cullen's things were gone. He had been told by another friend that Cullen had moved in with a local television anchorman who was a little better-looking than Maurice and had a fatter checkbook. Making matters worse, it was Maurice who had boasted to the television personality how great Cullen was in bed and how blessed he was.

Cullen didn't leave a loving note or make a phone call about his departure but texted Maurice a few minutes after he discovered he suddenly had more closet space. And though it has been over five years since the incident, I saw something change in Maurice that night, even though he called me the next day with his voice full of laughter, acting as though Cullen Hartwell never existed.

I'd been tied up the better part of the morning in a meeting with Brad Pitt's Make It Right Foundation, presenting some design ideas. The board was excited about my proposals and told me they would get back to me after Brad and his donors had a chance to look them over. Maurice, of course, had no idea where I was and needless to say did not like to be kept waiting. Whatever he had to tell me was urgent enough for him to call three times in two hours, so I phoned him the minute my meeting ended.

He picked up on the second ring. "Where have you been?"

From his jubilant tone, I knew right away that his urgent news had to be good.

"I was visiting this agency I'm thinking about doing some volunteer work for," I replied, more defensively than I'd intended. "I just picked up all your messages at once and was afraid something bad had happened. What's up? Is everything okay?"

The smile in his voice was audible. "Oh, old friend of mine, things couldn't be better. I have some delicious news. Are you sitting down?"

"No, the meeting just ended, and I'm still in their office. Hang on while I step outside."

I waved a quick goodbye to the executive director, as she stood to the rear of the hallway speaking with a colleague who was getting her signature. With Maurice on hold, I passed behind the receptionist seated at his orderly desk in the small but immaculate lobby, where half a dozen would-be tenants waited for appointments, and exited the glass door.

I stopped at the curb, where I laid my portfolio over the top of a public mailbox and removed my sport coat. "Hey, Mo, I'm back," I said, beginning to roll up my sleeves. "So what's the big news that's so important you couldn't wait another second to tell me?"

"Guess."

"Look, with you, I never know. I'll end up standing out here all day in the heat guessing unless you tell me."

He allowed for a dramatic pause, one in which I was no doubt expected to die from curiosity. "Well, since you can't bear the suspense, here goes: I'm going to throw the biggest motherfucking Labor Day party this town has ever seen. All the stops will be pulled out, opulence out the ass, boys for days. In short, I will be the new hostess with the moistest. Atlanta's new grande dame."

"How are you going to do that? Labor Day is less than a week away."

"I know that, boo. I'm talking about next year. A bitch needs time to plan."

So this was the news that couldn't wait. I might have guessed it would be something out of left field. "What happened to Jackson Treat?" I asked, if only to sound invested in his excitement. "He's reigned over the big Labor Day party for years, and I somehow don't see him allowing you to snatch his crown."

I could picture the nasty grin that had to have materialized on his face at the mention of Jackson Treat. Jackson was a tall, ruggedly handsome philanthropist who was widely respected for his work against AIDS in the African American community. That he was also a principal heir to the largest black tabloid in America only set ol' Mo's teeth further on edge. His green-with-envy rivalry with Jackson, who was too much the gentleman to be pulled into a catfight with the likes of Maurice, was a one-sided battle. Although I wasn't in the mood to listen to more dirty gossip, the clownish spectacle Maurice unwittingly made of himself always had enormous entertainment value. This new gambit promised to top everything, and for once I was curious to learn to what new lengths Mo planned to go to unseat his imaginary rival.

In a triumphant voice, he answered, "The wicked witch of Atlanta is about to be dethroned by a much younger, more regal, and far more deserving newcomer than she. Mark my words: that weekend will serve as my official coronation as the new social butterfly of black gay Atlanta." Then he added, none too friendly and with a magisterial sweep of his hand, if I know Mo—"And Mr. Jackson Treat will be banished to wherever aging, balding, thick-around-the-middle black homosexuals with ugly boyfriends young enough to be their children go." At the mention of Jackson's downfall, his voice brightened again. "Now isn't that the best news you've heard in ages?"

Being Maurice's best friend, I thought this would be a good point to step in and try to break the spell he had fallen under. But how do you tell someone as crazy as him that he's lost his mind once and for all in words he might actually hear? The theatrical predictions of his swift ascension—and Jackson's equally swift demise—were comical to say the least. Although I'd attended just a few Labor Day parties over the years, I was well aware that for black gay men and lesbians, that weekend in Atlanta was a bigger holiday than Christmas. For as far back as anyone could remember, the festivities were kicked off Friday night with Jackson's black-tie soiree. His party was followed on Sunday afternoon by the smaller but no less exclusive Lavender Pool Party, hosted by Austin Smith on the estate of his Buckhead home. I simply did not see either man making room for— much less being trumped by—the "new social butterfly of black gay Atlanta." Just wasn't gonna happen, not on their watch.

For starters, Austin too was local black gay royalty. He was a rich entrepreneur who had been featured in the *Atlanta Journal-Constitution*, *Black Enterprise*, and *Ebony*, when they'd done an issue on black millionaire bachelors. The story in *Ebony* had been the source of endless conversation at cocktail parties since Austin was sweeter than a pair of Hostess Twinkies and didn't care who knew about it. Naturally Maurice loathed him for his accomplishments, in fact taking each of Austin's newly publicized feats as a personal affront. That resentment was compounded every year when Austin failed to invite the very obviously social-climbing Mo to his very obviously nouveau-riche party.

Just as I'd expected, Maurice had topped himself—or at least he talked a good game. I was rendered speechless by these absurd ambitions, but I couldn't help ask how he intended to sink not only one diva but two—and on the biggest weekend of the year, no less!

"Oh, don't you worry. I've not yet determined how best to stomp Mr. Jackson Treat, but I can safely say right now that Austin's pool party won't be happening next year—or ever again, if I have my way."

"Mo, what are you up to?"

A public bus thundered past me, advertising on its side the new hit TV series in which Blair Underwood starred as a preacher moonlighting as an amateur sleuth who solved crimes with the help of exotic birds. Jade was an avid fan and couldn't figure out why I refused to watch it. At the moment I had my hands full with the drama unfolding before me.

As if speaking to a child, he said, "Don't you remember that little scandal Mr. Smith got caught up in with the city councilman he was blackmailing for city contracts? I heard the bitch sent most of his money to the Dominican Republic and was building a villa over there. I also heard from a reliable source that he was dating some second-level pro football player who was looking for his ass after talking about their business. I'm told there's a video of them doing the do that's floating around and that Mr. Football wasn't too happy. Now that couldn't happen to a more evil bitch, if you ask me. But you didn't hear that from me."

"No one's asking you," I added quickly, trying not to get caught up in his gossip. Sometimes I had to let Maurice know the black gay social scene in Atlanta wasn't a big deal to me. "But how do you plan to pull off an event so big? A party of that level costs a lot of money. How do you expect to pay for it all?"

"I have my ways. Trust me, AJ. I'll get food and liquor sponsors. Honey, these companies know us sissies have lots of disposable income and they also know how and where we spend it. Paying for the party is going to be the easiest thing in the world. The real challenge will be deciding who not to invite. That list is going to be longer than the list of people who will get the invites! I think I'll call it the 'Glitter and Be Gay Ball.'"

In spite of his harsh remarks and the mean-spiritedness behind them, a small part of me actually sympathized with where Maurice was coming from. I'd never made the A-list either, and there were times when it felt as if these lavish parties were thrown to make ordinary people like Maurice and me feel like shit for not having made the grade. Make no mistake: I wouldn't have participated in those events even if I had been invited. The self-ordained movers and shakers of the black gay social circuit held about as much interest for me as a rodeo. But for someone who's as closely aligned with gay culture as Maurice, the sting of exclusion was clearly felt more sharply. What I couldn't sympathize with or fully grasp was the lengths to which he'd go to right whatever wrongs he may or may not have experienced. When it comes to Mo, it's impossible to know what's for real.

Rather than draw him into an argument about the low nature of this new enterprise, I chose instead to take a less confrontational route in the hope that I might talk a little sense into him. That was the thing you had to remember: Maurice was thin-skinned and quick to anger, but sometimes a well-reasoned talking to—brother to brother—worked wonders.

"I have to tell you," I began in my best therapist manner, "what you're planning is going to take a lot of time. What about your business? You can't neglect your work over this party. Besides, who really cares whether there's a 'fabulous' new party? To tell you the truth, I think there's too much of this stuff going on already in gay life. You can't open a magazine without being hit over the head with the offering of some new gay cruise or huge party. What we need for a change is some substance, something that you don't throw out the next morning when the next fad comes along."

"Child, boo," Maurice said. It was his favorite saying and was the ultimate gay-boy brush off. Like he was telling me, I can't be bothered by the likes of you.

If you could detect a smirk over the phone line, I would have felt it at that instant. "Come on, AJ, when you say things like that I have to ask myself if you're really gay. Do you know how many gay party planners there are in this city? They will be lining up to work this party! I was going to hold it at the penthouse of the Four Seasons but that's in Midtown and so last decade. I think I've finally decided to have it at the Mansion. Won't that be fabulous?"

Clearly what I'd just said hadn't registered. I looked at my watch impatiently, wondering how I might make a graceful exit from this conversation that was spiraling downward. "And why will the Mansion be fabulous?"

"It's only the grandest hotel in Atlanta, and it hasn't even opened yet. My extravaganza will be the first big event held there. Everyone is going to hear about it and wish they'd been there. Oh, I can't tell you how happy I am right now. I knew if I waited long enough revenge would be mine."

A pause hung in the air for a second, as if he were expecting congratulations, with the noise of the lunchtime street traffic instead filling the silence. I wanted to tell him flat-out that this was the craziest, most harebrained scheme he'd ever cooked up. That it was bound to blow up in his face, and I wanted no part of it. Rather than saying that, I told him, "I guess if it makes you happy, then I'm happy for you." The line went silent again, which I took as my signal to bow out of the call. "Listen, I need to run. I gotta few errands to take care of. Call you later?"

"Why you running off so fast?" he asked, sounding almost hurt. "There's more. The official announcement will be made tomorrow on the TT 2.2 blog. The tongues will be wagging— and I mean that in a good way!" Maurice was talking about Tay Tenpenney, or TT as everyone called him. Tay was the most popular black gay blogger in the country. His blog was called Unsweetened Tea, because Tay wasn't always kind to strangers—or friends for that matter. Nobody dared cross Tay. He not only dropped hot gay and straight gossip like all the other bloggers, but his blog—unlike all the others—was political as well. When people wanted to reach the black gay community, they went to Tay first. Mo knew this better than anyone.

"All of Atlanta will see tomorrow that I have arrived. And I don't just mean gay Atlanta but the whole fucking city, because I'm going to break with tired, old, sorry-assed gay tradition by inviting straight allies to the party too. No point in wasting all that good liquor on a bunch of faggots in black tie."

A young white woman pushing a child in a stroller walked up to the mailbox to post a letter. She smiled as a way of asking me to step aside, which I did with a polite nod. I felt almost relieved to be brought back into the real world by her. Once she'd finished, I returned to my call. "Can't wait to see what you pull together. Let me know if you need a hand."

"You better believe I need your help! I can't do all this by myself. I have something special for you in mind," he said mischievously. "I want you to help me audition the strippers . . . I mean 'waiters' for the party. We'll bring in the hottest boys from across the country for top dollar, then later have them serve me and my good, good girlfriends the 'house specialty' in the VIP area. And I mean the real VIP set. You always have to have a VIP area for A-list guests."

"I'm sure you can handle that all by yourself, Mo." I lifted my portfolio from the mailbox, preparing my exit. "Hey, congratulations. Seriously, I'll call you a little later, okay?"

"You don't sound very excited for me. I thought my best friend would be as happy about my plans as I am."

"I am happy for you, Mo, you know that. It's just that I was in that meeting most of the morning and have some stuff to take care of before the day gets away from me. I want to hear all about it."

"Child, boo," he said with playful sarcasm, "believe it or not, I can take a hint when it's handed to me on a plate, thank you very much. I'll let you go for now, mister, but you'd better

call me later. Don't make me chase after you. I can get ugly."
Then, as if lost in his own thoughts, he added to himself as
much to me, "Like the church queens say, 'God is good all the
time.' But don't piss him off."

★ His question came after the first set of leg lifts and if I
hadn't been sitting down I might have fallen over.

"So how long have you known Dray?" Cisco asked.

"Who?"

"Dray Jones, the new point guard for the Hornets. You must
know him. I found out that's who hired me as your trainer."

How had Cisco found that out? Dray went to great lengths to
avoid evidence of a connection between the two of us, even going as far as creating a dummy corporation to handle some of
the big purchases he made for me. No one in six years had so
much as a clue that we were connected.

"Uh, I did some work for him," I answered vaguely, avoiding Cisco's inquisitive eyes. I reached down for a towel to dry
my face.

"So are you guys close?"

"What do you mean 'close'?" I started the second set of leg
lifts, praying his inquisition would be over soon.

"You know, like bois, or maybe ya'll kinfolks."

"We're not family, but we cool." I tried to sound like someone from the hood, thinking I could pass us off as old college
buddies if pushed in a corner.

"You think you could introduce me to him?"

I thought for a second and said offhandedly, "Sure." I was
willing to do anything to stop his questions.

"Yeah, maybe he can hook up a brotha with some tickets or

a few of those crazy groupie bitches I know he be meeting in every city," Cisco said with a cocky grin.

"Okay, if I talk to him I'll mention it. And by the way, he's not paying you, I am. I just figured a professional basketball player would know the good trainers." Years of covering for Dray made it easy to think fast and lie through my teeth.

But this wasn't over just yet.

"So why did you move to New Orleans?"

Damn! Why was Cisco suddenly so nosy?

"For work," I said, finishing the last set of weights.

Cisco slapped my hand with a high five. "That's what's up. You ready to work your abs?"

"Yeah, let's do that," I said, my body crashing to the mats.

★ I was looking through a West Elm catalog when my phone buzzed to let me know a new text message had arrived. I looked at the screen and there in all caps was a message from Dray that read, "HEY."

I sent a text back: "Hey." This was his way of letting me know that he was by himself or just thinking about me. It was a small gesture but it always made me feel good. I thought Dray hated living a double life as much as I did, and in some strange way it created a special bond between us over the years. Those texts were especially important when I hadn't seen or heard from Dray for days.

A few seconds later, another message: "What are you doing?"

I wrote back: "Thinking about you."

Seconds later I read: "THAT'S GOOD."

I wrote back: "When will I see you again?"

He responded: "VERY SOON."

I sent back the letter "K" and tried to turn my attention to the catalog, even though furniture was the last thing on my mind now.

★ Jade stepped in my living room, her heels clicking on the hardwood floors. She paused in the middle of the room and nodded her head approvingly. "I don't know what you do, but you must do it well," Jade said.

A couple of days after our last meeting, she had called to tell me she'd worked her rent situation out and to see if I wanted to go out and get some dinner. I was getting ready to take one of the thick pork chops I'd purchased out of the freezer. I thought it was just as easy to cook for two as it was for one and so I invited her for dinner, which she gladly accepted.

"I do okay," I answered casually. "There are a lot of people in need of my services down here."

"Now what do you do? I forgot." Jade took a seat on my green-and-white-striped sofa.

"Interior design."

She ran her hand through her hair and then twisted her earring with a knowing smile, "I know that pays a pretty penny. Don't you need an assistant or something like the character on what's that show I used to like . . . *Will and Grace*?"

"I liked it too but I've learned from Grace's mistakes never to hire friends. I like you and I want to keep you as a good friend." The truth was I thought Jade might work well for me but Dray wouldn't like the idea of a female assistant. He said they were nosy and talked too much. I told him he was paranoid.

"But if you ever need me, to run a few errands or water your plants, I could do that until you find someone. I can run to the store and go to the post office, and you'd be helping me out because I can sure use the money. I might have to go back to giving facials and massages, because this girl sure isn't going to be trading pussy for rent."

"Does giving facials and massages pay much?" I asked.

"Yes, but some of those rich women got on my damn nerves. Although a few of them can be nice if they think you might come to their house to dust off those pulled-up faces." Jade smiled.

For the first time, I noticed a huge diamond ring on her hand.

"Looks like somebody is doing pretty well," I said, pointing to her finger. The ring didn't look like something a casino waitress wears.

"Oh, this old thing? It's not mine. It belongs to a friend who might be going through a divorce. She doesn't want her husband to know that she charged this on one of his cards before she drops the ball and lets him know that she knows he's been cheating. It's not as big as the diamond Kobe bought his wife. Are they still together?"

"Are who still together?"

"Kobe Bryant and his wife, Vanessa. Because I thought I'd heard they'd broken up. I bet that gold digger got to keep that ring."

"I don't really follow basketball that much," I lied.

"Me either, but everybody knows Kobe."

I looked at my watch and stood up. "I need to go and check on our dinner."

"Something sure smells good. What are you cooking?"

"Pork chops with stuffing and green beans."

"Are you a good cook?"

"I guess you'll know after dinner. You do eat pork, don't you?"

"I eat anything that's free," Jade said from the couch with a hearty laugh.

I went into the kitchen and saw that the food was almost ready. I opened the fridge and saw several unfinished bottles of wine and realized I wasn't being a good host.

I stuck my head into the living room. "Jade, would you like a glass of wine?"

"Do you have any beer?"

"I don't know. I thought you were a wine drinker. But let me check."

I ducked back into kitchen and I heard Jade's voice again. "I changed my mind. Let me have some wine. That's more lady-like."

"White or red?" I called out.

"What's the wine that's pink?"

"White zinfandel," I said.

"Yeah, that's the one. Let me have a glass of that."

I poured Jade a glass of wine and thought maybe I would give her a chance to help me out after all. Taking the glass into the living room, I thought that maybe since we were both new to the city Jade could serve a dual purpose in my life.

Something was up. I hadn't heard from Dray for over
a week and I was starting to worry. Now that we'd gotten past the L.A. incident, our life had returned to
normal. I had just finished a run through the Quarter with
Cisco, and the workout combined with the humidity had me
sweating like I had just come in from a heavy rainstorm. Sitting
up on the mat and limp from exhaustion, I could feel his muscular chest pressing against my back as he prepared to stretch
me out.

"So that's some good news about your boi?"

"What news?"

Cisco continued to push my back forward. "He and his old
lady are having a baby."

I turned around to face Cisco. "What?"

"Yeah, my boi Teddy, who's Dray's cousin, told me his old
lady is knocked up. I thought you knew. You two being tight and
all," Cisco said, with a hint of innuendo.

My heart was suddenly beating like a bass drum, my mind
reeling. I was speechless. Dray had told me they were going to

wait at least five years before they even thought about having a baby. That bitch was trying to get her claws deep into him by having a kid. I had always told myself that I would be number one in Dray's heart as long as Judi didn't have a child. I should have seen this coming. I couldn't help asking myself where this left me. If the news was true, it meant Judi had found a way to be in Dray's life permanently. This wasn't the marriage of convenience Dray had led me to believe it was.

"Are you all right, dude?" Cisco asked, clearly confused by my response.

I took a deep breath and said, "I need to take a shower."

"Man, I hope I didn't say the wrong thing. But it looks like all the color has drained out of you, and that's hard to do for black people. You look like you just saw a ghost."

I sprang off the mat and told Cisco to let himself out. I rushed to my bedroom to get my cell phone. I had to talk to Dray.

★ I closed the door and hit speed dial. The call went straight to Dray's voice mail, so I sent a text saying to call me immediately. I heard the door slam, which meant that Cisco was gone. He must think that I was one strange bird, or maybe he figured out there was more to my relationship with Dray than us just being bois.

The television in my bedroom was on mute but I stared for a moment, lost in thought, at the newly skinny Star Jones talking to the actress Vivica Fox, whose new television show *Court Television* was on the air for the first time. I was happy to see that Star had bounced back. Just as I was getting ready to turn on the volume and hear what they were talking about, the cell phone rang.

"Dray!"

"What's up, boi," he said cheerfully, as if all was right with the world.

"You tell me."

"It's all good. Now tell me who was that young lady I saw you at the Ritz with."

"I told you she just a girl I met in the coffee shop. We were just hanging out."

"You need to be careful who you hang with. Bitches are nosy as hell, boi."

"I know, Dray, and you have nothing to worry about. Now is there something you haven't told me?"

"That I miss you. Yeah, that's true. I really do miss you."

"Then why haven't you called me?"

His tone changed. He had to have guessed there was more to this call.

"Sorry, AJ, but I'v^ been busy. I'm dealing with some issues."

"Dealing with what issues?"

"Some stuff, but nothing that involves you. Just stuff with Judi."

Furious, I paused for a second before blurting out, "Is Judi pregnant?"

Dray didn't respond. He must have been almost as stunned by my question as I was to hear the news from Cisco.

"Did you hear me? Answer me, Dray!" I shouted.

"Where did you hear that?"

"Is it true?"

We sat there in silence, waiting for him to answer. It seemed like forever. I was consumed by feelings of anger and betrayal. How could he hurt me so badly? Finally, in a cold, deliberate voice, Dray said, "I've got to go."

Before I could say "WTF" he had clicked off.

★ I'd had a couple of martinis and was slumped lazily across my bed in a wifebeater and gray shorts. Dray had hurt me as much as he had angered me. I couldn't think of anything else the entire evening. I was about to switch off the flat-screen television and crawl under the covers when I heard the doorbell ring. I jumped up, figuring it was Dray and he had forgotten his keys. I was suddenly very happy and excited.

I rushed down the stairs and opened the door. Standing in a tight-fitting white T-shirt and a black baseball cap covering a red bandanna was Cisco.

"Cisco? What are you doing here so late?"

"I was in the neighborhood and I saw your lights on, so I decided to see what was up."

Cisco walked into the foyer as if I'd been expecting him.

"What's up?" I asked, puzzled as to why he was here.

"Just chillin'. You looked a little upset this afternoon, so I was just checking to make sure you were all right."

I was touched, yet a little suspicious. So I told Cisco I was doing okay. Something about him dropping in worried me—what if Dray had been with me? But maybe after all, considering where we left off with the phone call, there was little chance of that happening. I decided to be polite and offered him a drink.

"What you got?"

"What do you want?"

"How about some vodka, like some of that Grey Goose joint."

"I think I can do that. What would you like me to mix it with?"

"Some cranberry juice would be sweet."

I walked over to the bar, suddenly a little embarrassed that I was only wearing shorts and a T-shirt, but, shit, I wasn't expecting a guest. I fixed his drink and made another martini for myself. With him just standing there I realized how lonely I felt and how nice it was to have a man in the house.

"So you just chillin'?"

I handed him his drink. "Actually I was just watching a little television in my bedroom."

"What's on?"

"I don't know, some reality show."

"We can chill up there if it's cool."

"Yeah, that's cool," I said. I started to say maybe we shouldn't, thinking this would be a disaster if Dray did show up, but it would serve him right. The martinis had me feeling a little reckless for once.

I put out my hand in a gesture to let Cisco know he should walk up the stairs first, but in a very masculine move he placed his hand in the small of my back and said, "Naw, you go first." He had an almost sinisterly seductive smile.

I started up the stairs and could feel Cisco walking closely behind me. Even though I couldn't see his eyes I felt that he was staring at my ass. When we reached the bedroom, Cisco plopped down on the plum-colored chaise longue in the corner.

I turned the channel to ESPN and took a seat on the bed, quietly sipping my drink. The silence was finally broken when Cisco asked whether I minded if he smoked a joint. I didn't like people smoking in my house but said, "Yeah, go ahead." I thought this was funny from a guy who had given me the blues over drinking coffee.

The dim lighting in the bedroom gave a feeling of subdued elegance. All the while I could feel Cisco looking at me, not the television. After an uncomfortable few moments I looked over at Cisco. He took a puff and blew smoke circles between sips of his drink.

With me watching him, he turned his attention to the television. "So you like b-ball?" Cisco asked, without taking his eyes off the screen.

"Yeah."

"Is that how you and ol' boi hooked up?"

"Ol' boi?"

"Your dude who plays for the Hornets. Drayton Jones. The dude who getting ready to have a baby." He blew another smoke circle.

"I told you we just friends."

The mention of Dray reminded me how pissed I was at him and disrupted any guilty thoughts I was having about how it would feel to be seduced by Cisco. I knew that I wasn't going to let that happen, even if he tried. The funny thing about the strange relationship I shared with Dray that was different from a lot of gay couples I knew was that I was completely faithful to Dray. I saw fine dudes all the time, and it wasn't as if they didn't notice me. But I wasn't about to risk the life I had for a roll in the sack with some wannabe thug. Plus I was the old-fashioned type, never one to go around looking for something bigger or better. My mother raised me to be more responsible than that.

Still, I didn't see anything wrong when, after finishing his joint and following it with a strong-smelling blunt, Cisco asked me if I wanted a massage. I was feeling a little tipsy myself and

I knew where this could lead, but felt I had the will to stop it before it went too far.

I lay across my bed on my stomach and awaited Cisco's strong hands.

"Take off your shirt. You got anything like some baby oil?"

"I got cocoa butter lotion."

"Where is it?"

"I'll get it," I said, rising from the bed and locating the lotion under the bathroom sink. When I returned my eyes immediately met Cisco's and I looked away.

"Come on, you need to take your shirt off."

I followed his instructions and removed my wifebeater.

I handed the lotion to Cisco, whose intense brown eyes locked on mine. For a long moment I imagined what it might be like to kiss someone other than Dray but put that thought out of my head. I lay down on the bed. My body jolted when Cisco's hands and the warm lotion covered my back. In no time the strength of his hands relaxed my body into stillness.

"You're good at this," I groaned, filling the silence that hovered over the room. I realized Cisco had muted the television. Cisco didn't respond as his caresses sent a sensuous tingle all over my body. A few minutes later, I felt his hands casually pull down my shorts and soon it felt like his lips were teasingly brushing against the small of my back. When he palmed my left cheek with one of his hands I told myself it was time to stop but said nothing.

"So what happened? You took care of ol' boi before he got into the league and now he's taking care of you?"

"What are you talking about?" I asked, focusing on my massage.

"Come on now. I wasn't born yesterday. I think there is sumthin going on between you two."

"We're just old friends from college, like family. That's why I was surprised to hear about the baby from you instead of Dray."

As much as I wanted to stop the massage, I did enjoy him caressing my butt. It was all good until I suddenly felt a huge, lubed finger being stuck up my ass. I quickly turned around and said, "What are you doing?" It was then I noticed that Cisco was stripped down to his boxer briefs and in spite of my alarm I couldn't keep my eyes from moving down his body.

"You know what I'm doing. This is what you want. Right?"

"I thought you were just giving me a massage."

"That's what I'm doing. With a little extra. You know how we do. You take care of me and I'll take care of you."

"I think you should leave," I said as I sat up, looking for my shorts.

"You don't want me to do that. All I'm looking for is an extra couple hundred dollars. That's chump change to a man like you."

"Cisco, you need to leave," I said firmly, but the truth was that I was suddenly afraid of him and worried that he might hurt me.

"What? I'm not good enough for you? I know gay when I'm around it. I see how you be looking at me when we work out."

I slipped on my shorts. "So are you gay?"

"Oh, hell, naw," he said with a dismissive wave of his hand.

"Bi?"

"Nope."

"Then what are you trying to do with me?" It dawned on me

that he had come to my house looking for more than company or just a massage.

"Shit! A nigga gotta eat. This could be our little side thing. But you need to know I don't get fucked and I don't suck dick. And I was hoping you could break me off a little paper before I leave."

How did I let this get out of hand so fast?

"Cisco, please put your clothes on and leave," I said, trying to sound as reasonable as possible.

"So, it's like that, huh?" I couldn't tell if he was more angry or hurt.

"It's like that," I said. As much as I wanted him out of my house, I couldn't not look at what seemed to be his big semi-erect dick peering from his white boxers.

"Okay, but I think you're going to be sorry," he said, thrusting a finger at me threateningly. Cisco slipped on his black warm-ups and left without a goodbye.

Ten

After a couple of long, lonely days, Dray bounced into my town house as if everything were cool as a spring breeze. I was not amused. He was wearing a hip-hop outfit of warm-ups, a long white T-shirt, and untied sneakers.

"So what you been doing?" he asked, taking a seat on the edge of the chaise in the living room.

"Waiting to hear from you, asshole," I snapped. It wasn't what I planned to say, but it just came out.

"Come on, Aldridge, don't give me a hard time. You know I have a lot going on. I'm adjusting to a new coaching staff, getting settled in the house, and getting ready for my baby."

I couldn't resist this opening. "I wondered when we were going to get around to that."

"Get around to what?"

"The baby. When were you going to tell me? Do you know how humiliating and hurtful it was to find out about it from my trainer, or better yet the newspaper and the Net?" Cisco's face flashed in my head and I wondered if I should tell Dray how he had tried to seduce me. I still wasn't sure what all that was about, but maybe that would make Dray jealous and he would realize he could lose me. That's one thing that sometimes annoyed the hell out of me. Dray was so damn cocksure he had me in the palm of his hand, and it might do him some good if he knew I had other options.

"I was going to tell you. But no time seemed like the right time. And I didn't want to tell you over the phone. We see each other so little that when I'm here all I want to do is hold you and make love to you. Besides, do you know how hard it was going to be for me to tell you Judi was pregnant? I already have you feeling sidelined in my life, so I knew hearing about the baby would upset you. There was no easy way to come out and say it."

"You're doing pretty well now, and clearly I'm not the only one you've been making love to." I knew I sounded like some high-school bitch that wasn't getting her way, but I couldn't help myself. I had to know that this was bound to happen. That's what married people did.

"Come on, boi. Married people have babies, and to be honest I'm so happy I don't know what to do. I'm going to be a daddy. Why can't you be happy for me? You feel like I've stuck you in the background and pull you out whenever I like, but without you . . . I don't know how I'd get by. Judi give me things I need sometimes, but what I have with her . . . it's not what we've got. A lot of this stuff is bigger than us. It involves my family, my career . . . shit, you know all this already."

I stood over him for a moment in semi-shock. Here was the man who I had basically given my life to be with gloating over the fact that his wife was about to give him something I never could. The whole world was going to applaud the happy couple while I came up empty-handed. How was I supposed to be happy about that?

It was as if my soul had finally broken, like the New Orleans heat had with the arrival of fall. I should get out of this relationship now while I still had a teaspoon of dignity left.

Dray smiled and took me in his arms. "But don't worry, nothing is going to change between us. We will always be there for each other. You know that."

"Yeah, right. I guess it means I'll just see less of you. Maybe it's time for me to move on," I said.

"Move on? What do you mean by that? You're not talking about leaving me, 'cause that ain't going to happen, AJ."

"I mean just what I said. Maybe I've been fooling myself. Judi's not gonna stop with just one kid. Before you know it you'll have so many kids you won't know what to do. How long do you expect me to live in the margins of your life?"

"What's wrong with kids? You knew I wanted a big family. My dad wants grandkids."

"How do I fit into all that?" I asked, exasperated by his denial. I was about to tell him he'd given his parents a home, let one of his other siblings give them grandkids, but I didn't.

"You will always be a part of my life. Aldridge, you know how I feel about you. Don't you?"

"I thought I did," I said softly, sitting down next to him. I wanted him to hold me and say that everything was going to be all right. But somehow I knew it wasn't going to be that way, even if he said so.

Dray moved close to me and put his head on my chest. His head felt as heavy as my heart. I didn't know what to say. I didn't really want to move on, but I didn't want the life I had or where I saw myself heading.

"Trust me, Aldridge, I will make everything work."

"But how?" I pulled away. "Dray, did you hear me?"

"Yes, I heard you. And if you stop asking these questions, I'll leave you these drawers I'm wearing now. I know you'd like that."

"Then . . ." but before I could finish my sentence our lips met and not another word was spoken.

Eleven

On a bright September Saturday, I was enjoying a juicy cheeseburger and a beer with Maurice in a midtown Atlanta sidewalk cafe. After my encounter with Dray, I decided I needed to get away and one call to Mo convinced me that Atlanta was the place.

I was looking for support and Maurice was the only really close friend that I had. I often passed up potential friendships because I didn't want to risk bringing new people into my life who might find out about Dray. Cisco proved how easily someone new could blow up in my face.

I'd left the airport and checked into the Intercontinental Hotel in Buckhead, and with nowhere to go and no one to see that first day, I'd done a little shopping at Phipps Plaza. Maurice got back in town the next day after visiting family in Alabama, so this was our first time seeing each other since I arrived.

"I trust the boxes I sent got to New Orleans safely," Maurice said.

"Oh, yeah. I forgot to tell you. Thanks."

"I'm still wondering what exactly made you clear out practically overnight," he said playfully.

"Just needed a change of scenery."

"So do you miss Atlanta?" Maurice asked between bites of the chicken wings he'd ordered.

"Yeah, sometimes. I do miss seeing all the lovely bois in every part of the city."

"You look good, bitch. I think you want to be one of the stars of my party. Are you still working out?" Maurice asked.

"You know me, I'm gay so I got to keep the body tight."

"I'm glad I got almost a year to get my fat ass in shape before the party. Is your trainer any good?"

"Yeah, but I think I might have to find a new trainer."

"Why? You aren't falling in love with him, are you?"

"Actually my trainer kinda came on to me and I turned him down." I took a sip of the ice-cold mug of beer.

"Was he fine?" Maurice asked hopefully.

"He was okay," I lied.

"Then why didn't you give him some of that famous anus?" Maurice laughed.

"Because I'm not like that. I'm a one-man man. You know that."

He pointed his fork at me. "No, child, you're a fool. That's where men are different from females. We aren't built to be faithful. It doesn't matter if you are straight or gay. So if you want to play Goody Two-shoes, give me his digits. I'd sit on that dick and think nothing about it. Do you know how much free dick I'm going to get the closer we get to the party?"

"I'm sure he'd never admit that he came on to me," I said.

"I guess trainers are the new models when it comes to seducing the kids and taking all their coins." Maurice smiled. "A few of them have turned your sister here out. But not anymore. You can get dick just by having power and clout."

"I guess so, because he wanted it to be perfectly clear that he was not gay and not sucking my dick."

"Yeah, right. They all say that. But why didn't you give it a go since you said he was okay? I know that most likely means he was fine as hell."

"Maurice, you know I'm in a relationship."

"You are. Even though I know nothing about this alleged relationship you seem to love hiding from me, your best friend. Have never ever been given the slightest clue as to who he might be or why you're hiding him. But don't mind me. I'm only your best friend. How is that mystery man doing? Maybe I should hold your invitation until you tell me who he is."

"He's fine. As a matter of fact, he's expecting his first baby and I don't know how I feel about that." Maurice was the only person besides Dray I'd confessed this to. I didn't expect him to really get where I was coming from, but it felt good to talk about the situation. "I hope this baby doesn't change things," I said as I watched a group of gay white bois stroll by the restaurant.

"Well, you can't give him a baby unless you're keeping more secrets than I think. I wouldn't worry about it. Those men are usually preoccupied the first three years and then it's back to their old tricks."

"You think so?"

"Child, boo. Just wait until he has to stay home and change dirty diapers."

"I'm sure his child will have a nanny."

"That's right. Your man is rich. Stupid me," Maurice said, playfully hitting himself upside his head. "It's the one thing I do know about him. How could I forget? Maybe I should get a rich man. No, they think they can control everything. Pretty soon I'll have my own money with all the sponsorships I'm getting for the party."

"I thought that money was for charity."

"It is, but there are consulting fees for all my time. Events like this are a lot of work and I need to be compensated," Maurice said.

We ate our meal in silence while the sun beat down on our faces. After a few minutes, Maurice looked at me thoughtfully. "Listen, all kidding aside. Does this guy really make you happy? I mean happy enough to hide a part of your life from your closest friend?"

I thought about his question for a few moments and then said, "Most times."

Maurice shook his head disapprovingly, "When you play with fire, sometimes you get burned, baby."

"He wasn't married when we met."

"So why didn't you leave him when he hooked up with fish?"

"I don't know. Do you ever think of Cullen?"

"Child, boo. Cullen. Please. What do you think?"

Before I could respond, my cell phone rang. I saw that it was Dray calling and I hit the IGNORE button, which would send the call straight to voice mail. A few seconds later he called again and then again. I didn't usually take his calls when other people were around, but I thought this might be urgent.

"Excuse me, Mo, I need to get this. Hello?" I said, standing up. I heard Maurice mumble to himself, "I bet you do."

"Where are you?" Dray yelled.

"What?"

"Damn it, didn't you hear me? Where are you?"

"I'm having lunch with a friend. What's going on?"

"Where? Are you in New Orleans?"

"No. I'm in Atlanta."

"What are you doing in Atlanta?"

"Seeing a friend."

"I need you to come back to New Orleans now, AJ, and I mean right now."

"Why?" Images of my aborted trip to Los Angeles flashed in my head and I became angry all over again.

"Don't ask any questions. I need to see you right away. I need to know who you've been talking to about us."

"What are you talking about?" I walked away from the table and headed toward the entrance of the restaurant. I noticed Maurice's eyes followed me all the way to the door and kept watching from clear across the restaurant.

"Somebody is trying to blackmail me," Dray said.

"Blackmail? Are you sure?"

"You heard me. I got a letter in a FedEx package threatening to go to the press and my family about our relationship."

"Did they mention my name?" I asked as I looked over at Maurice, who was now pointing at his watch to let me know he didn't have all day.

"Hell, yeah. They didn't have to say your name. The letter said something about my 'little boi toy' who I moved to New Orleans to be with me. Who have you been talking to?"

"Dray, you know me. I would never do anything to jeopardize your career. Damn it, haven't I proved that to you by now?"

"How else could they find out about us if it's just our secret? You think I told somebody?"

"I don't know," I said, totally flustered. Who could have

found out? Cisco threatened that I'd be sorry. Did he have anything to do with this?

"You need to bring your ass back to New Orleans so we can figure this out before I have to respond to this mutherfucker."

"Okay, I'll get the first flight out tomorrow."

"No, today. It's still early. Get on the next flight tonight."

"But . . ."

"Do it!" Dray yelled, and hung up the phone.

Twelve

I walked into my house and found Dray pacing like the expectant father that he was, but I knew this didn't have anything to do with no baby.

"What took you so long? It's past midnight. I have to get back home. I need to talk to you," Dray shouted.

"I took the next flight I could get, Dray." I put my bags near the closet door. "Tell me what's going on." I'd given the situation a lot of thought on the flight home and felt more and more frightened for him, than for us. Whatever any blackmailer had in mind was going to hurt Dray far worse than it could ever hurt me. I tried rubbing his arm to reassure him, but it seemed to make him even more agitated.

"Look at this," Dray said, handing me a white piece of paper.

"What's this?"

"Read it."

The words weren't handwritten or typed out, but spelled with letters someone had cut out from magazine and newspapers and pasted to the page.

*What will your fans say if they knew you were on the low
    with AJ?*
What would the owners of the New Orleans Hornets say?
What would your father say?
And what would your wifey do?
*If you don't want to find out, then I would get ready to reduce
    your big bank account by one hundred thousand dollars.*
Will be in contact soon Mr. DL Basketball Superstar.

My heart dropped to the bottom of my toes. Whoever this
was knew way too much and wasn't afraid to use it. But how had
they found us out?

"Dray, this can't be real. It's most likely somebody being
nosy." As soon as those words were out of my mouth, I didn't
believe them any more than I could see Dray did.

"Easy for you to say, but tell me who you told," Dray said,
grabbing me. "You sure you didn't tell your little friend Maurice in Atlanta?"

His grip was tight. "Let me go. I didn't tell anyone. I promise," I said.

"What about that girl I saw you with in the restaurant?"

"Jade? I haven't said a word to her."

"Are you sure? You two looked pretty cozy when I saw you."

"Dray, I haven't told Jade anything about us. Now let me the
fuck go."

He continued to hold on. "But you said she knew you were
gay."

"Yes, she knows I'm gay. I've never mentioned your name to
her or anyone."

"Then did you send this? Are you trying to get some more
money from me? Is that what this is about?"

Now I was the one ready to get tough. "I'm going to act like you didn't ask me those questions, because I know you know me better than that." I broke loose from him and felt like walking out on his ass right there.

"Then who sent this letter? Someone knows all about me. Somebody is trying to ruin my career." Dray nearly broke down in tears. I'd never seen him like this.

"What do you think the owners of the Hornets will say?"

"Fuck the owners. I'm not worried about them. I'm worried about what my father will say or do. This could kill him. And what about Judi? What about the baby? This could destroy me and everybody I love."

I couldn't keep Cisco a secret any longer. "How well do you know the trainer you hired for me?"

"Who?"

"The trainer. How well do you know him?"

"I don't know him at all. I told you my cousin recommended him." Dray stood up unexpectedly. "Why, do you think it could be him?"

"I don't know, but maybe he has something to do with it."

"Did you say something that could have tipped him off?"

"No, I didn't tell him anything. I was careful as always. But when he told me that you were about to become a dad, well, maybe he read something in my reaction. Hearing the news from anyone but you was like getting hit in the gut with a stack of bricks. I couldn't help but look devastated. There was no way to hide it."

I wondered if I should tell Dray how Cisco had tried to seduce me and how I'd turned him down. But this wasn't the time to get into all that.

"Did he ask you if we were lovers?"

"Not in so many words."

"What does that mean?"

"Could your cousin have told him about the baby?"

"I haven't told him," Dray said.

"Who have you told? Besides, I'm sure it was in the papers."

"I don't know how it got in the papers. These reporters feel like they own me. I told my parents, naturally. That's been it. My wife wants to wait until she's at least four months into the pregnancy. She had a miscarriage before."

"So she's been pregnant with your child before?"

"Yeah, but that's not the point. The only people I've told have been my parents."

"Maybe your mother told somebody. Who is this guy, your cousin?" Dray was always so tight-lipped about his family and I knew he'd be touchy about my insinuating that they might be behind the blackmail.

"Our mothers are sisters."

"Are they close?"

"Sure," he said, massaging his neck.

"Maybe she told her sister and she told your cousin."

"But Butchie wouldn't blackmail me," Dray said, turning and pacing the length of the room. "I give that nigga whatever he asks for. He ain't got any reason to be trying to hit me up for money."

I went over to him and looked him dead in his eyes and asked, "Why?"

"Why what?"

"Why do you give him whatever he asks you for? I thought you said your agent and business manager told your family and childhood friends no when they asked you for money."

"Butchie is my boi and family," he said defensively. "We grew up together. We learned how to play basketball together. Matter of fact he was a much better player than me."

"Then why is he not playing now?" I asked.

"Could never get a good score on the SAT, so he just sort of lost interest."

"Then I think you should double-check with him and ask him more about Cisco. I bet there's a whole lot more going on here, Dray."

"Can't you ask this Cisco dude if he knows anything about it?"

"No, he quit," I lied. "Said something about going back to Atlanta."

"Why didn't you tell me that?"

"I haven't had a chance, Dray," I almost shouted. I tried calming myself before I said something I'd regret. "And it wasn't that important. I was either going to work out by myself or get another trainer."

Dray collapsed into a chair. "I don't know what the fuck to do."

"I think you're overreacting. You've only gotten one letter from this person. Why don't we wait and see if anything else comes?"

"Let someone threaten to go to your father and see how you would feel. I told you about my father. He doesn't understand gay people." I'd remembered Dray telling me about something that happened when he was in seventh grade. His father found out his cousin was gay and forbade Dray to ever spend the night with him. But Dray didn't need to remind me about his dad. I've been his boyfriend for years and he's bent over backward to keep me apart from his family. For a moment I wondered about what would happen if someone exposed Dray and ended this lie once and for all. At least then we could finally live our lives openly and honestly for the first time. But I knew that as closeted as Dray was, even if the truth came out, I was kidding myself by thinking we could live our lives freely.

"Go home and get some sleep and let's see what happens tomorrow," I said.

Dray looked so defeated but picked himself up. "Yeah, you're probably right. Maybe it is a prank," Dray said.

"Now you're talking. Let's wait and see," I said, rubbing his arms again. This time it seemed to calm him down a bit.

He embraced me tightly. "I'm sorry for thinking you had something to do with this, AJ. I know how much you care about me," Dray said.

I hadn't felt this needed by Dray since the news broke about the baby. I was determined not to let him down. I prayed that he wasn't being blackmailed because of something I'd done. I knew this was impossible since I'd never breathed a word to anyone. I had written about our affair in my journals, but I kept those safely hidden in a sealed box.

Dray looked exhausted. "I'll see you tomorrow," he said, and kissed me on my forehead. "I'm under a lot of pressure here but things will be cool soon."

"I know, boi, I know."

 The moment I saw Jade at Willie Mae's Scotch House, home of the best fried chicken lunch in the state of Louisiana, I could tell something was different. She looked especially vibrant and vivacious and her eyes were twinkling almost mischievously.

"What's going on with you?" I smiled, taking a seat across from her.

"I'm getting close to the prize," Jade said as she rubbed her hands together like she was getting ready for something real good, and I don't mean the fried chicken.

"Close to what?"

"Close to meeting Reggie Bush, and then it's gonna be on! I met one of his teammates at the casino where I work and of course he asked me for a date. I asked him if he knew Reggie and he told me he was one of his best friends. So the way I figure it, I'm bound to meet him."

"Who's his teammate?"

"His name is Steve Slater. He's an offensive lineman, which was clear the moment I saw him. That boi got a big ol' ass and a big head to match. He's cute but not Reggie Bush cute. But I can date him for a minute."

The place was packed, so our waitress hadn't acknowledged us yet. The restaurant had been closed down after Katrina and had only recently reopened. I guess the people in New Orleans missed their chicken.

"Does he know you're after Reggie?"

"Of course not, silly," she said with a smirk. "Do I look dumb to you? This guy Steve is married but his wife is still in Michigan. So there ain't anything I could do with him even if he was my type." Jade looked around impatiently. "What does a girl have to do to get some service around here?"

"How did you find out he's married?" I asked. Dray came to mind all of a sudden. I'd left a message when I woke up, but I hadn't spoken to him today. I wondered if he'd cooled down since yesterday.

"I find out lots of information before I pounce," Jade said. "Besides I'm not going to sleep with him."

"You're not? What if he pressures you?"

"I can handle myself. I'll make it clear I'm not that kind of girl."

A plump girl with a pad, plenty of lip gloss, and a lot of attitude approached us. "My name is Latrelle. May I serve you?"

I set down my menu. "What's the special?"

"Chicken," she deadpanned.

I turned to Jade. "How does gumbo and the two-piece lunch special, dark meat, sound to you?"

"Sounds good to me."

"Anything to drink?"

"Two sweet teas?" Jade said.

"Okay. Salad bar is over there," she said, pointing to the rear of the restaurant. "It comes with your meal."

"I don't want any salad," Jade said, but the waitress had left already.

I couldn't resist asking Jade what she was going to do if Reggie wasn't interested in her.

"Oh, that won't happen." Jade smiled. "You should see me when I fix myself up. It's something to see, honey."

I gave her a little laugh. "Have you ever failed at getting the man you wanted?"

"Just once," she said, holding up her index finger.

"What happened?"

Jade crossed her arms on the table and leaned forward with a sly grin. "Let's just say he fell out the closet when I tried to give him what most guys want all the time. It seemed I didn't have the equipment he needed." Jade laughed to herself.

"Oh, I see." I smiled back.

"What kind of guys do you like?" Jade asked me.

"I don't have a type," I lied.

She sat up and looked me square in the eye, as if she were about to get serious. "C'mon, do you like feminine guys or those homo thugs? What about the down low men?"

"I don't have a type," I said again, and smiled.

"I don't believe that," Jade said with a wave of her hand. "I bet we like the same kind of bois."

"And that would be?"

"Jocks. Right?"

"How you figured that?"

"I told you I'm psychic, silly."

As if on cue, my phone rang. It was Dray. I asked Jade to excuse me for a second and stepped outside the crowded restaurant to take the call.

"Dray, I've been waiting on your call all day. How are you?"

"I got another note," he said, cutting to the chase.

"What?"

"I got a note demanding money and this one had my father's cell number. It said they would be calling him if I didn't meet their demands immediately. I told you this shit was real, AJ."

"Wait a minute. How did they get your father's phone number?"

"I don't know. But it doesn't matter because they have it. I need you to get over and help me figure this out."

"Where are you?" Why didn't this man figure out it had to be somebody in his family? Who else had access to his father's phone number?

"At your place. Where are you?"

"Having lunch with a friend. Do you need me?"

"Yeah, I do, boi. Just hurry up and get here."

"I will."

I clicked off my phone and went back inside. Two sweet teas sat on the table where Jade waited. I told her I had an emergency and was going to take my chicken lunch to go.

"Call me later?" Jade asked with concern in her voice.

I flagged down the waitress as I slipped on my jacket. "I will."

"I got your back, baby," Jade said.

"Thanks, Jade. That means a lot."

Fourteen

I arrived home to the sounds of Kanye West blasting throughout the house. I expected to meet Dray in the living room, but his sneakers were the only sign that he was somewhere close by. I followed the music upstairs to the bedroom, where Dray was lying shirtless on the bed.

For a man in crisis, he looked surprisingly calm. He had one leg crossed over the other and his hands behind his head. Dark glasses covered his eyes. When I walked into the room, Dray didn't budge. Maybe he was sleeping.

"Dray, what are you doing? I rushed right back from the restaurant."

"What up, boi?" he replied. Was he drunk or high?

"Can I turn down the music so we can talk?" I said, moving to the CD player.

"If that's what you want to do, but I don't think there's much to talk about." Gone was the panic in his voice from just a while before. Now there was a calmness that was almost more disconcerting than his panic.

"What about the letter with your father's phone number?"

"Kanye's new CD goes hard," Dray said, avoiding my question.

"That's cool, but I didn't rush away from my lunch to come and talk about Mr. West." I was totally confused by his sudden indifference to what only a half hour ago was a crisis.

"You didn't have to leave your lunch."

"You said you needed me."

"I always need you, AJ. You know that."

I sat on the bed and laid my chin on his muscled stomach. "I was worried about you," I whispered. "What happens to you happens to me too. We're in this together, and to be honest I'm scared for the both of us."

He stroked my head. "Don't worry, I'll make sure nothing happens to us." Dray took off the dark glasses to reveal watery, red eyes. He'd obviously been crying.

"So what are you going to do?" I asked.

"I'm going to give them the money," he said matter-of-factly.

"Just like that."

"You heard me. What other choices do I have?"

"How did the note arrive?"

"FedEx. Like the first one."

"Do you have any idea how they got your father's phone number?" I realized suddenly that whoever was behind this had something even I didn't have in Dray's father's cell number. The blackmailer had to be someone in Dray's family or a friend of the family. But how did they find out he's bisexual?

"No idea whatsoever. But it is his number."

"I bet it's someone in your family." Why didn't Dray see that?

"I doubt that," Dray replied quickly, sounding almost insulted. "My family and I are tight. They wouldn't pull some dumb shit like that."

Right. So tight you can't tell them about me, I thought.

"I don't think you should give them the money. I think you should call their bluff."

He sat up. "Why?"

"If you make this easy on them, they may come back for more money or demand something else."

Dray stared at the ceiling, lost in thought.

I sat next to him. "You don't have to play along, Dray. They have no evidence. All we have to do is deny their accusation."

"I thought about that, but I can't let my pops find out." There it was again. Dray's unbreakable devotion to his father and his family.

"Then tell him," I said. "Who knows, he might be cool with it."

Dray looked at me like I'd lost my mind.

"Are you fucking serious? You want me to tell my father that I like dudes? Tell him that I got a boyfriend that I take good care of? Do you know something about my father that I don't know?"

"Like what?" I asked, wondering where this was leading.

"Has hell frozen over? Because that's the only way my pops will accept some shit like this."

"So you got jokes? I'm serious, Dray. Tell the truth. Then we could be together every day and not have to hide. Lead normal lives just like everyone else."

"That is not going to happen. I'm getting ready to have a baby. I'm going to need my father to help me be the best parent that I can be."

"If he's the man you think he is, he will be there for you, Dray. So will I."

"You're talking fantasy bullshit, AJ. This isn't as easy as you make it sound. Do you realize that I got eleven teammates to deal with as well? The NBA ain't ready for somebody to be that truthful. You should hear the shit in the locker room about dudes who came out. I'm not ready to be a spokesperson for nobody but my family and me."

I wanted to say that if Dray's father was as closed minded as he sounded, then he would be the last person to teach Dray how to be a good parent, but I knew despite his father's conservative ways that Dray would always idolize him.

"So what are you saying, Dray? Are you ashamed of me?"

"Aldridge, this isn't about you. This is about protecting my rep. We can't have all this if I'm not playing ball," Dray said as he waved his arms around, gesturing to the town house.

"Well, it's not your rep when it's a lie," I said defensively. Suddenly this was more about our future than the blackmail threat.

"I don't want to talk about this anymore, AJ. I'm going to pay the money. I'm just glad I followed JB's advice and set up a BM account."

"JB? That's your agent, right? And what in the hell is a BM account?"

"Yeah, that's my agent, and he told me I need to have an account set up just in case any unwanted baby's mama shows up and we need to take care of it. I don't think JB had anything like this in mind."

"Promise me you will think about this before you do anything. Maybe we could go to the police quietly and they'll devise some kind of sting."

Dray stood up and turned to face me. "When you gonna get it through your thick skull that this isn't about us? This is about me. My career and future. Don't nobody give a shit if you're gay or straight." Dray's voice was restless with anger.

"So you're saying I'm a nobody? What happens to you has nothing to do with me?" I asked. "Fuck you, Dray." How stupid was I to sit there and try to help this asshole who's telling me that nobody gives a shit about me? I felt like a fool.

Dray grabbed his shirt from the nightstand and put it on in silence. He glanced at me in disgust. As he tucked his shirt into his warm-ups, he looked around the room for his sneakers and then headed for the stairs.

I couldn't let him leave like this.

"Dray! Come on, dude. Let's talk about this," I said, calling after him.

He had nothing more to say. Instead he stormed out of the house without a word.

Fifteen

I needed to get a life.

My own life. Real bad and real quick.

I stepped out of the shower. It had been three days and no word from Dray. Not one phone call, text, or surprise visit, and I was worried that he'd done something stupid. Drying myself off, I wondered if Dray's disappearing like this might help make it easier not to miss him too much if one day I decided to leave him. The thought crossed my mind now and then. But thinking about it was a lot easier than actually doing it.

I spread cocoa butter all over my body, and then slipped into some pima cotton lounging pants with a matching T-shirt. I prepared myself for another day of surfing the Internet and waiting for a man who obviously wasn't coming. Maybe I should go down to the Ninth Ward and see if I could help out there. Make myself useful, as my mother would say.

I logged onto the sports board to see if there was any news about Dray besides his upcoming bundle of joy or the new contract. Not that I expected to find anything out about Dray being blackmailed, but there was one site called Ballersblog.com that sometimes included gossip about professional athletes. You never knew what would pop up there.

Just as I had pulled the site up, my cell phone rang.

"What's going on, AJ?"

"Hey, Maurice, what's good?"

"Oh, nothing, just looking over some fabrics for some of the outfits I'm going to wear to my party. I plan to change clothes every hour on the hour. Also trying to decide what champagne to serve, and it's going to be hard since all the big companies have sent me free cases. Oh, have you seen Tay's blog today?"

"No, I haven't. What's going on over there?"

"Just a little more mention of the party, which is great because every time I'm on the site I hear from more sponsors. But Tay's going to drop a bombshell that will have the sports world rocking. I think I know what it's going to be."

"What?"

"I can't say because Tay will know it came from me and I can't have that diva mad at me. Speaking of the diva, he's calling me now. I need to take this, hon. Talk with you later."

"Okay. Keep me posted if you are allowed to share anything," I said. As soon as I hung up with Maurice my phone rang again.

"Hello?"

"Hey, you, is everything okay?" It was Jade. I hadn't talked to her since I left the restaurant in a rush several days before. Although I still didn't know her very well, it was comforting to hear her voice.

"I'm fine," I said in my best attempt to sound that way.

"I thought you were going to call me. You missed some good food."

"Remember, I brought my grub home, and it was great. How are you doing?" I asked, changing the topic as usual.

"I'm doing great. I mean, they working me like a slave at the casino, but I've been meeting some nice people. Hey, do you like basketball players?"

"What do you mean?" I asked.

"Do you like basketball players? You know, is that your type?"

"Why do you ask that?"

"I went out a couple of nights ago with the guy who's going to make sure I meet Reggie Bush and we were hanging out with some of his boys. After we'd had some drinks they started talking about some guy who plays in the NBA who's gay and who's about to come out. They didn't say who, but I think he might play in New Orleans."

I couldn't believe my ears. This wasn't happening, I told myself.

"Did they say a name?" I asked, trying like hell not to sound as frantic as I felt.

"I don't recall. They said it was a basketball player, or maybe I had too much wine." Jade laughed.

"Are you sure?"

"I can find out," Jade offered, "I'll just ask Steve. I'll tell him I want to make sure my girlfriends don't date him if he's on the low."

"It's probably just idle gossip. Believe it or not, guys talk just as much as girls," I said, trying to act normal.

"Yeah, you're right, but I just thought about you, especially if the guy's somebody nice. Remember me and your love life?"

"Yeah, I forgot. Thanks for thinking about me, Jade," I said, rushing her off the phone. I needed to get off the call quickly. "Hey, can I call you back? There is someone at my door."

"Sure, but don't let me have to track you down again. I don't want to feel like I'm being a pest, but I do worry about you. We all we got in this crazy city."

"I appreciate your concern and I promise to call you, Jade."

"Okay. Have a nice day, sweetie."

"You do the same."

When I clicked off my cell phone, I immediately phoned Dray. It went straight to voice mail.

"Dray, call me ASAP. Please. It's urgent."

"What you need to talk to me about?" Dray stood a few feet behind me.

I threw my arms around him. I was so happy and relieved to see him. "Where have you been?"

"I've been taking care of some business," he said, barely returning my embrace.

All my excitement over seeing him drained right out of me.

"What happened?" I asked.

"Hey, I don't want to talk about it. I'm exhausted. I just came by to chill, not have another argument."

I wanted to say "Hell no" but I could tell from the deep worry in his face and the tightness I felt from his body that he was probably tired from emotional overload. This was one of those times where he needed me to be supportive instead of harassing him about his personal life. I also saw this was not the time to share with him the gossip I'd just heard from Jade.

I reached out to him. "Okay, come over here and let me take your shoes off and we'll take a nap."

"I knew you'd take care of me. Nobody can make me feel better like you, AJ."

"I know, Dray," I said, loving the warmth of his embrace.

"I'm sorry I left like that the other day and had you worried, but I just couldn't take it anymore. To be honest, I was afraid for the both of us. You forgive me?"

"Yeah, of course I forgive you. What's happened over the last couple of weeks would make anyone crazy."

Dray sat down on the love seat in the bedroom. I got on my knees and unlaced his sneakers and took off his shoes and white socks. I rubbed his feet gently for a few minutes, then instructed him to stand up.

I took off his gray "Hornet Basketball" T-shirt and pulled down his black warm-ups. Suddenly, there he stood in just his blue plaid boxer briefs with the hint of an erection.

"Hey, Aldridge," Dray said, sounding to me as vulnerable as a little boy. "I really am sorry. I know you think I'm trippin' and maybe I am, but I couldn't hurt my pops like that. He is everything to me. You never knew your dad, so you might not understand. When I was a little boy, he lost his job and could only find work in Mobile, which was almost six hours away from our home in Mississippi. Seeing him gone all of a sudden, everybody in my neighborhood thought he was like most black men we knew, that he had left his family. But that was not the case. He called us every day and when I had basketball games he made every one of them. My pops told me it was important to him to set an example to me and my siblings so we would become adults he and my mother would be proud of. I'm not saying he's right about everything, but there are certain things I could do that would hurt him, and nothing is so important to me that I would hurt my father. Does that make sense to you?"

"Perfect sense," I responded, touched by his attempt to explain the situation.

"Do you forgive me?"

"Come with me," I said, and dragged him over to the bed. I

pulled back the comforter and Dray climbed under the covers.
I took off my pants and got in bed with him. I placed my back
against him in the spoon position and pulled his arms around
me. I felt his face nudge against my neck and I smiled to myself
because suddenly everything was right with the world.

About five minutes later, I heard Dray snoring and the
weight of his dick against my ass felt hard enough to drill a
brick. He missed me. When Dray finished his nap everything
would be like it was when he held me so tight. Suddenly I'd be
back in a world where everything was magical and perfect.

Sixteen

A couple of weeks passed and everything had gone back to normal. Still, I held my breath the whole time, waiting for the other shoe to drop. But no word from the blackmailer, which I took to mean he'd gotten all he was after.

I woke up late one morning with a dreamy sluggishness and for a moment didn't realize where I was. I knew I wasn't in my own bed, but I felt a body close by. I turned over and there was Dray sleeping beside me. Then I remembered.

He had called me the evening before and told me he wanted to see me, so I did what I always did. I jumped on a plane and checked into the hotel the team was staying at and waited for him to call. We were in Washington, D.C., at the Ritz-Carlton near Georgetown, where the Hornets were preparing to play the Bullets that evening. This was my fifth trip of the season; I'd already joined Dray in Seattle, Los Angeles, Miami, and Orlando. If the blackmailer had any plans to drive us apart, he was wrong. I loved that Dray wanted to see me more now than he had in months. But maybe there was more to it. He probably wasn't getting a lot of sex at home since his wife was almost six months pregnant. I didn't ask nor did I want to know for sure.

Whenever I joined Dray on the road, I usually got my own room on the club floor and hoped that he would be able to slip away from his teammates before I fell asleep. They didn't have curfews, but he usually hung out with his teammates until they had made their out-of-town booty call connections. Sometimes this lasted till two and three in the morning and it was all I could do to keep my eyes open.

I got out of bed, walked to the large bedroom window that overlooked Georgetown, and opened the curtains. It was going to be a beautiful day. Motionless clouds hung in a perfect blue sky.

"What are you looking at, babe? Come back to bed," Dray said.

"It's beautiful outside. I think I'll go shopping in Georgetown while you guys do your walk-through."

"That sounds like fun. Now come back to bed."

I kneeled down on the bed and whispered, "Are you hungry? Let's order a big breakfast and put it in the middle of the bed and eat just like we used to," I said, climbing back into bed.

"That sounds like a plan." Dray pulled me close to him and nibbled on my ear. Being in Dray's arms felt like old times and our recent scare felt a million miles away.

"You glad you came?"

"Yeah, Dray. I'm really happy to be here." During times like this, it was like Judi and her bundle of joy didn't exist. This was our world.

"I'm happy you're here too. I always sleep better when you're with me."

"For real."

"Real talk, babe."

"What do you want for breakfast?" I asked.

"Waffles, bacon, eggs, and maybe some cheese grits," Dray said.

"You must be hungry," I teased.

"For food, and something else," Dray said, grabbing my ass.

"I thought we took care of that last night." I smiled.

"Yeah, but I want some more."

"After breakfast."

"Okay, order the food. I'm going to shower and brush my teeth. The bus leaves for practice a little after ten." He hopped out of bed and ducked into the bathroom.

I heard my phone go off and I saw that I had a text from Maurice asking where I was. He said he'd been calling me with no answer. I sent a text back telling him that I was in Washington, D.C. I started to call him to see if everything was okay, but he texted back telling me to have fun at the Ritz. For a moment I wondered how Mo knew where I was staying, but realized he knew the Ritz-Carlton chain was my favorite.

I looked at the clock and saw that it was five after eight. I wasn't surprised we were off to a late start. Whenever Dray and I were together, we lost all track of time.

I considered the options on the room service menu and phoned in our order. Sitting there, I noticed the elegant room with its cream-colored walls had a stillness that was heightened by the sound of the shower. After all the recent drama, I appreciated the calm.

That quiet was broken when the hotel room phone rang and I picked it up, assuming it was room service checking our order. The Ritz was impeccable and was always checking to make sure everything was just right.

"Hello?" I said.

"Are you enjoying your little visit?" a deep male voice asked in a hard, colorless tone.

"Who is this?"

"Never mind who I am. Just answer my question."

"You have the wrong number."

"I don't have the wrong number. I called the hotel and asked for Aldridge Richardson and they put me right through."

"You have the wrong room," I said firmly.

"This is Aldridge, isn't it?"

"Tell me who *you* are."

"Don't worry about me. Is your basketball boyfriend nearby?"

"I'm hanging up," I threatened.

"That wouldn't be a wise move, playa."

"Why not?"

"Is your boyfriend there with you?"

"I don't have a boyfriend."

"Oh, yes, you do. And if you want to keep him then you're going to get me some big money. Otherwise I'm going to go to the press, wifey, and of course your boi's family. I'm also going to tell your mother what you did when you were fifteen. I don't think she going to like what I have to tell her."

The bathroom door swung open. "Who are you talking to?" I turned around and there stood Dray with a towel around his waist and a toothbrush hanging from his mouth.

"Wrong number," I said, hanging up the phone abruptly, hoping Dray hadn't overheard the rest of the call.

"Did you order breakfast?"

"Yep."

"How long will it take?"

"Twenty minutes," I said, standing up and nervously straightening the room.

"Are you okay?"

"I'm fine," I said without looking at him, "just eager to start the day. I'm going to call downstairs and see if I can get a car service to take me shopping."

"That sounds like a plan," Dray said. He stepped back into the bathroom and pulled the door closed. The phone rang again and I picked it up quickly.

I was in no mood for this. "Hello," I said confrontationally.

"Yes, sir, this is room service. I wanted to ask if you wanted strawberries or blueberries with your waffles?" a female voice asked. "The ticket has both checked by mistake."

"Strawberries," I said.

"Thank you. Your meal is on the way up."

"Thank you."

Just as I hung up, my cell phone rang. I looked down anxiously at the caller ID: Unknown. I let it go to voice mail, feeling I'd spoken to enough unknown callers for the day.

Seventeen

Sometimes even a twenty-nine-year-old man needs a hug from his mother. But since I was in New Orleans and my mother lived in North Carolina, I settled for the next best thing: a phone call.

I'd been home from D.C. for a couple of days, but I was still upset by the phone call I received at the hotel. I wasn't going to tell my mother what had happened, but I knew she'd make me feel better anyway. I dialed her number.

"I was just thinking about you," Mama said, picking up the phone without a hello.

"I guess we were both thinking the same thing, and how did we ever live without caller ID?" I laughed.

"Ain't that the truth. How are you doing, baby?"

"Okay," I said, halfheartedly.

"Are you sure?"

"Yeah, but why do you ask?"

" 'Cause mamas always want to know that their babies are okay, especially when they're not there in person to see for themselves. When am I going to see you?"

"Very soon. I was thinking about coming up this weekend. First I need to make sure I don't have any appointments with my clients." As always, I hated lying to my mother and wished I could have just said I needed to make sure Dray didn't need me.

"It would be nice to see you, baby." I could hear the smile in her voice. "Bella will be so excited, but I won't tell her until you're sure you can get away."

"I don't want to disappoint her. You think I should call her?" I asked.

"She always loves hearing from her big brother."

"Then I will do that," I said. A beep indicated an incoming call. The ID flashed "Out of Area." Fearing the worst, I took a deep breath.

"Well, let me know when you book your flight. I'll come and pick you up," my mother said.

"I will. Mama, I got another call coming in. I'll phone you in a couple of days. I love you."

"I love you too, baby. We can't wait to see you."

I clicked the phone over and paused to try to calm myself before saying hello. My greeting was followed with dead silence.

"Hello," I repeated, impatience in my voice.

"So I see this is the best number to reach you." It was the same male voice from the hotel suite.

"Who are you calling?"

"You've forgotten my voice already. That's not good, boo."

"Who is this?"

"I told you not to worry about who this is. Just wanted to know when you were going to have my money."

"I don't have any money for you."

"I don't believe that shit. You got plenty of money. Doesn't your basketball boyfriend give you ducats for all that good sex you give him?"

"Stop calling me. I'm reporting this call to the police," I said.

"I wouldn't do that," he warned very slowly. "But if you should contact them, you leave me with no choice but to release into cyberspace the little film you guys made."

"What film?" I asked. Dray and I were sometimes a little wild when we got down, but we never filmed anything. I'd used my digital camera to take a couple of pictures of him in his underwear, but that was it.

"The little film that was made when you were at the Ritz-Carlton. You guys really go at it. Y'all make Kim and Ray J seem like it was their first time."

"I didn't make any film at the Ritz and you know it. Cut this bullshit out."

"I didn't say you did it knowingly. I just said there was one made. If you weren't so quick to get off this phone and if you listen, then you might learn something. The skin-tight black underwear you had on was quite cute and your boyfriend is really blessed down there. I bet you love that."

He was right. I was partial to black underwear because Dray liked the way it looked against my skin. Flipped out by how this asshole would know this, I yelled, "Shut the fuck up. You don't know shit about me."

"Oh, I know a lot about you, faggot. Fuckin' slut! What will your mother think when she finds out about Mr. Wilson?"

"Who is this?" I screamed, finally losing my cool. Nobody and I mean no one knew about Eddie Wilson, especially not my mother. Shit, where was Dray when I needed him? What was this maniac talking about? Had I worn black underwear? I couldn't concentrate. This person had to be bluffing. My mind raced over the faces of people I'd met since I moved to New Orleans and the people I'd come into contact with at the hotel in D.C. There was the friendly bellman who seemed to linger in the suite as he helped me with my bags. The room service attendant and the maintenance man both had been in my room. Did one of them have a hand in this?

"Think of it this way: I'm your filmmaker and if I don't get paid, then I'm going to have to release this little gem."

Now it was my turn to bluff. "You don't have a film of me."

"Wanna bet? This little film is going to have more hits than the R. Kelly and Paris Hilton sex tapes combined. With it being a big-time basketball star and his boyfriend, everybody going to be downloading that shit. Don't you love this cybershit? Maybe I'll have that old-school jam 'Basketball Jones' playing in the background as you two get busy."

"Yeah, right," I scoffed. "You don't have shit." But he'd said it: *basketball jones.* Did this asshole know about my and Dray's secret password? How could he?

"You don't believe me? Give me your e-mail address and I'll send you a few frames of your first feature film."

"You got hold of my phone number. If you're so clever, try getting my e-mail address too."

"That won't be a problem. I think after you review your performance with your boyfriend, you'll change your tune."

"Fuck off," I said, and switched off the phone in a huff.

A wave of anxiety washed over me. I wanted to call Dray, but I didn't. I hadn't yet mentioned the hotel phone call to him because he'd been so excited after he'd hit thirty-three points, which included six three-point shots in a row. I always got a text after the Hornets won, but after that game I not only got a text but a phone call as well. Dray was so excited, happier than I'd heard him in weeks, that I didn't want to bring him down with more bad news. Truthfully, I thought maybe I could take care of this on my own. I just prayed this entire situation would go away.

This phone call meant that either somebody was playing a sick practical joke or that Dray and I were in really big trouble.

Eighteen

I flew to Atlanta for the day for a haircut and to get my teeth cleaned, since I hadn't found a good barber or dentist in New Orleans yet. Dray was busy worrying about his pregnant wife, so I figured he wouldn't even notice if I was gone for a day. Frankly, I was relieved to get away for some time of my own. I secretly hoped that when I returned all would be right with the world again.

My intentions were to fly down in the morning and come back on an evening flight, but instead I called Maurice for an early dinner and he convinced me to come to his house for dinner and then spend the night. Since I didn't have any plans, I gladly accepted.

After eating some delicious down-home Southern food takeout from Justin's, Maurice and I retired to his den to catch up over a couple of bottles of wine. Dray had been so much on my mind that I'd forgotten to take care of myself. Maurice had been there for me over the years, and I missed these times and our talks more than I realized.

Maurice poured his fourth glass of white wine, chattering away about his party, which he no longer referred to as simply "the party." In a nod toward grandeur—real or imagined—he had given it the illustrious-sounding name "Glitter and Be Gay Ball." Whatever he called it, there was much about the whole setup that still puzzled me. Apart from how Mo planned to pay for everything, even with sponsors, there remained the unanswered question of how he and TT had become so tight. Everyone knew that TT was the gossip to end all gossips and that there was no depth so low that he would not dig for dirt. But what I'd heard also was that behind TT's flashy-trashy persona was a big, snobbish old queen who thought he was royalty; in other words, exactly the kind of "uppity bitch" Mo railed against. Although I enjoy a word of gossip now and then, as a rule I steer clear of this type of gay man. People like him made me grateful to be with Dray, no matter the obstacles and occasional pain involved. Maurice, however, was not altogether outside this world. In fact, I sometimes thought the only thing that separated him from the likes of TT was that he didn't have his fame or money. But it was more than this that distinguished them. Mo didn't run in TT's celebrity circles, and breaking into that group was about as easy as crashing a party by scaling a barbed-wire fence wearing a tuxedo; you could give it your best, but chances were you'd end up getting shredded.

I was mulling all this over my wine when it occurred to me that this might be the perfect moment to do a little digging myself. Up till now he'd purposely kept the details of his sudden connection to TT ambiguous, which for him was like waving a red flag. Maurice had been going at the bottle pretty good, and his tongue by now had to be at its most loose.

Trying my best to sound nonchalant, I asked offhandedly, "Hey, Mo, tell me again how you and TT got so tight? Where did you meet him?"

A smile of superiority flashed across Mo's face, indicating he was about to share a story that he quite obviously enjoyed but wasn't entirely sure he should tell. As much as he enjoyed this story, however, he enjoyed his wine even more. I therefore knew it wasn't a question of whether he would spill the beans but how many he would spill. Given his current state, I wagered it would be the whole pot.

"Like everybody these days, we met online. But not on one of those gay dating sites," he hastened to add, as if that were something beneath him. "I simply wrote TT an adoring e-mail, saying how much I admired him for what he'd accomplished, how I followed his blog religiously and worshipped at his shrine. He wrote back almost immediately, we exchanged a few friendly notes—including one with a picture attached of me looking particularly stunning—and then just like that he invited me to lunch. The Capital Grille, of course. It was all so simple that I couldn't believe he fell for it."

"What do you mean? Fell for what?"

"You know me, child," he said with a playful slap on my knee. "You have to get up pretty early in the morning to trick a diva like me, but do I ever know how to work these star fuckers. All I had to do was oh-so-casually drop the names of one or two people who knew."

"Knew what?"

He grinned once more, then looked me in the eye as if to heighten the moment of suspense. Then he added bluntly, "About his sordid little life in Miami before he moved to Atlanta and became the black gay grande dame. How he got the money to finance his rise to the queen of the gay gossip blogs."

Leave it to Mo. Yes, he could be low-down and devious, but at times like these, I have to admit, he had me in his corner, fascinated by what new mess he had concocted. I smiled to myself in anticipation, while Maurice finished off his wine glass and poured himself another. I knew that wine was like a truth serum and since I had been drinking, my so-called moral code disappeared along with the wine.

"Tay grew up down in Miami, right outside of Little Havana, and was a hustler coming out of the womb. When he graduated from high school, he moved to South Beach, where he was dating this thugged-out nigga who also happened to be one of the city's biggest drug dealers. The dude had bank and nobody ever knew he was on the low, but they had been messing around for a long time. Well, old boi used to like to slap Tay around like he was a real bitch after he'd had too much Henny, and I guess one day Tay got tired of being smacked like he was a rag doll. And so like any diva, Tay started plotting his revenge."

"How the hell did you find that out?"

Settling back into the black leather sofa, Maurice paused. Whether this was for dramatic effect or he actually was attempting to gather his thoughts, I couldn't say. I'd seen him toasted before, but he wasn't quite there yet. That was only a matter of time. More than likely this was part of his performance, and knowing Mo, he relished it. Here I was, his captive audience.

"You see, a couple of years ago I met this guy through a site that posted profiles of prisoners looking for pen pals. You have to pay to get their addresses and stuff but the company that runs the site stands by all the profiles and pictures as being legit—not like most of these sites, where everybody is serving up fake pictures. Anyway, I was intrigued, so I wrote to about ten guys—all the same letter, naturally—and eight responded. Most of their letters were barely legible, but they were hot! Men in prison ain't got no shame while they in the joint."

I'd been listening so intently that I'd almost forgotten I was holding a glass of wine, so I took a sip. "But what does this have to do with Tay? Was he in prison?"

"No, honey. We both know Tay wouldn't last a night in prison. No, it was his boyfriend Dillard Lewis, better known as 'Big Dil,' who was in prison. I know because he was one of the inmates I wrote to. He had a body to die for and I'm telling you, I'd have held out waiting for him over the two years he claimed he still had left to serve. Well, you know these guys. They'll tell you anything to keep you on the line. Wasn't any two years— more like forever. But I didn't know that when we first met."

Maurice then leaned in toward me without a word, the way they do in movies when someone is about to deliver the goods. I followed suit and leaned toward him expectantly. Our heads inches apart, he said, "And can I tell you this man wrote me some letters that made me wetter than morning dew! I'm telling you," he squealed, throwing back his head at the memory, "I used to get hard just walking to the mailbox. Where he came up with this shit, I'll never know, but I was falling for this nigga—and just through his letters! That nigga made your sister wet with his words, baby."

He let out a little laugh, perhaps embarrassed to have revealed himself to me so suddenly, but that wasn't Mo's style; more likely he was turned on all over again just talking about those crazy letters. He then took a white cocktail napkin from the table and dabbed his glistening brow. I couldn't help but wonder how Mo had held out telling me this story—one he obviously prized—for so long.

"Things progressed from there," he continued. "Soon I was put on his phone list, and suddenly I was getting calls from him at least twice a week. Phone calls from prison are expensive but worth every penny when they talk nasty. And if that man could write dirty, Lord, you shoulda heard him talk dirty! AJ, as God is my witness I was done! I mean, sold on this motherfucker. People joke about this prison-love shit all the time but, I swear, when it happens to you, it's a whole other story." Maurice was the only person I knew who for emphasis could turn "whole" into a six-syllable word. "Asking no questions, you pick up and go meet your man. So the next thing I know, I'm heading down to some skanky prison in Florida I'd never heard of to meet my new husband. You'd have loved it. I drove the entire way with the top down, feeling just like Whitney Houston in *Waiting to Exhale*. I was going to meet my man."

Now it was my turn to laugh. I shook my head in disbelief. "I'm speechless, Mo. I mean it. I'm outdone. You gotta tell me what happened when you met."

"Well, for starters, he was even better-looking in person than in his pictures. I would have sold my grandmother back into slavery to touch him but of course they didn't allow that shit in prison. It's fine for those guards to stand by while some dude gets gang-raped, but when it comes to two grown men giving each other a hug, forget it! But believe me, I went back every chance I got. What can I tell you? I was obsessed, maybe even possessed. I couldn't get enough of the man. If you saw his picture, you'd know just what I mean."

"Where does TT come into all this?"

"I'm getting to that, be patient. Let the diva have his mo-

ment. One day I told Big Dil about me moving into a new apartment in Atlanta, and he said rather ominously that when he got
out he was coming to Atlanta to settle a score. When I asked
what he meant, that's when I found out about him and Tay."

"What about them?" I asked, surprising myself by how invested I'd become in the details.

Maurice simply sat there for a moment, swirling the wine in
his glass. "It seems old Tay is a very smart diva indeed. He
wanted out of the relationship, but there wasn't any way Big Dil
was going to let him go just like that. Remember, he used to
knock him around but good. Tay must have gotten desperate
because he cooked himself up a nice little plan. There came a
weekend when he knew Big Dil would be driving up to Orlando
to see one of his baby mamas. Totally on the sly and without Big
Dil having so much as a clue, Tay packed a suitcase full of drugs,
guns, cash, you name it, then stuck the suitcase in the trunk of
Big Dil's car. Next Tay tipped off the authorities, who stopped
Big Dil on the turnpike, and Mr. Big Dil hasn't seen the stars in
the sky ever since. Tay set him up big-time."

From the zeal with which he spoke, Maurice obviously
bought the story, but it rang hollow to me. I didn't doubt that a
relationship that fucked up got out of hand and crazy games
were played out, but it all sounded far-fetched, even for a drug-
dealing thug and his boi.

I chose not to put any of this into words and instead went
along with Mo. "Wow! That's an incredible story. It's almost
hard to believe. This really happened?"

"Please believe, child. I thought it was kind of crazy at first
but it all makes sense when you think about it. Doing so much
illegal dealing, Big Dil didn't trust in banks, so he kept his
money at home, and eventually Tay got his hands on it. It

doesn't take a genius to guess that someone at Big Dil's level of dealing thought nothin' of leaving millions of dollars lying around. But who'd have figured Tay had the balls or know-how to pull off the job? Big Dil didn't know it then, but he sure as hell knows it now!"

"That's a big job all right." I set my glass down on the table, intent to get to the bottom of this, if there even was one. "But what was that about him telling you he was getting out in two years?"

"Yeah, that's what he told me when he had me under his spell, but it didn't take long for me to figure out he was lying. That nigga is gonna be in jail for a long time."

"For how long, do you think?"

"Right now he got life or something, which means I ain't never gonna get any of that dick. He told me he has close to twelve inches and thick."

"That's what I'm talking about." With the mention of Big Dil's off-limits foot-long, Mo's story somehow felt much sadder to me. But I wasn't going to get sidetracked on dick gossip. "So he's sure Tay set him up?"

"No doubt about it, and get this: that crafty bitch took all the money that he didn't put in that suitcase and moved to Atlanta, where he completely remade himself and started his now thriving business. When he found out over lunch that I knew Big Dil, he was ready to deal. To put it plainly, I need him to bring down Austin, which is no skin off Tay's nose. What choice do I have? Nobody would give a shit if the information about Austin came from me. Who'd listen? Despite what this sounds like, it's not blackmail. Even I got to draw the line somewhere. I don't want any of Tay's money, just a little bit of his power. He scratches my back and I rub his."

"That's some story," I said, wondering how much of what he'd spilled would be remembered in the morning.

"Yeah, it's one motherfucking story all right," he concluded with self-satisfaction. Then Maurice sat straight up. He looked serious all of a sudden, as if he'd realized he'd talked too much. "But it's our story, AJ, and if you tell anybody—I mean anybody—both our asses will wind up living in Idaho in witness protection. You can't breathe a word of this to anyone. Do you hear me?"

"You ain't got to tell me but once," I said. "Besides, I'm pretty good at keeping secrets. Even better than you know."

Maurice nodded his head in appreciation, raising his glass in a toast. Whether this was in recognition of our friendship, the party, his dealings with TT, or all three, I'll never know.

★ "Why do I have to change my plans?" I asked.

"Because I really need you to be in Chicago with me, babe. You bring me good luck," Dray said, taking my hand.

"But I promised my mother. I won't cancel on her twice."

"The Chicago game is big. It's for first place and you've been my good luck charm lately. I've been scoring thirty points or more every game and it's because you're in the stands. I'm convinced of that. Besides, I get to hold you all night."

Dray had come by after his morning practice and we were having blueberry smoothies in the living room. I had decided to tell him about the new threats but when I saw how geeked up he was from practice, I must have lost my nerve. Instead of telling him about the phone calls, I said I was going to North Carolina for the weekend.

"I'm not the reason you're doing so well. You've been playing well all season. You're a great basketball player, Dray."

"Come on now, baby boi. Chicago is a wonderful city and I might see if I can stay a day extra, since we don't have a game until three days later. Maybe we can find a spa outside the city and do something special." He smiled.

"You guys play Chicago later next year. What if I come then? I really need to get home."

"I don't know," Dray said. His face softened with disappointment. He took my hands and rubbed them together as he thought it over. Finally he let out a sigh, then turned to meet my eyes. His face broke out in a grin. Dray moved in real close and traced my lips with his tongue. I'd longed to taste his tongue all morning, but I decided to let him kiss me first.

"Those are kind of tasty," Dray purred.

"My tongue tastes better," I whispered.

"I bet it does." Suddenly his strong tongue entered my mouth forcefully and we locked in an embrace.

We kissed passionately on the couch until the phone went off in the next room and shattered the moment.

"I need to get that," I said, pulling away.

"No, come back here. You can't leave me like that. I want more," Dray pleaded.

"Only if you say I can go to North Carolina this weekend. If you do that I promise to join you in Toronto for the next game." Dray knew that was my least favorite NBA city because it was so cold, although it was the one place where he didn't mind venturing out with me for window-shopping.

"Okay, you win. But if I have a bad game in Chicago, it's going to be your fault," Dray warned.

The phone stopped ringing but immediately resumed seconds later.

"Let me take this. It might be a bill collector." I laughed.

"Yeah, right. You don't have any bill collectors. I make sure of that. But you go ahead. I'll be upstairs taking a shower. I expect you to join me in a few minutes."

"Okay, I'll do that," I said, giving Dray a quick peck on the cheek. I hopped off the sofa and sprinted toward the hallway where the phone was located.

"Now hurry up," Dray said as he walked up the stairs.

"Sooner than you think. You just make sure you're ready." I waited a beat, then clicked on the phone. "Hello?"

"I see your boyfriend is there to offer a little afternoon delight. How special is that?"

I was not about to do battle with this guy while Dray waited, so I simply clicked off the phone and headed toward a stress-reducing shower upstairs.

*Nineteen*

I walked through the automatic doors of the Raleigh-Durham airport and into the cold North Carolina night. The fresh air against my skin reminded me how chilly Raleigh got this time of the year. But just being back home warmed me with nostalgia. I crossed the sidewalk, passing several cabs, when I spotted my mother waving and blowing the horn of her ruby-red Cadillac. Her smile immediately made me glad that I had passed on Chicago.

"My baby's home!" Mama sang as she got out of the car and hugged and kissed me.

"Hey, Mama. So good to see you and be back home."

"And we're so glad you're back home."

"Where is Bella?"

"Having pizza with one of her friends from dance class."

"A female friend I hope."

"You know my rules, Aldridge," Mama said, cocking her head. "Bella doesn't date or take phone calls from the opposite sex until she's sixteen, and then only if her grades are right." She slipped her arms over my shoulders. "Come on and put your luggage in the trunk. We need to move fast because I'm parked illegally and I don't want to argue with the rent-a-cops."

Mama popped the trunk and I laid my garment and overnight bags over her tennis rackets and Bella's worn ballet slippers. I couldn't help but notice a bag of golf clubs and thought how wonderful it was that my mother had taken up the game in her fifties. It pleased me that Mama finally had her own life apart from Bella and me.

"You want me to drive?" I asked.

"You might not remember how to get around this town. Raleigh is really growing," she said, turning over the ignition. "Before long it might be too big for Bella and me."

"I bet I can still find my way around this town."

"You can certainly borrow my car if you decide to go visit some of your friends."

I thought for a moment and realized that no one I wanted to see lived there anymore. Like me, most of my classmates had left Raleigh, for Atlanta, Washington, D.C., or Charlotte. Besides, the people I'd been close to during my senior year at East Side High weren't my classmates or from Raleigh. I suddenly remembered Devin Gossett, the track and field star from Shaw University. I'd met him coming from my summer job at Bank of America before my senior year in high school. Devin was my first serious romance and I couldn't help smiling at the memory of sneaking out of the house and into his dorm room after I was certain Mama had fallen asleep. At the time she was working two jobs, so I could usually count on her being out cold by 8:30. Sometimes I would ride my bike to the campus or Devin would borrow one of his teammate's cars and meet me blocks away from Mama's house.

The last time I'd heard from Devin was several years ago, when he had gone back home to the Bahamas to compete in the Olympics for the national track team. He told me then that he was marrying a girl from the islands, not because he was in love, but because it was what his parents and country expected of him. Little did I know this would become the story of my life. That was cool with me because I liked Devin a lot but never felt in love with him like I did with Dray.

Meanwhile Mama was talking about her golf game, the new outlet malls, and how she wanted to come down to New Orleans and help Katrina victims. Every now and then I would look over and catch a glimpse of her brown eyes, which were soft and full of a mother's love. She was wearing a rose-red sweater, with an ivory skirt and lipstick that matched her top. Mama was a petite woman, short, just a little over five feet, with no visible waist. As a kid, I thought she was the most beautiful woman ever. She's still striking all these years later.

About twenty-five minutes later, we pulled off Highway 85 South and drove down a few dark roads until we came to the gate of a charming neighborhood. On both sides of the street stood two-story homes with spacious yards dotted with leafless trees. I remember the look of wonderment on my mother's face the first time she saw her new house fully decorated by yours truly. It was a look that I would never forget, and it had brought me great joy to be able to purchase a new house for my mother and sister. Thanks to Dray's generosity, I'd been able to pay cash for the house and decorate it with stylish furniture that had always been out of Mama's reach. He knew how much family meant and told me to pull out all the stops if it was going to make Mama happy. I loved Dray even more for allowing me to make that happen.

Mama's place was a white two-story house with a long brick walk leading to the door. We pulled into the driveway and into the garage; I got my bags from the trunk and followed Mama through the garage door and into the kitchen. The sudden aroma of the kitchen was almost as welcoming as my mother's hug and kisses, but not quite.

"What's that I smell?" I asked, laying my bags on one of the chairs in the breakfast nook.

"You know I had to cook some of your favorites." Mama went over to the stove and took a big wooden spoon from the counter and stirred a simmering pot.

"You left food cooking? Now you know better than that. You could have burned this house down," I scolded.

Hands on her hip, she gave me a "Who do you think you're talking to?" expression. "I knew that your flight was on time, so I left it on very low. I wanted it to be hot when we got home."

I joined her at the stove, "I thought we'd have pizza like Bella, but is that what I think it is?"

"What do you think it is? Or better yet, what does it smell like?" Mama asked as she lifted a silver lid from the big steel pot.

"Is it your world-famous stew?"

"You got it, baby. I know what my number-one son likes."

Mama was known for her white bean stew with duck sausage. My favorite dish was seasoned with chopped onions, minced garlic, fresh thyme, and miniature tomatoes. She usually served the stew with a warm spinach and bacon salad along with garlic cheese bread on the side. I could tell from the fragrant aroma that this had to be the exact menu. Mama knew me so well. I had even been thinking about the stew as the plane took off.

"Bella's gonna hate that she missed this." I laughed.

"That girl doesn't know what good food is. I told her she wasn't assured my good genes and she needed to start eating healthy if she wanted any kind of serious dance career."

"She'll be all right. I think we both know she got good genes."

"Sit down, son. Let me fix you a bowl," Mama said.

"You want me to help? I can get the salad plates." I looked around the kitchen, trying to remember which cabinet Mama kept them in.

She waved a dishcloth at me dismissively. "Sit down. You know my rules. You're a guest on the first night, but first thing tomorrow I'll go back to treating you like family."

"Do you have any red wine?" I asked.

"I do, but don't let me have to tell you to sit down again. I will get it when I finish serving the food."

I sat down at the table and unfolded the white linen napkin and placed it in my lap. I watched my mother ladle the stew into a white bowl, and somehow the joy she felt in having me home came through even in the small gesture of fixing my plate. All of my problems back in New Orleans felt a lifetime away.

There really was *no place like home.*

A couple of hours later, I was in my bedroom on the computer, trying to see if the Hornets had won and whether Dray had had a good game. The Hornets Web site said that they had lost the game and Dray had scored twelve points—not bad, but certainly not the scoring tear he'd been on recently. I wondered if he was going to be upset with me. I picked up my phone and sent him a text message. "Keep your head up boi. Y'all will get them the next time. Sleep well. AJ."

I then sent Jade a text reminding her to check my mail and water my plants. She texted me back immediately telling me it was already done.

I then got a text from Dray: "See I told you so. Next time you should listen to me boi."

I texted him back a simple "K" and then got up and walked over to my suitcase, which was lying open on the bed, when suddenly the door opened. A delightful, fine squeal of a teenage girl exploded in my room.

"My big brother's home! My big brother's home!" Bella repeated as she raced toward me, nearly tackling me onto the bed.

"Bella, you look so pretty," I said, kissing the top of her head. She had on a light pink leotard, a blue hoodie, and pink sweatpants that I'd sent her months ago. Her hair was in a ponytail and her skin so smooth and silky that if I hadn't known better, I would have sworn she was wearing makeup.

"AJ, how long are you going to be here? Maybe you can come to my dance studio or we can go shopping at Belk's. Did Mommy tell you that I'm taking voice lessons and that we're going to get an interview coach or maybe a life coach?"

"A life coach? An interview coach? What's that? Sweetheart, when did you get a life?" I joked.

Bella eyed me sternly. "I will be a junior in high school next year. And the interview coach helps me with my pageants, taking me through mock interviews."

"Are you ready for that?"

"Ready? My book bag is packed. I can't wait to go to a new school and leave some of those petty middle-school girls behind."

"So how is that going?"

Bella picked up one of my magazines and let out a sigh.

"They just hatin'. I guess it's to be expected. If Paris and Nicole can endure it, then I guess I can as well." Bella sounded quite the grown-up. I regretted that so much of my time was spent away from her and Mama. Here she was becoming a young woman and I was missing out on all of it.

"Paris and Nicole? Are they in your class?"

"No, silly. Paris Hilton and Nicole Richie from *The Simple Life*. I love those girls."

"I don't know if those are good role models, Bella," I said skeptically.

"I know they do stupid stuff like drink and drive, but they're going to stop doing that. I wrote Paris on her Web site and she actually sent me a letter back." Bella was clearly impressed by the connection she'd made. I didn't want to tell Bella that most likely Paris's assistant or some secretary had penned the response.

So I said simply, "That's nice."

"How long are you going to be home? I wish you would move back here so you could see me dance all the time."

"Maybe someday we'll live in the same city. The three of us."

"Mommy said we were going to watch a movie tonight. Which one?"

"I brought *Dreamgirls*. Have you seen it?"

"Have I seen it? Please," she said, looking at me sideways. "Only ten times and I know all the songs and dance steps. I tell my dance teacher all the time that I'm going to be the next Beyoncé." Bella dropped back onto the bed and waved her skinny arms.

"Why don't you just be the first Bella?" I suggested.

"Yeah, that's what I'll be. Everyone will just call me Miss

Bella." She giggled, staring at the ceiling. "And I'll make so much money that I'll be able to take care of you and Mommy like you take care of us."

I closed the suitcase and sat it on the floor. "Well, Miss Bella, why don't we go in the kitchen and microwave some popcorn and get something to drink."

She popped off the bed. "Okay, and I'll even make some of my famous Bella's pink lemonade."

"What am I gonna do with you?" I teased, slapping her butt playfully.

Bella stretched her arms out playfully and sang, "And you, you . . . you. You're gonna love me. Yes you are. Ooh . . . love me."

"Hey, I thought you wanted to be Beyoncé not Jennifer Hudson," I said, pulling my little sister out of the bedroom and toward the kitchen to prepare our snacks for movie night.

★ I had been home in New Orleans for a little over thirty minutes when the phone rang. I looked at the caller ID, recognized Jade's cell number, and clicked on. "Hey, Jade."

"So you made it back safely," she said. "Did you enjoy your trip? How are your mother and little sister?"

"They are doing fine and it was a really good trip. I'm glad I went home."

"Glad to hear it. What's your little sister doing? Did you tell her about how you're planning a sweet-sixteen party for her?"

"She's into school and her dance. I didn't mention the party because I want it to be a surprise." I settled on the couch. "What have you been up to?"

"I've been keeping myself busy. I picked up some night shifts and even work the VIP room at the casino. They've been calling me a little bit more at some of the spas to do facials, so I guess the rich people must be moving back to New Orleans. I have to go to some woman's house in a little while. I guess the bitch too rich to leave her house." Jade laughed.

"It's good to hear the rich people are returning. Maybe the city is on its way back at last. Anything important looking come in the mail?" I asked.

"Nothing looked urgent. I checked your e-mail too and I printed everything out and set it on the table in the hallway."

I looked at the narrow table right off the living room and noticed a lovely assortment of colorful flowers. "Hey, thank you for the bouquet. It's nice to come home to fresh flowers."

"I thought you'd like them."

"I do. I may have to leave town more often if it means flowers will be waiting."

"Listen, I need to start getting ready for my appointment. Do you need me to bring your key by today?"

"It can wait. Thanks for looking out, Jade. Don't forget to send me your invoice."

"I won't forget that!"

"Maybe we can get together soon and grab a bite to eat," I suggested.

"That would be nice. Maybe I'll try to learn how to cook something." Jade laughed.

"If you expect to marry a football player, you might want to work on that," I teased.

"You're probably right."

"Is that all you want from life, Jade?" I asked, suddenly thinking about Bella and myself.

"What do you mean?"

"Do you think marrying a ball player will make your life wonderful?"

There was silence for a moment and then Jade said, "I got big dreams, AJ. I want to own an exclusive dress shop, carrying

dresses I design myself. I'm pretty good at it. But most important, I want to be happy and in love. Now if that happens to be
with a street sweeper, that's who I'll marry."

"For real?"

"AJ, you haven't figured it out. I'm a lot of talk, but I'm
really a good girl."

"I know that, Jade."

I heard the beep indicating I had another call. "Oh, Jade,
make sure you marry a man who brings you flowers," I said.

"I always wanted to live in a house where flowers were waiting on me, so you don't have to worry about that."

"I'm glad to hear it. Bye, sweetheart," I said, and clicked
over to the other line.

"Hello?"

"So, I see you're home." It was the blackmailer back to
haunt my ass. Anger welled up inside me and I wanted to throw
the phone against the wall.

"What do you want?"

"We'll get to that later. Have you checked your e-mail?"

"No."

"I think you should do that and then we'll talk about how
you're going to give up all that money that doesn't belong to
you."

I'd listened enough and clicked off in a fury. I walked
straight to my home office. My hands were shaking from a
combination of nerves and anger as I punched the power button on the computer. It took a minute for the computer to boot
up and then I logged on. The silence was broken by the auto-
mated voice saying, "You've got mail."

Several new messages had arrived that morning, but one

e-mail captured my attention immediately. The sender's name was BLACKMALE and the e-mail came with an attachment. The message read, "Thought you might like to see this before the rest of the world does. Mr. Wilson would be so proud of you."

I couldn't begin to imagine what I was about to find, and part of me wished I could shut my eyes and make the whole thing disappear.

When I opened the attachment, a pop-up appeared at the bottom of the screen.

I clicked on the PLAY button, which started a film clip showing two men in bed. I looked closely. Even though I couldn't see the faces clearly, I realized that it was me and Dray at the hotel in Washington, D.C. There was no audio and the screen was so tiny that the movement was hard to make out. But it was clear to me that it was us, just as it would be to anyone else who knew what we looked like.

Dray and I were passionately kissing and undressing each other, something we did often when we had the chance to be alone. Someone had invaded the most intimate, cherished space of our private life and I felt sick to my stomach. I quickly shut down the e-mail and rushed to the bathroom. Standing in front of the toilet, I didn't know whether I was going to cry or throw up.

I looked into the mirror and couldn't help but notice the look of fear in my eyes. I had tried to keep it cool and thought I could handle the blackmailer all by myself. Suddenly I saw how wrong I had been. But I didn't need to see my reflection to know I was scared. I turned the cold water on and splashed my face repeatedly, trying to calm myself with deep breaths.

I dried my face and headed toward my bedroom to do something I hadn't planned. I was going to tell Dray it was quite possible that he was about to join the elite club of celebrities who had a sex video on the Internet.

⭐ "Dray, please call me when you get this message. I need to talk with you right away. I know you have a home game tonight. Maybe you can stop by. It's urgent." As soon as I hung up, my landline rang. I knew exactly who it was.

"So what did you think of my little film?"

"What do you want?" I asked in a surprisingly calm voice, even though my pulse was beating so fast I could feel it in my neck.

"I'll tell you what I want. I want you to get me a quarter of a million dollars—don't breathe a word of this to anyone—and then I want you to get your faggot ass out of New Orleans," he said with mounting anger.

Had I done something to this guy to offend him personally? My mind ran through all the people who might have a score to settle with me, but I came up blank. But maybe it wasn't me but Dray they were mad at, and I was caught in the middle. Was Dray holding out on me? Did he have somebody else in his life besides Judi and me? "How soon am I supposed to do this?" I asked, not knowing what he meant by getting out of New Orleans. This was so far out of control now that I wondered if it was time for Dray and me to go to the police. This situation didn't appear to be about the money, and what assurances did I have that this guy still wouldn't release the video even if I followed his orders?

"Just stay by the phone," he warned. "I want the money in

cash and I'm warning you, if you tell anybody or show up with someone you and your boyfriend are going to be the talk of cyberworld. Do I make myself clear?"

"Yes," I said.

"I guess you're smarter than I thought," he said smugly.

"How do I know this still won't end up over the Internet after I've paid you?"

"Guess you'll have to trust me."

"So when I give you the money you will get me the original copy of the video?"

"That's the deal."

I knew full well that even if he gave me the original it was no way of preventing him from double-crossing me. This idiot was right about one thing, I was going to have to trust him.

"When do I get the video?"

"As soon as I get the money and I know your ass is out of town for good."

"Why do I have to leave town?" This part of his demand was worse than extorting money from me. While I didn't much care for New Orleans, I cared for Dray deeply, and if Dray moved to Timbuktu I'd have followed. This man wasn't intent on just taking our money: he was hell-bent on tearing us apart and destroying our lives.

"Because that's the way sh . . . because I said so. Stop asking so many damn questions," he said.

The practical details involved in moving so quickly came to mind. "I might not be able to sell my house very quickly," I said, wondering why I was talking real estate to this total stranger.

"It's not your house. Your faggot boyfriend bought it. Remember?"

I'd had enough of this guy and my patience ran out. "Look, let's get this over with. Where do you want to meet?"

"Jackson Square," he said, just as my cell phone started ringing. It was Dray, and a protective calm settled over me even though I should have been more scared than ever. Maybe together we could beat this guy.

"I'll wait on your call, but I will need some time to get the money."

"You better not be trying to stall. All you got to do is go to the bank."

"I got to go," I said.

"Expect my call soon," he said, and hung up.

I immediately clicked on Dray's call.

"Dray. You got my message?"

"Hey, baby boi. No, I haven't listened to my messages yet. I just left the locker room on my way home but I thought about you and so I just called. What was your message?"

"Not so good," I said, wondering if I should tell Dray over the phone.

"What happened?"

"I don't think I should go into it over the phone."

"Okay. Hey, guess what? I felt my baby kick today. I went with Judi to her doctor's visit and I felt him kick. He'll be here before you know it." Dray sounded like he was beaming.

"It's a boy?" I asked, trying not to sound as deflated as I felt.

"Yeah, that's the other good news. I'm going to have a boy."

I sank back into my sofa speechless, my mind reeling that not only was Dray going to be a father, but this woman was going to deliver a boy. Just what Dray had hoped for. What else could go wrong today? I asked myself as I stared at the back of the front door. I felt so alone all of a sudden. I wanted to walk out that door and out of this whole sordid mess and into a life where I was the star, or at the very least costar.

"Aldridge? Hey, are you still there?" Dray asked.

A few more moments and I finally said, "Yeah, I'm still here."

"Isn't that great news? My parents are so proud. My dad is already talking about teaching him how to play basketball like he did with me."

"Yeah, Dray, that's wonderful news," I said, forcing myself to sound as supportive as I could. "Can you come by tonight?"

"Naw, dude, I promised her that I was coming home right after the game. I'm going to have to play ghost for the next couple of months because she's going to need me a lot more. But don't worry, I'll make it up to you soon, or maybe you can come to Phoenix next week when we play the Suns. Do you want to do that?"

"If you want me to," I said halfheartedly. Sure, she needed him. I wanted to pour out all my news about the blackmailer and say, "See, I need you too, Dray." But just as I done a thousand times before since he met Judi, I held it in.

"Hey, I'm pulling into my garage. I will text you before I go to bed."

"Yeah," I said, feeling tiny tears begin to slide down my face. "Why don't you do that, Dray?"

Twenty-one

After several martinis all by myself I lay down to sleep, but instead only dozed on and off. Was I really about to lose everything? I could stand losing the house and I could even stand losing all Dray's money if it came to that. But the thought of not having Dray in my life was something I couldn't fathom. I needed him and I hoped Dray needed me too.

I woke up and found there was a text from Dray saying he was going to try to sneak off and come see me. So when I heard the doorbell a short time later, I figured he'd run off without his key.

"What the hell are you doing here?" I demanded.

"I wanted to see how you were doing. We didn't leave on such good terms," Cisco said.

I couldn't believe that this asshole, who had to be behind the blackmail of Dray and me, had the nerve to show up at my home. Maybe he didn't think I would be home and was coming to my house to plant some kind of movie camera or listening device to further his plan.

"Aren't you going to ask me in?" Cisco wore a Puma sweat suit that was a kelly green color with yellow stripes I hadn't seen a lot of men wearing. Funny that in the heat of anger I noticed something as dumb as that.

"Why would I want to do that?"

The expression on his face suddenly changed from all smiles to a deep frown. "So it's like that," he said, taking a step back and looking me up and down like I wasn't shit.

"Yeah, that's the way it is." If I could have popped him upside his head, I would have.

He looked visibly alarmed.

"So, are you still working out?"

"Are you kidding me? I can't believe you'd have the nerve to show your face. Did you come to pick up your money? Is that what you're here for? You guys aren't giving me much time. I ought to call the fucking police right now."

"Police? What are you talking about, dude? You don't owe me any money."

"Come on and stop playing with me. I know you're the one who blackmailed Dray, and now you're doing the same thing to me." I eyed my alarm system to the left of the door and made sure I knew where the panic button was in case this fool came after me.

"Blackmail? Dude, you trippin'. I'm here to apologize, but if a brotha can't drop by to admit that he was wrong, then I will just take my happy ass home."

I scrutinized Cisco to see if he was possibly telling the truth. He had to be behind this scheme, and most likely one of his bois was helping him out. I didn't know how they were getting their information but I figured their street smarts could carry them only so far. But if he really was behind all this, why would he come to my house? The terms had been laid out by the blackmailer, so why would he risk exposing himself by seeing me in person?

"So," I said, my arms crossed against my chest, "you're saying you didn't contact Dray and threaten to tell his father if he didn't give you $100,000 and then turn around and put your bois up to do the same thing to me? You didn't threaten to release some little video of us if I didn't comply? Are you saying that wasn't you?"

Cisco stepped closer, as if to plead his case. "Look, man, that ain't the way I roll. I make my own money. I might not ever have bank like you and Dray, but my moms raised me better than that."

Don't ask me why, but somehow I knew there was not a trace of a scam about him. Maybe he was telling the truth, and here I was acting like a crazy person.

I followed my hunch. "You sure?"

"Look, Aldridge, my word is my bond. I don't know what you're talking about. I came over here to apologize for coming on so strong a few weeks ago. I was wrong and that was unprofessional." Cisco stood there a moment, looking expectantly, as if my believing him was the most important thing in the world to him.

Frankly, I didn't know who or what to believe anymore. My nerves were fried and I didn't have the strength left to fight this alone. I had to talk to someone.

"Come in," I said, opening the screen door.

He backed away hesitantly, playfully, putting both hands in front of himself defensively. "Are you sure?"

"Yeah, I'm sure." I laughed. "Things have just been crazy lately. Come in."

Cisco slid into my living room like a stray cat who might get tossed out at any second.

"So will you accept my apology? I think you're a cool dude and I can help you find a good trainer. I just wanted you to know that you didn't do anything wrong and I'm working on some issues in my own life."

"No hard feelings," I said, shaking his hand. "You owe me an apology? If anything I owe you one."

We took seats facing each other across the coffee table.

"So what's all this about being blackmailed? That's some serious shit."

Now that I'd gone and told him about the blackmailer, there was no turning back. I couldn't exactly turn around and say this was some type of joke I'd planned just to pass time. I had to play it cool enough not to tell him too much, but just let him know what I was up against. "Yeah, that's the real deal. At first they came after Dray, and when he paid them a hundred thousand they came after me."

I went on to tell Cisco about the guy demanding money and meeting him at Jackson Square.

"I wouldn't be meeting any niggas in any park in New Orleans carrying a suitcase full of money. Dude, this sounds like some television or movie shit. And you thought it was me? That's funny," he said, shaking his head, amused by the idea. "I ain't got the smarts or the heart for that kinda shit. My ass don't want to end up having the state of Louisiana providing my housing."

With Cisco out of my lineup of suspects, the field was suddenly wide open. Only it made less sense than ever.

"Who could be behind all this?" I said, thinking out loud.

"Sounds like some shit these junior playas in New Orleans might try. Punk asses." Cisco leaned forward. "Do you need my

help? I got my bois that could put a little pressure on these people," he said, slamming his left fist in his open right hand as a
show of power.

"What can you do? What are you saying?"

"I'm saying I got some associates who can bring the wood
and ain't nobody got to know."

"Let me think about it." As much as I loved the idea of the
blackmailer getting his ass kicked, I didn't want to get involved
in anything criminal that was going to get my ass into trouble
that Dray's money couldn't get me out of.

"Okay, man, but all you got to do is to say the word. I will hit
up my boys and it will be on like *Donkey Kong.* Shit, I ain't
busted up a pimp in a long time."

I laughed in spite of myself. "I'll let you know, Cisco."

"Okay, that's what's up. I'm going to bounce, but hit me up
if you need me. My cell number is still the same."

"I appreciate that," I said.

"That's what's up," Cisco said, and leaned over and gave me
a brother-man hug. I walked him to the door.

"Thanks for coming by. I really appreciate your concern."

"No doubt," Cisco said with a smile that belied his tough-
boy demeanor.

★ An afternoon rain was beating down on the roof of my
town house when Dray walked in, soaking wet.

"You miss me, baby boi?" he asked, seemingly unaware of
the irony that he was about to have a new "baby boi" all his own.
He removed his T-shirt, his six-pack glistening.

"Yeah, I missed you."

"How you gonna show me you missed me?" Dray asked. He

was oblivious to all the new drama, and that would have been almost funny if I hadn't felt so afraid and alone.

"You want a massage?"

"That could be a start."

"I'll do whatever you need, Dray. You know that." I knew where this was heading and I started to tell him what I really wanted was to just crawl in bed with him, maybe read to him until we both fell asleep. I needed him to hold me like old times when we were in college, to tell me that everything would be fine just as long as I was in his arms.

Dray unbuckled his belt and his jeans slid down. In seconds he was butt-ass naked. His dick looked as big as a telescope.

"Come here, babe, and show me how much you missed me," Dray said devilishly. I needed to talk to Dray more than I needed to make love to him, but his awesome body was dictating the conversation. After all these years, this man made me hard as brick any time we were together.

I walked over to him and he wrapped me in his massive arms. He began kissing me and his kisses were so deep it was like he was making love to me with his lips. I was ready to climax right there in his arms.

"Let's go into the bedroom," I suggested, removing my sweat suit.

"Naw, let's do it in here," Dray whispered in my ear, which he proceeded to nibble like some exotic delicacy. He was feeling frisky and I needed to be made to feel safe. I gave in to his passion. Before I did, however, I picked up the remote to my music system. I clicked it and the melodious sounds of Keyshia Cole filled the room.

Dray was sprawled out with an expectant smile. I crawled over to him and started to lick him like he was covered in chocolate syrup. As I got to his groin, I could smell the heavy scent of his arousal. He cupped the back of my head to pull me in closer, moaning, "Come here, AJ baby, and let Dray show you how I really feel about my boi."

Dray's massive dick was fully erect, begging to be stroked and tasted. I slid my hand over his mushroom head and down his long shaft all the way to his balls. He closed his eyes, lost in pleasure, moaning, "Oh, baby, that's it." I repeated the gesture, running my tongue over his dick head at the same time. Finally I couldn't stand it any longer and took him in my mouth in one quick motion. Dray shuddered and opened his eyes. He mouthed a silent "O." I closed my lips tight around his dick and then went all the way down on him, coming up only to kiss his balls.

When it felt like Dray couldn't stand it anymore, he stood up and went to the French Provincial desk where I kept my condoms and pulled a couple of the gold packets out. Then he came over to me from behind and began to grind on me as he played with my dick until it was brick. He turned me around to face him and he bent down and began kissing my chest until I was ready to explode from excitement. He began kissing me deeply and then he turned me back around. Moments later, I suddenly felt his latex-clad dick plunging into me like someone was pushing a balloon up my ass. I gasped, half in pain, half in disbelief that this man could slide inside me so fast. I offered no resistance, pushing my ass into him, wanting every inch in me. As he began to grind, the pleasure intensified and I didn't want him to ever stop as he sent a sweet excitement through my body.

I closed my eyes and enjoyed the cool slipperiness of the lubricant before letting out a long breath of pure pleasure. I could feel Dray's warm breath against my neck and the faint smell of his deodorant as he continued with his powerful strokes. As he pumped harder I reached back to touch his plump, muscular ass like I was trying to press him deeper inside me. As the ripples of pleasure streaked through my body, Dray and I were moaning as our sweaty passion increased.

"What you want me to do now, baby?" he whispered.

"Oh, Dray, keep fucking me. Come on, boi!"

"You like that big dick, boi?" He began to stroke me deeper and faster, mounting me doggy-style.

"I love it," I said, trying to hold up my nut.

"Like you love me?"

"Yes . . . yes," I said. I lost myself completely at the sensation of having Dray inside me.

"Tell me."

"I love you, Dray." I could barely get out the words, he had me so breathless.

"What else you love?"

"You."

"What else, AJ?"

"I love this dick," I moaned.

"How much?"

"I can't live without it . . . oh baby, that is it!" Dray's muscled body enveloped mine, squeezing tightly. In a moaning and pumping crescendo, we suddenly climaxed simultaneously.

As we both lay on the polished cherry floor, limp from exhaustion, there were so many unspoken questions dancing in front of me. I looked over and admired Dray's eyes and lips, and his dick lying on his belly like a turkey drumstick. I wanted to kiss him but I resisted. Dray looked at me and asked if I felt all right and I simply nodded my head. I wanted to ask Dray if

Judi made him feel as good as I did. Did she love him the way I did? Could he be himself when he was with her? Could he tell her every thought that crossed his mind? I wanted Dray to promise me that we would always be together. That he would always love me. But nary had a word left my lips. Although we lay there wrapped in an embrace, I could feel my man slipping away between my fingers.

Twenty-two

The big day arrived and I was nervous as hell. How exactly do you walk into your neighborhood Bank of America and withdraw a quarter million dollars in cash? Although I told myself that I was going to do it no matter what—after all, what choice did I really have?

Still, somewhere in the back of my mind I resisted. Maybe this wasn't the answer. Dray had paid off this guy before—what was to stop him from coming back again? I still hadn't told Dray a thing and kept asking myself if that wasn't a mistake.

It wasn't as if he knew how to handle the blackmailer all that well. He had caved in at the demand, anything to save his ass. But even so, we had been in that together and for some reason that had made a difference, made the situation feel a lot less scary than it felt this time around.

I told myself that I kept Dray out of it because I loved him with all my heart or I was scared of what he might do. Whatever the reason, I was going through with my plan without a word to Dray.

. . .

★ I walked into the bank loaded with identification and an empty Louis Vuitton duffel bag. I decided to make my transaction at mid-morning, when I thought it would be less crowded. The last thing I needed was someone nosy overhearing my business. There were enough people spying on me as it was.

There were only three people in front of me and they couldn't move fast enough. When my time came, a young African American woman with two-toned hair asked how she could help me.

As calmly as I could, I said, "I would like to withdraw two hundred and fifty thousand dollars from my SmartMoney account, and I would like it all in hundred-dollar bills." No matter how I tried to psyche myself up for that moment, I couldn't quite get it right. I'm sure I looked as suspicious as I sounded. I had more than enough money in my account, but I was still nervous about taking out such a big withdrawal and walking around with it.

"You want to do what?" she asked with one of those "sister-girl-child, please" looks.

Just as calmly, but no less nervous inside, I repeated, "I would like to withdraw a quarter of a million dollars from one of my accounts and I would like it in hundred-dollar bills."

"I guess you want crisp, new hundred-dollar bills," she wisecracked.

"That would be nice, Nikita," I said, looking down at her name tag.

"I'll need some identification."

"I have three pieces," I said, handing her my Louisiana and old Georgia driver's licenses and my black American Express card. For good measure I had my dog-eared social security card on stand-by.

She looked at my identification, then at me, and then once again at the cards.

"Where did you open your account?"

"In Atlanta," I said.

"Is that where your signature card is?"

"I guess so."

"What's the last four numbers of your social?"

"Eight-one-one-nine," I said, from memory.

She clicked my information into the computer in front of her. "What is your verbal password?" she asked.

"Basketball thirteen."

"Hmmpt. There it is," she said, sounding surprised. She sized me up, as if to figure out where I got all this money and what I was going to do with it after I made the withdrawal.

I gave Nikita a quick smile, hoping to speed the transaction along.

"I have to talk to my supervisor, and this may take a minute."

"Take your time, Nikita," I said. "I'm not in a hurry."

About ten minutes later, Nikita came back, smiling, with a middle-aged white female. I could see a middle-aged black security man out of the corner of my eye. Nikita sat back down at her computer and proceeded to explain my transaction in detail. Then the supervisor looked at me and asked politely, but sounding concerned, "Mr. Richardson, is everything okay?"

"Everything will be just fine once I complete my transaction," I said firmly.

"I understand. We're waiting for your Atlanta branch to fax us a copy of your signature card since you're not a regular customer at our branch. I expect it any moment." She smiled again, eyeing me more than a little suspiciously.

"And how long will that take?" I asked.

"Not long. But I hope you understand, we're trying to protect you," she said. I started to say, "Yeah, by keeping me from

my own money," but I didn't see any advantage in playing my
angry-black-man card, so I simply smiled back politely. Nikita
still looked at me with a hint of suspicion, like she was thinking, What is this nigger up to?

"Why don't you sit in my office while we get this finished for
you," said the supervisor, who identified herself as Mrs. Curtis.

"That sounds like a great plan," I said as I looked to the glass
office off the lobby that she pointed to.

"I'll join you in a few minutes," Mrs. Curtis said.

"Fine. I'll be waiting," I said, heading toward the office.

Inside the office I noticed a couple of certificates on the
wall. I learned that Debbie was her first name and that she had
an undergrad degree from the University of Alabama and a
masters from Southern University. I'd heard that there were a
lot of white people in the area who'd gone to the graduate and
professional schools of the predominantly African American
Southern University. Somehow I couldn't picture Debbie Curtis being one of them. Just as I was getting ready to look closer
to see what kind of degree Debbie received from Southern, she
walked in, carrying a blue bag and noticeably friendlier. She
closed her door quickly and took a seat behind her desk.

"Thank you for your patience. I was able to verify everything
and complete your transaction, Mr. Richardson," she said as she
began to remove hundred-dollar bills from the bag. "This sort of
transaction, in such large amounts of cash, is highly unusual for
us. I hope you understand." She laid out the stacks of bills in
front of me. Once the surface of her desk had nearly been covered with money, she said, "I would advise you to count it, although I can confirm with absolute certainty it's all there."

After ten minutes of counting under Mrs. Curtis's watchful
eye, I nodded to her as if to say, "That's everything." I opened

the duffel bag and began to place the bills inside. She had gotten clearance but her demeanor told me she couldn't figure out what the hell I was up to.

"Would you like me to get one of our security officers to walk you to your car?" she offered. "That's a very large amount of money."

"Thanks, but that won't be necessary." I had my own security in the form of Cisco waiting on me right outside the bank. He had offered to be my bodyguard when I handed over the money in the park. Although I figured this asshole wasn't about to try to hurt me, having Cisco close by did offer some comfort.

"Well, thank you for banking with Bank of America, Mr. Richardson. Maybe sometime soon you can come in and sit down with someone from our brokerage. We might help you to invest some of your remaining funds. We'd be happy to speak with you anytime," Mrs. Curtis said, offering me her slender hands.

"I'll think about that, but I have someone handling my investments for me right now. Thanks for your help with this matter."

I headed out of the bank with Nikita's eyes following me, a smirk on her face.

★ When I got back home, I waited for the phone call with further instructions. Clearing out wasn't going to be easy. I looked around the house and thought I would miss this place. I recalled the first time Dray saw the place decorated. He walked in and his mouth dropped open. He said that I'd outdone myself and maybe one day we'd share a place like this.

Dray and I had had some good times here and I really believed I could be a lot of help in rebuilding the city. But somebody else didn't think so and wanted me gone, baby, gone.

Right at noon my landline rang.

I took a deep breath. "Hello?"

"Did you get the money?"

"Yes, I did," I said.

"Good. Now I want you to meet me right in front of the fountain on the square at five thirty sharp. Don't be late and the money better all be there."

Ignoring his threat I asked, "When will I get the disc?" I wondered why he wanted to meet in a place so public. There would be dozens of witnesses. Could he be afraid of me?

"I told you when you'd get the damn disc."

"Oh shit," I said, suddenly remembering that I had a seven o'clock flight to Phoenix to meet Dray for his game.

"What's wrong?"

"Can we meet a little earlier? I have something I have to do early this evening."

"Hell no, and make sure you don't tell anybody or you'll really be sorry."

"No one knows," I lied. Cisco made me promise I wouldn't attempt the drop-off alone.

"If anything seems funny to me the whole deal is off and that won't be good for you."

"How will I know you?"

"I'll be dressed in black," he replied quickly.

"What am I supposed to do when I get there?"

"I want you to sit on the bench on the west side of the fountain with the bag with the money right next to you. Just look straight ahead the whole time. You'll know it's me when I arrive. I will take your little package, make sure everything is straight, and then I'll give you what you want. You do what I tell you and this won't take long."

"Okay," I said, looking at my watch. I wondered how I was going to explain missing my flight to Dray. Where would I begin? "Sorry I missed my flight. I had to meet my blackmailer." I needed Dray more than ever.

"Be smart and all your troubles will be over."

"Five thirty?" I said.

"Five thirty sharp."

I clicked off and suddenly I found myself wondering what you wore to a blackmail drop-off.

★When I arrived at the square, I saw no one dressed in black. Instead there was a group of young guys throwing a football and the usual smattering of tourists strolling through the park. I saw in the distance—across from the square—Café Du Monde and thought of Jade. She'd been the one reliable, good friend I'd made in town. I felt lousy about ducking out without telling her. Until that moment I'd not realized how much I'd miss Jade.

As instructed, I took a seat on a bench on the west end of the fountain. It was well past 5:30 but no one had shown. Just as I was wondering if this was some kind of joke, a black man, about five-ten and close to two hundred pounds, walked toward me wearing all black. This fool had a tarnished gold-colored grill in the front of his mouth. The first thing that came to mind was that there's no way this idiot was smart enough to pull this off by himself. Would he even be able to count the money to see if the amount was correct?

He stopped and looked at me cross-eyed and then down at the black leather bag I'd transferred the money into. I nodded as if to say, "That's the money, idiot." He stared at me, then coldly threw a white envelope toward me, grabbed the bag, and started to haul ass through the park.

He almost bumped into Cisco, who was sitting on a bike, shirtless, drinking from a bottle of water looking like just an ordinary guy out in the park for an early evening ride.

So this was the guy who'd turned my life upside down? I shook my head in disbelief and watched the rich evening sunset cover the city. I let out a deep breath, glad that this episode of *The Streets of New Orleans* was over. I could now head home and get ready for my trip to Phoenix. For the first time in weeks, I was going to be able to enjoy my time with Dray.

I walked a few feet toward the lamppost where Cisco was stationed when I bumped into a woman who was quickly rounding the corner without looking where she was going. When I turned to apologize, there was a moment of instant recognition. Her face was a little fatter and I almost didn't recognize her, yet I knew who she was. Those olive-green eyes were just as cold and her styleless bleached-blonde hair just as messy as when I spotted her at the mall. Still, it didn't make sense. What was she doing here?

Confused, I asked, "Do I know you?"

She had a look of deep loathing yet at the same time a self-satisfied smile on her face. "You know me, asshole," she said with an icy tone that matched her eyes.

She was obviously pregnant, with a pumpkinlike stomach sticking out of her yellow Empire dress. What in the hell was Judi doing in this park, giving me so much shade?

"Who are you?" I asked, trying not to let on I knew exactly who she was.

"Stop playing, Aldridge. You know damn well who I am. I'm your boyfriend's fucking wife, you little idiot."

"My boyfriend?"

"Cut the crap."

"Who are you talking about?"

"Drayton Jones. You know who that is?"

"Yes I know Dray, but he's a friend. So you're his wife? Nice to meet you," I said extending my hand.

She brushed it away and said, "You think you're cute."

"I haven't a clue as to what you are talking about. What are you doing here all alone?"

"Just making sure that our transaction came off without a hitch, and to give you my own personal message," she said with a steely directness.

"What are you talking about?" Was this *bitch* behind all this shit?

"I'm talking about you and my husband. If you don't want your D.C. escapades broadcast all over the world, then you will leave him alone and I mean for good. We are getting ready to start a family and we don't need your ass in the picture." She moved in closer. "You better be glad that I let you keep some of Dray's money, but if you contact him in any way from this moment forward, I will take it all from you. That would be very easy for me to do. I'm his wife, not some pathetic faggot boyfriend he keeps on the side. That money belongs to me anyway. Do I make myself clear?"

As crazy as this episode had been up until now, never had it been crazier. My heart hammered away in my chest and I took a deep breath before speaking. "I don't know what you're talking about," I said, making eye contact with Cisco. I wanted to let him know that I wasn't in any danger but I still needed him close by.

"Don't be coy and cute with me, Aldridge. Or should I call you AJ? Yeah, I think I will. I knew all about your little affair before I married Dray but figured it would end when we left Atlanta. You're not dealing with some sista girl," she said, snapping her fingers in mockery, "who's too stupid to not know that the man she was about to marry had a boy on the side. But I will say this for you, AJ: you're persistent, so I had to deal with you the way my daddy deals with his business partners, and that means hitting you in your wallet." She stepped closer to me and raised her jeweled finger and waved. "Do not contact Dray under any circumstances or not only will I release your little sex tape on the Internet, but I will put your sick phone conversations and texts on full blast. Then for the pièce de résistance I'll tell Dray's parents about all this madness. And we both know they would be crushed and so would Dray. So if you love him like you say you do, then it's time you show it."

So this is what everything came down to. Some cheap blonde who managed to trap Dray called the shots for the guy who loved Dray with all his heart. At the same time, I didn't know what made me madder—that this woman was giving orders or that Dray had settled for such a low-down piece of trash. He'd never spoken of her in anything but adoring terms, so maybe Judi would make a fine actress.

I didn't respond, but a silent rage started to warm my body. I wanted to slap the shit out of this woman, but I could flash forward and see my ass sitting in a jail cell for hitting a pregnant woman, and a white one at that.

"So do I make myself clear? I don't want to have this conversation again. I need my husband to turn his full attention to me, our child, and the few good years he might have left to make millions. You understand me?"

Recalling my promise to Dray never to reveal our relationship, I said, "I don't know what you're talking about."

Although she flashed a fake smile, I could tell she was not amused. "So that's how you're going to play it? Well, let me leave you with this piece of advice: if you dare to get on that plane to Arizona tonight, you're bringing Dray's life, as he knows it, to an end. I'll be on the phone to Mississippi so fast that his family will think another Katrina has hit."

I'd had all I could take. "Nice seeing you, Judi. I hope the rest of your pregnancy is a stress-free one."

"I can live stress-free as long as you do what I say and have no further contact with Dray. And if you think for the slightest second that I'm not serious about doing what I just said, then you are sadly mistaken."

I turned around and realized that Cisco was now only a few feet from us. I guess the conversation had gone on long enough to signal trouble.

"Is everything all right?" Cisco interjected.

Judi turned in disgust. "Who is this? What kind of person are you? Are you two-timing my husband with somebody else's husband?"

"Aldridge, is everything cool?" Cisco asked again.

"Everything is cool. Are you ready to roll?" I shot Judi my death look, warning her that she'd fucked with the wrong guy. She might have had the upper hand right now, but that could change at any moment. I wasn't going to roll over that easily.

As I started to walk out of the park, she shouted, "Don't force me to make those phone calls, Aldridge, because I will. Nobody messes with Judi Ledbetter and just walks away. Do you hear me? Nobody!"

When we were safely out of the park, Cisco asked if I wanted to talk about what had just happened.

"I really don't want to get into it right now."

"That's cool, but who was that pregnant white chick and why was she all up in your grill like that?"

I turned to face him. "I said I don't want to talk about it."

Cisco let it go and we walked a few blocks in silence. My nerves had calmed some and I had the urge to tell him what had gone on, as much to process my anger as to share the whole story.

"That was my boi's wife, and it seems like she's the one who's been blackmailing both of us." There, it was out in the open at last. Since I wasn't going to see Dray anymore, I had no need to protect our secrets. Judi was the kind of low-class bitch who would tell his father and Dray would never forgive me, knowing I could have prevented that.

"How did she find out about you two? You guys are together, right?"

"Yeah, we're together. Have been for seven years." I was surprised at how easily I released the secret I'd kept for years.

"But how did she find out about it?" Cisco asked.

"I guess that's the million-dollar question."

We turned onto a street. "Are you going to tell him what happened?"

"Nope."

"Then who was that dude who left with the money?"

"Someone Judi paid to do her dirty work. But taking my money, my boi, and my house wasn't enough. When she saw me, she couldn't resist letting me know she knew what the deal was," I said.

"Bitches all the same no matter what color they are."

I didn't need to hear that and was relieved to reach my town house where I could finally be alone.

"True. Good looking-out."

"No problem. Do you want me to come inside and make sure everything is cool?"

"I think everything will be fine. I really appreciate your concern, but I got some things I need to take care of. Give me a call tomorrow and we can talk about resuming my workouts."

"That's what's up." Cisco surprised me by lunging forward and giving me a brother-man hug. He slapped my shoulder by way of saying goodbye, then climbed on his bike.

I turned the key to my door and watched Cisco disappear into the New Orleans night.

★ For the first time in a week, I walked into my house without dreading some danger that might await me. Strange as it seems, I felt safer knowing who the enemy was. I picked up the phone and called my cell phone provider, canceling my three cell phones. I got a new cell phone number but made sure that it was private. I confirmed twice with the customer service representative that no one would be able to gain access.

"No one can get it unless you give it to them," she assured me.

Next I called my mother and gave her my new number. When she asked if everything was okay, I lied and told her yes. I explained that I was getting too many telemarketing calls in the middle of meetings. I promised to try my best to make it home in two months for Christmas.

I called Jade but got her voice mail. "Hey Jade, I'm taking off for a couple of weeks and I had to change my phone numbers. Don't worry about me. I promise to reach out once things settle down a bit."

I then phoned Maurice. I knew I couldn't hang around New Orleans for long and would have to find a place to stay for a couple of days. I needed to be around a good friend as I figured out what I would do next. Of all people, he knew how it felt to lose a man.

"Come on, child, I could use the company," Maurice said.

"Are you sure it won't be a problem?"

"If it gets to be a problem, then I'll put your ass out," he joked.

"I think I'll leave here first thing tomorrow."

"Does this have anything to do with the phantom boyfriend?"

At first I began to resort to the usual lies to cover my tracks, but to my surprise I said, "Up until now everything had to do with the phantom, but not anymore. Not anymore." Just speaking the truth so spontaneously felt like a new beginning in some small way.

"I'm glad to hear that, child. I'm sure he wasn't good enough for you. Men ain't shit. Never have been, never will be. It's all about the dick for them. That's real talk, honey."

As Maurice continued to ramble on about how lucky I was to be rid of my boyfriend, I felt a deep regret rise within me. I had an aching sense of sorrow. I felt like I had lived most of my adult life in a dream. A dream that died that evening in the park with Judi. Now I had to go and live in the real world. And my friend Maurice was as real as it got.

Twenty-three

I woke up to what was going to be my last day in New Orleans for a while. I'd not spoken to Dray since the drop-off and I struggled with my tremendous feeling of loss. With my phone shut off and him on the road and unable to just drop in on me, I pictured him deeply concerned. At least I hoped he was worried. More than anything, I imagined he was pissed.

Morning had settled in cool and secure, a mild drizzle falling outside the bedroom window. I got out of bed and emptied the contents of my closets into three suitcases I had lined up on the floor. The stuff that didn't fit in the suitcases I put in two big boxes to give to the local Salvation Army. I'd loved shopping for all those clothes, yet it was surprisingly easy to let them go. After all, I reminded myself, they're just clothes.

As I packed, I was overcome with flashes of anger at what Judi was doing to Dray and I fantasized about getting revenge. I desperately wanted to get the bitch back, but she had me over a barrel.

I thought about calling Dray and telling him what had happened and giving him an ultimatum. I knew he loved me, but was that enough to give him the courage to face his fans and, more important, his family? Was that asking for too much?

Then I thought how selfish I sounded by thinking this little love affair was more important than Dray's career and family. He would never forgive me if I forced him to make that decision, and so leaving and following Judi's orders was most likely the wise move.

Just as I was going into the kitchen to get something to drink there was a knock at the door. What if it was Dray? What explanation would I give him about the suitcases? I wouldn't put it past Judi to show up at my door for round two. I walked into the living room and through the side window looked outside and saw Jade.

Relieved, I opened the door.

"What are you doing here?"

"I got your message. What is going on?" Jade asked with a look of genuine concern. "You can't take off just like that."

"Everything is fine," I said.

"But where are you going?"

"Atlanta, to help out a friend of mine."

"Is he or she sick?"

"No, just dealing with a little love issue."

"Oh, he's got the love jones," Jade said, understanding in a snap.

"Yeah, I guess you could call it that."

"Is it your friend Maurice that you were telling me about?"

"What about Maurice?" I asked.

"Is he the one in love?"

How had she remembered his name? I couldn't have mentioned him more than twice, but I guess women remember insignificant shit like that.

"Yeah," I stuttered. I appreciated her concern but was in no mood for company all of a sudden.

"Are you sure?"

"Sure about what?"

"Are you sure no one is messing with you?"

"Why would you ask me that?"

"I don't know. I just have a funny feeling," Jade said vaguely.

"Trust me, Jade, everything will be fine."

"Do you need me to take care of things while you're away?"

I hadn't gotten around to that. "Yeah, Jade. Thanks a lot. I'll pay you when I get back. I hope that's okay."

"I'm not worried about that. I just hope everything is all right and you can get back here soon. Besides, I think my ship is getting ready to come in."

There it was again. It was as if she knew a whole lot more than she was saying.

"What's going on?"

"Oh, nothing," Jade said quickly. "Just make sure you call me when you get settled."

"I will." I couldn't shake the feeling that something was strange with Jade changing the subject. I asked, "What do you have planned today?"

"I have a couple of in-home appointments and I'm going to try and get to the gym."

"Okay, give me a hug and I'll see you soon," I said as I moved close to Jade and hugged her tightly. Just before I released her, she whispered, "You know I'm here if you need me."

"I know," I said as slow, small tears formed in my eyes.

.   .   .

★ After meeting with a real estate agent to put my place on the market, I took one final look around the living room and my eyes landed on the phone. I knew it would be cut off soon, but I suddenly had the urge to make a call.

I was relieved when I heard a dial tone and I immediately began dialing. After a few rings there was the familiar voice that always brought a smile to my face.

"Bella," I said.

"AJ, I was just thinking about you!"

"What were you thinking?"

"How I couldn't wait to see you again."

"And I can't wait to see you, sweetheart. Is Mama at home?"

"Yes, she's in the kitchen cooking, I think. You want to speak with her?"

"Yes, darling."

"Okay," Bella said.

"I love you, Bella Lynn."

"I love you too."

As I waited for my mother to come to the phone, I thought about how lucky I was to have my mother and sister in my life. I didn't want to admit it, but I was going to need them more than ever as I worked my way through this nightmare of a breakup. I wasn't about to dump the whole mess in their laps, but Mama was smart enough and knew me so well that I wouldn't have to say much for her to get the general idea.

"Hey, baby," my mother said. "Is everything all right?"

"I guess so," I said somberly.

My mother could always tell from my voice how I was feeling and so I guess it had betrayed me again.

"It will be soon."

"Is there something special I can do? Do you need me to come to New Orleans?"

"No. I just called to tell you I'll be in Atlanta for a couple of weeks."

My mama was no fool. "What's wrong, baby?"

"Oh, Mama, I'll be all right." I paused to consider what I was about to say. "I just need you to pray for me."

"I always do. You know that. I don't know why you would even ask me."

"I know you do, but I might need extra prayers the next couple of months."

"Does this have anything to do with your special relationship?"

It was as if she'd struck a nerve. I suddenly felt tears running down my face. "Yeah," I mumbled. "It does."

"Do you mind me asking what happened?"

"There's too much to go into, but it's over and that makes me really sad," I said. Mama didn't know the half of it.

"Have you been crying?"

"Yes," I said.

"Baby, let me give you a little piece of advice that my mother gave me the first time a boy broke my heart. I want you to hear this, so first stop crying."

I wiped the tears with the back of my hand and asked my mother what my grandmother had said.

"Don't cry because it's over. Smile because it happened."

Twenty-four

Christmas Day arrived in Atlanta, cold and wet. The city needed the rain, but I didn't need the gloomy weather to take me further into a love hangover—no, make that a depression. Leaving Dray hurt just as much today as it had when I made the seven-hour drive to Atlanta.

Maurice had told me the night before Christmas that he hoped the holidays would help snap me out of my funk in time so I could enjoy the New Year. Besides, he said, he didn't want his best friend carrying doom and gloom to his Christmas dinner. He had invited about thirty of his friends over for a huge Christmas dinner catered by S.T.E.P.S., an event-planning company that hosted most of Atlanta's elite affairs. I guess business had picked up for Maurice because he wasn't cutting any corners this Christmas. Or maybe he was still auditioning people for his big party.

I admired the way he poured his heart into his design firm, party planning, and everything he attempted. Failure was not a part of his vocabulary.

Maurice had hired someone to decorate his ranch-style

home in Jonesboro with lights and pageantry outside as well as inside. When I woke up Christmas morning, the chef was busy preparing dinner, but he wasn't too busy to make omelets and fresh blueberry muffins for Maurice and me.

"I hope you're not going to walk around here all day with that long face," Maurice said as he took a sip of hot apple cider. The breakfast nook where we sat was full of the cider's delicious aroma.

"You know the real reason I'm having this little Christmas party, don't you?" Maurice asked as he took a pinch of his muffin and smiled a sly grin.

"Because it's Christmas and you love giving parties."

"Yes, that's true, but my list for the big party isn't where it needs to be. Still way too many people, and so I need to make some cuts before the New Year. So I invited some people who are at the bottom of the list and might find themselves with no invite or on the waiting list. You can help me make cuts. Won't that be fun?"

"I don't know if I'd be good at that," I said, wondering how Maurice took pleasure in cutting out people who were about to be his guests at Christmas dinner.

"Don't worry about that. I'll teach you. Pay close attention to their conversation and wardrobe. If they can't dress well for the holidays, then there is no hope."

"Do they know that they're being judged today?"

"Child, boo. They don't have a clue. A couple of them have already been telling people they're in."

I didn't say anything for a couple of moments as Maurice rambled on about the Christmas party and the big one for Labor Day. Every now and then I heard him call out names and say things like, "Make sure you watch her because she can be shady." Finally I broke from my trance and said what I was thinking.

"I know, I should have gone to North Carolina, but I didn't want my mother to worry about me," I said.

"I still don't know what happened, and I know you're never going to tell me, but there's a new year coming, Aldridge. You need to try to put whatever happened in New Orleans behind you and start the year out right," Maurice said. "You deserve some real happiness."

"I think finding a new place to live will be the first thing I'll do," I said.

"Well, you picked the right time. It's a buyer's market. I'm going to buy some of the foreclosures in Midtown and rent them out."

"With the economy being so weak, you sure are doing well," I said, taking a bite from a muffin.

Maurice smiled, obviously satisfied with his life. "Yeah, things have picked up, but that's because I haven't limited myself to decorating houses. You know me, boi, I'm always working on a bigger plan," Maurice said.

"That's smart."

"Go spruce yourself up, child. Maybe Santa left you a new outfit and you'll meet your next boyfriend today."

"I promise not to be a drag on your party. I'm almost looking forward to it. It's been so long since I've been on my own at Christmas," I said. I couldn't help but remember the Christmases Dray and I had spent in various cities. Usually there wasn't a game on Christmas Day, but if they had an away game the next day, the team would arrive on Christmas Day. Dray always had several gifts for me. The thing about Dray was that although he was preoccupied and demanding, he still paid attention. One year he gave me a Rolex watch with 13 on it, his jersey number and the date we met, simply because, he said, he knew it would make me smile. We used to talk about the day when we would be able to spend Christmas together in our own home. For the longest time, I held on to this hope and truthfully I think Dray did too. Neither of us knew how or when this would come about, but we held out hope. Now that was never going to happen and I needed to give up that dream. But that was not going to happen overnight.

The Hornets had a game in New Orleans the day after Christmas, so I knew Dray was spending the day with *her.* Having come face to face with Judi in such an ugly way, I couldn't begin to guess how he could stand to look at her at all, much less start a family. From the beginning I couldn't understand what he saw in her, and now it was impossible to even guess.

I wasn't looking forward to my return to New Orleans the next week, but there was a buyer for the town house and I needed to be there to supervise the packing of my prized paintings. The realtor thought leaving them up would help speed up the sale.

I sat watching yet another Christmas parade on television in Maurice's guest room when I heard the first few guests arrive. One of them broke out with a loud "Girl, you got Christmas up in here in this camp for sure!" which set my back up. Even in the best of times, I didn't know if I was ready for a bunch of queens on Christmas, much less now that I was mending a broken heart. I'd promised Maurice I wouldn't be a drag, so I told myself to pull it together.

I moved through the kitchen and dining room and tried to give polite smiles and nods to the guests. They all appeared to be black gay men in their thirties and forties, handsomely dressed, but there were definitely too many Christmas ensembles with dangling handkerchiefs. From first glance, Maurice wouldn't have a hard time getting his invitation list down. Damn, I was starting to sound like his best friend.

They stared at me approvingly, as if I were a gift who'd just jumped out of a box. Having older men cruising me was the last thing I had on my mind, so I excused myself and moved back into the kitchen.

The Christmas spread looked like it was ready to be photographed for a food magazine. There were two golden-brown turkeys, a standing rib roast, and a honey-baked ham in the center of the table. Bowls of macaroni and cheese, candied yams, dressing, rolls, cornbread, and salad completed the feast. There were two handsome waiters in tuxes attending to the food and ready to serve the all-male dinner party.

By 3:00 all the guests had arrived. They seemed to know one another, giving warm hugs and kisses as each entered the room. It had been ages since I'd been alone with so many gay men, even longer since I'd been to a gay dinner party. I felt like an outsider in a room full of men you would think I would have had so much in common with. Maurice moved from one guest to the next with a bottle of champagne, refilling empty glasses as he went. Little did these poor fools know they were being judged by their host.

I noticed his ease with gay men and thought about how I never quite got on with them, not even in the beginning, when I was young and just coming out. I seldom saw myself reflected in that new gay world, and when I did it was usually some silly snap queen who had nothing in common with me other than being another black man who preferred sex with men. It made choosing as my partners men who didn't identify as gay but slept with men that much easier.

Watching the genuine fondness these guys at the dinner party displayed openly and unambiguously for each other, I felt tenderness for them, for the tough path any black gay man had to walk. But as much as I was touched by their camaraderie, I couldn't quite reach it. Their world and the one Dray and I lived in were as different as South Dakota and South Beach. I imagined what Dray would say walking into this scene, and I smiled without intending to. He'd have felt as out of place here as at a bridal shower.

Looking for a place to hide out and watch a game, I located a television in the study. I soon found myself thinking only about Dray as I watched the Miami Heat compete against the Cleveland Cavaliers. I was slightly amused as LeBron James's mother was interviewed and revealed to the national television audience that she'd purchased some diamond cuff links for her son, but only after his stylist had approved them. I thought of two Christmases before, when I'd purchased the exact same thing for Dray and how happy he was with them. When he opened the black velvet box, he was so excited that he couldn't wait to slip them into his shirt and model them for me.

Maurice came into the room looking a lot less festive.

"Well, making the cut is going to be easier than I thought. I can't believe the nerve of that bitch," he said, still holding the green champagne bottle. "Sloane Mouton came to my party. That bitch was not invited. If he thinks he going to get an invitation to my party, then the bitch is crazier than I thought. And trust me, I'm going to have top-notch security there."

"Who is that?"

"This guy who I went out with a few times. Everything seemed great, but then he just stopped calling me without explanation. He wouldn't return my calls either. I heard he was trying to hit on Tay, so I guess he was looking for a sugar daddy. But I got his ass. I had all his utilities cut off and tried to cancel his credit cards, but I realized the bitch most likely didn't have any. I don't know if he knows I did it, but I paid his ass back good," Maurice fumed.

"Did he come with someone?"

Maurice poured himself more champagne. I hoped he didn't get drunk or else this party could take a nasty turn.

"His new boyfriend, Lyon, who I invited only because I was going to make a play for him, or at the very least have him as eye candy for the Labor Day party. Lyon didn't mention he had a boyfriend. I should throw both of their asses out. Lyon may have just got cut from the list even if he fine as hell."

"It's Christmas and this is your party. Just ignore them and enjoy the rest of your guests."

Maurice thought about what I'd said, let out a deep theatrical sigh, and rejoined his guests.

After the game was over, I switched off the television and contemplated returning to the party. I got as far as the hallway, where I overheard one of the conversations. Of course they were whispering about who would get an invitation to the big party. Several men were talking about the movies: *Dirty Laundry*, a rare black gay family comedy starring the straight hunk Rockmond Dunbar, and the new Denzel Washington movie *The Great Debaters*, which Oprah Winfrey produced and promoted heavily on her talk show. One guy mentioned the new Will Smith movie and how much money it had made, and how Will was now one of the hottest male stars in Hollywood.

Eavesdropping further, I heard from another corner of the room, "We taking over, child, and if Obama wins this election, white folks are going to be heading back to England."

I casually entered the den, trying not to appear aloof but not wanting to get drawn into a conversation either. I also dodged the heavy cruising taking place right and left. It felt strange being young and single again. As depressed as I was over the breakup, realizing that I was a good-looking young guy with his whole life ahead brought me hope suddenly. I grabbed a handful of almonds from the side table and paused when I heard the subject of football come up. A couple of guys spoke about how dreadful the Atlanta Falcons were and how their coach had recently bolted the team to coach the University of Arkansas. I heard them say it was all Michael Vick's fault, but they admitted they missed seeing the handsome black man leading the home team and lamented that Vick had played his last game in an Atlanta Falcons uniform.

A few minutes later, the dinner bell rang and Maurice summoned his guests to the dining room for a moment of giving thanks. We all stood around the huge maple table holding hands as he led his guests in prayer. I wondered which of these guys were Lyon and the new boyfriend. As Maurice went on and on like he was delivering a sermon, I snuck a peek at the tree and noticed about thirty blue Tiffany boxes under it. Now this was big-time, and I could only imagine what the parting gifts would be come September. If Mo was living this good, then maybe I could make it on my own in Atlanta too.

When Maurice finally finished, the chorus of amens that followed sounded more like sighs of relief than blessings.

In spite of the glamour of the affair, this wasn't a formal sit-down dinner. The table couldn't possibly have accommodated the large number of guests, so an elegant buffet with servers had been set up. I fixed myself a plate and then retreated to the study. I said a prayer of my own that nobody

would miss or join me. I sat all alone watching another basketball game.

For about twenty minutes, it seemed my prayers were answered. I was relieved that I wouldn't be stuck at a table between chatty dinner companions. Then a tall, slender man with
a plate in his hand walked into the study. Damn, how did he
know I was there?

"What are you doing in here all by yourself?" he asked playfully.

"Just watching the game," I said politely, but with as little
enthusiasm as possible.

"Mind if I join you?" he asked.

"Come on in," I said, gesturing to a leather chair to my left.

He sat down and for a minute or two ate in silence, all the
while surveying the room like he was sizing up the place for an
estate auction.

"Who's playing?" he asked.

"The Lakers."

"That's Kobe's team, right?"

"Kobe plays for the Lakers," I said, overemphasizing the
obvious. I kept my eyes glued to the television, hoping he'd take
a hint.

"I'm Bobby. Bobby Lee," he said, offering his hand. "Are
you Mo's new roommate?"

"I'm his houseguest. My name is Aldridge," I said, shaking
his hand.

"Nice meeting you, Aldridge. So what do you think of Atlanta?"

"I've lived here before," I said.

He gently dug into the food on his plate. "What brought you
back?"

"I haven't decided if I'm coming back," I said.

"Where are you from originally?"

"North Carolina," I said, between bites, intentionally trying to sound noncommittal.

"Wow, me too. I'm from Gaston. What city are you from?"

"Raleigh."

"Isn't that funny—the first new person I meet at this little affair is one of my homeboys." Bobby laughed.

"Yeah, funny," I said, trying to refocus my attention on the game. I didn't want to hurt this guy's feelings, but all I wanted was to be left alone.

"I don't guess you're worried about getting an invitation to Maurice's big party, since you living with him."

"That's not the way it is," I said defensively.

"I heard he's not inviting a lot of the people here today. Is that true?"

"I don't know anything about the guest list."

"Oh. Can you believe New York is going to marry Tailor Made?"

"What?"

"Don't you watch the show *I Love New York*?"

"No, what's that?" I asked.

"It's a reality show about this girl whose nickname is New York. At first New York was on that show with that ugly-ass Flavor Flav and he broke her heart twice, and then she got her own show and the guy broke her heart. This year I was expecting her to fall in love with this fine-ass brother she had on the show, but she picked the white boy. Now they say they getting married. Ain't that some crazy-ass shit?" Bobby smiled.

"I wouldn't know. I've never seen the show," I repeated.

"It's like watching a train wreck," he said, shaking his head between bites. "Once you take a peek, you can't look away."

I leaned in closer to the television. "Whatever," I said. Hopefully Bobby would go and refill his plate.

There was an awkward silence, which I was actually grateful for.

"Who do you think has a better chance to be president? Hillary or Obama?"

"Neither one," I said. "We'll get another white man."

"You think so?"

"I know so," I said matter-of-factly.

"Do you like sports or do you watch for the cute boys?"

"I like sports," I snapped.

"I like the cute boys, but I don't like basketball so much with the long baggy shorts. I miss the good ol' days when they wore hot pants." Bobby laughed to himself.

If he wasn't going to leave, then I would. "If you will excuse me, I think I'm going to the kitchen to get some more food," I said.

"Do you mind bringing me a turkey leg and a little dressing? Oh, some gravy too," he said.

I wanted to ask him if I looked like a member of the waitstaff, but instead I told him it would be a while before I came back.

"Don't worry, I'm not going anywhere," Bobby said with a wink, eyeing me up and down like only a gay in heat can do.

★ I didn't go back for refills but instead went into my room and closed the door. After a short nap brought on by a case of "itis," as my mother liked to call it, I walked into the kitchen to find Maurice paying the caterer in cash. That looked like a lot of cash to have lying around, but leave it to Maurice to get the best deal by paying cash and holding out the carrot of possibly getting the contract for his big event.

"You did a great job," he told the caterer, a big man with a full beard dressed in a white chef's coat. "Everything Lou said about you was true. The best in Atlanta."

"Thank you. I left some extra cards on the counter, and please tell your friends about me. And I'd like to put in a bid for your Labor Day party."

"Of course you would," Maurice said. "And doing this party for a little over cost certainly makes you the front-runner."

"I'm glad to hear that. I've heard a lot about your plans."

"But not everything, I hope. I still got some surprises up my Dolce & Gabbana sleeves," Maurice said with a hearty laugh.

As far as I could tell, all the guests had cleared out. I went to the refrigerator to get a glass of pomegranate juice, which Maurice had convinced me was even healthier than green tea. This alluring scarlet fruit juice actually made me feel like it was stopping the aging process.

"So where did you disappear to?" Maurice stood with his hands on his hips, giving me a reproachful eye. "I looked around and you'd gone ghost."

I located the juice in a plastic jug, hiding behind the leftovers in large aluminum trays.

"The food gave me a case of the 'itis' and I needed a nap," I said.

"A case of what?"

"The 'itis,' as in prefaced by the n-word. That's what my mother calls it."

Maurice rolled his eyes. "So did you meet anybody you like?"

"Nope, I sure didn't," I said, hoping this would put an end to the subject.

"Did you *try*? What about Bobby? I saw you talking to him."

I turned and faced him. "Bobby, you're kidding, right, Mo? I told you I'm not ready to start another relationship."

Maurice placed his hand on my shoulder. "Who said anything about a relationship? Because that's not what I asked. You better locate you a friend with benefits or a nice piece of trade, because winter is upon us, child, and you don't want to sleep in that basement room all by yourself."

"I'll be all right," I said solemnly. My thoughts immediately went back to happier times with Dray. I'd struggled like hell to put him out of my thoughts, but that would take time.

"Are you thinking about him?" Maurice asked.

"Who?"

"Whoever you left or who left you."

"Not really. Well, maybe I was thinking about him just a little," I said.

Maurice poured himself a cup of coffee from the pot on the stove. "Look, Aldridge, I know you might be hurting now, but time will change all that. If this guy wasn't good enough for you to introduce him to your best friend . . . well, he just couldn't be that special."

I thought about what Maurice had said, and gulped down the juice. "Maybe you're right."

"I'm always right, doll, but I thought you knew that."

Twenty-five

It was New Year's Day, and while many use the day as a jump-off point for new beginnings, I couldn't seem to get out of bed. The house was empty because Maurice had decided on a whim to take a few friends of his down to the Dominican Republic for a week of sun and being chased and serviced by handsome Dominican men. I'm sure some more party cuts would be made as well. He had invited me to join them, but I wasn't interested in a trip for sex and sun. Actually, I looked forward to the opportunity of having the house to myself.

I dragged myself out of bed and over to the television. The E! channel had on its end-of-the-year review, and when they came to the part where they showed pictures of the many celebrities who had died during the year, I wondered how many of them, if any, knew a year ago that last year would be the beginning of the end for them. Damn, that was a morbid thought, AJ, I told myself.

But if anyone knew firsthand what a difference a year could make, it was me. I was of course missing Dray and remem-

bering the times we spent cuddled up in bed watching the
marathon of college bowl games. It wasn't that I loved football
so much, but spending all that leisure time in bed with Dray
made up some of the happiest moments of our relationship.

I'd been gone from New Orleans for a couple of months and
pictured Dray frantic about my sudden disappearance. He
might even have thought I died, but of course wouldn't go to the
police. I thought about dropping him a note to say not to worry,
that I was okay, but thought Judi might find out and deliver on
her promise.

Imagining Dray calling the hospitals to see if I'd been in an
accident made missing him all the sadder. People don't walk
out on a relationship when they're happy; they do it when they
want out, like my dad. Poor Dray was probably going through
hell worrying about me, and he could thank his loving wife for
that.

★ I hadn't been outside, but I could tell by the coldness of
the wood floor against my bare feet that it was a typical
January day. I loved the solitude of an empty house and was reminded that I needed to find a place of my own.

I decided right there that I would go to New Orleans immediately. Enough lying around and doing nothing. I was going to
see how the sale of the house was coming along—more specifically, when I might expect the cash I would need to buy another
house.

I pulled a couple of pairs of slacks and a couple of shirts
from the small guest-room closet and grabbed some warm-ups
and enough underwear for four days. When I got ready to pack
my shitload of toiletries and sneakers, I suddenly remembered

that the bag I used to carry them in was probably somewhere at the bottom of the Mississippi River, most likely discarded by Judi's henchman.

I started to head for Lenox Mall to pick up a new duffel bag but didn't really feel like going all that way and dealing with the crowds returning unwanted Christmas gifts, so instead I went into Maurice's bedroom to see if he'd left something I might borrow. I was sure he wouldn't mind and I planned to return before he did.

I opened the door to his bedroom and peeked around the door like I was expecting Maurice to be sitting there lounging on his chair.

The room was immaculate and decorated in sort of a masculine Laura Ashley that combined bold floral patterns with touches of leather, like the trunk that sat at the foot of the bed.

There was a new forty-six-inch flat-screen television on the wall above a maple dresser and pictures of Maurice's family and one or two old boyfriends. There were stacks of books with samples of invitations Maurice had spent hours looking over for his party, and stacks of comps of male models applying for spots as eye candy for the big bash.

The door to his large walk-in closet was slightly ajar and I figured this was the place Maurice might keep any luggage. I noticed a set of Louis Vuitton bags that I'd never seen him carry or brag about and figured it belonged to one of his friends, so I decided not to even touch it.

The closet, like the room, was well organized and had the feel of a color-coordinated sock-and-T-shirt store. I was almost afraid to touch anything for fear of messing up his stuff. In the corner of the closet, I spotted a couple of black leather luggage pieces and thought I was in luck.

The first one I saw other than the LV bags was a large leather bag the size and shape of a hatbox. Not exactly the piece I was looking for, but I pulled the top off to see how deep it was.

To my surprise there were various snapshots of young African American men in various stages of undress. Some were strangely sexy while a few were downright pornographic. Looking more closely at a few of the pictures, I decided I was intruding, so I closed the hatbox quickly.

I found an even bigger surprise when I opened the second leather bag. Instead of containing pictures, it had stacks of new hundred-dollar bills. Maybe this was money from donors for his party, but still I wondered what the hell Maurice was thinking. Surely he knew how dangerous it was to leave all that money lying around his place, especially with the rough trade he liked going in and out of his house at times.

It was way too much cash to leave around, especially considering the type of thug boy Maurice sometimes kept company with. I wondered if he was involved in some illegal cash-only venture or just wanted to keep his money close to him. It suddenly looked like I would be heading out to Lenox after all. I hoped that all the pissed-off people with bad gifts and the bargain shoppers were taking a break or had run out of money.

Twenty-six

I snuck back into New Orleans like a fugitive. I took a hotel room at the Hyatt Place Hotel, about thirty miles outside the city in a small town called Slidell.

I didn't venture into the city until the Friday after New Year's Day. Part of my choosing the remote location was because I didn't want to risk the chance of running into Judi or Dray, but also because all the decent hotels in the city were booked solid with the both the Sugar Bowl and the National Championship football games being played in the Superdome.

The only person I told was Jade, who had invited me to a chicken dinner at Willie Mae's Scotch House. It seemed like a safe bet since Dray wasn't big on fried food and I certainly couldn't see Judi having her ass up in the joint.

The place was packed, and we had to wait about forty-five minutes before we were seated. I didn't mind because it gave Jade and me a chance to catch up. She looked good and it appeared she'd added a few more tracks of hair to her well-kept weave.

"So," she began. "Two weeks turn into two months for you. What were you doing all that time? It looks like you lost weight. Have you been eating right?"

"I've been trying to lose some weight," I said.

"Sure you have." Jade laughed.

We were finally seated and handed menus.

"I must have a ton of mail."

"Got it right here," Jade said, reaching into a black leather bag. She handed me two stacks of mail held together by a rubber band.

"Thanks," I said.

"Now tell me again why you aren't staying at your fabulous place?" Jade asked suspiciously.

"I'm selling it and I don't want to be there when they bring in new owners. Might cost myself a sale if they see my black ass sitting up in there."

"I heard that." She laughed.

"Speaking of black, can you believe Obama won the Iowa caucus?"

"That was a shock. Do you think he can really win?" Jade asked.

"One day, but I still think we get a white boy this time."

"You ain't said nothing but the truth. All people need to do before they vote is to pay a visit down here. I know you read about how our kinfolks acted when they announced they were tearing down the housing projects."

"Yeah, I have mixed emotions about that. I'm still hoping to work with Brad Pitt's project, doing what I can."

"How is it going? I saw something on television about him the other day."

"I can actually see progress being made. It's really wonderful what he's doing. His people say families may be moving into the new homes before the end of the year."

"I'm surprised I haven't run into him. I usually run into famous people. Used to happen to me all the time when I lived in Los Angeles."

The restaurant was buzzing with conversation. Fortunately Jade and I had been seated at a small table, so we didn't have to shout to hear each other.

"Are you still working hard?" I asked.

"I guess you could say, 'Hardly working.' I was able to give up my waitress gig but I still do a few facials and massages here and there," Jade said. "I met someone and he takes pretty good care of me."

"Who? Reggie Bush? Did you finally meet him?"

"It's not Reggie but I did meet him. Reggie at last!" she said sarcastically. "Not quite what I was expecting. He's short and I think he doesn't have much love for brown sugar."

"Don't they all," I said with a smirk.

"That's why I found myself a basketball player."

"A basketball player? Who?" I asked, wondering if it was somebody I knew. Wondering if it was someone Dray knew.

"He doesn't live in New Orleans, so I might be moving to Cleveland."

"Is it LeBron James?" I asked excitedly.

"Ain't he married? Miss Jade don't do married anymore, baby. No, it's not him, but it's one of his teammates. I went to a Hornets game because one of my clients gave me tickets. My seat was with the wives, so I was sitting right behind the Cavaliers bench."

"So how did you meet him?"

Jade took a sip of her water.

"I was minding my own business, but I noticed him check-ing me out. I was dressed in a pale pink pantsuit and of course the pants were hugging my assets. So anyhoo, when I was leav-ing, this young guy runs me down saying that somebody on the Cavaliers asked me to wait for him outside the locker room. I knew it was him and I didn't have shit else to do, so I took a chance and waited to see what he was talking about."

"What happened next?"

"We went out for cocktails. I liked his talk and the next week I was on a flight to Cleveland. Just like that. And to think how I spent all that time chasing a man who don't even like my type." She grinned, recalling the meeting, and I sensed she enjoyed telling the story and finding the path to love.

I was so happy for Jade, but marveled at how differently the world played out for gay and straight people. I'd watched the wives section of the game countless times, feeling like I was as entitled as any of those women to be sitting there. But no mat-ter how much I meant to Dray, that could never happen for me. I never kidded myself that it would, but hearing Jade's story and seeing how easy it was for a woman to step into a man's life and be accepted so quickly made her news a little bittersweet.

"What's his name?"

"Paul Peters," Jade said.

"Is he a brother?"

She frowned. "Of course he's a brother."

"How tall is he?"

"Six-five," Jade said proudly.

"What do you like about him?"

"He's crazy about me."

"That's good." I smiled. "What else?"

"He is sexy as fuck." Jade laughed.

"How so?" I asked, suddenly interested in sex once again, even though it was the straight kind.

"Let's just say he can get the panties off without raising my skirt," Jade said with a sexy wink.

I'm sure I blushed at that. "I'm so happy for you," I said. And I meant it too. Jade deserved her sexy basketball player. Even if I couldn't have mine, I was happy for Jade.

The waiter sat two sweet teas on the table and I looked at him and mouthed "Thank you."

"I'm happy for me too," Jade said. "Seems like my little blackmail paid off well for me."

My heart stopped for a second. "Blackmail? What are you talking about?"

"Well, the woman who gave me the tickets was one of my clients. Bitch never gave me the time of day. I would go out to her house, one of those brand-new mansions, and give her a facial and massage, and she wouldn't even look my way. Bitch thought she was all that. You know how white girls can be."

Jade picked up the menu for a moment and then put it right back down on the table.

I felt there had to be more to the story. "So come on, tell me what happened."

"It seems her husband plays for the Hornets. One day, when I had finished her facial and massage, I was in the bathroom off her master suite washing my hands. When I walked back out into her bedroom, she was on the phone, all frantic. She kept saying, 'Are you sure it's not my husband's? What happens if he can tell it's not his when the baby is born?' I thought to myself, Uh oh, this is some soap opera shit."

"What was she talking about?"

"The bitch is pregnant and her husband ain't the baby's daddy. I heard the entire shit. I wanted to turn and leave but I couldn't move. When she turned around and saw me standing there, you would have thought the bitch was looking at a ghost." Jade laughed at the memory.

"Is her husband white?" I asked, trying to think of the white players on the Hornets.

"No, that's the kicker. Her husband is black. She was fucking around with one of her husband's best friends on the team, and he's the daddy. But I think the friend is either white or real light-skinned. When she realized I'd heard her entire conversation, she basically admitted it to me and told me she'd do whatever I asked. It surprised me, because she came off as this really tough bitch for a white girl, but I guess she's out of her mind worried about her husband finding out he's not the baby's daddy."

For a moment I couldn't wrap my head around Jade's story. Could it be who I thought it was? Rather, who I prayed it might be? Certainly Judi couldn't be so stupid, I thought. I knew Dray was close to a couple of his teammates, including a white center named Craig Wilson and a light-skinned brother with green eyes, Dalton Sharpe. Dray even once mentioned that one night when he'd gotten loaded with Dalton and Craig, he'd thought about telling them about us, but had quickly come to his senses.

"So what did you ask for?"

"Nothing. The bitch just started giving me shit. Giving me huge tips, tickets, and even some of her jewelry. She told me if I kept this to myself there would be a little reward for me after the baby was born. I don't know who she thinks I'm going to tell. As far as I'm concerned her husband deserves to get a cheating bitch for messing with those white girls in the first place," Jade said with a dismissive wave of her hand. "He doesn't mean shit to me."

"Can I ask you something?" I asked. My stomach began to rumble with nervous energy.

"Sure."

"What color is your client's hair?"

"Blonde, but I'm sure that it came out of a bottle."

"Does she have any kids now?"

"I don't think so. Why?"

"I was just wondering." My mind was racing a mile a minute. "So you still give her facials and stuff?"

"Yeah, matter of fact I'm going out to her place tomorrow at three for a facial. I wonder what she's going to give me this time," Jade said, tearing a small piece of a dinner roll from the breadbasket.

I couldn't wait any longer. I had to know if she was talking about Dray's wife.

"Jade, what's her name?"

"Judi. Why, do you know her? I hope she's no friend of yours! That girl is wack for sure."

"No, I don't know her." But I did know how her mind worked. I flashed back to Judi in the park, with her air of absolute confidence that she'd taken care of me. I flashed back to all the months of fighting back tears at the thought of losing Dray. That gold digger was the cause of all the heartbreak and depression I'd gone through. And now this valuable information had landed on the table at Willie Mae's Scotch House wrapped more beautifully than a huge box in Tiffany blue. I sank back in my chair, rendered speechless but concocting a plan of my own, and thought about bringing Maurice in to help me. He lived for shit like this.

Twenty-seven

Before I called Cisco, I checked on the Hornets Web site to see where they were playing. If Dray was in town, I couldn't have my revenge just yet. I was still lying low and didn't want to jeopardize my plan. I was relieved to see that they were playing in Charlotte that night and had a game in Atlanta two days later, which meant they would most likely head to Atlanta after the game rather than coming back to New Orleans.

Cisco showed up at my hotel a little after two, dressed in white warm-ups, a crisp white T-shirt, and a gray-and-black windbreaker. The weather was unseasonably warm, and when I reached for my leather jacket Cisco advised me that my long-sleeved shirt would be more than enough.

"I'm going to take this jacket off as soon as we get to the car," Cisco said. "Now where is it you need me to take you?"

"I need to go out to Kenner. Have you ever heard of a housing subdivision called Crescent Estates?"

"Yeah, I've heard of it. It's pretty ritzy out there. Matter of fact a lot of ballplayers live there. Is that where we're going?"

"Yep."

"Who we going to see?".

"I just need to take care of some business," I said mysteriously. I knew Dray and Judi lived in a gated community with a security guard but wagered that the guard might think the name Jade belonged to either a woman or a man. If Judi was expecting Jade, then I needed to get there before three o'clock. I was going to confront this bitch, make her give me back my money, and give me some of hers for charity. I had decided against trying to reach out to Dray to tell him what I knew because of how much it would hurt him. Besides, telling him his wife had been unfaithful to him with one of his friends wasn't going to get us back together.

As we drove down Interstate 10, I tried to picture Judi's face when I showed up on her doorstep. I smiled at the thought of justice being served.

"Looks like our boy might be getting out of jail sooner than everybody expected," Cisco said, playing with the button to his navigation system.

"Who is getting out of jail?"

"Mike Vick."

"How is that?" I asked. I smiled to myself at what Maurice had said about throwing a brick just to get put in prison. I thought how much he would enjoy this misadventure I was going through, and couldn't wait to sit down over some good brandy and tell him all about it.

"I hear he's entering some drug program, which will take some of his time off."

"Smart move and good for him," I said.

"You think the Falcons will take him back?"

"I doubt it. Atlanta is pretty conservative."

"Is it?"

"I think so," I said.

"That's surprising."

"Why do you say that?"

"Everybody calls it 'Black Hollywood.' And a lot of rappers and hip-hop people live there. I think if all the black people got together and said they wanted him back, they might let him come back."

"I don't think it matters what black people want. It's a white man that owns the team and he's going to be listening to what his friends say, and I don't think they want Mike back."

"You right," Cisco said in a low voice.

A sign on the freeway said it was five miles to Kenner, and my nervous stomach began to growl so loudly that you would have never known that I'd had fruit and cereal for breakfast a few hours before. I knew Cisco heard it when he looked over at me with a puzzled expression on his face. I gave him a small smile and was reminded how handsome he was. If I didn't get back with Dray, then maybe I could bring him out. But just as soon as the thought crept into my mind, I heard Maurice's voice chastising me for even thinking about getting into another relationship with a guy not willing to admit that he was sexually attracted to men. I wasn't about to make the mistake of taking Cisco's kindness as a sign that he was interested in dealing with me or his issues about men.

But damn, he was fine, with those big arms and honey-colored skin. He was a little boy and a thug all rolled into one. A nice thug boy.

Cisco interrupted my naughty thoughts. "I think this is our exit."

I noticed a sign for Crescent Estates. "Looks like the navigation system brought us to the right place."

He stared admiringly at the system on the console. "Man, this thing is the bomb. Even though I get sick of that bitch's voice when she trying to take me the long or wrong way. I find myself yelling at her to shut the fuck up because I know where I'm going." Cisco laughed.

We pulled up to a brick security hut, which had a half door on the entrance side. A middle-aged white man in a white shirt and black tie and holding a clipboard greeted us.

"May I help you, gentlemen?" he asked.

I lowered my head in Cisco's direction and said, "We're here to see Drayton and Judi Jones."

"Who shall I say is here?"

"Just tell her Jade," I said. Cisco looked at me like I was crazy. I guess he realized for the first time that I was up to something that might not be strictly legit. But then I didn't expect that would be a big problem for him.

"May I ask the nature of your business? I'm not being nosy—we're required to ask."

"Damn, this place is like trying to get in the White House," Cisco said.

"I'm the interior designer," I said quickly.

"They must be doing some big changes up there, because another designer just came about thirty minutes ago," the guard said with a laugh.

"They're taking bids," I suggested.

"Must be. Do you have their address?"

"2001 Creston Terrace," I said. I remembered the address from the time Dray showed me his new driver's license. He wanted to make me laugh by showing me the picture he'd taken with his tongue stuck out. I always had a good memory for simple shit like that.

"That's right. You just go down to the first stop sign, which is Jacobs Terrace, and make a right and then a quick left. The Jones house is at the end of the cul-de-sac."

"Thanks," I said, waving as we pulled away. As we neared their house, I wondered if I was doing the right thing. In my mad rush I hadn't really thought the situation through. What if she had a maid or somebody else who answered her door? Would I even get inside? It was too late to worry about all that. We pulled into the steep driveway of their two-story mansion. The house was made of cranberry bricks and had two beautiful glass doors. There was a candy-red Mercedes SL sports car with dealer plates from Buckhead Mercedes. I don't know why, but my eyes went to the expiration date on the tags, which read January 28. Somebody had gotten a real nice Christmas gift, I thought.

Cisco switched off the ignition and turned to me. "Now why are we here? Don't tell me it's some friendly visit."

My attention was on the house. "I need to take care of something, but looks like she might have company."

"You want me to go up and knock on the door and find out?"

"Not yet. Maybe we should pull out and wait and see if whoever is driving this car is leaving soon."

"I can do that," Cisco said, starting the engine and putting the car in reverse.

We pulled up in front of the house right next door to Dray's. Cisco and I sat in silence as we watched the house like we were some kind of undercover drug agents waiting for a deal to go down. After about ten minutes, I looked at my watch and saw that it was a quarter to three. The real Jade would be arriving any minute. It was time to make my move.

Just as I was getting ready to tell Cisco to pull back into the driveway, one of the doors to the house opened and a tall and slender light-skinned black man walked out the door. Was this Judi's lover? Jade had said that she thought it was a basketball player, and this person was too short to be playing in the NBA, unless he was a three-point shoot guard. He was wearing sunglasses and a brown warm-up jacket with a hood on his head. He looked carefully in all directions like he was making sure no one had seen him leave the house.

"What do you think dude is up to?" Cisco asked, nodding to the man with his chin.

"I don't know, but he definitely looks like he's up to something."

He jumped quickly into the Mercedes. I thought it was odd that on a day when you could ride around with your top down, this fool was covered up in a hood like a burglar who had just pulled a heist.

Suddenly I had cold feet. I couldn't stoop as low as Judi. Something about the way I was raised prevented me. My plans didn't seem like such a good idea. This was stupid and I needed to just carry my ass back to Atlanta and start over. If this was the person Dray chose to start a family with, maybe I really didn't need him in my life after all. Could be I would give a regular gay guy a chance at my love, find myself a job, and try to live a normal life finally.

We watched as the car slipped out of the driveway. The top started to rise, covering up the driver.

"So what are you going to do?" Cisco asked, almost as much out of impatience as curiosity. "Follow him?"

I looked down the street and saw a pink Volkswagen just like Jade's headed our way.

"Let's get out of here, man. I'm sorry I wasted your time."
"You sure?"

"I'm sure. Let's see if we can follow the Mercedes and find out more."

As Jade pulled into the driveway, Cisco sped off. Moments later we were right behind the Mercedes but at a safe distance, so as not to make ourselves look suspicious. It occurred to me that the driver couldn't be Dalton because he would be with Dray and the rest of the team. But I still wanted to know who had just left Dray's house.

"Why are we following this slow-driving S.O.B. in that nice ride?" Cisco asked out loud to himself.

"We won't follow him for long. Just to the freeway," I said.

"Just tell me what to do, dude."

"Just keep driving like you're doing now. You're doing fine, Cisco."

We followed the Mercedes as it came to the security station. The guard came out and talked to him for a few seconds. The car pulled off, and it was our turn to deal with security.

"That was quick," the guard joked. "I see you didn't stay as long as your competition," he said, indicating the Mercedes.

Cisco gave the security guard a smirk without responding, and then looked over at me. I just looked straight ahead.

When we pulled out of the crossway and headed back to the freeway, the Mercedes was right in front of us. Thank God we were now on a two-lane highway. Cisco sped past. A few blocks later, we came to a traffic light that went from yellow to red so quickly that Cisco had to slam on his brakes.

Looking left and then right, he wisecracked, "A brotha don't want to get caught out here doing nothing wrong." I looked at him and smiled from a release of tension and nerves; I was happy that I hadn't lowered myself into doing something that would embarrass my mother.

The Mercedes was now idling alongside us, just to my right. I hadn't yet looked over. I was curious to get a better look at the driver but didn't want to be too obvious about it.

Just as the light turned green, I leaned forward casually a few inches and took a look at the driver of the Mercedes. He flipped down the vanity mirror and dramatically brushed his face without looking in our direction, and then sped through the intersection. I was flabbergasted.

"Naw, it couldn't be," I muttered in disbelief.

"What?" Cisco asked.

Before answering I shook my head. Did I just see who I thought?

"Do you know that dude?" Cisco asked, gesturing to the Mercedes flying down the road away from us.

I didn't know how to answer his simple question.

I watched the Mercedes disappear. "I think that's the man I thought was my best friend."

"Word," Cisco mumbled as he sped onto the freeway and back toward my hotel.

Twenty-eight

A few hours later, I was boarding a Delta flight to Atlanta. As Mama would say, I was spent. Being blackmailed by my boyfriend's wife was hard enough, but seeing my best friend involved both hurt me deeply and left me enraged. I knew Maurice could be an underhanded and lowdown bitch when he chose to be, but never would I have imagined he'd turn on me. This realization also left me horribly confused, asking myself not only what I'd done to deserve this betrayal but how Maurice knew Judi. He lived outside Atlanta and it wasn't like he would ever show up for a game. No, this was some major shit that made no sense.

I was more pissed off than I'd ever been in my life, and my thoughts were spinning like a circus ride gone wild. When we'd gotten back to the hotel, I had thrown my clothes into my suitcase and Cisco drove me to the airport in silence. Although he'd repeatedly asked what was going on, I chose to wait to explain the story to him.

We shared a tender moment at the airport. Well, tender for a guy like Cisco. I had stepped a few feet from his car when I heard him call out my name. I turned around to find Cisco leaning his head out the window. With a huge smile, he said, "AJ, everything will be fine. I will make sure of that. I got you, man." He let out a little laugh, waved, and was gone.

My only thought was to get to Atlanta before Maurice did. I was going to pack all my shit and take whatever money he'd left in the closet. Money that belonged to me.

On arrival in Atlanta, I took a cab to Maurice's house and was relieved that it looked like I had beaten him back. Knowing Maurice, he was probably stopping at every small town between New Orleans and Atlanta, trolling the streets in his shiny new sports car looking for boys. He hadn't a clue I knew his deal, and so had no idea what awaited his return. As I pushed the code into the keypad of the garage, I tried to wrap my head around the day's events.

Although I hadn't figured how Maurice and Judi met, suddenly everything made sense. Maurice was the real blackmailer. Some of the information Judi knew about me was in my journals. The journals I'd left in Maurice's care when I moved to New Orleans. That evil sissy had warned me that he could be deceitful and crafty. Why hadn't I been smart enough to see he'd eventually turn his tricks on me?

How could I have been so stupid? Not only with my choice of friends, but about my love life as well? I made up my mind to call Dray and tell him what a fool he was. I was going to tell him that he'd let a good thing get away and nobody would love him like I did. And if he was happy with Judi, well, I was going to tell him they deserved each other.

My battle wasn't with Judi and her nasty ass. It was with the man I had put my trust in, given my love, and more important given my life up for. I decided at that moment, in the empty house I wanted to set ablaze, that revenge wasn't what I wanted. I wanted my own life back and I wanted it now, even if it didn't include Dray.

But first I had to get past something that had happened to me long before I met Dray, something that dated back to my childhood. I located the boxes that held journals I'd started keeping while in high school. Journals that held secrets I thought I'd kept to myself for so long. Journals so valuable to me that I always kept them close by, with the exception of my lapse in judgment when I'd first moved to New Orleans. I immediately found the first one I'd ever had. It was black leather, with yellow pages and blue lines. I turned the pages until I found the entry I was looking for, sat in the middle of the floor, and began reading it for the first time in many years. The memory of that night was now as fresh as a new layer of snow.

It was a winter night, cold and clear, when he showed up. I had just turned fifteen and Bella was two. I was babysitting as my mother worked her part-time job as a sales clerk at the Belk near our house.

His name was Eddie Wilson and I called him Mr. Eddie. He was a tall man, about six-six, light-skinned, with hazel-brown eyes and a five-inch Afro. He took my mother out to the local club a couple of times after meeting her when he came to install a phone line at our home.

I remember Mama telling one of her girlfriends how much she liked Mr. Eddie because he made her laugh, but she was concerned that he was a couple of years younger than her.

On that night I looked out the window and saw Mr. Eddie standing on the porch. I was a little surprised, since he and Mama only had dates on the weekend. I opened the door with hesitation. He asked for Mama and I told him she was working. He asked if he could come in and wait. I let him in.

He flipped through a magazine as I finished up my homework. Every now and then I would glance up at him when I thought he wasn't looking, admiring his handsome face. After about thirty minutes, he looked at me and asked what I was doing. I told him math problems and he walked over to the table where I was studying, saying he wanted to see what math was like these days and wondering out loud if he could do the assignment.

Moments later he was standing behind my chair, peering over me into my math book. I could feel the heat of his body because he was so close to me, and then I felt his breath on the back of my neck.

"Turn around," he instructed me. When I did my face was directly in front of his crotch area and it was bulging. He removed my pencil from my hand. Mr. Eddie then took my hand and placed it on his groin and with his hand on top of mine moved it up and down as he moaned. After a few minutes, he took out his dick and asked me to kiss it. I'd never done that, but strangely it seemed like the most natural thing in the world.

As Bella slept in the room we shared, Mr. Eddie took me to my mother's room and laid me on the bed on my stomach. He was careful not to disturb the bedspread or pillows as he pulled my pajama bottoms down.

"Have you ever done this before?" he asked.

I turned my head around and looked at him. He had removed his pants and his tantalizing thick dick was hard.

"No," I said.

"I'm going to try not to hurt you," he said as he gently

pushed my head into the bed with his strong hands. When he entered me, his delivery was painful but slow and careful. His body shook and he let out a primal scream as he came, pulling his dick out of me, part of his cum in his hand and the rest on my back and legs.

Mr. Eddie went into my mama's bathroom and minutes later returned with a warm washcloth and instructed me to wipe myself off. Then he left, and never returned to see my mother or me.

Reading the entry after all these years made me both sad and angry. Sad because I realized my boyhood innocence had been taken away from me prematurely and mad because the person who'd taken it, like my good friend Maurice, didn't give a damn about me.

★ My bags were packed and sitting by the front door as I surveyed the room. I wanted to be sure I had everything because I didn't want to have any reason to ever set foot in this house again. All was quiet for a second and in that moment I remembered all the laughter Maurice and I had shared here. The Christmas party suddenly felt like a lifetime ago. Now my mind wanted to bury those moments forever.

The place never felt more silent. I don't know if it was just me feeling especially lonesome after losing Dray and Maurice or whether I just wanted to get out of there badly, but the silence was pronounced.

I walked down the hallway into the living area when I heard the front door open. Maurice's voice shattered my solitude.

"I'm back," he sang out.

A bag of luggage hung from his shoulder and he had on a silly hat with a red-and-green pom-pom dangling from it. He wore a smile that I wanted to slap from his face.

"Did you miss me, hon?"

I stood there in a fury, unable to articulate my rage and deep, deep feelings of betrayal. I held so much resentment at that moment that I thought once I started going off on him, I might end up beating Maurice to the ground.

"Child, did you go deaf-mute while I was gone? I asked you if you missed me."

Coldly I walked passed Maurice and opened the side door that led to the garage. There parked was all the proof I needed: the shiny red sports car with the temporary license plate. I blinked back tears I was determined to suppress and went back inside the house.

Maurice still had on that smile and asked if I liked his new toy.

"How could you do this to me, Maurice?" I snapped. "You of all people. How could you do this to me? What have I ever done to deserve your trying to ruin me?"

"AJ, child, what are you talking about?" Maurice asked in wide-eyed innocence.

"You know damn well what I'm talking about," I shot back. "You and that bitch in New Orleans blackmailed Dray and me. And don't you lie to me. Don't you fucking lie to me! I know it was you. I saw you leave his house today."

He had been busted and it showed on his face. He couldn't conceal his look of surprise. If I had any doubts about him at all, those doubts were gone.

I reached for one of my bags. I'd never been so disgusted by anyone in my life. "I hope you're happy with yourself, but I hope you know what goes around comes around. So sorry I won't be around to see you get yours."

He snatched the hat from his head and yelled, "Don't you come in here all high and mighty with me, mister. You'll get yours too. It's one thing to be a faggot, but it's another thing to be with a woman's husband and let him take care of you like you're some beautiful white woman. Who in the fuck do you think you are? What makes you think you're so special?"

Maurice moved closer to me, as if he were about to hit me.

"You better move the fuck back," I said.

"Or what? You gonna hit me? Go ahead. I'll call the police so fast you won't have to worry about a place to stay because your ass will be in jail."

"Then get out of my way," I ordered. I didn't know anymore what he was capable of, but I knew Maurice well enough to know that he would follow through on his threat. I had to get out of there before I did something I'd never done in my life: spit in someone's face. He stepped to the side to let me pass and I bent down and grabbed one of my bags.

"Have a nice life, bitch," I said, picking up the second bag. Oh, I would have given anything to slap his ass so hard his head would spin, but I knew violence wasn't the answer. He'd hurt me so badly that I didn't know what could satisfy my fury.

"Oh, I will, thanks to you," he said with bitter sarcasm. "The cash that Ms. Judi gave me for all the information I supplied her with will keep me happy for a long time." He stepped around to my left. "Can you imagine how happy she was to give me some ends when I told her about you? Do you know how much fun I had reading about your little affair and how you couldn't wait until your boyfriend and you were together always? Well, it's not gonna happen, hon. Not now, not ever. Just think of the heartache I saved you."

I was beyond rage by this point. It was obvious I was talking to a madman. "You're sick, Maurice, and I should feel sorry and sad for your pathetic existence."

"Don't feel sorry for me, bitch, because I know who I am. It's you who's got the problem," he said, thrusting an accusing finger at me. "I feel sorry for *your* sick ass. I guess it all started for you when you took your mama's boyfriend. You had the gall to go around thinking you're better than everybody because you got some NBA player to fall in love with you? Just because you don't have to worry about shit, always talking about the charity work you're doing and how you were helping your mama and sister while my ass, like most of the sissies in Atlanta, was out here struggling, trying to keep the bank from taking back my villa."

The depths of Maurice's desperate envy truly shocked me. Sure, he had kidded me about living large, but never would I have guessed that he'd held all this resentment inside.

"You remember that time when I came to see you and you got so mad at me for coming to your house unannounced? Well, I was through with your ass then. I was done. But a bitch like me always got a plan for queens like you. I knew you were most likely sleeping with somebody's husband and I made it my business to find out. I learned about you and Dray almost a week later by camping out a little ways from your condo. I saw who was coming and going. I guess they didn't teach you in North Carolina to never cross a real dirty-south diva because we will cut you, and I mean deep! You sissies think you just hurt somebody and move on to the next victim. But Maurice will never be a victim. Never again, bitches."

Maurice's tirade grew louder and louder in a crescendo of jealousy and resentment. I didn't move, because I was stunned by what I was witnessing but also because I wanted to see how much more of his plan he'd reveal.

"And then you were stupid enough to leave with me all your sleazy little love journals with even more secrets, like how you once had a crush on one of your mother's boyfriends. Do you think she'd be so accepting of you if she knew you wanted to get with her trade? I don't think so." He smiled. "Yes, honey, I found Ms. Judi right before the wedding and we became good girlfriends fast. So she's known about you for a long time. We were both just waiting for the right moment to get back from you what you'd taken from her: her husband! My little film project at the Ritz in D.C. took care of that."

I'd never witnessed such viciousness up close and it was frightening. I felt like I was listening to a stranger who'd been eaten up by malice. This wasn't the world I lived in. We had nothing more to argue about.

"Okay, you win. I'm done," I said as I started toward the door. I was going to tell him that I had all the money he'd left in the closet but he'd find out soon enough. I was going to take the money and donate a portion of it to Brad Pitt's organization back in New Orleans.

"And don't you dare come anywhere near my party. I will have your ass arrested. Do I make myself clear?"

"Wasn't coming anyway," I said firmly.

"Yes, you are done," he called after me. "Now Judi and her little family can live happily ever after thanks to me. Who knows, she might even ask me to be godfather to the new baby."

It hit me right then that there might be a way to get back at both Judi and Maurice. I stopped in the foyer and turned to face Maurice for one last time.

"So I guess you know the baby's not Drayton's. I'm sure Judi told you, since the two of you are so tight, that she's pregnant by one of his teammates."

"What are you talking about?" Maurice asked.

I simply smiled and walked out the door. My work there was done. If I knew the real Maurice, Ms. Judi would soon feel the sting of blackmail herself.

Twenty-nine

I had one more thing to do before I could start my new life. So on the second Thursday in January, I sat in the lobby of the Ritz-Carlton Buckhead waiting for the Hornets team bus to arrive. I needed to talk with Dray and I knew they would most likely arrive, as they usually did, between two and three P.M.

The weather in Atlanta, like the rest of the country, was unseasonably warm but cool enough for me to get away with black straight-cut jeans and a thin white V-neck sweater and black boots.

For me this was a very bold move and something I'd never even contemplated. It had been two months since I'd last seen Dray and I was extremely nervous, yet confident that I was doing the right thing. After years of hiding out and covering up, I was finally closing the door on all that and opening a new one for just me.

Around half past two, the first tall African American man walked into the lobby dressed in an exquisitely tailored suit. He was followed by several men around his height and several shorter white guys carrying bags. The team had arrived and so I put the magazines I was reading back into my briefcase. I stood up and tucked my sweater into my pants, and the few wrinkles on my sweater disappeared.

A few minutes later, Dray walked in. Seeing him so suddenly felt like the time I saw him in college after his first training camp. And I was just as nervously excited now as then. Dray's head was down and he had headphones on. The first thing I noticed was that Dray was wearing the gray pinstripe Armani suit, with a pink shirt and light blue tie, that I had bought him almost a year ago.

I was about to call out his name to see if he could hear me above the iPod, but instead I just stood there. He passed by without noticing me and joined his teammates at the reservation desk.

After ten minutes Dray had finally reached the front desk, and a few minutes later he turned and started walking in my direction. He still looked as if his mind was somewhere else when he suddenly glanced up and saw me. At first he looked upset, his brow wrinkled in confusion or anger, I couldn't tell, but then his face softened almost immediately. Dray looked around, I guess to see if any of his teammates were close by, and then moved toward me.

"AJ! Where the hell have you been? I have been going crazy not being able to get in touch with you," Dray said in a low hushed tone.

"It's good to see you, Dray. How have you been?" I spoke so calmly that I surprised myself.

He moved closer to me, as if he were afraid I might disappear like a ghost. "I thought something bad might have happened to you. You might have been dead for all I knew. I called

all the numbers I had for you, even old numbers. I can't tell you
how many times I went by the place. You got some serious explaining to do, sir."

"Yes, we need to talk, Dray, but not in the lobby of the hotel," I said.

"Are you staying here?"

"Yes, and I'm listed under my name. Call me when you have
time. But if we don't talk before you leave to go back to New Orleans . . . well, I can't be certain we will get another chance."

Dray looked at me like he was trying to figure out who he was
talking to, as if a take-no-shit stranger had taken over my body.
He just stared at me in wonder and moved his neck back as if he
were really seeing me for the first time. "I will call you as soon as
I get into my room," he said. "Whatever you do, don't leave
without us talking. Please. I can't stand to lose you like that
again. I was in a living hell." One of the players called his name,
asking if he was coming upstairs. Dray nodded, then headed for
the bank of elevators. I waited a few minutes and did the same.

★ About an hour later, the phone in my hotel rang.
     "What room are you in?"

"What?" I asked, not really understanding what Dray was
asking me.

"What room are you in? I got about forty-five minutes before I have to get ready to leave for the arena. I want to see you."

"I'm in sixteen forty-eight."

"That's the club floor. You haven't seen any of my teammates in the private lobby, have you?"

"I haven't been there, but my room is at the end of the hall.
So we should be cool," I said.

"Okay. See you in a few."

I hung up the phone and took a deep breath. Why was I so worried? I had clarity about myself and my relationship with Dray more than ever before. I guess I was concerned that Dray might not appreciate this new self-assurance that I would make it on my own.

I went into the bathroom and brushed my teeth, held my hairbrush under cold water, and then pulled it across my head. I looked in the mirror to see if my teeth were clean, if my face was okay. I ran a cold washcloth over my face. I spread some moisturizer over it just as I heard a knock on the door.

I peered out the privacy hole and saw Dray looking down the hallway apprehensively. I pulled the door open.

"Come in," I said.

Dray walked in and wasted no time shooting questions at me.

"Where have you been? What happened to all your phones? Where you been staying? How could you just leave and not tell me? Man, this shit ain't cool. I've been worried shitless. I thought maybe something bad had happened to you. Damn, what are you trying to do to me?"

"Let's sit down and talk," I said, pointing to a pair of chairs. "Let me try to explain." I took Dray's hand and led him to the seats. But instead Dray pulled me close to him and hugged me as if his life depended on it. I inhaled the scent of his cologne as he began kissing me. It brought a load of memories rushing back, which I struggled not to let overtake me. His kisses were deep, like he was making love to me, and I couldn't help but think that maybe I was about to do the wrong thing.

Dray started to go for my zipper and unbutton my shirt when I suddenly stepped back from his embrace and told him to stop.

"What? You don't think we have enough time? I have forty-five minutes," Dray said, checking his watch.

I thought about giving it just one last time, but convinced myself that that was not why I'd come to this hotel. He studied my face and then he smiled.

"Dray, I can't do this anymore," I said.

"What? Meet like this?"

"No, I need to be on my own. What we are doing is wrong and I can't live like this anymore."

"What are you talking about, Aldridge? Have you met someone else?"

"No. It's not about anyone else. This about me and what I need."

"I thought you needed me? Let's not lose what we got."

I didn't answer, but instead stared at Dray for a moment, my heart still on the fence. It would have been the easiest thing to run into his arms right there.

"Answer me," he demanded softly. "Why can't I be with you?"

"Dray, you know I love you more than anyone in the world, but I think it's best if I just get on with my own life." Speaking those words, I realized that I had hardly ever told him I loved him. I think Dray had said he loved me maybe five times during our entire relationship. Somehow those words felt superfluous when we both knew what we felt in our hearts. Dray looked like he was on the verge of tears, but he didn't cry.

"We're not going out like that," Dray said, his voice quavering with emotion. "You mean too much to me. You're the only guy I ever had feelings for and it can't be over just like that. I won't let it."

"Then you have to make a choice. I can't share you any

longer. You have to choose between me and Judi." I hadn't come there to give him an ultimatum and quickly regretted it. What he wanted was no longer my concern. I'd come to tell him what I needed to do.

"You can't ask me to make that decision. I'm getting ready to be a father. I can't just leave Judi now. Give me some time. Let's not do anything until after the baby is born. After that we can talk." He reached out and took my hand. "I'll make things right for you. Haven't I always?"

This was the time I thought I should tell him the truth behind his wife's pregnancy, but I didn't. If I was going to have Dray for myself, it had to be because of how he felt about me, not because he'd married a liar and a tramp.

"There's no time left to talk, Dray. You've made a choice. I wish you well."

"You ain't leaving me. I'm your first and only love. We'll talk about this some more tonight after my game. We'll work something out, AJ, where everybody will be happy. But you can't leave me," he pleaded. "I need you."

"Do you?"

"Yeah, more than anything."

Dray pulled me into him and gave me a small kiss. "I really love you," he whispered. I looked up and saw his private, dreamy smile softening his face.

"I know you do, Dray. Listen, man, it's getting late and you've got to get ready for the game. Why don't we get together afterward?"

"Okay." He smiled as if he'd scored. "We'll order room service and have some great make-up sex."

"Great, babe. Have a good game."

"I know I will, now that I know you're all right." He kissed

me again, then headed out of the room. I sat there on the edge
of the bed by myself, realizing that I'd be gone by the time the
game was over. I felt a good cry coming on, but somehow this
time the tears would feel as if they were washing away my old
life. I had a whole new future ahead.

⭐ I closed my suitcase and prepared to leave my room. I was
lucky enough to book a seat on the last flight from Atlanta
to Raleigh and couldn't wait to surprise my mother and sister
that night.

As I reached the elevator, I suddenly had a question for myself. Is first love the only love? And if so, what did the future
really hold for me?

When I got to the lobby, I decided I'd check out by phone
the next day so that when Dray called he'd at least get the hotel
voice mail.

Walking into a winter night that felt like spring, I couldn't
help but notice a half moon hanging securely in the sky. The
moon to me was one of God's most romantic creations. I
thought about all the times I'd looked at that moon with Dray
and how I never would again. It was time to move on. I felt tears
coming once more, but with equal speed my mother's words of
advice entered my head and I began smiling a smile as bright as
the moon itself.

Don't cry because it's over. Smile because it happened.

Epilogue

I woke up early one May morning, torn out of a dream about Dray. For the past four months, I'd been staying with my mother and sister, sleeping in my old room. When I woke up suddenly, everything around me felt as still and quiet as a dream itself. It took a second to adjust. In the dream Dray and I were alone on a beach that seemed endless. Nothing but ocean and sand for as far as the eye could see. Walking hand in hand, we didn't say a word. We didn't need to because we were so happy together—happier than I remember us being for a long time. As I lay staring at the ceiling, I wished I could force myself to sleep and return to the dream. But I knew that was impossible.

Love can be like a dream in that way. You're all caught up in it and all about it and you think it will go on forever. You're happier than you've ever been before. Sometimes you don't realize just how happy until it's too late. You wake up, and when that love is over, there's no going back. You can close your eyes, remembering the best of times and maybe even convincing yourself that if you had it to do over again, you know you could make

it work, but ultimately none of that matters. You have no choice
but to move forward, and moving forward can mean leaving
love behind.

   That's how I felt without Dray. Leaving him was what I had
to do. I knew I'd made the right decision, but that didn't make
it any easier. Although four months had passed since we'd last
seen each other, I was reminded of him frequently. I couldn't
see a basketball in a sporting-goods store or pass a game on TV
and not think of him. Occasionally something I saw or heard or
read would send me into an especially bad funk that would take
hours to get over. It could be something as simple as a song that
would play randomly on my iPod or a newspaper ad with a
great-looking man. The problem was that I seemed able to recall only our good times together, which made the funk that
much worse. I'd begin to second-guess myself, asking if I'd
chosen wisely. As difficult as it was to overcome such painful
feelings, I learned to pull myself together at these moments.

   But it wasn't just obvious things like basketball that brought
Dray to mind. Had it been only that, getting over him would
have been a little smoother. No, there was also a bunch of stupid stuff that I'd never before associated with Dray but all of a
sudden connected with him in his absence. It was a lot like
when my grandmother died. Up until her death, peeling an orange was just peeling an orange. Once she was gone, however, I
couldn't help but remember how she used to peel one for me at
breakfast whenever I spent the night in her home. Today I can't
cut open an orange and not think about her. The smell and taste
of citrus reminds me of her every time. That's how it was for me
with Dray. Ordinary things like the feel of a pima cotton T-shirt
or the automobile section of the Sunday newspaper he used to
love reading or just some young dude bouncing into a fast-food

restaurant all happy could bring intense emotional flashbacks. Who'd have guessed? I hadn't realized till then that the end of a relationship could feel so much like a death.

I found a small amount of solace in the fact that Dray was still worried about my well-being, and realized that I wasn't going to jeopardize his career in the name of love. One day, soon after I arrived at my mother's, a very handsome man dressed in an Italian navy-blue suit and a sky-blue striped shirt showed up on her doorstep while I was alone. I was startled when I opened the door and saw this clean-shaven man with some of the most glittering, cat-gray eyes I'd ever seen on a human being.

He asked if I was Aldridge, and when I said yes he told me his name was John Basil Henderson, and I immediately recognized the name of Dray's longtime agent. My former lover never mentioned that his agent looked more like a highly successful male model.

John, as he told me to call him, went on to tell me that Dray told him about our little situation, and that Dray had instructed him to write me a check for whatever I asked for. At first I was insulted and angry, but I realized it was Dray's nature to worry about how I would take care of myself.

As John stood in the foyer off of my mother's living room, we eyed each other suspiciously, like players in a chess game, waiting on someone to make the next move. In the stillness and silence I was struck by the strangeness of the moment. I finally broke the silence and told him I didn't want any more of Dray's money.

"He really wants you to be taken care of," John said.

"I can take care of myself," I said confidently.

"I'm sure you can. I know it couldn't have been easy for you to give up what you two dudes had," he said with a voice of understanding.

"Is that it, John?"

"Yep. I'm done."

He gave me one of his cards and told me if I changed my mind or ever needed Dray's help, to give him a call. I took the card and before I closed the door on John, and Dray, he looked at me and said, "I'm not new to this kind of relationship, and for what it's worth, Dray told me he cares a great deal for you." I started to tell him I knew that, but I remained silent as I very slowly shut the door.

To help take my mind off Dray as best I could, I threw myself into helping my mother prepare an unforgettable sweet-sixteen birthday party for Bella. It wasn't a *My Super Sweet 16* type of party, but it was close. The quiet time I'd spent with my family had been good for all of us. We'd always been tight, but we hadn't seen so much of one another in years. When I went away to college, we were different people. Bella was a little girl and I was scarcely old enough for my mother and me to share the kind of adult conversations we'd been having all week. I wasn't willing to come out with my entire story—and I'm not sure I was yet emotionally equipped to do so even if I had been—but I offered up enough for her to understand that I'd lost a true love and been betrayed by a trusted friend. She listened patiently as I laid out my troubles. That's one of the things I loved most about my mother: she was so smart that you could tell her only a little, but she could read between the lines and understand the big picture. It couldn't have been easy for her to see her son heartbroken and betrayed, but she didn't let on. Mothers are strong that way.

It was ironic that I would dream about Dray the day I was returning to New Orleans. I'd debated for weeks whether it was the right city to start over in. I wasn't concerned about running into him. I knew it was safe to return when I read online that Dray had been traded to the Detroit Pistons after a locker-room fight. Apparently he'd become combative with team-mates following a nasty divorce. The article named his wife's infidelity as the reason for their separation, which meant Judi was going to have one hard time cashing in on her ex. I won-dered how Dray looked in his new uniform but was able to re-strain myself from going to the Pistons' Web site to look him up. No good would come of that.

Still, there were a number of solid reasons not to choose New Orleans. Apart from the memories of everything that had gone down between Dray and me, there was the fact that I knew virtually no one there. I had grown fond of the town, but won-dered if that was enough for me to settle there permanently. My project had been selected by Make It Right to help with home design, but it was only a three-month engagement. When I ex-plained this to Jade—who'd been pestering me to come back—she took the initiative and made a phone call to a friend at Xavier University, who helped me secure a teaching position in their design department. Jade, who was splitting her time be-tween New Orleans and Cleveland, added for good measure that the friend happened to be gay and single and was a dead-ringer for Rockmond Dunbar. Although I'd hoped that teach-ing at a historically black college might lead to some new friendships, I wasn't ready to date, even if the man in question was a knockout. I was carrying around too many unresolved is-sues that only time would heal.

However, I was surprised to find myself excited by the idea

of meeting a new set of people, and slowly I came to see that it wasn't making friends that was exciting but the realization that for the first time in years I was about to live openly and honestly. No more secrets. But was the exchange worth it? Would I have traded this new openness and honesty for a chance to have the old Dray back? I can't say, and I won't know until I've experienced some of what lies ahead for me.

It seems Judi wasn't the only one to fall on hard times. Maurice saw some bad luck as well. About three weeks ago, I went to Atlanta for the day and bumped into Bobby from the Christmas party outside a Midtown coffee shop. It turned out that Maurice had burned him too, and Bobby was therefore quite pleased to revel in the news that the Glitter and Be Gay Ball had been canceled. He must have noticed the look of surprise on my face because he paused to ask whether I'd heard the news. I shook my head no, adding that I'd been back in North Carolina. He laughed and said—wide-eyed with gossip—that the party being canceled was the least of Maurice's worries. Apparently he'd suffered a spectacular downfall that had set the town buzzing. Dying to know all the details, I asked Bobby to join me for a cup of coffee.

Bobby went on to explain that Maurice had been busted in a sting operation. He'd been getting information on bids for city contractors. His archrival Austin Smith found out about it and alerted the FBI. When questioned by the grand jury about his actions, Maurice—true to his evil core—lied under oath. The perjury charge didn't sit well with his party sponsors, Bobby assured me, and they wasted no time pulling out right and left. They all expressed public concern over how their money was being spent. We shared a good laugh over Maurice's misfortune, and said goodbye. My laugh was an uncomfortable one because despite what Maurice had done to me, I felt there was a person deep inside longing like us all to be really loved.

There was more to the story, I discovered after logging onto Tay's blog for the first time in months. In a posting dated several weeks back, Tay disclosed his troubled past and how Maurice had used it to blackmail him into promoting the party and smearing Austin. Tay also wrote that he was not the first to be blackmailed. Without naming Dray or me, he alluded to Maurice blackmailing a former close friend who was dating a professional athlete. Fortunately the wording was so vague that one would assume he was talking about a heterosexual couple. When he heard about Maurice's arrest, Tay said, he offered to cooperate with the prosecution in any way that might help their case. I pictured a line of cooperative witnesses waiting outside their door. If the prosecuting attorney gets her way, Maurice will be looking for another pen pal—only this time he'll be the one sending letters from behind bars!

I smiled to myself. Well, Maurice, you were always running after notoriety, and you've finally got some. How does it feel, boi? What goes around really does come around.

Boo, child, boo.

04906 4562

THE SCHOOL of GREATNESS

A REAL-WORLD GUIDE TO LIVING BIGGER, LOVING DEEPER, AND LEAVING A LEGACY

LEWIS HOWES

RODALE.

© 2015 by Lewis Howes

Simultaneously published as trade hardcover and international paperback by Rodale Inc.

Printed in the United States of America

Rodale Inc. makes every effort to use acid-free ♾, recycled paper ♻.

Book design by Joanna Williams

Library of Congress Cataloging-in-Publication Data
is on file with the publisher.

ISBN-13: 978–1–62336–596–7   hardcover
ISBN-13: 978–1–62336–714–5   paperback

Distributed to the trade by Macmillan

2   4   6   8   10   9   7   5   3   hardcover
2   4   6   8   10   9   7   5   3   1   paperback

We inspire and enable people to improve their lives and the world around them.
rodalebooks.com

To my family, this book is for you,
Diana, Ralph, Chris, Heidi, and Katherine.
Thank you for encouraging me to chase my dreams,
guiding me spiritually, showing me how to be
of service in the world, and teaching me grace, patience,
and most of all, love.

CONTENTS

PREFACE

You were born with potential.

You were born with goodness and trust. You were born with ideals and dreams. You were born with greatness.

You were born with wings.

You are not meant for crawling, so don't.

You have wings.

Learn to use them and fly.

—Rumi

For the last few years, I've felt like the luckiest guy on earth. Every week, my job has been to study at an elite and exclusive—but entirely unofficial—university, a mythical academy where the world's greatest men and women teach, lecture, and pay forward the amazing knowledge they've accumulated on their paths to becoming the best in the world at what they do.

My professors were Olympic gold medalists, award-winning musicians, *New York Times* best-selling authors, world-changing activists and philanthropists, enormously successful entrepreneurs, and inspiring experts and thinkers. I was fortunate enough to be their student, audit their classes, and learn things from each of them that I will carry with me forever. I consider this education the greatest gift I've ever been given.

Deep down, all of us suspect—we *hope*—something like this exists somewhere, but we just have no idea where it is or how to get in. Our world is swimming in information and data, unlike at any other point in human history, and for years that has been intoxicating to many of us. We could type anything into the Google search bar and we'd have a million answers in a millionth of a second. We could pick a topic and go down the Wikipedia rabbit hole for hours, if not days. But eventually, information for curiosity's sake wasn't enough. We needed more. We wanted to know how to apply it to the world and to our lives. We wanted knowledge and wisdom, not just 1s and 0s. We think that places like the World Economic Forum in Davos are maybe where we can find it. Or Summit Series. Or TED. I've been to a few of those forums and events, and frankly, they're not even close to what I've experienced over these last few years.

The place I am talking about is more like Plato's cave than the red circle on the TED stage. My amazing mentors did not speak to me for 18 minutes and then disappear into the ether; they sat across from me, literally and virtually, and brought me out from the shadows into the light of real knowledge. How did this happen? I'm still not entirely sure, but there is one thing I know beyond any doubt: They fired my passion to sit across from you, through the pages of this book, and share their teachings with you.

I've come to call this place the School of Greatness.

It's not your stereotypical school. There are no class-rooms. No homework. No principal or dean enforcing rules or even tracking attendance. Nobody pays tuition (except maybe the price of this book). Some of the "pro-fessors" would recoil at being called that. And when we leave to try our hands at the real world once again, there will definitely be no graduation ceremony and certainly no diploma.

Now to be clear, this school is great not because it admits only great students but because the teachers are and the students want to be. Both share big dreams. And as Wilma Rudolph, the Olympic champion who was once the fastest woman in the world, said, "Never underesti-mate the power of dreams and the influence of the human spirit. We are all the same in this notion: The potential for greatness lives within each of us."

With *The School of Greatness,* you will learn how to recognize and harness this potential. You will come to understand the importance of dreams and the tools that exist within you to make those dreams reality. *The School of Greatness* is not a bag of tricks and hacks. It's not a boot camp. It's a way of life, a way of living. When you want to lose weight and keep it off, you don't go on a diet, because diets are about artificial restriction. They're miserable. Instead, you change your lifestyle to match your goals. This is the same thing. *The School of Greatness* is a life-style for a lifetime that you are going to love.

Like the professors and students in *The School of Greatness,* I've chased big dreams my whole life. Ever since I can remember, I wanted to be an All-American

athlete. Growing up in Ohio, and then growing to be
6 foot 4, obviously meant football at the Ohio State University. That was every Ohio boy's dream. Everything I
did as I grew up was aimed toward accomplishing that
goal. There wasn't a day that went by that I didn't think
about it and work on it—and I made it, sort of. I went to a
smaller Ohio college after I transferred schools a couple
of times for better (and bigger) opportunities, and I even
set a number of records along the way. But it wasn't until
my fourth year that I finally became an All-American athlete—in the decathlon, of all things: a sport I'd never even
trained for. Never in my wildest dreams could I have
imagined that happening!

As soon as being an All-American became a reality—
first as a decathlete, then the next year, finally, in football—it immediately began to lose its luster, and I had no
idea why. I'd accomplished all of my goals, and I went
further than most people would have ever expected, but
that was little consolation. At a party celebrating my
achievements, the moment that should have been my
greatest triumph, I was miserable. I couldn't enjoy it
because my focus had already shifted to bigger and better things: turning pro. Eventually, I had a tryout in front
of a dozen NFL scouts at an indoor training facility at the
Ohio State University, my former dream school, along
with a number of future NFL players, including an eventual Super Bowl MVP. I performed well, but coming from
a smaller school, I had little chance of being drafted.
An Arena Football League team—which is technically
professional football—did pick me up, but 1 year is all

I played as my career ended due to a series of frustrating injuries and recovery setbacks.

Suddenly, those dreams of glory and fame came crashing down to earth. It wasn't pretty. I was 24 years old, washed up, broke, and sleeping on my sister's couch with my arm in a cast and a mountain of credit card debt staring me in the face. My dreams vanished. What I was living through at that point was a nightmare—and I feared that it was something I'd never wake up from. It was the lowest low I've ever experienced.

What I realize now, only in painful hindsight, is that I wasn't chasing the specific dream of being an All-American or playing in the NFL. Those were discrete goals. I was chasing a broader dream: being great. And what was missing from my life, on that couch with a broken wrist and no money to my name, wasn't talent or ability—it was a sense of a greater purpose, a feeling that I was working and striving for something bigger than myself.

I knew I wanted to be better, and I had all this passion and energy, but I had no outlet for it. I had to do something. So I reached out to others: friends of mine, friends of my family, coaches, my siblings. A new mentor suggested I check out LinkedIn, the social media Web site, which back then in 2008 was just starting to get traction among business professionals. I saw all sorts of potential to connect with high-profile business owners and other CEOs whom I never would've encountered otherwise. I began reaching out and connecting like a madman. I reached out specifically to people who worked in the sports business because I had just come from my own athletic experiences. I had a positive message to share, and I enjoyed helping people and relished becoming what Malcolm Gladwell calls a "connector."

I eventually built this presence on LinkedIn into an incredibly lucrative speaking, advising, and teaching business. I had no background in online business, but I had good instincts and was willing to work my butt off, and as I took some advice from mentors, the money started flowing in. After an initial period of figuring it all out, my first year brought in close to $1 million in sales. By year 3, that had more than doubled. Eventually, my business partner bought me out in a deal for seven figures.

There I was, not even 30, with more money than I'd ever seen before, having turned a vision into a lucrative reality and reinvented myself as an entrepreneur in the process. With some help and some hustle, here I was again, on top of the world. It should have been another moment of triumph—I had built a business from scratch and grown it to scale—and yet the call to something larger still haunted me. I knew a piece was missing.

One of my teachers, the author and journalist Steven Kotler, would later define greatness as "waking up every day and saying 'Okay. Today I'm going to move mountains.'" That's what I wanted. That's who I wanted to be.

I started over again, this time with the notion that I would seek out something larger, since it wasn't coming to me through these stereotypical markers of success. In January 2013, I decided that I would start interviewing some of the smartest, most successful, and *greatest* men and women in the world and ask them every question I could. I wanted to be around only those people who understood what it meant to strive for true greatness, who woke up every morning to move their respective mountains, pay it forward, and help others get to a better place. Part of my motivation was selfish—my own insatiable thirst for understanding how individuals seek and achieve this higher ground—but I also wanted to give readers and listeners access to this wisdom. What good was greatness if I couldn't share it?

The response was overwhelming. My little podcast, *The School of Greatness,* amassed a large audience with more than five million downloads before the first 2 years and hundreds of thousands of unique visitors every month. In a world with a seemingly infinite supply of available podcasts, *The School of Greatness* has been featured on the main page section of iTunes more than 10 times and has ranked number one on iTunes' Business and Health list.

Not only were these lessons resonating with listeners and readers but, as I was in the process of conveying them, they were also changing my life. They were the lessons I wish I had been given and understood when I was 16 years old, struggling to make sense of athletic gifts and struggling through a tense and often terrible family life. It's what I wished I could have turned to when, immediately after leaving the All-American podium, I was engulfed by depression and pain. They could have helped me make the most of my opportunity in professional sports—and they could have saved me hundreds of thousands of dollars in costly business mistakes.

Those lessons form the core of this book. The lessons in this book are not *my* lessons; they are my lecture notes from a unique and wonderful school. I'm simply lucky enough to be the messenger. As I was writing, I learned that there is a long tradition of this kind of book. From Aristotle's *Ethics* and Epictetus' *Discourses* more than 2,000 years ago to a more recent book like Peter Thiel's *Zero to One,* the great thinkers themselves didn't write those books: A student did. What survived was simply the lecture notes from an epic course we were not fortunate enough to have attended in person. Classicists have been kind enough to give author credit to the masters, and I hope you'll see that with this book, too. Although my name is on the cover, the names of my teachers should be as well. I couldn't have written this without them, and it is with the deepest gratitude that I share their wisdom.

INTRODUCTION

What Does It Take to Be Great?

Greatness is a spiritual condition worthy to excite love, interest, and admiration; and the outward proof of possessing greatness is that we excite love, interest, and admiration.

—Matthew Arnold

I'm a pretty good athlete, but there are legions who are far better than I'll ever be. Olympic gymnast Shawn Johnson accomplished more in sports as a teenager than I will in my entire life. I've done very well in business, but men like Angel Martinez, CEO of the billion-dollar shoe brand Deckers, and fellow lifestyle entrepreneur and angel investor Tim Ferriss aren't looking in their rearview mirrors for me. So I am not just talking about the kind of greatness that can be measured and assessed by a universal standard; I am talking about the greatness of exploring, reaching, and sustaining your potential—that is, the kind of individual and unique greatness that we are all capable of.

Greatness, as I've come to learn from people like Shawn, is "not just holding a gold medal at the top of a podium." It's about inspiring people, about sharing a message, about believing the truth in that cliché: It's the journey, not the destination to some perceived treasure or moment of adulation. In fact, there are a million ways to be great and a million more things to be great at. Most of them don't come with a medal or a giant check. Consider this list.

Being a parent   Being an advocate
Being an artist   Being healthy
Being generous   Being an entrepreneur
Being a leader   Being of service
Being a change maker

All of these are amazing dreams where greatness is a worthy and attainable goal. Those who have become great at any of them—irrespective of plaques on their walls or trophies on their mantels—are the people we can all learn from. In this book, we're going to learn from people who did stand on podiums—literally and figuratively—but were great at these things as well. They embodied excellence in many facets of their lives, and we can apply their approach to our own.

As Shawn put it to me, "Greatness means having pride in yourself, being happy with yourself, knowing you've worked for something and couldn't have done anything more. That is greatness itself." It is cultivating the character and habits that not only lead to success but also help you overcome any challenge or adversity. It's about lifting yourself up from the depths of despair and using mindfulness, joy, and love to harness your dreams. It is a progression through a series of lessons—eight areas of focus and continual improvement.

1. **Create a vision.** Most great athletes describe their ability to visualize the outcome they desire in a competition. They know what they want and where they want to go. It is as much a part of their process as any aspect of training. As the famed acting coach Lee Strasberg put it, "If we cannot see the possibility of greatness, how can we dream it?" Now, what is *your* dream?

2. **Turn adversity into advantage.** It's hard to find the story of someone who has achieved greatness who did not face some sort of significant adversity. When you look more closely, you see that this adversity actually helped them—it put them on the path toward a unique and individual form of greatness. What challenges do you face and how can you use them to develop greatness?

3. **Cultivate a champion's mindset.** What does it take to become a champion, and how does a champion see the world that she is trying to conquer? Visualization, meditation, mindfulness, and emotional intelligence are tools that help you understand who you are and where you are at any given moment in your life and allow you to find joy and fulfillment in the moment. This is where greatness takes root. How can you view the world through the eyes of a champion?

4. **Develop hustle.** We all face obstacles and seem to have an impossible amount we need to get done. Many get stuck at this wall, but what separates the greats from the rest of us is that they reduce the wall to a barrier and make it into something they can climb over. It's also important to never stop

hustling—even after we've accomplished a goal. Where will your hustle and energy come from?

5. **Master your body.** No one chooses the body they're born with, but almost everyone has the ability to build and maintain their physical assets far beyond what they imagined. It's all about thinking like a champion, training like a champion, and eating like a champion. Are you taking care of yourself?

6. **Practice positive habits.** How many hours *exactly* does it take to achieve mastery and greatness? It's not about a number, but great things will happen if you practice a certain skill over and over again. Building positive habits is a necessity to achieve your desired goals. And having a deep belief in something that can support those habits, be it religion or community or family, is a key ingredient in the recipe for greatness. What positive habits can you add to your daily life?

7. **Build a winning team.** You can't achieve greatness alone, period. Success is a shared process. Finding the right mentor and making the best use of that mentor or coach is a requirement. So is building a team of partners, employees, supporters, and fans. Success is all about developing and cultivating healthy and fruitful relationships—not just with your peers on the field of endeavor but also with those who can truly challenge you—in all aspects of your life. Whom do you need to join forces with?

8. **Be of service to others.** Trophies and rings and fat bank accounts have a surprisingly short shelf life when it comes to greatness. Research has shown

that the happiest and most thriving people are
those who spend their time giving back, helping
others, and participating actively in their communities. In fact, the best gifts are the ones you give;
they make your own achievements that much more
fulfilling. How are you going to contribute and help
others?

This book is the distillation of the eight master lessons on greatness that I have discovered on my journey,
with help from my network of mentors and coaches, colleagues and teachers. By studying greatness this way, we
will learn that it is a process of continuous education and
self-realization. It's something we'll follow for the rest of
our lives.

If you're like some of my podcast listeners or a lot of
people who read books such as this one, you are probably
saying to yourself, "This all sounds well and good, but
what is this book actually going to help me do?" That's a
fair question. I'm not here to waste your time or make
false promises.

What *The School of Greatness* is going to teach you is,
first and foremost, what is great and special about you.
Most people think greatness or being great is external to
themselves, that it's something you acquire or add on.
That is not true. Greatness is something that is unearthed
and cultivated from within. The lessons and the teachers
in *The School of Greatness* will help you find the greatness
in you.

This book will then inspire you to pursue it. It'll show
you how to be great—whether you're an athlete, an

entrepreneur, a mom, an organizer, a freelancer, or a
designer—at whatever passion you harbor deep inside.
They say "seeing is believing," but sometimes even that
isn't enough. Sometimes people need to be convinced.
They need to be inspired to have a vision, let alone pursue it with vigor in the face of countless unseen obstacles.
I was fortunate enough to have truly great men and
women draw out whatever potential I have inside me,
and now you and I and all the other readers are going to
work to become the best we can be—together.

GROUNDING

Before I do pretty much anything in life, I like to have
what I call a "grounding" moment. I originally experienced this process in sports. Before every game, the
coach would prepare us for the battle ahead by getting
our thoughts together and putting us in the right frame
of mind. I call it getting grounded. This is where I commit
myself to my vision, get connected to who I am, and focus
on what I'm intending to create in that moment. You may
already have grounding moments in your daily life and
not even realize it. Whether it's meditating in the morning to get ready for the day, taking a moment of silence or
saying a prayer before meals, or psyching yourself up
mentally and physically before a game or a speech or a
sales pitch or any of the other "big" moments we go
through in life, it's extremely important to find some
head space for whatever your ritual may be.

This grounding process is critical for your success in applying the lessons in this book to your life—and critical for success, period. If you don't give yourself a moment to visualize the clear results you want to create, then you are less likely to achieve what you desire. It's all about setting your intentions for what you want. Getting grounded can be one of the most powerful things you do if you apply this process to your daily life.

Each chapter will begin with my personal grounding statements to let you know what my intention is for you to get out of that chapter and to prepare you for what's to come. When my coaches would ground us before big games, it always gave me that calm confidence I needed to take on some of my most challenging competitors. I want to pass that calm confidence on to you. You have challenges and obstacles that stand in your way on a daily basis, and grounding in the morning and before any big moment is a habit that I know will support you tremendously.

The School of Greatness, in all its parts, is a framework for achieving real, sustainable, repeatable success. This book isn't just about making you feel warm and fuzzy. It's about giving you the tools, knowledge, and actionable resources to take your vision and turn it into a reality.

Who are you?
What do you stand for?
What's your dream?
What type of legacy do you want to create?
How can we become great together?

GET GROUNDED

In this chapter on vision, I want you to dream. Allow yourself to clear your mind and look at everything as a possibility— no dream is too big or too crazy. Imagine what you'd want your life to look like if you knew you could never fail. Let go of what someone else wants for you, what you think society wants for you, and what you think you are supposed to do because it's reasonable and "makes sense." You are here to live an extraordinary life. Think about what *you* want to do in your life and how *you* want to live.

The lessons in this chapter give you permission to design the life you've always dreamed of while living unapologetically. The exercises at the end will help you practice the lessons and exercises in the seven chapters that follow this one. If you're like I used to be, you might be tempted to skip these exercises because they seem like "work"—but that's the whole point. This can be an uncomfortable process, but it's one that finally shows you what life could be like if you choose to live in a world where "anything is possible."

Get ready, my friend. This is the beginning of a beautiful journey, and I'll be with you every step of the way.

CHAPTER 1

CREATE A VISION

*The only thing worse than being blind
is having sight but no vision.*

—Helen Keller

reatness is my passion, but vision is my obsession. Let
me explain. A clear vision can unleash extraordinary,
mind-boggling power. I've been known to get more than a
little intense on this topic. Let me tell you a story about a
guy I met named Steve who reminded me of my younger
self and was probably like a lot of you out there. He had
been friends with my girlfriend at the time for a number
of years, and she wanted us to meet up over dinner. I
went through the whole "where are you from, what do
you do" small-talk racket that you do when you meet new
people, and Steve told me he was in graduate school to be
a doctor of physical therapy and was finishing up in the
next 6 months. As an athlete who has been through his
fair share of injuries, I am familiar with physical therapy,
so I found this pretty interesting.

I asked him, "So Steve, what do you want to do after you graduate? What's the dream?"

Like most people who just got blindsided on a first friend date, he said, "I'm not really sure."

"Well, if you could have anything, what would you want? If you could have it all, what would it be?"

Steve started talking about working with the military and doing physical therapy on wounded veterans and enlisted soldiers. The benefits would be good, and he could support his family. There's a big military hospital in Germany, so maybe they could see some of the world that way, too.

"That's really cool," I said. "Has that been what you've always wanted, or is there something else?"

Very quickly, Steve said, "I used to be a football coach. So I'd love to be a physical therapist on a pro sports team and work on these great athletes."

Now he was speaking about something I knew well, and I could tell he meant it. "That's awesome, Steve. So is that what you really want?"

He thought about it and said, "You know, actually, it'll probably be a lot of hours, like 80 hours a week. And I'd have to work my way up. And it'd be a lot of time and energy. So maybe working for a pro team is just one of my options, like plan B or C."

"Okay, so you don't want to work for a pro team?" Now I was confused. "Then what is it you really, really *want*? What's your vision?"

I laugh every time I think back to this dinner conversation, because I feel so bad for Steve. When he ordered his meal, he had no idea it came with a side of interrogation, especially from someone who seemed to be getting frustrated with him. And believe me, I was getting frustrated, because I was asking him to focus in on what he really wanted to do with his life—what he desired—and instead, like so many of us who have not yet recognized the inherent potential for greatness within ourselves, he was listing all the things he could do but probably wouldn't.

I learned about desire—the distinction between what we *can* do and what we *want* to do—and how to uncover it from the unstoppable Danielle LaPorte. She's a phenomenal motivational speaker and author who has graced us with her presence on *The School of Greatness* podcast a couple of times. The first time she came on, she said something that still spins around in my head to this day. She stated, "You need desire to be fully alive and you need vision to fulfill your desires." How amazing is that?!

Together with *The Desire Map: A Guide to Creating Goals with Soul,* which she published in 2014, Danielle changed my perspective on vision and is mostly responsible for turning it from an interest to an obsession. And now, every time we speak, she hones and clarifies my understanding of vision and desire a little more. The last time, she described her book this way: "*The Desire Map* is about helping as many people as possible get clear on their core desired feelings."

That was exactly what I was trying to do with Steve: pushing him to get clear on how he felt about life so he could figure out what he truly wanted to do. Finally, he got real: "To have my own practice by the beach. And work like 5 hours a day. And then be able to be there to support my family."

That is a vision—it was practical, it was real, and though he'd been afraid to be direct about it earlier, now you could hear the sincerity in his voice. I was eager to ask him how he felt after saying that out loud, but I didn't want his dinner to get cold, so I let it go until dessert. We all dug into our entrées, and, between bites, Steve added one final thought that sums up the entire reason that holds people back from excelling in the School of Greatness:

"I just don't know if that's possible."

Yes, it is absolutely possible, and it has nothing to do with ability. As the renowned leadership expert John Maxwell says, "Successful and unsuccessful people do not vary greatly in their abilities. They vary in their *desires* to reach their potential." (emphasis mine) The reason I know this is true and that Steve's dream is possible is because of my time with one of the School of Greatness's greatest teachers: Angel Martinez.

I met Angel Martinez in Goleta, California, at the new headquarters of his company, Deckers Brands, a fast-growing, billion-dollar global footwear company. I'd heard of Deckers from the same mentor who introduced me to the power of LinkedIn, but I had little understanding of the company's size or track record before connecting with Angel, Deckers' CEO. From the looks of the company's beautiful new campus, with its glass walls, intricate woodwork, and gleaming granite floors, it was doing pretty well. It turns out, like millions of other people, I was more familiar with two of their best-selling brands: UGG and Teva. When you think about the uniqueness of those two shoes and then you meet Angel, a guy who looks more like a jazz musician than a CEO, you understand why his motto for Deckers is "We want to inspire the unconventional."

Angel took an unconventional route to greatness. It would be difficult to find another CEO with a similar résumé and worldview. An iconoclast and footwear industry legend, Angel was a founding member of Reebok—its third employee—and the catalyst for the company's explosive growth back in the 1980s. He single-handedly pushed Reebok into the budding aerobics marketplace by combining style with function and designing the world's first aerobic shoe for women. Driven by sales of that shoe (called the Freestyle) and lines of improved tennis, running, and basketball shoes, Reebok became the fastest-growing company in history up to that time and blew past Nike for the dominant position in the US athletic shoe market.

Angel went on to serve as CEO of the Rockport Company, a Reebok subsidiary, before eventually leaving the footwear giant to pursue his own ideas and passions. He later helped found Keen, the popular outdoor footwear brand, and joined Deckers as CEO in 2005, when the company had $200 million in sales. Under Angel's watch, in less than a decade Deckers' revenues have soared to nearly $1.5 billion. Fueled by his entrepreneurial vision, the company has expanded around the world with popular retail outlets, new brands, and record growth. If greatness is built upon insight, acquired wisdom, and a unique vision, Angel is the embodiment of that path to success—a path that begins in prerevolutionary Cuba.

Born in Cuba in 1955, Angel was sent off to live with guardians in New York when he was a toddler, never to return to his native country and never to live with his father or mother again. His mother had left her young family when Angel was born, and because of the revolution in 1959, Angel would not see his father again for 34 years. Raised in a tenement in the South Bronx by his elderly aunt and her disabled husband, Angel always felt like an outsider who never quite fit in.

His first brush with footwear envy came when he was in grade school and yearned for a pair of Converse Chuck Taylor All Star high-top sneakers, the Air Jordans of the day. To be cool, you had to have Cons. At $6.99 a pair, they may as well have cost a million dollars. His aunt offered to pay $1.99 for sneakers—the price of cheap sneakers at Woolworth's—but Angel was determined to get his Cons. He collected bottles that he redeemed at two cents apiece until he earned enough for them. So precious were those shoes to him that he walked the four blocks home from the shoe store on the sides of his feet so as not to get the bottoms of the Cons dirty.

"It was a moment of epiphany, the perfect confluence of attaining something I'd dreamed about for a long time and having it turn out to be just as good if not better than I had hoped for," Angel recalled. "It was my first taste of

the power of a product to provide emotional and psycho-
logical comfort."

LESSON #1:
BE SPECIFIC

This was also Angel's first positive lesson in the power of
vision. More important, it was a lesson in the power of a
clear, specific vision. He didn't want just any shoes. He
didn't ask his aunt for "a cool pair of shoes." He knew
exactly what he wanted: the $6.99 top-of-the-line Con-
verse Chuck Taylor All Star sneakers in the iconic black
canvas with white laces and toe guard. He dreamed
about these shoes so vividly that he could feel them on
his feet and would do nearly anything to have them.

As the award-winning Brazilian novelist Paulo Coelho
wrote in his bestseller *The Alchemist*, "People are capable,
at any time in their lives, of doing what they dream of."
And it's that much easier to accomplish when you know
exactly what your dream is. It might seem odd to you that
a goal as small as having a pair of nice sneakers of his own
would be considered a dream—most of us have never had
to struggle so hard for such a small material possession—
but for Angel, growing up poor in the Bronx, it put him on
the path he followed the rest of his life.

Angel's story blew me away. From my time in the
business world after college, I always knew vision was
important, but to see the power of a clear vision on one
person's life like that was a transformative moment for
me. Not only did it guide him toward achieving that first

small dream—as a kid, no less—it shaped his entire life. If Angel hadn't obsessed over his Cons to the point that he collected two-cent bottles for months in order to buy his first pair for himself, would he have ended up in the shoe business? Would he have become a founding employee of Reebok or the CEO of Deckers? Probably not. Such is the power of a clear, early vision.

After talking with Angel, I started thinking about my own past. Did I have a big, outsize dream that I was obsessed with while growing up in suburban Ohio? What were my $6.99 Cons? Then it hit me. As I talked with Angel, the entire memory came back to me in a giant flash. I was 6 or 7 years old, sitting on the living room sofa with my dad watching an Ohio State football game. I don't remember who they were playing or who won, but I remember the announcers talking about an Ohio State linebacker named Chris Spielman who'd graduated the year before and been chosen by the Detroit Lions in the second round of the NFL Draft. They said he was a two-time All-American. I had never heard that phrase before.

"Dad, what's an All-American?" I asked.

"They're the best players in all of college," he answered nonchalantly, unaware of the future impact of what he was about to say. "There are only a few of them. They make all the big plays."

Wow, I thought, *one of the guys from my favorite team is one of the best in the entire country?!*

I remember sitting there staring into the television, listening to these announcers talk with energy and passion about Spielman and the other All-Americans on the field that day. *Who are these guys? What makes them so special?*

For those unschooled in the splendor and glory that is Ohio State football, here's a quick lesson. Practically the entire state shuts down on Saturdays in the fall when the Buckeyes play. Their stadium, called the Horseshoe, holds more than 100,000 people, and it's always filled to capacity with screaming fans dressed in scarlet and gray. Many of them are wearing the jerseys of All-American Buckeyes past and present. They're all there, I realized, to see these All-Americans—guys like Chris Spielman—do amazing things and lead their team to victory.

At such a young age, I didn't have the words to describe that feeling, but in that moment, I became obsessed with greatness in sports. I wanted to be like all those All-Americans. I wanted to be *one of the best.* I wanted to be great. Thinking back to that day and then to all the years of practices, workouts, eating regimens, supplement experimentation, games, injuries, and physical therapy sessions, I realized becoming an All-American wasn't just an idea that popped into my head one day. It was the name for the dream I'd had since I was a little kid.

Like Angel's dream for his first pair of shoes, being an All-American can sound a little silly or even a little cute if you don't have the context and you don't know how that singular vision guided decades of our lives. Having a goal that feels attainable but slightly out of reach provides focus and direction. It prevents you from getting distracted or discouraged when things don't go your way. Angel wanted those Cons as soon as humanly possible, but seven dollars' worth of bottles at two cents a pop is a lot of bottles for a little kid. I wanted to be an All-American, but I had no idea how to go about doing it, and neither did anyone I knew. It wasn't as if that kind of greatness was living next door, the way that Steve Jobs lived near the famous Packard's garage or the way it might be for a kid who hopes to succeed his father as CEO of a family business or graduate from the college his parents went to. Our goals felt outsize to those around us, and our timelines were different, but they both were well defined with a clear end point. If you want to be great at anything, you've got to have a clear vision of exactly what you want, why you want it, and when you want it to happen.

All greats do this, including the greats you will hear much more from over the course of the rest of this book. It was an essential component to Shawn Johnson climbing the medal stand in Beijing, Kyle Maynard climbing Mount Kilimanjaro, Rich Roll going from overweight lawyer to world-class ultramarathoner, Scooter Braun building one of the most successful music management firms in the industry, and my brother climbing the ranks of the world's great jazz musicians, to name a few. Now, having a vision isn't all you need to be great, happy, or successful, but it's absolutely true that you can't be those things without one.

LESSON #2:
LET YOUR VISION BE YOUR IDENTITY

We focused first on creating a vision because it's the most important step to getting anywhere and achieving anything you want in any area of life. But we also have to be clear about what a vision is. A vision is not just a dream. A powerful vision emerges when we couple our dreams with a set of clear goals. Without both, we are apt to wander in a clueless and purposeless fog, because a dream without goals is just a fantasy. And fantasies are the bad kind of visions—the hallucinogenic kind, not the real kind.

A powerful vision emerges when we couple our dreams with a set of clear goals.

Without a real vision, we lack identity. Having a real vision isn't just about clarifying what you want; it's about defining what and who you want to be. My vision was to achieve All-American status when I was younger, but what I really wanted to *be* was great.

For Angel, the Cons were about being like all the other kids—being equal—at a point in his life when he felt unlike any of them. Most of us can relate to wanting something stylish that our friends have, but few of us can probably understand what it's like to literally and figuratively struggle with identity from such an early age. On Angel's first day of school, his guardian introduced him

to the principal as Angelo, even though that wasn't his
name. In the 1950s in New York City, it was easier to get
by if people thought you were Italian rather than Cuban.
It wasn't until he was on his own in college that he could
finally convince people to call him what he wanted to
be called.

"I just made up my mind," he told me. "'No, that's not
my name. Angel is my name. You can call me 'angel' until
you figure out how to pronounce my name, but I'll make
it easy for you and just give it to you. It's Angel [An-hel].
I'm not even asking you to do it with an accent or anything.'"

But it was about more than people pronouncing his
name correctly; it was about making a life. Having his
own name was something he needed. He craved becoming someone on his own terms, in line with his vision for
who he was (and is to this day), not what some public
school administrator said he was on a piece of paper,
even if his guardian had the best of intentions. See, what
might seem conventional to some of us today—the idea
of going to college, getting a good job, having a nice
house—was, for someone with Angel's background, not
just unconventional but downright crazy when he was
growing up. Especially if he insisted on embracing his
Cuban immigrant heritage just as the Cold War really
started getting chilly.

Listening to Angel talk about his childhood made this
distinction clear to me. It revealed a relentless ambition,
a life of striving for true accomplishment. To be equal, to
be somebody, to be great. But not great in the more tradi-

tional, achievement-based way that I was trying to be great. His was greatness in life, in living.

It might seem like Angel had two completely different visions—one to be just like everybody else, the other to be his own man—but actually they are two sides of the same coin. They unify what he wants with who he wants to be. That is the essence of identity. Just as pairing your dreams with your goals is the essence of a real vision, unifying your vision lets you blow past what other people think your limitations are. Beyond those limitations is where greatness lives. If you don't figure out what you want in life and who you want to be, you will most likely feel trapped within those limitations. No path to greatness has ever involved settling for less than what you really want.

Let's go back to the dinner where I met Steve. Steve thought his dream was to be a physical therapist, maybe with the military or a pro sports team. In fact, his dream was to live near the beach and work from home a few hours each day so he could always be there for his family. No wonder he was confused. He wasn't sure it was possible because he didn't realize that being a physical therapist wasn't his dream; it was just a goal on the path and a means to achieving his actual dream. What he was after was control over his life and the luxury of seeing his kids grow up. Once you clarify this, then it becomes possible to develop a real plan for getting there.

"The challenge," Angel told me as we discussed his childhood, "is to be able to project yourself into a future that you have no reference point for. If you grew up in a well-to-do, solidly middle-class family where you got a new car, you lived in a nice house, you took a nice vacation once in a while—I'm not talking about anything exotic, I'm talking about the middle-class American dream—well, for me growing up, that was absolute fantasyland. That was something I saw on TV, on *Leave It to Beaver.* That house on TV was a palace to me, and it was a challenge to convince myself that I belonged there, too."

The famed World War II general and French president Charles de Gaulle is reported to have said, "Greatness is a road leading towards the unknown." And he was right, but only in a particular sense, I think. It's not that you don't know what it looks like; the unknown part is what it's like to *be there.* This is something so many of the students in the School of Greatness—myself included—struggle with when we first get started. Greatness is for those people over there—they've been there and done that. They deserve it for whatever reason. Who am I? What have I done to think I can achieve these great things? I'm just Lewis from Ohio or Steve from LA or Angel from the Bronx.

LESSON #3:
TURN THE TELESCOPE AROUND

The key is to understand that the vision creation process doesn't end when you've clearly articulated what your dreams and goals are. There is another part to it—the part where you envision what it's like to have achieved those goals and live that dream. I learned this, too, from Angel Martinez.

"When I was a kid, I came up with this idea while playing with a telescope," he told me. "I realized that you could look through both ends. When you look through the small end, everything is far away. But when you look through the big end, you say, 'Wow, that looks totally different when I turn the telescope around.' I would tell people who doubted themselves, 'You might just be looking at your life through the wrong end of the telescope.'"

Could you have the same problem? That outsize dream that seems so far away is often a lot closer than you think. It just seems distant because we look through the wrong end. Angel's point of view was so absolute and so unusual that it made me reconsider my own story. Then he said something that struck a chord:

"I came to the conclusion that it's easier to come from a place than to go to a place. At Reebok, I thought we were better than Nike," he recalled. "We just hadn't done it yet. I didn't come to Deckers because I wanted to stay in the funky old building we were in before this new one was built. I was already at the other end of the telescope for this company. I saw this as a multibillion-dollar company because of the quality of the people and the products and the brands. I realized, you become what you envision yourself being."

You become what you envision yourself being. If Mike Tyson hadn't ruined face tattoos for everyone, I would tattoo that phrase backward on my forehead so I could read it every morning when I got up and I looked in the mirror. Because that is the true power of a vision on the path to greatness. It's not a destination or a specific achievement or an amount of something—it's a state of being that encompasses all of the goals you've set for yourself along the way.

You become what you envision yourself being.

One of the amazing things about doing what I do and getting to spend time with these teachers in the School of Greatness is leaving every encounter with far more wisdom than I arrived with. It's a great gift, and sharing it with the world is at the heart of my mission. It's why I've carefully chosen the stories I share with you. For instance, Angel Martinez is one of those rare individuals who could fit into pretty much every category on my list of traits that form the foundation of greatness. But I started the book with his story—a story of true vision in every sense of the word—because he is the kind of inspiring person we can all use as a reference point when we doubt our dreams or ourselves.

Angel has been driven by a vision that has propelled him out of bed every day for more than 50 years, long past the time he's earned enough money to stay in bed as late as he wants. Your job is to create a vision that makes you want to jump out of bed in the morning. If it doesn't, go back to bed until you have a bigger dream.

I have discovered and developed these powerful exercises to help you get crystal clear on what you want, why you want it, and when you want it to happen. To pursue and achieve greatness, you must truly become the author of your own destiny, and the writing starts with these four exercises.

EXERCISE #1:
Your Certificate of Achievement (COA)

Write down your goal. Print it. Frame it. Hang it somewhere you will see it. Every day.

Writing down your goal is a powerful thing. Declaring your vision and putting a date on it, as though it *will* happen (or, as Angel would say, like it already did), is even more powerful.

This exercise is about getting total clarity on what you want (like I did with Steve) and why you want it, and then declaring that vision for yourself in the next 6 months or whatever date you have in your head, as long as it's specific. Your goal can be financial, personal, or health or career related. It almost doesn't matter what the vision is. There's only one rule: It should be something hard to achieve. It must be something that terrifies you when you say it out loud to someone you respect. At the same time, it should be something that is possible to achieve in the allotted time frame—provided you put in the work. And then you write yourself a new goal once it is completed.

I am not the first person to come up with the idea to write down goals. Many who have come before me have recommended something similar. But I didn't learn this from them. I came by it honestly, at a fairly early age, watching my coaches. As an athlete, I have played on more teams with more coaches than I can count. We've been good; we've been great; we've been bad; we've been horrible. On most of those teams, the difference between success and failure was razor thin. Rarely could you put your finger on why, and God knows our coaches tried. Over time, though, I noticed one thing that distinguished the good teams from the bad ones or the successful coaches from the unsuccessful. The seasons where coaches had us write out our team vision and our personal goals were the most successful seasons I ever had. That shared vision provided a foundation for the team. Without it, we were athletes playing without greater purpose. Having that purpose and knowing why we were playing enabled the members of those teams to sacrifice for each other in ways the visionless teams never could.

The power of a clear, stated vision struck me so deeply that after my sports career was over, I wanted to see if I could apply this exercise to business and to life. I started with something that had dogged me my whole life: public speaking. I was terrified of speaking in public. I could not get up to talk in front of people to save my life. Whenever I gave speeches in school, I was a sweating, shaking, nervous wreck. I decided I never wanted to feel that way ever again.

A year removed from my professional football career after a number of injury setbacks, I joined Toastmasters International, an educational organization that helps members with their communication and public-speaking skills. I went every week for a year, with the goal of getting over my fear of speaking in public. But that goal wasn't specific enough; the vision wasn't clear enough. "Getting better" was too vague. Toward the middle of the program, excited by my progress but not satisfied with my direction, I wrote down a scary goal: Make $5,000 for a speech. What made it so frightening was the fact that I wasn't able to achieve it in that moment. There was no way anyone was going to pay me to speak at an event, not that version of me. But I knew that stepping toward my fear, that's where the magic is created. I had doubts—*Who is going to listen to a young kid like me? What do I have to offer?*—but I gave myself a deadline to do it: 9 months.

I wrote it down on a piece of paper. I framed it and hung it on my mirror where I would see it every morning when I woke up. Just like writing down our shared team vision back in my football days, framing and posting my speaking goal (with the date!) gave me a purpose and a destination. It turned my telescope around. Not only did I achieve that goal in the time allotted, but today I am much more comfortable onstage and regularly get offered upwards of $25,000 for speaking opportunities around the world. And it all started with establishing a clear vision and writing down my goals. I've been doing this exercise for more than 15 years now. I started calling it my Certificate of Achievement to make it an official part of the quest for greatness, and it continues to serve me well as both an athlete and an entrepreneur.

Download your Certificate of Achievement at schoolofgreatness.com/resources and you will receive an easy template for completing this exercise in excellence. Once complete, print out your COA, frame it, and place it where you're going to look at it every day. Make it the focal point of your daily routine, always at the top of your mind and on the tip of your tongue as that singular thing you must achieve.

EXERCISE #2:
Perfect Day Itinerary (PDI)

This may be one of the most powerful exercises you ever do for yourself, so make it count. I've coached many wandering entrepreneurs through this exercise, and most of them have told me it changed their lives. I wasn't surprised—when I did it for the first time years ago, it literally set me up for creating the life I always envisioned and living it every day.

In this exercise, your job is to map out what your perfect day looks like along the path to achieving your vision. There are two parts to this exercise: the macro and the micro. First up is the macro part, where you figure out what your perfect day would look like at a general level. Not every day is going to be exactly the same. Each day will look a little different depending on what happened the day before. It should look a little different; otherwise life would get boring and monotonous. Still, you want to have a broad sense of what each perfect day feels like. This starts with a series of questions.

> How do I want every day to look?
>
> How do I want to feel every single day?
>
> What am I creating daily?
>
> Whom am I spending my time with?
>
> What places am I exposing myself to?
>
> What passions am I fulfilling?

Take out a blank piece of paper or open a new document on your computer and fill the first half of the page with the answers, in broad terms, to these questions.

Here was mine from my first time completing the exercise.

PART 1: MY PERFECT DAY

In my perfect day, I wake up next to the woman of my dreams and she's crying tears of joy because she's so excited about the life we have together. I'm preparing to compete in the 2016 Olympics with USA Team Handball, so I head to an intense training session with my coach to increase my physical strength and athleticism. Then I'm working on my TV show that's on a major network and supporting my company team with all of my projects that inspire entrepreneurs to follow their own passions and make a living around what they love.

Now, in part 2 (the micro part), write out a detailed itinerary for the next perfect day on the bottom half of the page. This should include everything you want to do and have to do and exactly how and when you want to do it.

Every successful sports season I had included detailed daily itineraries. We received one in the morning and one before practice, and they set us up to win. There was no more wondering what to do, when to do it, or how much time to spend on it. It was all right there, plain as day, laid out in the steps necessary to reach our end goal. This is true for every professional sports team as well. The successful ones have a daily plan designed to lead them to achieve their vision. Theirs are similar, if not in many ways identical, to what I'm asking you to create.

Here is a version of my daily itinerary while I was writing this book.

PART 2: TOMORROW'S PERFECT DAY

7:30 a.m. Wake up, meditate, and enjoy the views from my balcony.

8:00 a.m. Healthy breakfast with green juice or a smoothie.

9:00 a.m. CrossFit/kickboxing or private skills training session.

10:45 a.m. Check in with my team about projects of the day.

11:00 a.m. Complete the top three tasks that were on my list before bed.

12:00 p.m. Healthy lunch at home or lunch meeting with someone who inspires me.

1:30 p.m. Back to the top three on my to-do list, recording interviews, doing videos, or working with the team.

3:00 p.m. Physical therapy to increase flexibility (2 days a week).

5:00 p.m. Pickup basketball, hiking with friends, swim in ocean.

7:30 p.m. Healthy dinner at home or out with friends.

9:00 p.m. Read, movie, events with influencers on the town.

11:00 p.m. Make a list of what I'm most grateful for today, create a "completed list" of what I did today. Write the top three list of what I want to create tomorrow.

11:30 p.m. Meditate, sleep, dream, recover body.

If you let it, the PDI can be a powerful exercise that will set your year (and many years to come) to contain the best days of your business and life.

It also helps validate your vision and vice versa. If your vision doesn't fit in with your perfect day at either the macro or micro level, you need to either change your vision or be more open, honest, and creative about what it will take at a daily level to reach your vision.

EXERCISE #3:
Personal Principles Declaration (PPD)

The third vision exercise is the statement of who you will be and what you will stand for in your life, even in the toughest moments. I call it the Personal Principles Declaration (PPD) because that's what it is—a declaration. You're not making a wish list or scribbling down some nice thoughts. You are declaring to yourself and to your world that this list of five principles is what you stand for and live by, no matter what comes your way. When something goes wrong or doesn't happen the way you envisioned, you fall back on these principles instead of falling into a negative spiral or becoming a victim of circumstances. You don't let your bruised ego get the best of you, because your vision is bigger than your ego. You will never achieve what you really want if you let your ego stand in the way of your principles.

Here is my PPD.

1. Love myself, everyone, and everything.
2. Be in service to support others and the world.
3. Always give my best and strive for greatness in everything I do.

4. Live in abundance.

5. Create a win/win with everything.

Here is Angel Martinez's PPD.

1. Tell the truth.

2. Be there for your family and friends.

3. Respect the opinions of others.

4. Know that you don't have all the answers. Ask questions.

5. Have humility.

6. Persevere.*

Print out your PPD or write it on a card and keep it in your wallet. Read over your principles often. Your ego is strong and very convincing (at least I know mine is), especially when the chips are down, but when you hold fast to your principles, you cannot be deterred on your path to achieving your vision. It doesn't matter what kind of adversity comes your way—and it will come, especially the bigger the vision—your principles are a set of powerful tools that will serve you along the journey.

*Of course, Angel added one more principle for good measure. You don't get from where he was to where he is now by doing just enough!

EXERCISE #4:
Your Personal Statement Plan (PSP)

This exercise is designed to bring everything about your vision together into a plan of action. We can think and plan and hope and wish, but until we do something about our vision (as you will see in the following chapters), it will only ever be just a dream.

On a blank piece of paper, fill out the following worksheet (to download this document, go to schoolofgreatness.com/resources).

Your name _____

Today's date _____ 6 or 12 months from today _____

Answer these questions.

Who am I? _____

_____

_____

_____

_____

_____

What do I stand for? _____

_____

_____

_____

_____

_____

What is my vision for myself, my family, and the world?_____

_____

_____

_____

_____

_____

List your five principles (Personal Principles Declaration)

1. _____

2. _____

3. _____

4. _____

5. _____

This is an opportunity to get clear on what you want, but make no mistake—living your vision is a commitment. It demands time and dedication, so don't take it lightly. Pause for a moment, if needed, before you put the vision of your life to paper. But make sure to complete these exercises in the next 24 hours while they're fresh in your mind.

Write out the top three goals you want to either achieve or maintain for the next 6 or 12 months under each of the following categories: family, relationships, business, money, health, recreation, spirituality/ inner growth.

Below each goal, write a detailed action plan for how you will achieve that specific goal: Make it so annoyingly step-by-step and spelled out that anyone could read your plan, follow it exactly, and achieve it themselves. Here is a sample of how three categories might look.

FAMILY

GOAL #1:   VISIT PARENTS AND SIBLINGS TWICE A YEAR.

Step 1: Find time in my schedule every 6 months where I could fly home (in next 3 days).

Step 2: Call Mom, Dad, and siblings to see when they are free (in next 7 days).

Step 3: Save to my calendar the set dates we agree on and book flights (within 2 weeks).

BUSINESS

GOAL #1: **MAKE $10,000 A MONTH IN THE NEXT 6 MONTHS.**

Step 1: Calculate how many customers it will take to reach this (1 day).

Step 2: Break this down into how many sales this will take weekly and daily (1 day).

Step 3: Set up and host one webinar per week to current prospects to generate these sales.

HEALTH

GOAL #1: **LOSE 15 POUNDS IN 60 DAYS.**

Step 1: Find a workout plan I'll be excited about (within 24 hours).

Step 2: Find coach or accountability partner (3 days).

Step 3: Schedule workout days and times of workouts for the next 60 days (3 days).

Step 4: Begin training on this plan in 4 days!

Write down the type of person you will need to be in order to accomplish this in 6 or 12 months.

Example: "I will need to be committed. Most important, I'll need to let go of the pressure or stress and empower others around me to support me instead of doing it all on my own. I'll need to deepen my understanding about business and how the world works for me to be able to flow in it effortlessly."

I will _____

_____

_____

_____

_____

Now write down the breakthroughs you will create as a result of understanding who you need to be to accomplish your goals.

Example: "Letting go of reaction or defensiveness. Peace with myself, and understanding that everything at the end of the day is 'small stuff' and doesn't require me to react in a way that doesn't serve me if things don't go well."

    This is your living document that you will adjust over time. Every 6 to 12 months, you should revisit it and make sure you are on track to live your vision.

COACHING TIP

Your life matters, and so do your dreams. It's time you act like they matter. The best way to start doing that is to visualize and map out how you want your dreams to look on a day-to-day basis. The key to greatness is fulfilling what you want in your life first and being an inspiration to yourself. By creating an inspiring life that works, you inspire others around you to do the same. This ripple effect is powerful. Just imagine if everyone focused on making sure their lives were fulfilling and inspiring. What would the world look like then?! When you complete this homework, show it to a friend or someone you care about and tell them your dreams and what you stand for. Ask them to join you in completing these vision exercises as well, so you have an accountability buddy. Then post it on social media and use #SchoolOfGreatness so others in the community can support you along your journey. You've got this, and I've got your back. It's time to make magic happen, and it starts with you getting clear on exactly what you want in your life and why you want it. Let's go!

GET GROUNDED

With everything I've ever wanted in life—from wanting to be a great athlete when I was young yet getting picked last for teams to learning to start my own business from my sister's couch after a career-ending injury with no hope in sight to finding a loving relationship with my ego and insecurities getting in the way—it has always and will continue to come with an equally difficult challenge.

When adversity arises, you have two choices: (1) Do nothing, let it overwhelm you, and fall victim to your circumstances, or (2) embrace the challenge and move toward the adversity, making it part of your success story. Prepare yourself for these moments, because they are going to happen in all areas of your life whether you like it or not. When you understand this and learn to embrace adversity, then you can learn to overcome it and use it to your advantage.

When I face challenges in my life, I think about my friend Kyle Maynard, whom I write about in this chapter, and how he, along with others, shows me how much I have to be grateful for.

CHAPTER 2

TURN ADVERSITY INTO ADVANTAGE

Storms make trees take deeper roots.

—Dolly Parton

For most of us, it's difficult to imagine becoming a championship wrestler, a football player, a weight lifter, a mixed martial arts fighter, or a mountain climber. There are so many obstacles that stand in the way of each of those goals: money, opportunity, coaching, talent and ability, confidence. Any one of them could derail these impressive dreams at any time.

Now imagine becoming *all* those things before you cut the cake on your 30th birthday. A friend of mine did. His name is Kyle Maynard, and he is one of the most inspiring teachers I've ever met. When he was a young man, those physical feats I just listed were only a few of the goals on his bucket list—a bucket that would never go empty and would one day include inspiring others to do great things. Kyle wanted to achieve his goals as badly as any person who aspired to greatness has wanted something. And by the middle of 2012, at the age of 26, he'd accomplished all of them. He played football in middle school. He was a champion wrestler in high school and won 36 varsity wrestling matches during his senior year. He fought a full three-round mixed martial arts (MMA) fight. He climbed the nearly 20,000-foot Mount Kilimanjaro.

On their own, these might not sound like particularly lofty goals. I've met many other people who achieved these same dreams at a much higher level, yet none of them did it the way Kyle did. When they did it, ESPN didn't award them with two ESPYs for their accomplishments, the way the network did in Kyle's case. Why? Kyle's accomplishments stand head and shoulders above those of most other men his age—most other men, period— because Kyle himself stands only 3 feet 8 inches tall. He is a congenital amputee. A birth defect related to something called amniotic band syndrome deprived him of the fully formed arms and legs that most of us take for granted. As he describes it: "Basically, my arms end right where your elbows would be. For each arm, they're both about the same length, and my legs end slightly above where the knee is, and I have two feet. They're just a little bit different."

Amniotic band syndrome occurs when the blood clots in utero and fibrous bands constrict the growth of fetal limbs. Doctors have no idea why it happens or what causes it, but they peg the statistical chances of it happening in an otherwise normal pregnancy at 1 in 10 million. Growing up, Kyle did not just face the typical external obstacles all of us face at one time or another; he dealt with a whole unique set of struggles that were a part of his life from the day he was born. And yet he accomplished each of the things he had envisioned for himself.

IT'S ALL IN THE DOING

You should not feel bad for Kyle Maynard. Pity isn't a feeling he's searching for. What I learned from Kyle over the course of our talks brought my understanding of goals and greatness into a kind of focus I'd never had before. Creating a vision is about clearly defining what you want (your goals) and who you want to be (your dreams). But goals and vision are one thing—they are made in our minds. They are only hypotheticals. Anyone can tell themselves they have a vision for what they want to create in the world, but it is our actions that dictate what we create in reality, where anything can (and does) happen. It is in the doing that the goals become real.

To be good at something requires talent, vision, and action. Greatness is what remains when that talent and vision meet adversity—and persist in the face of it. This is what makes Kyle a great teacher, and it's why he can teach us more than just about anyone about overcoming adversity on the path to greatness. When it comes to greatness, he teaches us that there is no room in life for excuses:

"When I was younger, when I was 10 years old, I used to cry myself to sleep some nights because I would just wish that I would wake up and have arms and legs. And no matter how hard I would have focused on that forever, it never would have happened. So when we go and focus on those things that we have no control over, it brings us nothing but unhappiness."

This mindset is unsustainable and unproductive in the face of adversity. It gets us nowhere. How does that old saying go: "Wish in one hand, crap in the other, and see which one fills up first"? That was a reality Kyle was forced to reckon with at an early age. As he said, no amount of focus or wishing was going to change anything. Like many of the breakthrough moments I've had in my life around the issue of adversity, Kyle's aha moment came on the football field. He was 11 years old.

"I made my first tackle in a football game when I was 11," Kyle recalled. "It seems like a relatively simple thing, but my life changed forever in that moment. I stopped having so many concerns over what might happen in the distant future. I stopped being consumed with wondering what I would do with my life. I used to ask questions like 'Would I have to live at home with Mom and Dad forever?' 'Would I ever have a girlfriend or a job someday?' And the interesting part: It wasn't like I was given any answers to any of those questions. I was just playing football."

Kyle wasn't thinking or worrying or wishing, he was *doing.* At 11 years old, no less! It was in the action and the perseverance in the face of tall odds that obstacles started to dissolve and he took his first concrete steps toward greatness. It became almost a philosophy of adversity, one that he lived by from that day forward.

"My life has had its challenges since that tackle," he told me. "But the concerns and fears I had over the future continued to subside until they became relatively nonexistent. I mostly attribute that to putting myself in situations where I'm uncomfortable and staying with it until I become comfortable.

"When I was 19, I gave a speech to several thousand of the world's most successful business owners, sandwiched between then senator Obama and Dr. Steven Covey, best-selling author of *The Seven Habits of Highly Effective People*. Once I gave that talk, it's no wonder every speech since then has been a whole lot easier!"

Amazing! Think about that for a second: In 8 years, Kyle went from crying himself to sleep every night, wondering if he'd ever have a girlfriend or a job or a place of his own, to speaking to a room full of business luminaries between the future president of the United States and the author of one of the most successful self-help business books of all time. And it all started with a tackle on the football field—with one little action.

"We are our greatest ally in terms of our capability to get past adversity. We can be incredibly motivated," Kyle often says. It all lies in how we perceive and engage the adversity we face.

THE LANGUAGE OF INTERNAL ADVERSITY

One of the things it took me a long time to learn about adversity, especially in my own life, is that adversity isn't always external or physical. In fact, it usually isn't. I first started to understand this through my work on emotional intelligence with Chris Lee (whom we'll meet next chapter), but it wasn't until I sat down to talk with Nicole Lapin about money that my eyes opened to how broadly adversity can manifest itself in our lives.

Nicole is a finance expert who spent years as a reporter and anchor for networks like CNBC, CNN, and Bloomberg before striking out on her own to write a *New York Times* best-selling book called *Rich Bitch* about getting your financial life in order. Her book is fantastic, and—man or woman—if you've always had money or finance issues, you should definitely pick it up and read it cover to cover.

But what struck me about Nicole when we met was the story of her path to financial reporting that began, remarkably, at age 18. It was a journey that was almost over before it began, thanks to a whole different brand of adversity—the internal kind.

A first-generation American, Nicole grew up with immigrant parents who operated a 100 percent cash household. No credit cards, no loans, nothing that typically defined the average American's relationship with money. It was all cash, all the time.

"We didn't have the *Wall Street Journal* on the kitchen counter, we never talked about stocks or bonds or any of that, and I never learned it in school. So I was pretty clueless growing up," Nicole told me. "I was that awkward girl with no debit card who went out to dinner with girlfriends and either dropped a wad of cash or wrote a check."

The final straw came when she was in college at Northwestern University in Chicago and she needed to buy a last-minute airline ticket. The convenient thing would have been to hop on the computer and buy one online. There was just one problem: She didn't possess a credit card. Instead, she had to go to the bank, withdraw cash, and roll up to the counter at the airport and pay for the ticket with a wad of bills. "I said, 'Enough is enough. This is ridiculous.' I needed to take control of my life and my finances."

Except how do you do that? How do you take control of your financial life and set yourself on a path toward a career in business news when finance is essentially a foreign concept to you? When you can't learn from your parents? When you live in a country where they don't teach you how to master and manage your money—not in elementary school or high school or college, even if you take finance classes?

"That's when I realized, it's just a language, like anything else that's new. It's a very foreign language," Nicole said.

She was totally right! Every single new thing we attempt in our lives is like a new language. The language of MMA and mountain climbing probably scared the crap out of Kyle when he first thought about tackling those feats. The language of LinkedIn and the language of business scared me half to death when I was planted on my sister's couch staring at the end of my career in sports (a language I was very fluent in).

Getting started is always the hardest part of doing anything new. You have to overcome all those fears and anxieties of saying the wrong thing or looking foolish. There can be a lot of shame involved, and shame has stopped more than a few people from doing important things—things they loved. Nicole recognized this and decided to jump in with both feet. She took a job on the floor of the Chicago Mercantile Exchange.

"When you start to speak that language, you feel you're speaking Chinese in your own country," she confessed. "That's what happened to me when I started on the floor of the exchange. I had to learn the language really quickly. When I realized that it was just learning a language and that if I learned it I could join the conversation, I felt so empowered."

I knew exactly what she meant, because I experienced that exact feeling when I was learning how to salsa dance back in 2006. I was living above a jazz club that offered salsa dancing once a week, and I went down there committed to becoming the best tall, goofy, white-guy salsa dancer that I could be. I was petrified, but for 3 months, I trained and studied and had group classes, and I took private lessons, and I watched YouTube videos, and I practiced in front of my mirror by myself like I was dancing with a girl. If you think it's weird when I talk about it, imagine how weird I felt doing it!

But I remember the moment when I finally understood the language of salsa dancing, and believe me when I tell you that when I started, it seemed like a *completely* foreign language. Nicole nailed it; it was absolutely like speaking Chinese. When it clicked and salsa started to make sense, as though I could speak the language fluently, I felt like I could run up the side of a building. I could do anything I set my mind to no matter what obstacles—physical or mental, internal or external—stood in front of me.

Nicole helped me reframe my outlook on adversity—
not just what it is and where it comes from but also how
to address and overcome it. It's a lesson I will carry with
me into every new challenge, because if there is one thing
that is inescapable in life, to say nothing of the path to
greatness, it is adversity. We dream, and then reality
smacks us in the face. We create a vision for ourselves,
and soon enough we learn that the world is, at best, indifferent to it (and us). In some cases, the world seems to
want to do everything it can to get in our way. It shows
up at nearly every stage along our path: from the early
days of figuring out how to walk; learning in school;
messing up your first kiss; practicing sports; starting a
new business. We experience loads of pain, frustration,
and falling down.

No one understands this better than Kyle Maynard.
He taught me that not only is no one immune to adversity
but that enduring your fair share of it is not an entirely
bad thing. When we fail over and over in pursuit of excellence, it actually helps us learn and grow into greatness!
Granted, Kyle has endured more than his fair share, compared to someone like me—I don't have a congenital disability, after all—but I still had obstacles to overcome.

THE HIDDEN ADVANTAGE
OF ADVERSITY

My entire childhood was based around a singular vision:
Become an All-American athlete. I thought it would be in
football, the sport I'd lived and breathed for so many
years. I thought it would happen my sophomore year in

college when I set the record for most receiving yards in one game (418 yards) and ended the season with the second most receiving yards in the nation. But my team had barely a .500 winning percentage, and they don't typically award All-American status to players on average teams. Things only got worse from there, on and off the field, as our coaching staff was unable to do what it took to put us in a position to be great. So my senior season, I transferred to another school that offered a real opportunity to achieve my dream. It was a tough decision to leave, especially for someone like me who'd spent his whole life playing with and for the team, but this new school showed a lot of promise, and I couldn't deny the dream that had guided my whole life.

In the second game of the season with my new team, we were playing our crosstown rivals. I was having a good game, making plays, and at one point in the third quarter, I hauled in a slant pass over the middle and took a hard hit to my ribs from one of the linebackers. I felt some soreness at the time, but thanks to adrenaline and competitiveness, I didn't think much of it. Then 2 days later at practice, I went to make a quick cut in warmups, heard a huge pop, and crumpled to the ground in absolute agony. I'd never experienced that kind of pain in my life. It felt like someone was stabbing me in the side, twisting the knife, and then using a sledgehammer to pound on the wound. My teammates thought I was joking because nobody had touched me! Well, it turned out that I'd probably hairline fractured three ribs on my right side in the game, and the quick cut and turn in practice did the rest of the work, breaking them all the way. The cartilage had ripped from the bone and my muscles were twitching at the spot of the tear, chattering my ribs at the place of the breaks. I'd turned my rib cage into a wind chime, and every breath fluttered the chimes even more. Needless to say, I was out the rest of the season.

For a few months, I was in so much pain, I could hardly walk. I couldn't sleep, cough, sneeze, or laugh for at least 2 weeks. I had to have someone lift me out of bed because I couldn't engage my stomach muscles without needing to scream in pain. I had never taken pain medication before, so when I popped the pills the doctors prescribed, my body didn't know how to react to them and I threw them up almost immediately—which was a whole other level of pain to add to the mix.

Yet the physical pain paled in comparison to the emotional agony. I was completely crushed. My dream was slipping away—adversity had smashed my vision to pieces like that linebacker had smashed my ribs. It was one of the lowest points of my life.

Around Christmastime of that year, a few months after the injury occurred, I had recovered enough that I was able to run on a treadmill without pain. I was feeling a little better emotionally, too, but I still couldn't shake the fact that I was nowhere nearer to the goal that meant so much to me. I was a senior, and the football season was over, so becoming an All-American wide receiver was clearly no longer an option. I had to figure something out. There had to be another way.

That's when it occurred to me that I might try my

hand at another sport in the months remaining of my NCAA eligibility. Except for my still-healing ribs, I was in good shape, and I was a great track athlete. My freshman year, I jumped 6 feet 6 inches in the high jump and 22 feet in the long jump, and I'd nearly cracked 11 seconds in the 100-meter dash. None of those marks individually would get me within sniffing distance of a medal stand, let alone qualifying for the national championships, but together maybe there was something there. Track and field is a spring sport, so I called my old track coach (who had qualified for the Olympic trials and was a former All-American herself) between Christmas and New Year's and asked her what it would take to become an All-American in the decathlon—the 2-day, 10-event test of strength, agility, and endurance whose winner in the Olympics is often called the "world's greatest athlete." Was it even possible? She said it was, but training would have to start right away, and I would need to do everything she said for the next 6 grueling months. No shortcuts. No excuses.

To use Nicole Lapin's metaphor, it was a new language, but I didn't care—I was in. This new vision gave me the motivation and drive to refocus all of my energy toward doing whatever it took to make that happen. It brought a sense of purpose when before I felt helpless. It gave me that pep in my step that, just a few months prior on the football field, allowed me to distinguish myself as a top-flight wide receiver. I felt like a warrior preparing for battle again. A powerful vision gives us warrior-like strength, which is why it's critically important to find or recalibrate your vision as soon as possible after confronting major adversity.

I immediately began the arduous transfer process back to my previous school (Principia College, where my old track coach was based) and got to work. In the 6 months that followed, I ended up getting into the best shape of my life—probably my peak conditioning as an athlete to date—and not only qualifying for the national championships but making the All-American team. (I'll explain what happened in the next chapter.) Then, if that wasn't enough, I earned a fifth year of eligibility thanks to all the injuries, got back on the football field better than ever thanks to the decathlon training, broke a few receiving records and made big plays in big games, and earned my second All-American honors. This time— finally—in football, my goal all along.

I had unearthed the advantage hidden within my adverse circumstances. What I had dreaded and fought so hard against at first—my injuries—actually got me closer to my dream. In fact, it surpassed the original dream in ways I could have never imagined. How could that be? How could an injury, one that I never anticipated, literally double my chances to be an All-American, which I'd dreamed of since I was a boy?

I didn't realize it then, but it all became clear when I spoke to Ryan Holiday, my friend and author of the book *The Obstacle Is the Way.* Ryan is a best-selling author, the former head of marketing for American Apparel, and the founder of a marketing and strategy firm that allows him to live the life he wants to live. Ryan has faced his own fair share of adversity. He dropped out of college at 19 years old; was virtually disowned by his parents; went to work for a string of high-profile, very difficult, and controversial clients; and spent the better part of the next decade working his butt off to get where he is today.

"It is a timeless truth of history and philosophy," he told me, "that the hardships we face in life can be seen as terrible tragedies or opportunities." The Roman emperor Marcus Aurelius, one of Ryan's great influences, was fond of reminding himself that "the impediment to action advances action. What stands in the way becomes the way."

In fact, you can trace this foundational element of Stoic thought through many of the most revered individuals who ever lived. As young men, both Thomas Jefferson and George Washington read the Stoics—thinkers and leaders like Cato the Younger, Epictetus, and Marcus Aurelius—and it helped them with the adversity they faced during the creation of America. The explorer and writer Robert Louis Stevenson was a longtime admirer of Marcus Aurelius and Stoic thought. So were painters like Eugène Delacroix, writers and thinkers like Adam Smith, and statesmen like Bill Clinton. Tim Ferriss, the investor and entrepreneur and my personal friend, is also a public proponent of this line of ancient philosophy that has relevance for our modern lives.

All these folks faced adversity on their paths to success. Sometimes it was big; sometimes it was quite small.

As Ryan writes, there is "one thing that all great men and women have in common. Like oxygen to a fire, obstacles became fuel for that which was their ambition. Nothing could stop them, they were (and continue to be) impossible to discourage or contain. Every impediment served to make the inferno within them burn with greater ferocity."

YOUR PERSPECTIVE IS YOUR CHOICE

Kyle Maynard is a Stoic, too, whether he knows it or not. When he says, "Our perspective is always our choice," he is echoing what the philosophers have always claimed— that there is no good or bad but only our perceptions. As he tackled each of his dreams, undaunted, it was the philosopher-statesman Seneca's words that he took most vividly to heart: "It is a rough road that leads to the heights of greatness."

When Kyle started wrestling in high school, he recounted to me, "People would say, 'You'll never be able to win a match.' They wouldn't say it directly to me necessarily, but I'd hear it through the grapevine." A lot of that doubt came from people whose perceptions blinded them. They did not see the hungry dreamer in front of them, only what was missing from him. They saw only what limited him and held him back—not that it might have made him stronger or more determined or that it might have some tactical advantages on the mat!

Some of the doubt and negativity almost certainly came from a place of fear and insecurity that existed in the minds of his potential opponents. What if this armless, legless teenager beat them? How would *that* look? They were right to be afraid. Kyle not only won 36 matches his senior season but also finished 12th in his weight class at Senior Nationals, beating several state champions and higher-ranked wrestlers along the way.

Kyle used these fearful people's misperceptions and misunderstandings to his advantage. He found fuel in the haters. As Ralph Waldo Emerson asked, "Is it so bad, then, to be misunderstood? Pythagoras was misunderstood, and Socrates, and Jesus, and Luther, and Copernicus, and Galileo, and Newton, and every pure and wise spirit that ever took flesh. To be great is to be misunderstood." Obviously, I'm not trying to say that Kyle is on the same level as Socrates or Jesus or Galileo, but when it comes to guys who fought some uphill battles, you can find worse comparisons. Part of greatness is being doubted and facing difficulty, and it's precisely that struggle that contributes to their greatness.

A year later, Kyle decided he would try his hand at mixed martial arts and began the rigorous training. "MMA actually taught me a lot about myself," he said. "It was the first time that other people really voiced major disapproval with what I was doing." The State of Georgia attempted to ban his first match. The Georgia Athletic Commission refused to issue him a fighter's license—a prerequisite to compete in a sanctioned bout. The nay-saying grapevine from his wrestling days moved online, and they had no problem telling him exactly what they thought. Internet commenters were ruthless and relentless as they wrote about him in all of the major

MMA chat rooms and communities online. They threatened him; they called him a legless freak.

"One of my core beliefs is that you have to have things that you're passionate about to go after and live to your potential," Kyle said to me. "I didn't want to be a pro fighter. I had no delusions about that. I just wanted to experience it. Because 99.9 percent of the fans of the sport would never step into the cage, and that's okay, but I didn't want to be afraid. I wanted to go in there and experience it."

The great ones look at every situation this way. They look at adversity as the lesson that moves them toward their goal, not the obstacle that keeps them from it. Fear drove Kyle's opponents and haters to lash out at him. It also drove them off the mat and out of the cage. It drove Kyle to test his limits and pursue his dreams with even more energy and purpose. As the great Lionel Richie put it, "Greatness comes from fear. Fear can either shut us down and we go home, or we fight through it."

This is why adversity is so important and why it is the second lesson in this book. First we have our vision, and then we run into obstacles. The real greats don't worry too much about this—it's inevitable, it's not the end of the world. Instead, this dose of reality is simply used as a challenge. To learn a new language. To channel their energy into their true path. To adjust their vision from fantasy into an actionable, realistic plan.

It occurred to me that this was the common thread in Kyle's life, as he repeatedly said to himself: "Okay, what is it that I should not able to do, and how can I do it? How can I figure out a way to do it?" It applied to tackling a ball carrier in his adolescent years, to speaking among giants in his late teens, and to climbing Kilimanjaro in his twenties. He was born without arms and legs, so he's simply had to modify and adjust and be adaptive to everything, to everyday life.

In this way, we must be grateful for our particular form of adversity, since it is the precise thing that helps us get to where we want to be. *What stands in the way becomes the way.* For instance, I was shocked to hear that not only does Kyle spend a lot of time working with veterans who've lost limbs in war, but when he meets them, he feels a kind of gratitude. Not reluctance or kinship or pity, but gratitude.

"I don't have any idea what it's like to lose my limbs. I was born without my arms and legs, so I have no perspective of that," he said. This is how it's always been for him. He was spared the enormous sense of loss and fear that these veterans feel. He was spared their pain, too, and the lingering effects of injury. Just think about the perspective it takes to live with that kind of attitude—to be grateful for something like being born with a disability because there are worse ways to end up where you are. That perspective and attitude inspire me. Whenever I seem to be having a "bad day," I think about Kyle and realize how much I have to be grateful for as well.

This is something that great men and women understand—that the actual problem, obstacle, or adversity is irrelevant. It's their mindset and response to it that matter. They learn from these obstacles what it is going to take to accomplish what they've set out to do. They learn the importance of persevering toward their vision *despite* that adversity. They learn the language so they can tell the world what they want to do and who they want to become.

It's funny, when I was speaking with Angel Martinez, this came up almost verbatim. Like me, Angel ultimately became successful in business (way bigger than me, obviously!) through a combination of vision, talent, and perseverance, and he discovered early on that the path to self-esteem was sweaty and intense and competitive— and not where he first expected to find it. I thought I would find it on the receiving end of touchdown passes. It turns out it was at the end of 10 grueling track-and-field events. Angel thought it would be baseball.

"I wanted to play Major League Baseball, like every Cuban kid, but when I was a freshman in high school, I think I was about 5 foot 3 inches and 112 pounds. I couldn't hit or throw the ball out of the infield. I could field well, but that was about it. I could throw to first and second. That was okay when we were playing Little League, but when we got to high school, it was a whole other thing," he told me.

Like Kyle and me, one of Angel's childhood dreams ran smack into the unforgiving reality of physical limitations. And like us, he had to find a way around them. For Angel, it was running.

"What attracted me to running was that I could be as good as I wanted to be," he said. "In distance running, there's no coach who is going to bench you or tell you that you can't play. And the clock never lies. There's no subjectivity. I remember when I started running, the older guys on the team told me, 'We only have one rule. You can't stop. You can go as slow as you need to go, but you cannot stop. You can never drop out.' "

SLOW AND STEADY WINS A DIFFERENT RACE

If there is one thing you take from the School of Greatness about pursuing your vision and achieving your dreams, it should be this: You can go as slow as you need to go, but you cannot stop. You can never give up or drop out of giving your best in your life.

Angel unwittingly taught his own son Julian, a cross-country runner at Claremont McKenna College, this lesson. "He had always heard me talk about all this," Angel said of Julian. "Then I went to watch him at one meet, and he was about halfway through the 5 miles when he felt a really sharp pain in his shin area. He started slowing down, and I could see something was wrong. I went out there and said, 'Julian, what's the matter?' He was grimacing but he ignored me, and he finished the race." It turns out, Julian had broken his leg at the 2.5-mile mark. Two hours after the finish, he was in a cast. When Angel asked him why he didn't stop, Julian's answer was simple and obvious: "I don't drop out, Dad." Make no mistake, true greats never drop out.

Of course, you don't want to put yourself through any type of trauma or pain intentionally that will hurt you in the long run (more on the importance of experiencing pain in Chapter 5), but it is the idea and intention behind not giving up or dropping out on giving your best effort at all times. That is what we are talking about here.

"The lesson of running is about what it takes to be successful in life," Angel told me. "It is a metaphor for a lot of things you need to learn. Running, like life, is that constant confrontation of a challenge every day. Some days you don't feel that good; some days you feel great. Some days you're not inspired; other days it's pouring rain and freezing cold but you still have to go and run. As a kid, that's an incredibly important lesson to learn: that it takes commitment and you have to believe in yourself and that you can actually do whatever the hell you want. There's no limit to what you can do."

I discovered the same thing during my decathlon training, and I am reaping the benefits to this day as I train with the United States men's national handball team. There have been many moments when I didn't feel like training, especially after an injury. I've experienced many injuries over the past 4 years as I've trained for this new sport. I pulled my groin three times; I stuck a needle in my elbow multiple times to drain fluid; I've sprained ankles, broken fingers, and even took an elbow to the throat that had me spitting up blood for a week. The list of bumps, breaks, and bruises feels almost endless. But each injury taught me a lesson, and after each recovery, I took the necessary steps to keep moving and (hopefully) learn from them and use them to my advantage going forward. Once you experience the power of this triumph over adversity—over *yourself* in many ways—it's enough to get you off the couch and back into the game. Kyle Maynard experienced it, too. He has experienced it every day of his life. But it doesn't just get him off the couch, it puts him on the side of mountains in the middle of Africa.

Kyle ascended Tanzania's 19,336-foot Mount Kilimanjaro as part of a nine-man team in early 2012. Unassisted by team members and unaided by prosthetics, he essentially bear-crawled on his elbows for $12^1/_2$ days—10 days up, $2^1/_2$ days down. Half a dozen people (with all their limbs) die on that mountain every year. To summit it at all is a serious achievement. To do it like Kyle did it, well, I don't think there is even a word for that except for *greatness*!

Kyle would disagree, obviously, because that is not how he perceives his situation. In fact, the truly striking thing is that the climb wasn't about him at all. Born in a US Army hospital to an Army dad, Kyle has always had a passion for working with veterans. This mission up Kilimanjaro was for them. The goal, he told me, was "just to send a message to some of our troops that have literally sacrificed their limbs for our freedom that 'You may have had this happen to you, but you're still able to go and create the life that you want. It may not include climbing Kilimanjaro, but you have something that you want to do.'"

At some point, adversity happens in everyone's life. It usually comes unannounced, and it doesn't arrive with flowers and candy. It takes different forms and hits each of us differently, but learning to address and overcome it is all about bending but not breaking in the face of the daunting situations it presents. It requires connecting your head and your heart to that deep well of energy within to push you forward in a positive direction.

Kyle had to do it 4 days into his trek up Kilimanjaro as his elbows and feet swelled in incredible pain and nearly broke him. Angel Martinez did it as a runner, struggling to push himself through every mile. The problem he faced, as he tried to run faster and farther, was that the shoes his team wore weren't very good. To get halfway decent running shoes, they'd have to go into Berkeley (he eventually had moved from the Bronx to the Bay Area) and buy shoes that had been imported by a company called Blue Ribbon Sports. The importer? His name was Phil Knight, and he went on to found Nike.

Angel saw these people making a living solving a problem in the sport he loved and thought: *Why not me? Why can't I make a living by connecting my current passion [running] with one of my earliest childhood passions [cool shoes]?* Eventually, he started working at a small shop and bought half of it from the owner. A few years later, a couple of English guys walked in with a new brand they hoped he would sell. They called it Reebok.

This is what I mean when I say that the obstacle can be the way. If he hadn't been too short, if he hadn't felt like he had something to prove, Angel never would have found himself exposed to the business that changed his life—that became his calling. As Angel puts it, "There's always a challenge if you don't see yourself as a conventional person," so you'd better be prepared and ready for adversity—ready to make the most of it.

Whenever shit would hit the fan for me over the last couple years, I somehow automatically come back to Kyle and Angel and think, *Gosh, how could I possibly have anything to be ungrateful for?* Sure, like anyone, I have things I can be unhappy about. I am not talking about being a Pollyanna or staring at life through rose-colored glasses. This isn't self-delusion. What I am talking about is looking at things with your eyes open. When I was younger, I would get down on myself if something bad happened or get depressed if I felt things weren't going my way. Now I remember, in a way that is real and meaningful, that I have miraculous advantages that many others have not had. If Kyle can accomplish all that he has, if Angel can go from a Bronx tenement to the corner office of a billion-dollar business, I can pursue my own dreams and strive for my own version of greatness without giving in to a bad attitude when things invariably don't go my way. Whenever I face adversity, I'm always reminded of the examples they set, and I am thankful for our friendship every day because of it.

When you're looking at things with your eyes open, with a different perspective, it is then that you truly see the opportunities at your doorstep and how you can use them to your advantage. At the end of the day, if achieving dreams was easy, then everyone would have done it and no one would suffer from that nagging feeling that either drives or depresses us. What makes achieving your dreams and fulfilling your vision that much more special is the hard work it takes to get there. Proving that adversity is no match for you. That's what this is all about!

EXERCISE:
Embrace the Adversity (Internal and External)

Adversity is difficulty or misfortune that, for most people, creates an unmanageable amount of stress. Those who learn how to use adversity to their advantage, however, possess the power to turn that adversity into greatness. This is easier said than done, of course, because no one actually *likes* adversity. When you first experience it and you aren't prepared, what it feels like is failure. Adversity means failure, and failure means you must be bad at something. That's an awful feeling.

In reality, failure is simply feedback. It's not that you are bad or not good enough or incapable. Failure (or feedback) gives you the opportunity to look at what's not working and figure out how to make it work.

Everyone fails. Highly successful people fail many more times than the rest of the world and with much higher stakes at hand. Once we understand this, we can look at failure as something to fall in love with instead of something to shy away from. Thomas Edison endured 10,000 failures before he made the lightbulb, but each "failure" was feedback telling him that he hadn't figured it out yet and that this particular set of choices wasn't the right one for this particular task. His failures weren't evidence of his incompetence—if anything, they highlighted his brilliance and increased the likelihood that the next attempt would be the successful one.

Oftentimes the biggest obstacle we face is ourselves. Negative feelings, self-doubt, self-loathing; they all come from within to sabotage our vision. Adversity of all kinds will remain in your life until you adjust your perspective and embrace the messages failure is trying to send you. Listen to the feedback and apply it to your actions, and before you know it, adversity begins to melt away.

This is an exercise you can and should practice when those negative feelings threaten to overwhelm you. Consider it a daily practice until you fully start shifting and living consistently in a positive way that will support you and your vision instead of bring you down.

Step 1: Be Aware of the Adversity

Adversity happens to everyone, and though pain is inevitable, despair is optional. Discover precisely what the adversity is and why it is happening. This is your opportunity to take responsibility for every type of adversity that comes your way. Focus on the *why*—the root of it.

There are two types of adversity.

1. **The minor daily adversities that come up from time to time:** Fighting in your relationship, not getting the raise you want at your job, getting parking tickets, receiving poor grades on homework, feeling exhausted and stressed, feeling unsafe in your environment, etc.

2. **The major singular adversities that are more rare:** A death in the family, a car crash, injury or illness, a major breakup, losing your job, going bankrupt, etc.

When you become aware that adversity is inevitable, it allows you to prepare for it happening in the future.

What adversities do you face right now? What in your life feels like it is standing in the way of fulfilling your vision and achieving greatness?

Write your adversities down. Then identify whether they are chronic, daily obstacles that seem to grind your progress to a halt or big, singular moments of struggle that have thrown you off the path.

How have you been dealing with these issues to this point? How have you dealt with similar issues in the past? Have you overcome any of them? What did you do? There is wisdom and insight to be gleaned from your answers to those questions if not about what to do, then definitely about what *not* to do.

If you're anything like many of my coaching clients and some of the great teachers you will meet in the coming chapters, the thing you did most often in the face of adversity when you were first starting out was either try to ignore it or avoid it. Sometimes you might even pretend it wasn't there. I know I've been guilty of each of those behaviors in my own past.

Needless to say, this is something you absolutely cannot do. You cannot avoid, ignore, or deny adversity. Be aware of which adversities you are facing and accept the adversity for what it is. Avoid it or resist it and it will only persist.

Step 2: Write It Down or Share It

Now that you are aware of the adversity, write down how it's making you feel and why you think it's making you feel that way. This helps let go of the stress you are feeling to a certain degree and gets it out of you, where it can be the most toxic and do the most damage. It also allows you to have a written record of what you are feeling over time so you can look for patterns and see areas of growth. Write it down with pen and paper. If you don't have that, put it in your phone or on your computer. Over time, you'll want this all in one place so you can refer to it, so keep that in mind. Get it out! Embrace it.

For example: I'm angry/stressed/frustrated because I had an argument with my girlfriend; upset that I lost my job; still shaking after I got in a car crash, etc.

If you hold this inside, it will only bring more adversity to your life. Remember, what you resist persists.

If you prefer to verbally express yourself, then find a dedicated "adversity friend" whom you can go to anytime you feel frustrated by failure or you're struggling through adversity. Make an agreement with this friend that is reciprocal—you'll always listen to them without judgment so they can purge their emotions, and they will be your sounding board in return.

In the next chapter, you'll read stories and go through exercises that will support you in finding resolution in these breakdowns.

Step 3: Acknowledge Yourself

Once you let the negative feeling go, replace it by acknowledging yourself for all that you have done that day/week/month/year. You are up to big things! Even if they seem small to you, they are always bigger than where you were earlier in your life. Most of the time, we are comparing ourselves to others in our family or careers, and we do more harm by comparing ourselves rather than giving ourselves credit for where we are along our journey. Acknowledge yourself for reading this—knowledge is power. Your good intention is there.

Examples of things you can acknowledge yourself for: being on time at work, consistently going to the gym or working out, eating clean, being your word, etc.

Step 4: Express Your Gratitude

It's hard to be upset when you are focusing on what you are grateful for. Verbally tell your significant other, a friend, a family member, or just someone around you three things you are most grateful for in this moment; then ask them what three things they are most grateful for in their lives. Obviously, you don't have to tell the other people that you are beating yourself up on the inside right now, but just be aware in the moment and shift into a conversation of gratitude. When you give, you automatically receive. It's amazing what a compliment to someone opens up.

Examples: I'm grateful for my amazing friends. I'm grateful for my health and that I can walk, see, and feel. I'm grateful for my family and the support they give me. I'm grateful for the bed I get to sleep on.

Step 5: Reconnect to Your Vision and Take Action

Return your focus to what you want to achieve and why you want to achieve it: your Certificate of Achievement and your Personal Statement Plan from Chapter 1. Then figure out the next step to making your vision happen, and take action toward it. Momentum helps build confidence and positive thoughts and feelings, so it's important to spring into action when you are down on yourself or feeling adversity.

Whenever you are in breakdown or battling adversity in any situation in your life, this five-step process will help you fight off the insidious nature of self-defeating negative thoughts and chart a positive path toward achieving your vision and becoming great.

COACHING TIP

Learn to fall in love with adversity. Don't fall into a victim mindset and look at it as the thing that is holding you back, but instead find the part of it that can launch you toward achieving your dreams. Remember, no one has ever achieved anything truly great without going through extreme adversity. That doesn't mean you have to suffer through every challenge. Balance out the difficulties that adversity brings by being grateful for what is good in your life and treat yourself with gentle care. Give yourself time to heal, be messy, and experience the painful feelings you are battling. It's okay. You are human. Beating yourself up during adversity is the worst thing you can do, so make sure to love yourself and surround yourself with those who support you and lift you up. Tune back in to your vision, your Certificate of Achievement, and the principles you stand for. Once you are ready, take the next step toward your dreams and living that perfect day. It's within your reach; you are closer and closer to bringing it to reality. Accept and embrace adversity. Failure is simply feedback. Use it and stay committed to your vision through taking action at all times. Don't stop now. Keep moving forward. You've got this, and I've got your back.

GET GROUNDED

There is a big difference between the person who gets great results and the person who gets average results. And it begins with the conversations in the space between their ears—with how they believe in themselves. When you start to believe in the gifts you have within you, you are already halfway to becoming great. To do this, you must accept where you currently are along your journey and understand that if you are not happy, you have the power to change it. All you have to do is learn the necessary skills and put in the work.

This chapter is about teaching you the skills necessary to develop such a powerful belief in yourself that your mindset won't be shaken even under the most extreme challenges. Take notes and prepare to equip yourself with a powerful inner voice and a deeper understanding of what it takes to become a champion. This isn't just a lesson for sports; it applies equally to life, love, business, and spirit.

CHAPTER 3

CULTIVATE A CHAMPION'S MINDSET

I understand that nothing is easy.
I say everything happens for a reason.
I dream of one day the world is in peace.
I try to see the good in everything,
I'm a caring girl who loves to flip.

—**Shawn Johnson, seventh grade**

Michael Jordan, Serena Williams, Michael Phelps, Tom Brady, Janet Evans, Michael Johnson, Mia Hamm, Michael Schumacher (that's a lot of Michaels, but you get the idea). What is it like inside the minds of these champions and champions like them? From a distance, they appear superhuman or super lucky or both. They get all the calls, all the money, all the best parking spots. The ball always seems to bounce their way.

It's like they are living in a different world than the rest of us, and in a way they are. Their world is crystal clear. It isn't foggy and tumultuous and filled with self-doubt, like ours can be if we haven't clarified our vision, battled through adversity, and developed the proper mindset—the champion's mindset.

The champion's mindset is all about focus, flow, belief, and emotional intelligence. It is the complete dedication to your vision of future achievement. The way I have learned to describe it to myself when I do the visualization exercise you will learn at the end of this chapter is as a unique headspace that allows you to focus all your energy on putting yourself in the best position physically, mentally, and emotionally to be successful.

Don't misunderstand when I say the headspace is unique. I don't mean that only some people are capable of having it. I mean that the vision for greatness that defines your mindset and drives your effort is unique to you. I also mean that it is a mindset different than any other you will experience in your life.

I've tasted what it's like inside the mind of a champion. In fact, most of us probably have—we just didn't know it at the time. I didn't realize it the first time it happened to me; I just thought I was doing what needed to be done. I was simply focusing on the task in front of me, completely and totally. It turns out, that is a major component in the mind of a champion, and I learned it on the end of a 15-foot pole and a 40-meter runway.

It was the early summer of my senior year in college. I'd just spent the last 6 months stretching, pushing, pulling, lifting, and willing myself into the best shape of my life in preparation for the NCAA Division III track-and-field national championships in Waverly, Iowa. Held over 2 days, my event, the decathlon, would put all my hard work to the test. After breaking three ribs in the second football game of the season less than a year before, I had come back stronger than ever. I thought the injury had permanently derailed my dream of becoming an All-American, but the decathlon had breathed new life into the dying dream, and if I finished among the top eight competitors, that dream would become a reality.

When the competition began, I was pumped with adrenaline and feeling strong. On the first day of the 2-day event, I did well in some events and not so well in others. I entered the second day of competition right around ninth place, and I knew that I had to excel in the third event of the day, the pole vault, in order to reach the All-American podium.

In the pole vault, each competitor has to clear an opening height to score points. You get three attempts at each height after that, but if you fail to clear the initial height, you get a zero score for that event (which would essentially eliminate you from placing in the top of the competition). On my first attempt at the national championships, I opened at a height I cleared comfortably in practice: 12 feet. I was confident in my approach, ran down the runway, and leaped so high over the bar that I could have cleared 15 feet, but I ended up grazing the bar on the way down and watched it roll off the stands. No worries, though; I still had two attempts left and knew I'd make it on the next one. On my second attempt, I tried to run harder than before and in the process overstretched my footing and missed my mark. I stopped running about 2 feet ahead of my ideal takeoff spot and tried to compensate by lunging forward. I went straight up 15 feet in the air and fell straight back down on the runway, missing the bar completely. Suddenly, the third—and last—attempt took on unexpected weight and pressure. I was only 22 years old, but I felt like my entire life had come down to this moment. Make it and I have a shot at being an All-American. Miss it and my entire 22 years, along with the grueling 6 months of training to prepare for this moment, would be for nothing. That's how I felt. My dream of greatness came down to this.

The pole vault is all about strength, technique, and timing. For a decathlete, it is often a make-or-break event. In 1992, Angel Martinez's old company, Reebok, ran a giant advertising campaign in the lead-up to the Summer Olympics in Barcelona centered around American decathletes Dan O'Brien and Dave Johnson, called "Dan & Dave." They were two of the best decathletes in the world and favored to win medals. There was only one problem: Dan didn't qualify for the Olympics at the Trials. Want to guess why? He no-heighted on the pole vault, missing all three attempts. "Dan & Dave" became "Dave . . . and all those other guys."

My coach looked at me with a calm confidence through her piercing eyes, and strangely, instead of panicking, I began to visualize back to when I was 6 or 7 years old, sitting on the couch with my dad, watching football together and his explaining to me about the All-Americans we were seeing and what it meant to become one of them. The sense of honor and purpose, above the athletic achievements, stuck with me. It cleared away my current confusion and distractions. It lifted the lead weight from my feet. I was aware not only of exactly what I had to do but also of exactly who I was and what I was capable of. That moment put me into intense focus as I sprinted down the track with the pole, hitting my mark and launching myself over the bar with ease. Relief and joy hit me simultaneously. I went on to make a personal best, clearing over 14 feet, that day in the pole vault, and I finished strong in the next two events.

I became an All-American that day.

I have felt versions of that laser focus a handful of times over the past decade in many areas of my life besides sports, including business and relationships. It's addictive. Yet some of us have never felt it—we may not know that it is absent and what feats we're missing out on because of it. Some of us haven't even come close to feeling that state of peak performance and excellence.

I never performed remotely close to my best before that day in the pole vault. That isn't to say I didn't do well other times, but the difference between being good and being fully in the zone—truly in the head space of a champion—is a crucial ingredient in greatness, whether we're talking about sports, business, or life. And it was that day, lying on the vault mat, looking up at the bar still in its blocks 12 feet above my head, that I realized the power of accessing the zone for all areas of your life. I am calling it "laser focus" now, but I didn't fully recognize what I'd been channeling in that moment until I spoke with two amazing people: Steven Kotler and US Olympic gymnast Shawn Johnson—both fully tenured professors of greatness as far as I'm concerned.

Steven Kotler is the author of *The Rise of Superman: Decoding the Science of Ultimate Human Performance*. To say that his book is the one that I had been waiting for my whole life is legitimately an understatement. Growing up a skinny white kid in middle Ohio, all I ever wanted was to figure out what advantages I could get as an athlete to raise my game to the next level and perform at my peak in every sport. I wanted to know how to get in the zone like the All-Americans and world champions I admired— or, as Steven refers to it, the "flow state."

"Flow," Steven told me, "is an optimal state of consciousness, where we perform our best and we feel our best. In flow, we are so focused on the task at hand that everything else vanishes. Time either speeds up, so 5 hours will pass by like 5 minutes, or it slows down, like that freeze-frame effect in a car crash. Your sense of self, your sense of self-consciousness disappear completely, and all aspects of performance, mental and physical, go through the roof."

Yes! That is exactly how I felt as I sprinted down the runway on the track in Waverly, Iowa, drove the pole into the pit, and vaulted myself over the bar and closer to my dream. Talking with Steven, I realized I was wrong about one thing, though: This wasn't my first experience with flow. I'd had a similar experience on the football field as a sophomore 2 years earlier, in a game where I just felt invincible—unstoppable. It was my record-breaking game.

I remember in the first quarter they put one defensive back on me. Before I knew it, there were two on me and then there were three, with the safety shading over. Eventually, it felt like the whole team had been assigned to cover me, but it didn't matter how many people they put on my side of the field, what they did, or what they tried to do. The ball was still coming my way, and I was catching every one of them. I felt like one of the Green Bay Packers wide receivers in the Monday Night Football game against the Oakland Raiders in 2003 when Brett Favre played the day after his father died. They caught everything, no matter where he put the ball. That's what it was like.

The funny thing was, we actually lost the game by a touchdown (42–35), and I remember at the end of the game being more depressed than anything, feeling like I didn't catch enough balls or get enough yards. I had no clue what my stats were or what I had done, yet everyone was coming up to congratulate me as we were taking off our pads in the locker room. "Man, you had an unbelievable game. How many catches do you think you had?" I had no idea. I thought 8, 10 maybe, which was a good game for me or any wide receiver. But I didn't want to think about it. So finally I hit the showers, beating myself up, thinking, *What could I have done better? How could I have been a better teammate?* I was the last one out of the locker room, just wallowing in my own misery of this loss, and my coach came up to me and said, "I just wanted to say congratulations. You actually broke a world record for the most receiving yards in a single football game: 418 yards."

Four hundred eighteen yards on 17 catches, including four touchdowns, to be exact. Yup. I was in a flow state. The kind that champions live in and greatness results from. To be honest, I was a little in shock at that moment. I was happy to hear the news that I accomplished something that had never happened before in the history of collegiate football (or any level), but I also felt responsible for our loss and was preoccupied with figuring out how I could have done things better. It was a bittersweet moment, but one I'll always remember, not only because of the record but also because I felt like Superman in that flow state, and I knew I wanted to feel that way all of the time, on and off the field.

Fortunately, flow doesn't happen only for athletes, I learned from Steven. The consulting firm McKinsey did a 10-year study of top executives in flow. They found top executives in flow are five times more productive than when out of flow. That's 500 percent more productive. DARPA* did a study with snipers, inducing flow artificially using transcranial direct stimulation and teaching snipers target acquisition skills. The snipers learned the skills 230 percent faster. In a separate nonmilitary study, DARPA also induced flow artificially and cut the time it took to train a novice sniper up to an expert level by 50 percent.

So that's what flow is and what it does, but how do you get it? How do you achieve the kind of flow state that leads to 418-yard receiving games, 230 percent increases in learning, or 500 percent increases in productivity?

---

*DARPA is the acronym for the Defense Advanced Research Projects Agency. It is essentially the R&D division of the US Department of Defense. Lockheed Martin has its Skunk Works; the Defense Department has DARPA. Most famously, DARPA is responsible for the creation of the Internet.

"It's twofold," Steven explained. On the one hand, it happens "out of necessity. Meaning the level of performance has gone up so much that in the case of athletes, at least, if you are not in flow when you're performing, you're going to end up in the hospital or dead." I could definitely relate to that. With three guys covering me, if I go over the middle for a pass and I am not in flow, I am on the ground with the wind knocked out of me or with another case of cracked ribs.

The other reason it happens is because you've surrounded yourself with all the necessary flow triggers. True greats have basically created the most high-flow environment they possibly could. Everything in their lives is triggering flow. Psychologists talk about it as the source code of intrinsic motivation. Another way of putting it is that the five neurochemicals you get during flow—norepinephrine, dopamine, anandamide, serotonin, and endorphin—are the most addictive chemicals on earth. They make you quicker, faster, stronger, and more motivated. According to Steven, they do the same thing for your mental output that they do for your physical output.

Talk about an aha moment.

What Steven was saying is that flow is really all about mindset—how you perceive your situation and how you receive information. To be in flow, to sidestep adversity like it is nothing and vault yourself toward your vision, you need to have a champion's mindset.

There's a great quote by Bruce Lee in John Little's documentary *Bruce Lee: A Warrior's Journey* that explains flow, when he talks about becoming like water: "I said empty your mind. Be formless, shapeless. Like water. You put water into a cup, it becomes the cup. You put water into a bottle, it becomes the bottle. You put it in a teapot, it becomes the teapot. Now water can flow, or it can crash. Be water, my friend. Like that, you see." The champion's mindset, to me, is becoming like water.

Though I'd tasted it in my life and found confirmation of my feelings with Steven, it wasn't until I met my next teacher that I saw these ideas in the living, walking flesh. You'd be hard-pressed to find, pound for pound, someone with a more powerful champion's mindset in the world than Shawn Johnson. At 4 feet 9 inches and 90 pounds and just 16 years old, with hundreds of millions of people watching live and on television, she won an Olympic gold medal in the balance beam and three silver medals in the team, individual all-around, and floor exercise disciplines at the 2008 Beijing Olympic Games. Then, as if to prove her remarkable determination was no fluke, Shawn gave the country a seminar on how to translate the champion's mindset into other areas of life by winning season eight of *Dancing with the Stars* not long after she returned from Beijing.

From the moment I met Shawn, I knew she was the professor who could teach me how to cultivate the right mindset. I'm 6 foot 4 and she is a shade under 5 feet tall, so naturally we went and did a CrossFit workout together one day to see who could beat out the other in a battle of the fittest. This is my book, so I'm not going to say in print that she whipped my butt, but let's just say that she beat me (and the rest of the class) so badly that it was embarrassing. Not that it should be—this is a woman who has performed and won at the hardest level of sports, in front of billions of people, all before she was old enough to vote. Obviously she is physically gifted, but I think we would both agree that her triumph over me (oh, and the entire gymnastics world) had as much to do with the power of the right mindset as anything else.

"Gymnastics taught me everything—life lessons, responsibility, discipline, and respect," Shawn told me. Imagine the training and discipline she had to embrace at an age when the rest of us were playing video games and hoping for our first kiss. Imagine the focus and the clarity of purpose and the self-awareness it required. This is all part of the champion's mindset. For years, I tried to imagine it, but that part always seemed to be missing from my game. It was the part I could see in the greats and the athletes who practically lived in a flow state and to whom I'd always compared myself (all those Michaels). Yet I struggled with it, and continue to periodically, in life and business, even today.

The reason, I think, is because the champion's mindset is fundamentally about belief. If there's one thing I know about champions, it's that they all have a strong belief in something. Usually they believe they are the greatest thing in the world (like Muhammad Ali) or they believe they have been graced by the guiding hand of a higher power. All you have to do is listen to an athlete being interviewed after a big game to see this in action. The announcer says to them, "Congratulations on the win, you were amazing out there today! How did you do it?" And the player usually responds one of two ways: Either they say, "I want to give thanks to God for giving me these gifts and being by my side, as all the glory goes to him," or they grab the mike, look directly into the camera, and go on and on about how hard they trained and how no one can beat them and how they are the greatest competitor to ever walk this earth in their sport (think Floyd "Money" Mayweather Jr. in boxing). Regardless of the ego involved, it continues to be true that most of the *greatest* athletes have such a powerful belief in themselves and their desire to accomplish their goals that nothing can stand in their way. Not even failure. It's this 100 percent confidence that they will achieve what they want that is a difference maker on the path to greatness.

I have accomplished a lot of goals since my days in Ohio. I've achieved success, earned a lot of money, but for years it was driven by anger, ego, and resentment. That's what fueled my passion to be successful, and it resulted in a lot of ups and downs. There'd be big moments, and then there would be vast lows of hurt, pain, insecurity, frustration, and loneliness. It was because deep down I didn't believe in myself and wasn't sure if others believed in me, either. I had a clear vision, I had more than my fair share of adversity, but this lack of belief prevented me from creating the kind of champion's mindset that would make flow state more readily accessible and greatness inevitable.

Another amazing person in the School of Greatness, 27-year transformation coach and leadership expert Chris Lee, talked to me in depth about this very issue. "I believe that the most powerful work we can do with ourselves is develop the strategies to uncover, redesign, and reinvent our belief system," he said. "Because the only way you're going to have your business be successful, the only way you're going to have your relationships be successful, the only way you're going to have your life be successful, is by elevating who you are being. You bring that into what you're doing, and that affects what you have. Because if we keep repeating the same thing over and over, we're going to have the same result."

Chris highlighted an issue that many of us face in our pursuit of greatness. We keep doing the same thing, oftentimes blaming external factors for our dissatisfaction, instead of looking within at our beliefs—at our mindset. There is a flip side to a strong belief in self, however, and it is one of the most powerful lessons I learned from my conversations with Shawn Johnson. It was about humility. The champion cannot allow ego and confidence to devolve into self-delusion. Belief in yourself has to be a weapon in your arsenal whose power you respect and revere; it can't be used like impenetrable armor that creates a sense of invincibility or superiority. That distinction can be the difference between achieving your dreams and being blindsided by failure (or getting to the top, then falling quickly once you are there).

Shawn used her belief as a weapon on the balance beam in Beijing. "She takes command of the apparatus," the commentator said as she worked through her routine atop the 4-inch-wide beam 4 feet off the ground.

"You can see, she is in charge." She won gold because she was in charge of her belief in herself and therefore everything she encountered. This is not always the case for a lot of people.

"I've seen the type of belief in self that can be destructive," she told me. "Because if you are that person who says, 'I believe so strongly that I'm going to win, and I believe so strongly I've given my all,' you're not opening yourself up to be able to see and respond to what other people are doing in the actual competition. When that happens, it can become a cop-out when you run into adversity."

That is why an equally important part of the champion's mindset is the pursuit of perfection and excellence, independent of external results. This is very different from a drive to "win." Shawn, like many athletes, isn't obsessed with winning so much as she is with doing her absolute best: "I never focused on winning. Especially when I started out and I was in 30-something place out of 39 people. It was never about winning. I couldn't have cared less. I just always wanted to do better. I think the only thing that really made me want to work more and get on top of the podium was the feeling of pride you have when you're successful. It had nothing to do with a medal; that was just extra. It was knowing I had done my best and I was being acknowledged for it. It was about knowing at the end of the day that I worked as hard as I possibly could, and even if a score is worth the very last place, I couldn't be any happier."

Cultivating the mindset of a champion is not an overnight task. Vision, focus, discipline, belief in self, humility, and the pursuit of greatness are all the products of developed emotional intelligence—a fine art that requires a lot of practice. You never "arrive" at this point of knowing and having it all. Greatness is not something that is delivered to you or you are delivered to. It's something you have to work on daily. It takes years of dedication, discipline, and drive that persist in spite of any and all of the constant changes that inevitably occur with your health, business, relationships, and the world around you. If you commit to the process of developing this mindset for yourself, you will blow past every limit you thought was unbreakable.

Steven Kotler has shown us what flow is and why it happens. Shawn Johnson has given us the elements of the champion's mindset that are a prerequisite for flow and for greatness—foremost among them focus, dedication, and a belief in yourself that is tempered by humility. Chris Lee has implored us to reevaluate our personal belief system, the ideas and principles that undergird everything we are trying to do and become. Oftentimes it is those things that are impeding us on our journey toward greatness, not the external factors we love to blame when we run into adversity.

In fact, it wasn't until I had fully absorbed all these lessons that my podcast really started to take off. What most people don't know is that *The School of Greatness* podcast began as an extension of my online business; it did not start with a grand plan. Fortunately, it gathered a little bit of steam over the following couple of months, thanks to the network I'd built up on social media. Still, it wasn't really going anywhere that I could point to because I hadn't truly articulated a vision for it (I had for myself—I wanted to pick all these great teachers' brains—but that wasn't enough), so it was impossible to develop the kind of focus I needed. As a result, any adversity I faced felt like a mountain instead of a molehill. Beginning with my work with Chris Lee, I started to turn things around and really focus on doing shows that reflected my personal beliefs and helped as many people as possible. Being in a space that I was very comfortable with not only gave me confidence in myself but also tapped into the energy and desire I had previously felt only on the playing field. Then, before I knew it, the podcast started taking off and now here we are.

But you might be asking, "How do you do it? What is the process?" Like Shawn Johnson, thousands of champions have turned inward to develop these positive attributes. Through visualization, meditation, mindfulness, and a focus on cultivating emotional intelligence, they have learned to tap into a powerful belief that they can succeed; that their vision is clear, their obstacles are surmountable, and their path to greatness is a reality.

I've developed a number of great exercises to help you with each step in the process: visualization, meditation, mindfulness, and emotional intelligence. Do these and the building blocks of a champion's mindset will begin to stack themselves.

EXERCISE #1:
Visualization

The purpose of visualization is to see the results you want to create, before they happen. This is something I did in sports every season (and continue to do in life on a regular basis).

In football, I wanted to be a great wide receiver, and I loved watching Jerry Rice. I'd watch his highlight reel over and over and visualize myself doing the exact thing he was doing.

The night before games, I would see myself on the field. I'd review every play in my head and imagine how I would run the routes perfectly, catch the ball perfectly, and run into the end zone every time.

A few hours before the game, I'd physically walk the field and see myself in position doing what I visualized and experience the feeling of making the big plays and winning the game. This process got me ready for any-thing and everything that might come my way and put me into position to create with my body what I had already performed in my mind so many times.

I do this every week for my personal life and busi-ness as well. This book is a perfect example. For years before writing this book, I would visualize myself walk-ing into bookstores and seeing my book front and cen-ter on the big front tables right inside the doors. I would see myself at book signings, speaking in front of thousands of people and spreading these key lessons of greatness to leave a bigger impact on the world. I did this for years before I ever sat down to write one word of this book.

I also practice visualization before I call people on the phone, whether it's personal or for business. I envision what I want to create from the exchange—perhaps a particular result for a business deal, a feeling or experience I want the other person to have at the end, or how I want a controversial situation to resolve. I visualize the whole process.

Each night, I visualize what I want to accomplish the following day. Before giving speeches onstage, doing online webinars, and so on, I visualize what impact I want to have. You could do this before going on a date with someone, preparing a meal you want to create, or anything else you want to do in your life. Visualization is a powerful process. It puts your mind in a place to set you up for success.

Your Visualization Process

Create a clear space with no distraction. I prefer it to be in nature, which for you might mean at your favorite park or on the beach. Or you can do this in bed before you go sleep and right when you wake up. I've also been known to do visualization in the shower with the water rushing down and imagine myself in a waterfall.

Allow yourself to relax and be calm. Breathe relaxing breaths. Now visualize whatever you want to see as complete. Nothing negative, only positive outcomes.

If your vision is to be a father, visualize yourself holding your newborn baby, what that looks and feels like.

If it's to have a relationship with your soul mate, visualize yourself embracing that person, both of you smiling, and being whole and complete in that moment.

If it's to have a successful business, see yourself making the deals, walking into your office, helping your customers.

In each process, really dive into what it feels like: What does it smell like and taste like? What color is it? What sounds are you hearing?

The key to visualization is to see whatever it is you are envisioning as complete. Then ask yourself how you feel in that moment. What do all of your senses feel?

You can play music in the background if that helps you relax, or the process can just be silent.

I recommend you do this for at least 5 minutes every day, visualizing the outcome you have set out (no vision is too small or too big for this process). I also recommend doing this before attacking any big opportunity in front of you. Take a moment to visualize what you want to create before you enter that moment.

EXERCISE #2:
Meditation—The 15-Second Centering Breath

If the point of visualization is filling the mind with an image of where we intend to end up, meditation is about clearing the mind of everything else—all the extraneous distractions, obsessions, doubts, and trifling matters that keep us from focusing. It is something we need to do every morning when we wake up and every night before we go to bed (at least I find my days more powerful and intentional when I do it morning and night). You live the day of a champion by beginning as one and ending as one.

The key to meditation is to focus on your breathing and be aware of your breath. You want to unplug and simply breathe. Breathe in joy; breathe out stress. In joy, out stress. Allow yourself to feel connected to the world, to the universe, and, most important, to yourself. Anything that gets you disconnected from business, career, stress, and the rat race is great for you.

My favorite breathing exercise is something I've taken from another of the greats I've had the privilege of learning from, sports psychologist Jim Afremow, PhD. In his book *The Champion's Mind: How Great Athletes Think, Train, and Thrive,* Jim talks a lot about the importance of breathing to perform like a champion.

"Under perceived pressure, we tend to hold our breath, and then we not only don't have the oxygen to our system that we need but also our muscle tension increases," Jim told me when we talked. "Muscle tension is the number one enemy in sports. If you're a swimmer, you're going to go slower. If you're a pole vaulter, you're not going to jump as high. Deep breathing helps to clear our mind of stress and expectations, and it relaxes our body. I think it's important to have either a meditation practice or, at the very least, to take a deep breath throughout the course of your day and notice whether you're breathing easily and deeply."

15-Second Centering Breath Process

1. Breathe in through the nose if you can for a count of one, two, three, four, and five, expanding the belly.
2. Then hold it for a count of one and two.
3. Then breathe out through the mouth for a count of one, two, three, four, five, six, seven, and eight, releasing the air in the belly.

Be prepared, this is a big breath. It's not something you're doing all day. This is just to reboot your breathing. But the key is the exhale. It's a little bit longer than the inhale, and that's where you get the relaxation response.

"When we think about taking a deep breath, most of us just think about the inhale—taking that big inhalation. That's actually the stressful part," Jim made me understand. "Getting all that air out, that's the relaxation part and really helps you to feel your best."

You will be surprised how you feel if you do this before bed or before an important meeting or event. When we focus on our breathing instead of the things that stress us out or that we are afraid of, we don't allow the stress or fears to creep in. Go ahead and try this exercise right now and repeat it for four cycles (1 minute in total). Let me know how you are feeling at the end of it by sending me an e-mail at lewis@schoolofgreatness.com. Anytime you are feeling overwhelmed or stressed, come back to this breathing process for 60 seconds. It will give you the clarity you need to take your next step, wherever you are.

If you want an another free guided meditation from

me to get you in the right frame of mind for your day, then check out schoolofgreatness.com/resources for additional resources.

EXERCISE #3:
Mindfulness

If you don't already have one, I want you to start a gratitude journal. I want you to write down your thoughts and express gratitude. Each night in your gratitude journal, be mindful of what's really working for you and what isn't working. Take the time to jot down everything you are proud of and excited about and to acknowledge yourself for these amazing things you've done. Then write down what you are committed to doing to move those things you are proud of forward.

For example:

Today I closed the biggest deal of my life. I'm proud of myself, and it's a dream come true.

Tomorrow I will continue to bring my [product/service/ message] to the world to help more people.

Next write down all the things that you reacted to or that weren't effective and failed to get you the results you wanted. Look at what was missing from you in those moments (patience, love, courage, confidence, etc.). What are you committed to creating and who are you going to be moving forward in those kinds of moments?

For example:

Today I didn't close the sale.

What was missing was that I didn't have the confidence in my product and I was too pushy about the result of the sale instead of showing my care for the potential customer.

I wasn't committed to being in a relationship with that customer. I will be connected the next time to understand their needs and wants instead of focusing on the result I want.

We think about these things in our heads constantly, but rarely do we ever speak them out loud or put them down on paper. Verbalizing and writing down these thoughts allow you to be aware and mindful of what you are creating on a daily basis and see what's working and what's not working in your life. Over time, you will create a record of what has worked and what has failed; what you have done to make things better and what you have (or haven't) done that has made things worse. You will spot patterns that will blow your mind. So even if you don't see results right away with this mindfulness exercise, recognize that you are doing the work to make results happen in the near future, when you will be ready to see and accept them.

EXERCISE #4:
Emotional Intelligence—Be Present and Know Thyself

The first key to greatness is having a vision for your future, but the best way to supercharge that vision is to be emotionally present so that you can give your full attention to the moment.

I love to salsa dance, and not just because it involves beautiful women who know how to move. I love it because it's something that forces me to be totally present and in the moment. If you are worried about how you look, whether you are doing something wrong, not being good enough, or if you're thinking about literally anything else other than that moment in that place, then your partner will be able to tell (and so will everyone watching you). To be good at salsa requires that you be present, that you be connected to what you are expressing in the moment and fully connected to your partner so you can lead them (or be led) to the next step or move during the song.

In that way, life is a lot like salsa dancing. You must be present, connected, and focused on making someone else smile if you want to create something meaningful each day. It's not always easy. Sometimes it can be scary to focus and put yourself out there like this, but it's extremely powerful and can create magical results!

You must learn to be confident with who you are and believe in yourself. All champions, even if they are scared, fall back on their belief in themselves and the work they've put in to get them where they want to be.

Emotional intelligence involves being able to shift in the moment and be aware of your emotions so they don't control you or hold you back; rather, you use them to move you forward. The more you develop emotional intelligence, the better able you will be to handle emotional situations in all areas of your life—with yourself, family, friends, and intimate relationships and in your career.

In short, emotional intelligence is the ability to understand and regulate your emotions and the emotions of others and be able to use that power to guide your thinking and behavior.

One of the key aspects of emotional intelligence is knowing yourself: your strengths and your weaknesses. Feedback is the vehicle you can use to achieve that. Feedback is information about how you are showing up to others and in the world. With that information, you develop greater, more highly tuned awareness of your strengths and weaknesses.

Step 1

List your five strengths and five weaknesses.

Some examples of strengths

Powerful	Loving
Passionate	Committed
Disciplined	

Some examples of weaknesses

Controlling	Fearful
Lack of discipline	Judgmental
Overanalytical	

Step 2

Contact three people who will be brutally honest with you and give you feedback about what they believe are your top five strengths and five weaknesses. When you have this information completed, put those lists side by side and identify what they have in common. This will let you know what you need to reinforce in your life (your strengths) and what you need to work on moving forward (your weaknesses). Also, it will let you know how calibrated your opinion of yourself is. Do you view yourself more or less the same as others view you, or are you completely delusional in either the positive or negative direction?

If you can be brutally honest with yourself, and you can find good people who will be brutally honest with you as well, this exercise is sure to give you a lot to reflect on.

Bonus exercise: Call someone from your past with whom you once had a strong bond but are now no longer in contact (a former partner in an intimate relationship, a friend from your past, or even a family member you lost touch with). Ask them as well to share what they consider your strengths and weaknesses with you. Their responses may surprise you, and I dare you to do it to see what lesson you gain from that conversation.

COACHING TIP

You have always been great, because you are unique, and *you* will never happen again in the history of the universe. Most people don't believe in themselves or their abilities because they don't understand how insanely special they are. In fact, we all are special, and only we have the ability to believe in ourselves. Others can be there for us and cheer us on from the sidelines, but even with all the support in the world, some of us still sabotage ourselves. In the game of life, we hold the controls. We are the players who make the plays. Our inner voice—our belief in ourselves—is what determines our mindset. And our way of thinking sets us up for failure or success.

You have a choice. You can think average and get average results or think like a champion and reap remarkable rewards. Which one do you want? It actually takes only a little more effort to believe in yourself than it does to put yourself down. Make the decision to spend that energy on improving your mindset and doing things that give you confidence rather than bring you down. Always come back to understanding how unique and powerful your gifts are in this world. You are the one who needs to understand this first before anyone else can. Now go make it happen!

GET GROUNDED

If I could attribute one thing to my success, it would be the topic of this next chapter: hustle. It started all the way back in seventh grade with the middle school basketball team. All I wanted was to make that team, to be part of something, and to contribute in a positive way. I wanted to be accepted and valued. I think we all want to feel worthy in the eyes of others, like we matter and that what we do is meaningful. This basketball team was my first opportunity to experience that in an organized fashion. Neither my body nor my skills had developed by that point, but more than anything, I didn't want to get cut (getting picked last was a big fear of mine, as it had happened before), so I ran around like a madman, dove everywhere on the court, and showed that I had all the passion and hustle in the world (a dream quality to any smart coach). I was willing to sacrifice my body unlike any other kid out there. While others didn't want to look stupid or were afraid to get hurt, I had a different vision. My efforts paid off. Not only did I make the team but I worked my way into a starting spot on my first-ever team sport.

It takes more than just hustle to be great, but you can't be great without that burning desire to do what others are unwilling to do. Sacrifice, in some form, will be a necessary part of the process, and whoever is more willing to sacrifice for the hustle will always succeed in the long run. Prepare yourself, as it's time to embrace the underdog within and step into your greatness.

CHAPTER 4

DEVELOP HUSTLE

No one is going to hand me success. I must go out and get it myself. That's why I'm here. To dominate. To conquer. Both the world and myself.

—Unknown

In 1991, a college sophomore studying music in the American Midwest made the mistake of selling some drugs to the wrong person. Until then, he hadn't done much more than smoke pot and sell some of it to his friends. Petty vandalism at his high school was as high stakes as his criminal career had been. Then, as these things tend to go when you're just 18 years old, he tried to push the envelope and test his boundaries. He started experimenting with hard drugs like LSD. But he was naive, and the brashness of youth got the best of him. He sold some of that LSD outside his circle—to an undercover policeman. And as if his luck couldn't get worse, like a scene out of a TV movie of the week, the judge, under pressure to make an example out of this young man, sentenced him to 6 to 25 years in prison.

It's a faceless, timeless story that transcends race, class, and region. A young kid makes a mistake that forever changes their lives and their family's lives as well. We are all too familiar with how stories like this usually end: The kid spends their most impressionable years behind bars and comes out worse than when they went in. Life on the outside is too difficult to contend with; habits learned on the inside are too difficult to shed. They reoffend; their crimes escalate. The cycle continues.

This story, however, is a little different. Because this young man didn't go back to jail. In fact, after being released in less than 5 years on good behavior, he went on to become one of the best jazz violinists in the world. He left prison with a fire lit underneath him—to practice, to repent, to humble himself, to hustle, and to do whatever it took to make something of his life. No task was too small, no gig was too tiny, no potential fan was too disinterested for him not to give it everything he had. And he did.

The story is a little different for another reason, too. That young man's name is Christian Howes. He is my older brother.

Chris's journey taught me one of the most important lessons I ever learned about greatness: *how to hustle.* No, not that kind of hustling—selling drugs on the streets. The good kind. The kind that makes you sweat and makes other people nod their heads and marvel at your work ethic. Of course, like most lessons in hustle, it did not start as all silver lining and no black cloud. It was born where necessity met adversity.

Chris went to jail when I was just 8 years old. It was a shock to all of us. I remember sitting in the car outside the courthouse, asking my mom what was happening and her just crying. I remember asking her why it was happening, but my parents wouldn't tell me, not until after he got sentenced. When the news spread and the neighborhood found out—which doesn't take long in a small suburban Ohio town—none of the mothers would let their kids play at my house. I was in second grade, and despite having my parents and my sister still there, I felt alone and helpless.

In retrospect, Chris's situation should not have been a surprise. Despite the musical genius that certified him a child prodigy, he'd been a troubled youth. "I hadn't been motivated," he said. "I didn't have goals. I was just coasting. It was jive." Still, none of what happened to him made any sense to me. It didn't feel real. I thought that only people who killed other people went to jail. Chris hadn't done anything like that. Plus, he didn't look like what I thought prisoners would look like when I was a little kid. He didn't have a smashed nose like a Bugs Bunny gangster. He didn't have a wild beard and crazy tattoos across his back like an outlaw biker. He was just Chris, my big brother, whom I looked up to. He was still a great guy, he just made some dumb decisions. And what's more, when I saw him in person, behind bars, he was still a hero to me.

That didn't alter the fact that this was a stunning and traumatic part of both of our lives. Prison isn't something a family usually comes back from intact. Chris would always be a convicted felon. I would always be the kid from the broken home with the older brother who went away. We'd always be "that family" down the street. If Chris had fallen into the trap that so many others do, he could have absorbed the trauma and spent his years in prison getting angrier and more resentful of the world around him. He could have blamed the cops, the system, or our parents. He could have just given up. The list of places outside of yourself to lay blame is virtually endless if you look hard enough. Instead, he made a clear choice: to overcome the stigma and the setback of his incarceration by resurrecting his life.

He rededicated himself to his musical gift. "When I got in there," he told me later, "I had a purpose. I knew I wanted to be a better person. I wanted to be a man and do something with my life." Music was going to be that something. He persevered against the monotony and put himself in the right mindset, scheduling time with the prison band every week. The only white guy in a group that played gospel, rap, R&B, and soul (Chris grew up playing classical music), he embraced the challenge and earned what would be considered a kind of prison master's degree in music appreciation and the resilience of the human soul. He developed an unrivaled set of skills— both mental and physical—that would set him apart in the world of jazz and spark his unlikely ascent.

To survive in prison, you have to overcome your own mind and protect yourself from everyone around you who is trying to take what's yours (your stuff, your dignity, your sanity, your freedom). You have to be strong, not just physically but also mentally—you can't give in to despair and lethargy. To have a chance on the outside once you're released, the challenge is the opposite—to break through the walls of people who don't want to give you anything you need (respect, opportunities, the benefit of the doubt). When Chris got out, he had to overcome the reality of being a convict and the opinions, biases, and fears of people he encountered as he tried to build his career. He did this with a freakish combination of passion and hustle—both in prison and out.

SHAMELESS URGENCY

There's a great quote from Publilius Syrus, a former slave in Roman times, who became famous for his wisdom. "Do not despise the bottom rungs in the ascent to greatness," he said. He was basically saying, you are not too cool for school. That was Chris. When he first got out, he would perform anywhere. He started by playing for free at local restaurants just to put himself out there and build a name for himself. Then he'd do hotel lounges, late-night dive bars, tiny jazz clubs with five people in the audience. He would play whatever time slot they'd give him for however long they needed him to play. He would put 100 percent of his blood, sweat, tears, and soul into each performance to blow the doors off the place. His passion ended up blowing the doors off places that didn't even have doors.

"When I got out, I was not afraid to promote myself," Chris said. "Most people can't get over that fear. In the arts world, you're supposed to stay cool, man. Just do your music, and it will come to you. I said, 'Fuck that. I know what I want to do. I want to be a great jazz violinist, to go onstage with great musicians,' and so I pursued it zealously."

After his final number in every set, Chris would get back up on the mike and promote the hell out of himself. He would thank them all for listening to his music, then grab his stack of CDs and go up to each person at each table in the club trying to sell copies. He was not afraid to put himself out there. Once when I asked why he sold his work so hard, never taking no for an answer (even when the person was saying, "Not a chance!"), he told me: "There's no shame in my game." And he was right. He was shameless but genuinely putting himself out there, and it worked—people bought his music.

Chris was tapping into something that I think 18-time Olympic gold medalist Michael Phelps described best when he talked about his swim training with Piers Morgan on CNN: "If you want to be the best, you have to do things that other people aren't willing to do." I watched with amazement as Chris pulled out all the stops, persuading customers to invest in his recordings and his future. It was about survival for him, about providing for his young family by doing work that he was fortunate enough to be exception- ally passionate about. He was willing to do whatever it took: "You have to chase opportunity whether you are an entrepreneur or an artist—especially for me, because I had to make up for so much lost time."

The irony is, we're all making up for lost time. That is the essence of hustle in the pursuit of greatness— doing whatever it takes and chasing opportunity with great urgency, like your life depends on it. Because it does. Greatness is really the survival of your vision across an extended timeline, based on your willingness to do whatever it takes in the face of adversity and to adopt the mindset to seize opportunity wherever it lives. After all, greatness is not something that comes to you; you go to it, and it's always moving. You slow down, and it moves farther away. You stop, and it disappears over the horizon.

Since those days in tiny jazz clubs and no-name festi- vals, Chris has toured the world, been on the cover of magazines, played Lincoln Center and Carnegie Hall, and collaborated with greats like Les Paul, Greg Osby, D. D. Jackson, and Spyro Gyra. His list of collaborators and clients is literally as long as my arm. He was a professor at the prestigious Berklee College of Music and set up a highly successful jazz violin camp where professional vio- linists from all over the world come to learn from him. All of that should have surprised me, but it never did, because he understood the importance of hustle in the pursuit of greatness.

GET UP AND DUST YOURSELF OFF

I was not a happy kid during Chris's years in prison. I was never the smartest kid in class. In fact, I was the opposite. I was ugly and awkward (at least until high school). I was lonely. I didn't have friends. I was picked last for everything. I remember telling my teacher a number of times, "I wish I was dead." I got called into the principal's office once in elementary school because I'd been getting into trouble. I said it to him, too, right there in his office: "I don't know what the point is. I probably shouldn't be alive." I didn't feel like I was ever going to matter.

I was 12 years old and smack in the middle of the worst period for most young guys—middle school—when Chris was finally released. It was the best day of my life. He called us on my dad's car phone in a 1988 Oldsmobile. "Order us a couple large pizzas, bro!" he said. "I am coming home!" When he walked in the house, he gave me this huge hug, and it was everything I needed. I had been so filled with all sorts of frustration and painful, confusing feelings. I finally had someone around whom I looked up to, whom I admired, who had also gone through pain and turmoil.

But it wasn't commiserating over our bad luck that was so important—it was his response to the negative circumstances and his ability to lift me out of the hole I'd sunk into. He didn't lie down and cry, like I so often wanted to (and did) as a little kid. He got up and hustled his ass off. He said to me at one point, "I can't go down any farther. I've already been to the bottom. I've embarrassed myself and my family and let everyone down. There's nothing I'm afraid of now, especially looking bad." In those early days, when he was playing at restaurants for free, it's not like he was calling ahead to schedule with a booking agent. He would just show up. He would go door to door until someone said yes. He created something from nothing. He had to. His back was against the wall. He was committed to his vision of being the best jazz violinist he could possibly be, and no amount of adversity was going to stand between him and his ability to make a full-time living at his passion.

Watching him do that—sitting there by his side as he defined his dream, knocked down every obstacle in his path, and then doggedly chased down greatness—was utterly transformational for me, almost more so today, now that I understand how special it was. Chris's passion for music and the hustle he displayed reaching fans and making new ones are what inspired me to get off my sister's couch in Columbus all those years later. For more than a year, I slept on that couch, 6 months of that time in a full-arm cast after a career-ending wrist injury that led to a painful surgery during my first season playing professional football. With no money to pay off my credit card debt and student loans and no college degree, I was left wondering if I had any hope of regrouping and figuring out why I was put on this earth, let alone of defining and achieving the greatness within me. My whole existence had been built on a foundation of becoming a highly successful athlete, and even though I had achieved those early All-American dreams, I was now languishing in self-pity because I'd washed out of professional sports. My vision was dashed; I was depressed and lost.

What Chris's hustle after prison made me realize was that I wasn't depressed because my vision was dead. I was depressed because I hadn't done the work to pick myself up, dust myself off, and figure out what was next. The hustle wasn't over; it was just different and shifted in a new direction.

Soon after that epiphany, I reached out to a number of people for guidance—my father's friends, coaches, my brother (obviously, why not go right to the source?), even the headmaster of my university, a man named Stuart Jenkins. I admired his wisdom and his moral courage. Stuart was hired to make changes and improve the university, and his decisions to cut underperforming members of the faculty were not popular. But his efforts vastly improved the academic standards of the school, and he proved to be an effective leader. He would often say to me, "Is this serving you?" rather than telling me what was right or wrong.

During that period of uncertainty, Stuart suggested I check out LinkedIn.com, the social media Web site, which back then was just starting to get serious traction among business professionals. I saw all sorts of potential to connect with high-profile business owners and other professionals there, and I began connecting with people like a madman. I reached out specifically to people who worked in the sports business because I had just come from my own experiences playing professional football, and I figured that would be a strong connection point to people I'd barely heard of in some cases and, in each case, never met. Lucky for me, I was right and got a high rate of acceptance.

In the first year, I made 10,000 connections! It was crazy but incredibly exciting. I became what Malcolm Gladwell called in his best-selling book *The Tipping Point* a "connector." It didn't happen overnight—I built these relationships one by one with passion and energy. I would meet people in person, talk to them on the phone, introduce them to others seeking their skills.

It was around this time, with my professional sports career over and my cast off, that I started making a little bit of money by hosting "LinkedIn networking events" around the country. Over the following year, I hosted 20 events in major cities, where 300 to 500 people would attend. They were amazed at how this 24-year-old former pro athlete kid with no degree was able to get so many people to show up at these professional networking events. What they didn't know was that I was literally e-mailing my LinkedIn connections one by one to ask them to come to my events or join one of the groups I'd created to bring everyone together. I adopted the approach Chris took right after he got out of prison—there was nothing I wouldn't do. I'd already reached my bottom, so the only direction was up. E-mailing everyone individually wasn't sustainable at the rate I was growing, obviously, but it kick-started everything I'm doing now and taught me valuable lessons about hustle—first and foremost that you have to be willing to do the work that others are unwilling to do if you want to succeed when starting from a position of disadvantage.

I eventually built this presence on LinkedIn into an incredibly lucrative online business. I had no background in building a business, but I pulled myself up by the boot-straps, went with my gut, took advice from mentors, and worked my ass off. There were no days off, no coffee breaks. I applied Chris's hustle strategies to the launch of the business, adjusting his tested methods to the practical realities of building a different kind of business from the ground up. The end result: The money started flowing in, when only a couple years earlier, I had no clear idea how I would ever make any money.

My inner frustrations and early fears are what drove me to hustle. I didn't want to be a failure. I didn't want to remain unseen. I was going to work my butt off and go through as much pain as I needed to bear. This, in part, is what powers me through a bad meeting or a failure even today. Even more so today, I'm driven by my vision to inspire others to reach their greatness, and it's what keeps my hustle so strong even in my darkest, most difficult days.

THE CURSE OF DAVID: WORKING HARDER *AND* SMARTER

The best hustlers are all underdogs. Even if they're not, they view themselves that way. They have a chip on their shoulder, or they chase something bigger than they are, because it's harder to hustle—to give it your all—when you're in the lead. You have nothing to judge yourself against or chase down besides the finish line. You're

always more productive when you're the underdog—
when you're David, not Goliath.

Just ask Tom Brady. Brady is arguably the best quarterback in the NFL. He is a no-doubt Hall of Famer; he
has four Super Bowl rings, three Super Bowl MVPs, two
kids, and one beautiful supermodel wife. Yet he plays
with the fiery, junkyard-dog intensity of a Davidian
underdog every game because he's got a Goliath-size
chip on his shoulder. Not only did he come to the University of Michigan and land *seventh* on the depth chart (the
lowest-ranked quarterback on the team), but once he
battled his way into the starting job as a junior, he had to
fight off another quarterback, Drew Henson, whom the
coach platooned him with the entire first half of his senior
season. Then, in the 2000 NFL Draft, despite setting
records at Michigan and earning Big Ten all-conference
honors, he wasn't drafted until the 199th overall selec-
tion in the sixth round—a compensatory pick, no less—
by the New England Patriots. Actually, to say that the
chip on Tom Brady's shoulder is Goliath-size is an understatement. It is the size of the 198 guys picked before
him and the 29 teams who had four or five chances to
draft him but chose not to. He works harder than everyone to show all those people what's what. He is a true
David in that sense.

My middle name is David, so I've always naturally
gravitated to that biblical story and the position of the
underdog. In fact, I've felt like an underdog at nearly
every point in my life—ever since childhood, when I was
picked last for sports teams or, worse, not at all and

forced to play by myself alone after school because no one wanted to be my friend. It is part of what has driven me to outtrain anyone and be better than everyone, because I'm not always going to be the biggest, strongest, or smartest. And when that happens, I still have to figure out a way to win no matter the circumstances, whether that means having the most energy, passion, or desire. If I have to, I'll be like a banshee out there. I'm always willing to put in the time and energy because I remember what it was like in elementary school to be picked last for every- thing and feel like life wasn't worth living.

Hustle isn't about working smarter instead of harder. It's about doing both. Hustlers are better *and* badder. They take their place in this world, they don't wait or hope or pray for it to come or for someone to hand it to them. And it's that Davidian underdog chip on their shoulder that often gives them the extra push when greatness seems at its most fragile.

In this way, Chris is literally and figuratively my brother-in-arms. But my sister-in-arms is Marie Forleo. Marie is an author, a TV host, and a business coach. She calls herself a "multipassionate entrepreneur," which is another way of saying she's a junkyard dog who attacks everything she does with passion and hustles her butt off, even the stuff she doesn't love to do or she knows isn't going to be what she does for the rest of her life. And she does it for a reason.

"So many opportunities have come from me training myself to show up like a champ wherever I was," she told me. "I got my first job on the floor of a Wall Street trading firm because I did such a good job on this one person's cappuccino at the place I bartended during college. He was like, 'You care so much about what you're doing, what do you want to do after you graduate?' I told him I was a finance major but I couldn't see myself in corporate finance or behind a desk. He said, 'My brother works on the floor; give me your résumé.'"

Part of me couldn't believe that was all it took to get a job on Wall Street, but the other part of me knew from watching my brother, Chris, that you can never underestimate the power of hustle. It can unlock a ridiculous amount of opportunity and potential. Even after Marie left her Wall Street job, she continued to approach her life with the same energy.

"I taught hip-hop at Crunch [a fitness center], and I didn't think I was going to teach hip-hop forever, but I wanted to be the best hip-hop instructor I possibly could be. And because I taught a good class that was always filled, the higher-ups chose me to audition for a new Nike program."

The result? Marie became one of the first four Nike "elite trainers"—a group who got to travel all over the world. She didn't wait around hoping someone would recognize her talent. She shoved it right in their faces and made it impossible for them not to see.

"The opportunities that can come when you do that, you can't even predict," she told me. "When you show up with that attitude of 'I'm going to master this, I'm going to bring my A game,' you feel better. You have more energy, and the results are going to be better."

Once Chris got out of prison, he wasn't waiting for anyone, either. He didn't expect anyone to feel sorry for him or give him the opportunities he always dreamed of—nor could he in his industry—so he went out and hustled to make his vision a reality. Les Paul, the famous guitarist, once remarked, "It used to be you could hardly find a good jazz violinist, but nowadays there are four or five really good players." I think that competition from all these players who hadn't lost 4 years on the inside was what drove my brother to be the best. It's what made him hustle—to try to carve out a space for himself. And if Les Paul is any judge, Chris's work has paid off, because even though there are now four or five really good players, he also said, "There is nobody better than Christian Howes." If there was such a thing as a mike drop in jazz violin, this would be it.

FALL IN LOVE WITH THE ART AND PAIN OF THE HUSTLE!

A Japanese proverb says, "Vision without action is a dream. Action without vision is a nightmare." You need both vision and action to achieve great things. Vision guides you; action propels you. But most people settle for the dream, because it is free and easy. It doesn't require action or hustle, which comes at a heavy price sometimes. Most aren't willing to pay that price. This is yet another place where true greats distinguish themselves. Muhammad Ali once said, "I hated every minute of training, but I said, 'Don't quit. Suffer now, and live the rest of your life as a champion.'" Training? Suffering? That is the hustle.

Earlier I joked that if you don't have a vision that gets

you out of bed in the morning, go back to sleep until you find one that does. I mean that—it's absolutely critical. At the same time, truer words have never been spoken than by Jonathan Swift when he said, "I never knew a man come to greatness or eminence who lay abed late in the morning." Your vision is what makes you want to get out of bed. Ultimately though, you have to do it. And you have to do it over and over and over again with every ounce of energy that you have, even on those days when you hate the suffering the most—especially on those days, in fact.

Do you think during the high school football preseason I enjoyed doing three-a-days in the heat of the summer while other kids were off at the pool flirting with girls? Hell no! It sucked like no other. But I'm a two-sport All-American, I became a pro athlete, and, as a result, I play for my country with USA Team Handball, the men's national handball team. Those guys who were taking it easy at the pool when I was killing myself . . . what are they doing now and what do they have to show for that? I have no idea, and neither does anyone else. And that's the point.

If there is someone who has a right to hate the hustle more than anyone, it's Kyle Maynard. Born with profound physical limitations, every day that he perseveres against the adversity laid before him should be a victory. But not for Kyle. His vision for greatness required not only that he stand up to those who stood in his way but that he put in the work to prove them all wrong and succeed in spite of them. The authorities who didn't want him to fight mixed martial arts and the parents who objected to him as a high school wrestler were no match for someone who was zero percent talk and 100 percent walk. He pushed through day after day and was so earnest in his efforts that he got his shot in both arenas. ESPN didn't just magically hear about Kyle's climb up Mount Kilimanjaro—he didn't wait for good things to come to him. He went out and hustled, promoting it to whoever would listen. He brought attention to his cause with unrivaled passion because he believed in it and wanted his message to get out.

Shawn Johnson talked to me about hustle and passion, too, particularly with respect to talent. So many people think they can skate by on talent to reach their goals and accomplish their dreams. She is firmly in the camp of Team Hustle. Why? "You can be the biggest or the most talented person in the world, but if you don't love what you do, then it's not going to show and it's not going to work. And you don't necessarily have to have the greatest talent, but if you work for it and you love it, then you'll have better results." She is absolutely right.

If Shawn is on Team Hustle, then its captain has to be Angel Martinez. He is pure hustle. He was a great runner not because he was naturally talented but because he was willing to work harder than everyone else. He had grit. It began when he was a grade school kid in the Bronx picking up hundreds of two-cent glass bottles to buy a new seven-dollar pair of Cons. It continued to work for him on the cross-country team in high school as much as it did years later when he was going from meeting to meeting trying to turn Reebok into a global footwear brand.

The difference, I have discovered thanks to so many of these great mentors, between those who achieve greatness and those who cannot get beyond mediocrity is very closely tied to how hard they hustled. My brother showed me the power of hustling to change even the most challenging of circumstances. Chris wasted his natural talent for years, getting distracted by drugs, trying to impress too many losers at school. He went to prison and nearly lost everything. But his passion for music and becoming a better man to make something of his life gave him the direction and the energy that propelled from a prison cell to the practice room every day for 20 years.

I know that's easier said than done. So far, I've only given you the Nike approach to hustle—Just Do It. But hustle is somewhat of a difficult discipline for people to wrap their heads around (most hard things are). It's not something you can learn. It's something you just have to put into action.

The question is, what holds people—what holds you—back from developing it? It's usually not a lack of energy. Everyone is capable of hustling. But we always seem to leave something in the tank; we go at half speed. We don't have that sense of shameless urgency. We won't get up and dust ourselves off. We won't embrace the harder, smarter work of David to the Goliath of our competitors or our haters. We won't just grin and bear it and do the work. Why? In a word: *fear.*

Fear of looking bad: We don't want people to see us sweat or struggle, and we are afraid of what people think about us.

Fear of failure: We must remind ourselves that we will fail 100 percent of the time we don't try.

Fear of success: At times we fear our success greater than our failures, because some of us don't want to be put in the spotlight or be required to lead when we succeed.

So how do we step away from these fears in our heads and step into action? Part of the process is understanding, as the 18th-century English writer Samuel Johnson did, that "true greatness consists in being great in little things." Baby steps, essentially. Turning small things into great advantages through hard work by flexing the hustle muscle. It's a skill all the professors in the School of Greatness have mastered at some point along their paths. They understand that you don't just go from starting quarterback of your high school team at 16 years old straight to the Super Bowl, because even if it were allowed, they know you aren't ready for it at that age. You must go through the necessary progression to gain experience, wisdom, and years in college before you are allowed to compete at the NFL level. Then only a small percentage of the best players in college football make it to the NFL. Then only one team a year can win the Super Bowl. It takes years and years of doing the right things to set yourself up for the chance to achieve greatness for something at that level.

All that being said, it's never too late to start. It's never too late to hustle in pursuit of your vision. In 2011, the Jazz Journalists Association nominated my brother, former inmate #260873, for Violinist of the Year. In 2012, he was selected for the prestigious Residency Partner Program from Chamber Music America for his educational outreach work with school music programs. In 2014, the US Embassy in Kiev invited him to tour Ukraine and serve as a cultural ambassador. It wasn't raw talent that got him there; it was his relentless drive to make up for the lost time he'd frittered away as a young man. And that is the lesson that has made all the difference in my life. If I could give one piece of advice to a budding entrepreneur, it would be that—just one word: *hustle.*

EXERCISE #1:
What-If Scenarios

When my students notice their minds falling to any of these fears that hold them back, I give them an exercise to calm their thoughts and get them back to a grounded place of principles and vision that will lead them into action.

With pen and paper or a journal, find a comfortable and quiet place where you won't be interrupted.

Think about your vision and your goals. Imagine the hustle required to make them a reality. Now write down all of the things you are afraid of if you throw yourself headlong into the hustle. Allow yourself to experience the feeling of fear while you write these things down.

What if I look stupid?

What if I mess up?

What if I lose my investment?

What if I go broke?

What if I ruin the relationship?

What if I get fired?

With each what-if, write out all the things that could go wrong, including the worst-case scenario. *What if I get fired* . . .

. . . and my wife leaves me?
. . . and we lose the house?
. . . and we have to live in the car?
. . . and my friends stop talking to me?
. . . and I can't find another job?

Let it all out onto the paper. Experience the fear with each possible outcome. Now redirect each what-if into a potential positive outcome. *What if I get fired* . . .

. . . and it turns into a better job in a few months?
. . . and I can use the severance to take a well-needed family vacation?
. . . and I can spend a month reconnecting with my kids?

Turn every what-if into a positive redirect of "what could" be created instead. Again, your vision won't come to life without your assuming some risk or taking some action. Mistakes will happen no matter what. It's part of the game; it's part of life! Fear is a necessary component of that—it helps you calculate the risk—but you can't let the fear make the decisions for you. You must feel the fear, process it, and do what you need to do to achieve what you've set out for yourself.

A lot of times we don't hustle because we are afraid of the negative potential outcomes. But if we use that fear, process it, and shift our thinking toward the positive potential outcomes, we can turn that fear into faith. When people hustle, it's not because they have no fear—

it's because they've harnessed it instead of letting it harness them.

EXERCISE #2:
Working the Hustle Muscle

There is a popular saying in entrepreneurial circles that goes something like this: "Entrepreneurship is living a few years of your life like most people won't, so that you can spend the rest of your life like most people can't." What they're talking about is hustle. Hustle is about taking consistent action over a period of time in order to build momentum and create the kind of leverage that makes things easier in your life over time. Not surprisingly, this is also the recipe for greatness. It's achieved through consistent action over a long period that begins well before the season begins or opportunities arise.

Everything I've ever been successful at has involved, whether I knew it at the time or not, massive action by being clear about my vision and doing whatever it takes to achieve it. But hustle isn't just about taking consistent, massive action every day toward what you want—it's about taking smart action as well.

There are four smart areas everyone can and should be hustling in:

1. Your body
2. Your mindset
3. Your relationships
4. Your skills

Hustle is a muscle. It's something that takes time to develop into a powerful momentum-building machine. To develop your hustle, you must embrace it and fall in love with the process. The daily journey of developing yourself is, in fact, hustle itself, and over time you'll see massive results from it. Here's how I approach it, plus an exercise on how to develop your hustle muscle.

1. Your Body

Do one thing every day that makes your body healthier and stronger. Something that is painful (the good kind of pain) and requires you to push yourself physically at the gym, on the bike, or during your run. Something that makes you feel uncomfortable, that you'd rather not do. It's this consistent habit of doing something that is painful and uncomfortable that will increase your pain threshold and make you stronger in all areas of your life (in Chapter 5, we cover the steps to mastering your body even more).

2. Your Mindset

Do something every day to improve your mindset and your way of thinking. The greatest minds question everything. They see the world where anything and everything is possible (even if it sounds absolutely crazy). This process could be:

- Reading a thought-provoking book
- Listening to an inspiring podcast
- Going to a workshop
- Learning from a coach or mentor

- Asking questions about everything (allowing yourself to be curious)
- Understanding that you can learn something from everyone
- Studying meditation and different philosophical ideals

3. Your Relationships

A leader is someone who understands that relationships are the key to success in business and life. How well you understand people, your compassion, and your ability to flow through others' emotions in stressful situations influence how deep you can go in relationships. But it's also important to know and be known by the influencers in your industry to achieve greatness in your career, business, or brand. If you follow any of the following steps, you'll be setting yourself up to win in the area of relationships.

- Connect with three new people each week in your industry in person, by phone, or online.
- Connect with three influencers each week (any industry).
- Share a meal with three people each week (breakfast, lunch, or dinner), like the great Keith Ferrazzi recommends in his book *Never Eat Alone*.
- Go to one group event every month—a networking event, breakfast meeting, mastermind group, etc. (Mastermind groups have been a key ingredient to my making seven figures in my business, and I dive into how to join and start your own mastermind in Chapter 7.)

- Send video messages online or via phone to your connections. Don't do this just on birthdays but also make it a point to follow up to see how you can support them with anything they are doing, and ask what their biggest challenges are right now. For example, I like to e-mail friends and just let them know how much I appreciate all of the work they are doing in the world, and I talk about something specific I see them doing at that time. Don't ask for anything in return or do it for any reason other than to show how much you care. This will stand out in their minds and deepen the relationship.

- Ask questions and make the conversations about others, not about what you want. When you focus on giving support to those you trust and believe in, they will almost always want to offer support in return.

- Show up at industry conferences, trade shows, and summits.

For many of you, this will come naturally, but for others who are more introverted, this will require stepping out of your comfort zone and developing a stronger mindset (as in Chapter 3). If you are going to events in person and feel uncomfortable at first, simply find a friend whom you can attend with to ease the anxiety, or start with smaller group events and grow from there (more on relationship building in Chapter 7).

4. Your Skills

Whenever you are in transition or you feel stuck, it's not the time to hunker down, it's the time to hustle and learn new skills. The more skills you have, the more you have to offer in any situation—it's like you've added a new tool on your tool belt to handle any situation in business and life. I'm constantly learning to master new skills and taking on new challenges each year. These are just some of the skills I've picked up over the past decade based on the dreams and passions I have in my life.

- Learning the guitar
- Salsa dancing
- Joining Toastmasters and improving my public speaking
- Picking up a new sport (Team Handball)
- Learning how to write books
- Learning how to build Web sites and grow a following through social media
- Learning to be a coach and workshop facilitator
- Podcasting and editing
- Learning meditation
- Learning acrobatic yoga
- Learning CrossFit, yoga, and different styles of strength and fitness training
- Learning how to make money
- Learning how to invest money and start and launch a business
- Learning how to manage my emotions and let go of my reactive ego
- Learning breathing techniques
- Learning how to hire a powerful team for my business

All of these are things I didn't know how to do when I was growing up or in college. It took time to learn and master these skills, but now because I can pull them off my tool belt at any time and access them in different areas of my life, I'm able to get where I want to be much easier and faster.

Write a list of 10 skills you want to learn. Start with the one that excites you the most and create a game plan for how you will learn it over the next 6 months. It could be a new language, graphic design, a new instrument or hobby. Also think about the skills that will support you in your relationships, your mindset, and your body, as those will be key to supporting you on your path to greatness.

COACHING TIP

Will Smith once said in a sit-down interview with the great Tavis Smiley, "The guy who is willing to hustle the most is going to be the guy that just gets that loose ball."

Most people get stuck in life because they are obsessed with what could go wrong. I had the opposite experience growing up. Everything was already going wrong. I was made fun of a lot, I was picked last for stuff, I didn't feel accepted. Worrying wasn't an option. I had to take action to improve myself and overcome my fears if I didn't want to feel that insecurity anymore.

When you experience fear, move toward it. When you feel doubt, take the necessary actions to build your confidence. When you are afraid of being wrong or looking bad in front of others, be humble and vulnerable to create real human connection. The hustle takes action. It requires getting over yourself and how you look. It can be a beautiful journey if you give yourself permission to hustle like a maniac because what else are you here to do other than make the most of what you can be?

GET GROUNDED

Your body is everything. You may think being a little over-weight isn't that big of a deal, but on the road to greatness, it affects your overall energy and can be that one thing that holds you back with everything. Each body is different, but we all respond positively to a certain set of guidelines and philosophies. Throughout this chapter, you'll hear about these lessons from some incredible teachers who've studied the body (and the mind) far more than I have in all of my years as an elite athlete. I've been in great shape, and I've been in horrible shape, so I can speak to how much better my entire life is working when I'm on the path of body mastery. Your body is your home; it's time to learn how to keep it clean and free of clutter to fulfill the vision within you!

CHAPTER 5

MASTER YOUR BODY

If the body be feeble, the mind will not be strong.

—Thomas Jefferson

Rich Roll was a former NCAA Division I swimmer on some of those amazing Stanford University teams in the 1980s that produced a number of Olympians. After he graduated, he went to Cornell Law School and became a successful entertainment lawyer. He had a beautiful wife, a happy marriage, and a luxurious home near the ocean in Malibu Canyon, California, yet like so many fortunate, accomplished people who appear to have it all, he was not happy. It felt like there was a giant hole in his life from which his spirit and drive and passion steadily leaked out.

Despair is the word a lot of us would use to describe that state, and it can happen whether we have success or not. It's depression. Burnout. Exhaustion. Sick and tired of being sick and tired!

Rich was almost 40 years old and felt stalled out when he should've been at the top of his game. He knew he wasn't living up to his full potential. It's a phase that can hit at nearly any age. Midlife crisis. Quarter-life crisis. Whatever caused it, whenever it happens, it is the opposite of greatness.

"I was just unhappy," he said. "I felt ripped off, cheated. I'd done everything right and should have been celebrating, but instead I was unhappy."

Rich was working 80-hour weeks and bingeing on junk food. It was the only thing he had time for, and at the same time, he was so overworked, the idea of the self-control required to diet seemed laughable. He never had the time to work out and consequently gained 50 pounds. He broke 200 pounds for the first time in his life and kept going. Rich was in denial and rationalizing his deteriorating physical and emotional health.

One day he was climbing a flight of stairs at work, and halfway up, he had to stop. He was out of breath, felt tightness in his chest, and couldn't make it to the top. As a former athlete, this really hit Rich in the stomach—his increasingly flabby stomach.

We've all been there, where having given up on something or run into adversity we can't bear to face, we just pretend. We pretend we don't have a problem and just plain ignore it for so long that it takes an event like this at a moment like this to pierce through our delusions. We sit there paralyzed by grief and confusion: *How did it ever get like this? What happened between then and now that could possibly explain why I can no longer walk up a flight of stairs or play with my kids or sit comfortably in an airplane seat?*

At different times in my life, I've oscillated between

exercising like a madman and wanting to just say screw it and be lazy. Being healthy can be a lot of work, and it can be so tempting to procrastinate and kick the can down the road. But if you want to do great things, that is absolutely the wrong attitude. The path to greatness means being responsible to yourself and others.

In that moment, we have a choice. Unfortunately, too many of us choose to do nothing. To continue to pretend.

But Rich did not.

TACKLING THE IMPOSSIBLE

"I'm 39," he said to himself right there, "and I had to take a break walking up a simple flight of stairs. Something is really not right. I need to make some changes."

He decided in that moment this would be a new beginning in his life. It was this choice that put Rich *back* on the path to greatness.

What he did *not* do was decide to make a small change. A small change or an incremental commitment is too easily forgotten or abandoned. "I'll cut out soda." "I'll eat a salad for lunch." "I'll start Monday." Instead, he started fresh immediately—with a full cleanse to clear his body of the toxins and waste he'd been shoveling into it. He'd been treating his body like a toilet instead of a temple, and now he had to flush it out—and then repair the plumbing. He did this by cutting out all of the junk food and meat and eating a completely plant-based diet.

"The first couple days, I was buckled over, sweating, like I was in rehab," he told me. "It felt like detoxing off heroin or something; it was terrible. By the last couple days of it—and I don't know if you've had this experience—I felt incredible. Better than I'd felt in 20 years or maybe ever. That told me just how resilient the human body is. In a matter of a week, after treating my body so horribly with a terrible diet for so long, I felt better than ever."

The famous English billionaire businessman and adventurer Richard Branson has been asked for his best piece of business advice. His answer is always one word: *exercise.* Why? Because if you don't take care of yourself, you can't take care of your business. A stroll through the Forbes list of the world's billionaires is, with only a couple exceptions, a testament to this idea. Nowhere is the connection between physical health and business wealth more pronounced than with the current generation of entrepreneurs, represented most completely by author, angel investor, and human guinea pig Tim Ferriss.

Tim is best known for the number one *New York Times* best-selling book *The 4-Hour Workweek,* but he is just as passionate about human performance as people like Steven Kotler. His second book, in fact, was called *The 4-Hour Body* and introduced the world to a number of amazing ideas and practices. It shouldn't shock you that physical activity is very important to him, on many levels. "I find sports very helpful as a bookend to close out the day," Tim told me, "to do training at 6:00 p.m., where you are absolutely protecting that time as much as you would protect any other type of conference call or anything else. Not only does it set your body up physically for dinner and the rest of the night, but it also forces you to prioritize your day in order to get all your work done before you head to the gym." The energizing effect of both those things—getting your work done and getting the blood flowing—is a huge asset on the path to greatness.

I think Rich was feeling the truth of all that advice, because he was finally starting to fire on all cylinders again. He loved the way he felt so much that he decided he would stay clean. For him, this meant that he would become a vegan. A significant number of monumentally successful businessmen and leaders have done this over the past 5 or 6 years to get healthier and more productive: Steve Wynn, Bill Clinton, Mort Zuckerman, Al Sharpton, Russell Simmons, Biz Stone, and John Mackey, the CEO of Whole Foods Market. Even Mike Tyson went vegan, and he was an ear-chomping killing machine!

With all the junk out of his diet, Rich made a commitment to exercise again. Not a little bit but a lot. His wife bought him a bike. He started swimming again. He hired a coach, because he was so serious about getting healthy that he wanted to surround himself with experts and good energy. It started off gradual, but at the end, Rich was putting in 25-hour training weeks. It became like a second job, as he had cut back on his law practice significantly to pursue his new lifestyle practice. In a relatively short time, he was an athletic machine nearing the best shape of his life.

And that's when it hit him: He was going to do an ultramarathon—which is essentially any distance-running event beyond a traditional 26.2-mile marathon.

"Two years prior, I couldn't make it up a staircase, and here I was. I had never done an Ironman; it wasn't like I was a seasoned triathlete. I'm a complete newbie. I was very inexperienced at this. I had a level of confidence that I could complete it, but I also had a responsible level of humility about what I was about to do. I wasn't there to win or anything like that. I was there to celebrate the fact that I was sober, that I had lost this weight and changed my life. That was really it."

Despite that humility—or perhaps because of it—Rich didn't just finish the race, he placed 11th. In his very first ultramarathon. You don't need to be an extreme sport enthusiast or an endurance athlete to appreciate the audacity and ridiculousness of Rich's accomplishment. It would be like taking up rock climbing as a New Year's resolution, training on a rock wall for a few months, and then going to Yosemite on the first day of spring and sprinting up the face of El Capitan like a spider monkey.

I found this transformation to be so inspirational and profound. Rich had mastered his body and taken back control of his life along the way. What I love the most about this is that Rich found his calling in life, and a new vision was born in the process. He's built an ultrasuccessful lifestyle business out of his passion. Now a best-selling author, he educates and inspires millions around the world through his books, widely popular podcast, vegan health products, speeches, and more. He turned adversity into advantage and ran with it, literally!

Rich said, "My whole life, I had chased the carrot. Go to the best school. I got in all the Ivy League schools; I studied hard." But where did it get him? Overworked, unhappy, and, worst of all, out of shape. "I was at the point in life where I was supposed to be celebrating everything that I had built," he said. But he couldn't. In his position, who could? Greatness isn't about working a lot or making a lot of money. It's about having purpose and being the best that you can possibly be. And how can you jump for joy when you struggle to walk up a damn flight of stairs?!

YOUR BRAIN ON JUNK

All the teachers in this book mastered their bodies in one way or another. I also spent some time learning from Daniel Amen, MD, a leading American psychiatrist, a brain disorder specialist, director of the Amen Clinics, and *New York Times* best-selling author, which added another layer to my understanding of why mastering the body is so important. It's not just about muscles. Your brain matters, too. Your mind and your body are connected; they are both part of your body. Are you taking care of them? As they say, garbage in, garbage out.

"Your brain is literally involved in everything you do. How you think, how you feel, how you act, how you get along with other people, and when it works right, you work right," he told me. "When it's troubled, though, for whatever reason—toxic exposure, head trauma, drug abuse, lack of oxygen—that's when you start getting sadder, sicker, poorer, less successful."

The problem so many of us have is that we completely ignore the role of our brains in the health of our bodies. "If you never look at the brain," Dr. Amen warned, "you may never know what is going on with you." And when that happens, you can find yourself in a nasty cycle of poor physical health leading to poor emotional health, which in turn leads to worse physical health, and so on and so on.

When I was bummed in my own life and career, I went through a similar bout of lethargy and felt that slow slide toward unhealthiness. What was really tough about it was that it happened so gradually. I steadily gained a pound a month for close to 2 years. To make it more confusing, I also started to become successful (financially and in my business) around that time. That made it harder to see through my own carb-driven haze and question my habits. After a 2-year period of hustling, barely making much each month, I remember making $6,200 on my first webinar and feeling like I was the richest man in the world. I started eating like a rich man, too. After that moment, the money started to roll in, and so did my fat rolls. I was eating 7,000+ calories a day (to be fair, I was working out, too, but it was all out of balance). Worst of all, I had sugar after every meal, which is a huge no-no even if you're interested in only a basic level of health. I just wasn't taking care of my brain or my body. When I look back on it, I know that I wasn't the best I could be. I wasn't thinking or feeling as clearly as I could have.

It turns out, according to Dr. Amen, that when your weight goes up, the size and function of your brain go down. It wasn't until my move to New York to pursue Team Handball and my dream of representing the United States in the Olympics that I finally snapped out of this slump, and it was only because the waistband on my underwear finally snapped back at me. I knew I was getting pretty heavy. My face was so wide my family and friends started to joke about it—they called me "Flewis" . . . *Fat* Lewis—but when I couldn't wear my underwear anymore without the waistband snapping back and rolling down under my belly like a slap bracelet, that was enough. I stepped on a scale for the first time in a long time, and the digital display shouted "254" back at me in big, red, angry numbers. I decided in that moment to cut out everything bad for the next 30 days (Rich Roll–style).

I didn't have any sugar, gluten, or dairy for 30 days. I'm not saying this is for everyone, nor was it recommended to me by any health expert or doctor; it's simply something I wanted to do to create a new habit for myself, because I understood the power of creating positive habits when something isn't working the way you want it to (more on this in Chapter 6). I lost 28 pounds in the first 28 days and felt better than ever, so I decided to do it for another 30 days and dropped a couple more pounds. I didn't change anything else, and I was still working out the same way . . . it was all from cutting my intake of the stuff that wasn't working for me. I dissolved Flewis by drinking (and falling in love with) green juice every day, eating foods that were organically grown and taken directly from the ground, and eating organic, grass-fed meat. Between choosing the right foods and remaining dedicated to my workouts, I've never since worried about gaining the pounds back.

I now have sugar and sweets from time to time, but my diet is much more balanced, and my weight (and health) is where I want it to be. My life is better every day because of it. And the work I put into mastering my body has made all the other decisions I have to make and the work I have to do that much easier.

But naturally—and my brother, Chris, was an example of this—people put a lot worse stuff in their bodies than sugar: drugs, excessive alcohol, and nasty chemicals. We deprive ourselves of sleep or even have "natural" addictions like gambling and sex. This has a real and tangible effect on your ability to perform. Forget about the kind of flow state that Steven Kotler describes in his books—that's way outside the realm of possibility with these negative influences at play, because they can quickly and easily destroy your body and tap-dance on your brain. So stop abusing yourself!

SLEEP YOUR WAY TO THE TOP

Just like Rich Roll, 5 years ago Ameer Rosic, Canadian kettlebell champion and an expert on sleep optimization, was in a bad place. He suffered from deep depression, he dabbled in alcohol and drugs, and his outlook on life was horrendous. "I had no meaning in life at all," he told me. "I felt like there was a dark hole, an abyss, in my heart. Then life hit me on the head with a hammer."

The epiphany came when he woke up and realized that much of his struggle was due to a lack of sleep. He was up into the late hours nearly every night partying, getting very little sleep, thinking he was a superman who could take on anything. His physical and emotional health began to suffer, and with that his life suffered tremendously, too. He knew he had to do something, so he began to learn about circadian rhythms and the importance of getting the proper amount of sleep. "Everybody needs to realize, we are like batteries," he said. "Sleep recharges you. It increases and balances hormones, strengthens your immune system, gives you clarity, gives you focus, and so much more." The more he researched, the more Ameer realized that sleep was the pivotal factor in achieving optimal health, ahead of diet, ahead of exercise, ahead of everything.

And for Ameer, the turnaround could not have been more stark. "I have somehow encapsulated so much passion in my soul, in my being, and it is because of the way I sleep, the way I eat, and the way I treat my body, because when you treat yourself first, everything else follows and everything else is greater," he said.

The impact of proper sleep wasn't just physical either. Ameer raised his IQ, became the Canadian biathalon champion in kettlebells (the national sport of Russia—don't ask, I was as confused as you are), and built a business helping others optimize their health. Ameer put it best when he said, "If you want to run a business and you want to do good in this world, if you want to deliver value in this world, it's all about treating one's self first. When you treat yourself first and you create that perfect vessel, you then have the ability to affect so many more people globally."

It's crazy how important a foundational habit sleep is! As Shawn Stevenson, sleep specialist, author of *Sleep Smarter: 21 Proven Tips to Sleep Your Way to a Better Body, Better Health, and Bigger Success*, and another great mentor whom I have had the privilege to learn from, put it: "Sleep is something our genes expect of us." He calls it vitamin S, which perfectly explains the additive and restorative role of sleep in our lives. When he talked to me about the information in his book, he could not overstate just how detrimental a lack of sleep can be to every aspect of life.

"We have a thousand things going on in our lives, and sleep is often one of the first things we tend to omit," he warned. "We don't understand that by lacking that high-quality sleep, we're actually *demolishing* our ability to achieve at a high level in everything else in our lives." (emphasis mine)

This is especially true for entrepreneurs, many of whom wear their marathon coding sessions or back-to-back all-nighters as badges of honor in the race to start-up success. To you folks, Ameer has some shocking news that you need to take to heart: "Around 2013, a study came out that showed people who stay up 48 hours or more, which many people do in these crazy stressed-out days we're living, have the same blood sugar as a diabetic." As a diabetic! "Now can you imagine," he continued, "what happens when this gets compounded? Day in, day out, year after year after year. It's going to end up in something not very beneficial."

I think we can nominate that last sentence from Ameer for the Understatement of the Century. It was

definitely a "holy crap" moment for me, I can tell you
that.

If you're like a lot of people who are struggling with
turning your dreams into reality, with realizing your
vision for greatness, right now you are probably saying,
"Look, I have a demanding job. I have kids. I can't exercise
25 hours a week like Rich Roll or go to bed at 10:00 every
night and sleep 8 to 9 hours like Ameer Rosic. I don't have
the time, I have commitments." Well, Rich did, too. "We
need to be extremely selfish a few hours a day and take
care of ourselves and our bodies," he said. Echoing Ameer's
point, he continued, "You can't help someone else if you
are not taking care of yourself."

I've learned that it's a lot like when you're on an airplane and they say, "Put your own mask on first, before
assisting others." You can't help anyone if your brain is
oxygen starved or, worse, you're already dead. The same
principle applies to taking care of ourselves so that we
might help others. We need to make sure we're really
taking care of our bodies, physically, mentally, and emotionally. We need to make sure we're getting all of our
needs met, that we're going after all of our wants and
desires. Those don't come last, they come first—no matter how selfish that might feel. When they come first,
everything else follows quickly after.

Rich said, "I'm a better person when I'm taking care
of myself in this way. There's a certain part of me that
feels like that's what I'm supposed to be doing. I'm wired
for it. I'm happier, I'm more productive, I'm a better husband, and I'm a better father when I am training and taking care of myself in that way."

WHAT IS POSSIBLE WHEN YOU MASTER YOUR BODY

Chalene Johnson, a *New York Times* best-selling author and a world-renowned fitness coach, has trained hundreds of thousands of people and sold millions of copies of her workout videos. She witnesses firsthand what's possible when you take ownership of your health. Her students send thank you messages on a regular basis sharing what they've created in their family lives, careers, and personal relationships due to her training. Some people find it difficult to change their lifestyles with years and years of bad habits; trust me, I get it. But Chalene, now a close friend, said to me, "Anything and everything is possible with a plan. If this [healthy body] is what I'm interested in right now, what am I willing to give up?" If you want to make a change, then something needs to actually be different in order to get better results. Meaning, what vices in your life would you need to remove to improve your health and your body and gain all that is possible with a mindful lifestyle?

For Rich, his relationship with his family improved when he made physical health a priority. He was content. He was happy. Much as Ameer's work with sleep became more than just a curiosity, Rich's success at training and running quickly became more than a hobby. He built an entire lifestyle business out of it, for crying out loud, and he became *great* in more ways than one to boot.

I know this sounds crazy, but I am convinced that a major reason many people don't achieve greatness or even reach for it is because they just don't have the energy. They aren't taking care of themselves. We all need to do a better job of this, for ourselves and in support of others. Remember, it doesn't matter how great your vision is, you cannot muster the will to overcome adversity or marshal the energy to hustle tirelessly if you're out of breath or stuck on the couch.

Your greatness problem might just be a health problem.

And just because you haven't taken care of yourself in the past doesn't mean you can't and shouldn't start right this second. Rich was 40 when he got serious. We can't turn back time and start over, but we can choose how it will end, and it is never too late to take the first step in the right direction. That's what mastering your body is about. The past is irrelevant—what matters is where you go now. Maybe your road will end on (or include) many miles of high-endurance running. Or maybe it's just getting in better shape so you can play with your kids. Or maybe it's eating right so your head is clear and fresh so that you can think without the fog.

Regardless, mastering your body is a fundamental, foundational part of your journey toward greatness. It is the engine that powers the runaway train of your vision, pushes you over obstacles, clears a path for you to focus, and fuels the hustle that takes your dreams even further than you imagined possible when you first dreamed them. Do not take advantage of your body. Do not take your brain for granted. As Ameer described it to me, "We are like banks, and there's a mechanism in our brain called sleep debt that actually accumulates the seconds, the minutes, the days that we miss out on sleep. And just like with a loan that doesn't get properly serviced, one day the bank will come knocking on your door, saying, 'Hey, Lewis, well, you owe us about 2 to 3 years of catch-up time.'" And just like with real banks, that knock almost always comes at the worst possible time. In the pursuit of greatness, mastering your body is all about not letting your body write checks that your brain can't cash.

The idea of entering a CrossFit gym or training like an elite athlete may be as terrifying to you as giving a speech was to me when I went to Toastmasters the first time. But that doesn't let you off the hook from mastering your body in the School of Greatness. If you want to play a big game in life, you need the energy it requires physically and emotionally to take on every challenge and obstacle that stand between you and your vision. Here are three things you can do to master your own body starting right now!

EXERCISE #1:
Take a Picture of Your Body . . . Naked!

If you really want to inventory how you view yourself—what you like and don't like—there is one place to start. See yourself naked, literally, and then take a picture.

Accepting (and loving) your body is the first step. Take a picture of yourself naked and evaluate the parts you love and the parts you want to improve on, and write them down. Notice where you're putting your negative energy and focus on accepting those aspects of your body. Only then will you have the positive energy you need to make the improvements you want.

Without your accepting responsibility for your body the way it is at this moment, the unhappiness or negative energy becomes a source of your results. Anything that's based on fear ends up in fear. By accepting and loving my body, I've got the positive energy I need to stay on a workout plan and lifestyle diet that others might struggle with. When you love your body—or maybe more accurately, the person *inside* your body—it's much easier to stay committed to a vision than to do something out of fear and self-loathing. From this place, you are able to choose to lose weight because it matters to you, not because how you look matters to others.

EXERCISE #2:
Develop a Fitness Lifestyle Plan That You Love

My goal for this book is to open you up to any and all possibilities. No matter where you are on your fitness journey, each step can be one in the right direction. Know that your body should not hold you back but only move you forward in achieving your vision.

First, carve out the time—write it down in your schedule. This should be a minimum of 5 days a week for at least 30 minutes per day. This will create a routine and reinforce a commitment to physical health as part of your lifestyle. It doesn't matter what time you exercise during the day; at this point, the most important thing is to do it at the same time every day to make it a consistent habit. Pick a time that works well for you and your lifestyle. I prefer mornings because it kick-starts my day and puts me in a positive mental space, since I've completed something before I've really even begun my day. As my mom says, completion is powerful.

Second, start moving and get active. I always incorporate things that I love into my fitness program, because that is the easiest way to get and stay motivated. As an athlete, I play a lot of pickup basketball, go running, do sprints, lift weights, swim in the ocean, and try different boot camp–style workouts because that's what gets me excited when I exercise.

This doesn't mean you need to spend 2 hours crushing your body every single day. The important thing is not to get paralyzed by the overwhelming expanse of the fitness industry. Whether it's jogging in the neighborhood, walking with purpose to the café to get your daily tea, or stretching for a few minutes in the morning, every little bit of movement counts. Remember, this is a journey, not a destination.

Third, find an accountability partner for support. This could be a friend, spouse, trainer, or even pet (yes, make a commitment to keep your dog in shape as well!). You are that much more likely to commit when you have someone else holding you to your word. Many people hate working out, which is why they don't stay with it. If this is where you are, then an accountability partner might be the perfect thing to help you stay committed and make working out more fun.

Last, I've learned to do one painful exercise every day so that I can expand my comfort zone and take my body and mind to new levels. So do something each day that makes you uncomfortable. This doesn't mean you should go and try to pull a muscle because it's painful. You essentially want to do something new and/or difficult that is consistent with what you are striving for with your body. Although I love certain things about my workouts, I never keep to the same routine for too long. Change is good. I always push myself to a level of discomfort that eventually becomes painless and rewarding.

This probably sounds like I'm telling you to search out crazy, exotic exercises that target muscles you didn't know you had. Nothing could be further from the truth. Your goal when it comes to painful exercise is really doing anything that makes you sweat and sends your heart rate up—doing pushups (or any lift or exercise) to failure, repeating hill sprints with minimal rest, or simply working out harder than the previous day. It's simple: *Push yourself!*

I'm personally a big fan of interval training. This includes making your own workout of four to six exercises that you'll do for 45 seconds at a time with a 15-second rest between each exercise for as many rounds as you want.

Example of an Interval Workout

45 seconds: pushups	15 seconds: rest
15 seconds: rest	45 seconds: lunges
45 seconds: air squats	15 seconds: rest
15 seconds: rest	45 seconds: situps
45 seconds: jumping rope	15 seconds: rest

Do this for four rounds (or adjust the rounds and time for each exercise to push yourself however you want). You can get as creative as you wish with this simple workout plan and add in any type of exercise, with weights or just your body weight. You can do this at home, at the gym, or wherever is most convenient for you. Make sure to change things up and keep it fresh. Depending on how many rounds you do, the workout will take roughly 30 minutes with light stretching before and after.

The key here is to do something that you enjoy (even though it will be painful) and find someone to make it fun with you. For more workout resources and options, go to schoolofgreatness.com/resources.

EXERCISE #3:
Find Out What's MISSING

Aubrey Marcus, my good friend, a health expert, and CEO of the nutrition company Onnit, designed this exercise exclusively for you! With his focus on total human optimization, his method for mastering your body begins with finding out what's missing from your health and lifestyle. It's so important that he has turned it into an acronym to guide your progress (MISSING). Figuring out where you are physically and physiologically in each of these seven areas is critical to your health and your ability to effectively pursue your vision on the path to greatness. Use this exercise as a guide to see what's currently missing from your health and adjust each area as needed.

M—Mineralization

The body is made up of a variety of minerals. Every single system in our bodies requires adequate minerals to function properly. We get these in the foods we eat. Ask yourself where your foods are coming from. Are your fruits and vegetables organic and locally grown? Is your beef grass fed? If the answer is yes, you're on the right track. Trace your food back to the source.

One of the best ways to return minerals to your daily diet is to use Himalayan salt. Regular table salt contains only three minerals: sodium, chloride, and iodine. Himalayan salt has anywhere from 65 to 85 trace minerals. The expression "worth one's salt" comes from Roman times, when soldiers were given an allotment of salt as their *salarium*, which is where we derive our word *salary*. To function efficiently, it was essential that soldiers replenish the salt lost by their bodies during long marches. Having the right salt could mean the difference between life and death.

I—Inflammation

A lot of top doctors now are saying that pretty much all disease stems from some type of inflammation. The reason is that the body has to combat inflammation, just like you would combat any other type of pathogen. When the body is using resources to deal with inflammation, it has far fewer resources to deal with immune response and proper function, and thus disease can grab a foothold. Managing inflammation is incredibly vital.

Paying attention to those inflammatory processes is important. Inflammation can even come from poor digestion! One thing that can be valuable in dealing with inflammation is using proteolytic enzymes. Proteolytic enzymes go through the body and start to break down any kind of dead proteins that are lying around the body and stimulating inflammatory responses. Utilizing a good proteolytic enzyme can be a major benefit to mastering your own health. (My personal recommendations for enzymes are at schoolofgreatness.com/resources.)

S—Stress

As discussed in Chapter 2, stress is a part of the human experience that we need to manage. We don't realize the physical cost of being under chronic stress. Stress releases a hormone called cortisol, which reduces immune function. Stress is fine if temporarily you need to run away from an animal, hit a deadline at work, or do something that requires a short burst of all of your focused energy. If the stress is chronic, however, the body is severely limited in how effectively it can deal with any number of stressors. Stress will eventually burn out your adrenal glands, and through a variety of chemical processes and substitutions, you'll start to produce fewer of other hormones that are essential for optimal living. So managing stress is incredibly important.

Now take time to write down what you do to manage stress. One of the simplest ways to reduce stress goes back to our meditation exercise in Chapter 3. It's been shown scientifically through a number of studies that deep diaphragm breathing will naturally release your stress. So focusing on your breathing is an important way to release stress.

Here are a few examples of what I personally do and don't do to manage stress.

DO	DON'T DO
Meditation	Smoke
Physical activities	Drink
Listen to music	Binge on TV
Change my environment	Overeat
Dance	Oversleep or lounge for days

S—Sleep

Sleep is probably the most important health tonic you can provide your body. It is the time to repair, restore, recover, and rejuvenate. Sleep is the key. There are great books, like *Sleep Smarter* by Shawn Stevenson, that talk about the different ways to improve your sleep. First and foremost is understanding that the body is designed to sleep during the night and be awake during the day. If you can optimize your schedule to get 7 to 8 hours of sleep during the night so you are fully awake during the day, you've taken the first big step.

Once you've gotten yourself on a better schedule, the next step is to optimize sleep itself. Photosensitive elements of the eye trigger melatonin production—that's the hormone responsible for letting you know that it's time to sleep and for helping the body fall asleep. Additional light in the late-evening hours short-circuits the melatonin process. So minimize artificial light sources like late-night TV and smartphones. No electronics in bed! Track your sleep nightly. Early to bed, early to rise, and get 7 to 8 hours of sleep nightly. It's that simple.

I—Inhalation

Our meditation exercise should reinforce the importance of breathing. Inhalation is one process that we do constantly throughout the day, and if we stop, we're dead. We don't realize how crucial getting oxygen to our body is. We just take it for granted. But not all breaths are equal.

If you're taking shallow chest breaths, you're not adequately oxygenating your body for optimal health and

stress management. So paying attention to your breathing, using that as a rudder to navigate different health
modalities, is key. Breath can help you deepen your meditation, it can power you in your workouts and in your
training, and it can keep your body more alkalized, which
will improve your mineralization. Breath is incredibly
important and too often overlooked in the health picture.

If you get the chance when you have an extra minute
(maybe while sitting in traffic), simply focus on your
breath—those full diaphragm breaths that go deep down
into your belly. The benefits to your health can be massive. Are you breathing optimally? Could you use more
cardiovascular fitness? It starts here.

N—Nutrient Density

Nutrition in America has been calorie focused for a long
time. What we have learned over the past couple decades,
though, is that calories are not as important to health
and having a great body as nutrient density. You can get
500 calories from sugar or you can get 500 calories from
a grass-fed rib eye; your choice will have a vastly different effect on your body. How many nutrients are you providing your body? How many green vegetables? How
many healthy fats, like coconut oil and avocado and olive
oil, with their omega-3s and omega-9s? What kind of
nutrient density does your food have? What doesn't have
nutrient density? Make sure your meals are balanced and
rich in nutrients. Water is the most essential nutrient;
without it, human life cannot survive. Make sure you are
staying hydrated. Are you drinking enough each day?

G—Gut Health

The gut is the cauldron of health. This is where your digestive system works to convert minerals and nutrients into fuel that will sustain a healthy body. From the very first doctor, Hippocrates, to doctors in the present day, medical practitioners have always been aware of gut health, but it's something that is only now getting its proper respect. Matter cannot be created or destroyed, so how do we grow or change? We grow by assimilating nutrients from our food and building our bodies and regenerating our cells by using those nutrients. Poor digestion can lead to inflammation and what's called leaky gut syndrome, where food particles escape through the gut barrier and trigger an inflammatory response.

Gut health is influenced by the probiotic flora in your gut, also known as the gut biome. These microorganisms are important for digestion. Additionally, many of the neurotransmitters and hormones that are responsible for your mood, your happiness, and everything that makes you feel great are either affected by or originate from the gut. Most of our serotonin production comes from the gut. Our immune cells are produced in the gut. Having a healthy gut biome—one that works symbiotically with the body—is vital for your immune function, for your mood, and for your health.

So when you're looking to master your body, pay attention to what you're MISSING. When you aren't missing anything, only then can you say you've mastered your body. Your goal at that point is to maintain where you are for as long as you can!

For the complete guide to figuring out what's MISSING from your health, along with resources on supplements and products to optimize your body plus my personal fitness plan, go to schoolofgreatness.com/resources.

COACHING TIP

Listen, I'm not perfect. My weight goes up and down sometimes. I don't always eat perfectly. Like most people, I love sugar and sweets. But I'm sick and tired of seeing people who have given up on themselves! The only difference between those people and me (and you, I hope!) is that I'm willing to put in the work and experience the pain necessary to keep my body and mind in shape so that I can perform throughout the day on a high level, live the life of my dreams, and pursue my vision come what may.

If you aren't getting what you want in life and you are out of shape, don't think for a second that those two things are unrelated. It's time to say, "Enough is enough." It's time to admit, "I'm sick and tired of feeling sick and tired." It's time to get up and do something every single day that makes you sweat and gets your heart racing. Put yourself through some type of daily discomfort, whether it's for 5 minutes or 50 minutes. Do something that is so uncomfortable that it starts you on the process of getting your body where it needs to be, and then maintain that by falling in love with the feeling of that pain. Yes, your vision and relationships and dreams depend on it, but most important, so does your life. It's time to step up and make your body great!

GET GROUNDED

Our habits shape who we become and the results we create in the world. In my life, I've cultivated habits that supported me and others that brought me down. We've all been there. Unfortunately, most of us don't know how important our habits actually are. The most successful, fulfilled, and vision-focused individuals in the world have daily rituals and habits to which they attribute a significant amount of their success.

If you want to achieve greatness in your life or your business, then everything you do needs to be done with a purpose and for a reason. It doesn't take long to form a new habit, but it can slip away from you just as quickly. True greatness comes from the intentional act of doing something positive over and over and over again. It's time to take a look at the habits you've been forming and begin forging a new path right now by applying some of the habits of the most successful people in the world.

CHAPTER 6

PRACTICE POSITIVE HABITS

Successful people are simply those with successful habits.
—Brian Tracy

Armchair quarterbacks love to yell at athletes who "waste their potential" or "take their gift for granted" or "don't hustle" or "don't act like a good role model." This is usually just empty projection, aimed at great men and women who have accomplished more than the fans can ever dream. But sometimes there is truth to it.

Anyone who has ever tried to make it in sports can tell you that while they were out at practice leaving everything they had on the field, there were other athletes using merely a fraction of their capabilities. Guys like NBA All-Star Allen Iverson (who, during an infamous press conference where he was being judged for missing practice, said, "I'm supposed to be the franchise player, and we're sitting here talking about *practice*?!") and National Football League All-Pro Charles Woodson were notorious for giving the bare minimum to get by until the lights came on. Woodson's ability as an All-American, Heisman-winning, All-Pro NFL cornerback was so freakish, so otherworldly, that he didn't dial up his practice habits until 10 years into his now 18-year professional career, and even then he only did it because he realized he was setting a bad example and creating bad habits in some of the younger players who looked up to him. He didn't do it because he didn't need it to compete at an elite level—a fact that drove his coaches on every team he ever played for stark raving mad.

This is not a story unique to the playing field. Poor practice habits—or preparation problems, as I like to call them—transcend the world of sports and affect us in our jobs and our relationships. Doing the bare minimum at work. Rushing to complete a task at the 11th hour because experience has taught you that you don't need the previous 10 to get it done. Forgetting your partner's birthday and running around the day of for a present that doesn't feel like you forgot. Crash dieting to lose 10 pounds before going on a beach vacation. We do these things because we've gotten away with them in the past. We were fast enough, smart enough, young enough, lucky enough. We lean on experience and ability, not on proper preparation. We have poor habits, and sooner or later our luck is going to run out.

One of my most inspiring teachers let his poor habits get the best of him. He is actually a guy with a story very similar (minus the fame and millions of dollars, of course) to Charles Woodson's. His name is Graham Holmberg, and I played college football with him. Practice after practice, week after week, season after season, I watched him get by purely on his physical prowess and agility, a substantial gift he was bent on wasting. I was glad he was on our team (you don't want to be on the other side of the ball from a guy like Graham), but I was also jealous and angry at the same time. Despite what seemed like unlimited athletic potential, reaching for true greatness didn't seem to be on his agenda. Instead, Graham preferred to party, chew tobacco (on the sidelines during practice even!), stay out late and sleep in late, chase women, and enjoy himself. He had no ambitions beyond being pretty dang good and having fun.

You might be saying to yourself right now, "Wait, that sounds pretty awesome!" And it is, or it can be, at least for a while. Who doesn't like to have fun and tear it up every once in a while? But that's the operative phrase: *every once in a while.* If that's all you do, eventually it gets boring, especially when it doesn't produce anything lasting or when talent can no longer bridge the gap that bad habits create.

Now others of you might be asking a different question: "Well, what if you don't have any talent? What then?" First of all, that's garbage. Every single one of us has talent churning away inside; you either have misdiagnosed yours, denied it, or taken it for granted. But second, talent—at least of the kind I'm talking about with Graham—isn't destiny. Sure, talent can make greatness easier to achieve, but greatness is not the exclusive domain of the talented. Greatness is the result of visionaries who persevere, focus, believe, and *prepare.* It is a habit, not a birthright.

Unfortunately, because he was so supremely talented and so much had been given to him at birth, Graham ignored the power of habits that his parents, teachers, and coaches tried futilely for years to drill into him. Or maybe a better way of saying that is, he let his life be ruled by those bad habits. And as I have come to learn after talking with true greats like Angel, Shawn, Ameer, and my brother, the number one way to waste your talents is to allow bad habits to take over. The consequences of a life led by bad habits are inevitable.

TREADING WATER

Now you wouldn't think that Graham would be the teacher we need. He never approached the kind of greatness we all saw in him, and over time he became deeply unhappy. But Graham's story doesn't end there—it gets worse and then better. When he left school, he didn't go pro. He didn't go semipro. He didn't go anywhere! He stayed right where he was, like all those people who peaked in high school, never left, and watched life unspool in front of them. It was almost like Graham was the real-life Al Bundy from the famous 1990s sitcom *Married with Children,* whose greatest achievement in life was scoring four touchdowns in the 1966 city championships for Polk High. And it was all downhill from there. Like Al, Graham was basically treading water. Treading water is not a growth strategy. It doesn't get you anywhere. There is no progress with treading water. All you're doing is fighting to stay in one place, with enough of your head above water to keep from drowning.

That was exactly where Graham was one day a few years later, when he learned that a close cousin had been killed in a car crash. Something in Graham clicked. It was like he finally woke up from the stupor he'd put himself in, and instead of treading water, he began to kick and paddle with purpose. I've never seen someone turn his life around as quickly as he did, giving up all his vices cold turkey and going to the gym nonstop. On this new path, he developed the workout and lifestyle habits that would eventually turn him into the world champion at the Cross-Fit Games and earn him the label "the world's fittest man."

But the greatness he achieved in fitness is not what we can learn most from, or at least what I learned most from. Graham's turnaround was rooted in his mind. He became intensely spiritual and devoted to his faith. He became a baseball coach at the high school his beloved cousin had gone to. He opened his own CrossFit gym, where he offered Bible study on the weekends. He married and started a family. He turned the adversity that stopped him cold in his tracks into a new vision where positive habits fueled an amazing transformation that affected all areas of his life.

"It was like, I don't want to be a hypocrite to these kids, and inspire them and coach them up and teach them the right habits, if I'm doing bad stuff as well. I made a decision to just wipe that stuff out of my life and not let it control me anymore," Graham told me.

For Graham, that meant cutting out everything from chewing tobacco and drinking to other less tangible but equally toxic sins: jealousy, anger, ingratitude, ego. That is the tricky secret about habits—they are best built or changed one by one, but eventually, you have to get to all of them if you want to be great. In the quest for greatness, there is no substitute for developing positive habits.

AN OLD GREEK'S ADVICE

Aristotle said, "We are what we repeatedly do. Excellence, then, is not an act but a habit." That old Greek understood how important positive habits are to overcoming adversity and enduring the quest to become a champion. I have learned that champions aren't just born; champions can be made when they embrace and commit to life-changing positive habits.

Having known Graham for more than a decade and watching how he made a conscious shift to that new path, I decided to examine my own habits. I saw how quickly positive habits built strength and resulted in a deeper sense of belief—in myself, in my vision, and even spiritually.

This process wasn't easy at first. I never got into any of the obvious things we think of when we talk about bad habits—drugs, drinking, or smoking—because from an early age I saw what they did to my brother and realized I didn't want to make those same mistakes. I wasn't perfect by any stretch (and achieving greatness isn't about being perfect anyway), but my bad habits were less clear to see or less straightforward to understand. Thanks to a lot of introspection and coaching from greats like Chris Lee and Tony Robbins, I finally came to see all the bad habits I'd developed starting as far back as my time on the middle school basketball team.

- Beating myself up
- Being ungrateful
- Failing to acknowledge positive growth
- Being overly judgmental (toward myself and others)
- Disrespecting my parents and family
- Staying in unfulfilling relationships too long
- Eating poorly
- Not exercising regularly
- Keeping a messy living space
- Swearing like a sailor
- Staying up all night
- Sleeping in all morning
- Cheating on homework and tests
- Reacting to situations in a way that upsets others
- Getting by without practicing

It took a lot of time and constant feedback to realize what wasn't working in my life, and it will be an ongoing journey until the day I die. Over the years, I began adding positive habits and noticed a dramatic change in my results and the way I felt internally as well. Some of these include:

- Constantly expressing gratitude
- Smiling at as many people as possible

- Going to bed early
- Getting 7 to 8 hours of committed sleep
- Making my bed in the morning
- Staying organized
- Acknowledging myself and others
- Loving people wherever they are on their personal journey
- Eating clean
- Training my body
- Saving and investing my money wisely
- Meditating
- Visualizing my results and creating a game plan
- Respecting others
- Investing in my personal growth
- Preparing before big moments
- Surrounding myself with inspiring people

Staying consistent with positive habits can be a challenge. I still go back and forth on them. There have been many times where I was working out intensely and in the best shape of my life, and then for whatever reason, I got off track. Before I knew it, 3 or 4 months would go by, and all of a sudden, I'd find myself in the same position as Rich Roll—exhausted halfway up a flight of stairs!

The key to surviving and then thriving after these moments is to not beat yourself up when you do break a habit. Rather, you need to reconnect to your vision to refamiliarize yourself with why it's important to stay true to your positive habits in the first place.

A habit and its results can change fast, so it's crucial

to set yourself up to win and do what works for you to stay on track. For some, that's journaling the habits you kept and the habits you broke and creating rewards and consequences for yourself when you do. For others, that's hiring a coach to keep you accountable or finding an accountability buddy or friend with whom you can work on these things together. For still others, it's finding a mastermind group where you are all constantly challenging yourselves to stay on track.

The tricky part about habits is that any one of them (good or bad), when you look at them individually, doesn't seem all that critical. It's when you take them in combination or as a whole that they become incredibly powerful. They can easily and shockingly thwart the same amount of progress that they can create. This is why we admire people with great self-discipline. It's not because they were born great. It's because they learned the power of habits and applied that power to create a lifestyle that supports the best version of themselves.

Almost everyone knows the famous (and mythical) story about Michael Jordan getting cut from his high school basketball team. Not only did he use that as motivation (in reality, he got demoted to JV as a sophomore), but he cultivated an entire regimen of positive training habits that built him into the greatest basketball player to ever play the game—including spending every off-season adding a new move to his repertoire to make himself more unstoppable.

James Altucher, the great entrepreneur and writer, has talked openly for years about hitting rock bottom over and over again. His brilliant book, *Choose Yourself!*, is all about the positive habits he's developed to pick himself up off the floor and be more successful than he was before—from writing down 10 ideas every day to his now famous "daily practice" in which he works on and calibrates his physical, emotional, mental, and spiritual health. My former teammate Graham Holmberg did the exact same thing to turn his life around.

Now, I don't want you to think this is all about morals. Though morals are important, this is really about human optimization—not avoiding sin. Ironically, it was Eric Thomas, the inspirational speaker and "hip-hop preacher," who made this clear to me when he pointed out a simple bad habit that almost everyone has: getting distracted. Think about how hard it is for us to stay on task these days; from social media to e-mail, there is an endless pull on our time.

So Eric set out to change that tendency in his own work. He told me that he practices a "no interruptions" policy when he is being creative: "When I get started, I don't care if it's my wife, my children, they know that from a certain time frame, I'm going all in. And I can't go all in answering the phone. I can't go all in watching TV. I can't go all in with those kinds of distractions swirling around me." This has helped him craft messages that have reached millions of people around the globe.

Meanwhile, he pushes back at entrepreneurs and artists who can't seem to create work that resonates.

"It's because you're not in abstraction," he said to me. "You don't have that moment of your day—I don't care if it's 10 minutes or 4 hours—where you shut the entire world out. No Twitter, no Facebook, no Instagram, nothing. For that time, you're going all in. Once you come out, then we can do Instagram. And I'll be honest. Your content probably would be stronger if you had that time of isolation, of solitude, where you give yourself a chance to think. You give yourself a chance to go in, and when you go in, you go 120 percent. That's my ritual."

Really, it's a habit. An excellent habit. The beauty (and curse) of habits is that once they are formed, they are hard to break. Consciously pursuing great habits consistently will click you into autopilot on the path to greatness.

MAKE YOUR BED, CHANGE YOUR LIFE

I'll give you another example just to make it clear how simple and small good habits can be: Make your bed. In 2014, Admiral William McRaven gave an amazing commencement address at the University of Texas at Austin. In the speech, he focused on the critical nature of making and inspecting a sailor's bed each morning. This might seem like some petty, officious quirk of military regulations at first. After all, isn't that what your mother bothered you about every morning? But when you hear it from Admiral McRaven, it becomes the definition of a positive habit. It's a way to start off your day with an accomplishment and encourage you to keep tackling the tasks of your day. And furthermore, as Admiral McRaven said, "Making your bed will also reinforce the fact that little things in life matter. If you can't do the little things right, you will never do the big things right."

Admiral McRaven was not the first person to stumble onto the power of making your bed every day. Gretchen Rubin, the habit expert and number one *New York Times* best-selling author of *The Happiness Project,* has talked on her blog about making your bed since way back in 2007! In fact, of her millions of readers who worked on their own "happiness projects," she reported that making the bed had the biggest impact on their happiness. Her explanation for why this was the case, which she wrote about a few months before the release of *The Happiness Project,* echoes Admiral McRaven's words in many ways.

> First, making your bed is a step that's quick and easy, yet makes a big difference. Everything looks neater. It's easier to find your shoes. Your bedroom is a more peaceful environment. For most people, outer order contributes to inner calm.
>
> Second, sticking to any resolution—no matter what it is— brings satisfaction. You've decided to make some change, and you've stuck to it. Because making my bed is one of the first things I do in the morning, I start the day feeling efficient, productive, and disciplined.

I have to be honest, when my first company had its first million dollars in sales, one of the few splurges I made was to hire an assistant. I'm embarrassed to say that one of the things I had that assistant do every morning was make my bed (hey, at least someone was developing the habit!). But as I learned about the importance of positive habits, I stopped this. I realized that by having my assistant do a task like this for me, I was depriving myself of an opportunity to practice a positive habit that could kick-start my day on my own personal path to greatness. And now, every morning when I wake up, I make my bed—starting my day with some satisfaction and discipline.

HABITS OF HIGHLY SUCCESSFUL PEOPLE

Here is the thing about positive habits: It isn't that important which habits you practice, as long as they are beneficial and they work for you. What matters is that you commit to them and that you do them every day. Just like developing hustle is really about doing the work, practicing positive habits is about committing to a routine. A routine guaranteed to move you closer to greatness, especially if you develop positive habits related to the other lessons in the book: creating a vision, overcoming adversity, cultivating a champion's mindset, developing hustle, mastering your body, building a team, and being of service.

If you are like I was before I watched my friend Graham turn his life around and propel himself into the highest echelons of CrossFit like a blond-haired kangaroo, you might need help figuring out which positive habits are worth practicing. And to be honest, I still struggle with that at times. That's why, whenever I meet great people, I have a little habit (or I suppose it is a *meta*habit) I make sure I do. I try to observe them for positive habits to learn what made them great. I often explicitly ask about their habits when they appear on my podcast. The reason? I want to see which habits I should deploy in my own life.

In early 2014, *Entrepreneur* magazine ran a story about this very subject on their Web site. It featured a cool info graphic that showed the daily habits of the wealthiest people in the world. While making money is only one element of greatness (it is not everything by any means), there is something to be said for how their habits translate over to success in other areas of life.

These are their habits.

1. Maintain a to-do list.
2. Wake up 3+ hours before work (to set themselves up for the day).
3. Listen to audiobooks during commutes (or you can read, if you take public transportation, or listen to my podcast!).
4. Network 5+ hours each month.
5. Read 30+ minutes each day.
6. Exercise 4 days a week (I recommend 5 days myself, with daily movement, of course).
7. Eat minimal junk food.

8. Watch 1 hour or less of TV a day.

9. Teach good daily success habits to their children.

10. Make their children volunteer 10+ hours per month (I encourage you to do it with them to set the example).

11. Encourage their children to read 2+ books per month (I didn't read much as a kid and wish I would have).

12. Write down their goals.

13. Focus on accomplishing a specific goal.

14. Believe in lifelong educational self-improvement.

15. Believe good habits create opportunities.

16. Believe bad habits have a negative impact.

Following all of these habits won't guarantee that you'll become rich or that you will immediately achieve whatever form of greatness you are after, but they can't hurt, and they could very well be the springboard you were looking for!

I have incorporated a number of these habits into my life. Here are the daily habits I focus on the most.

1. Wake up early and say thank you for being alive another day (not 3 hours early, but it's an ongoing practice!).

2. Make my bed!

3. Meditate for 10 minutes.

4. Drink a green juice at breakfast.

5. Stretch and move my body.

6. Have a high-intensity training workout.

7. Eat organic, home-cooked meals.

8. Watch very little TV (for 4 years I didn't even own a set so that I would stay focused).

9. Focus on my goals and take action steps toward them.

10. Network with a purpose to give to others.

11. Acknowledge others and smile in every conversation.

12. Express gratitude throughout the day and the last thing before bed.

13. Work with a coach and mentors.

14. Constantly learn new information and skills.

Here are a handful of other habits I've picked up and adopted from some of the greats I've met along my path.

Be your word. I learned this when I was 11 years old from my father when he caught me stealing money one day. I remember lying to him about it and then feeling a tremendous amount of guilt and shame from the consequences of my actions after he found out the truth. He taught me that those emotions that made me feel sick inside were the result of not being your word. This meant simply doing what you say you are going to do when you say you're going to do it. Not lying is part of being your word. A friend of mine once said that as long as we are breathing, we will always be breaking our word. I'm not perfect, but it's something I strive for every day. The easiest way to make a person feel unappreciated or like they don't matter is to break your word to them or fail to follow through without a renegotiation (of what time you'll show up to a meeting, what they can expect from you, etc.). Being dependable to other people makes it easier for you to depend on yourself. Honoring your commitments to other people makes it easier to honor the commitment you have made to yourself when you created your vision for greatness.

Focus on gratitude. This is a habit I picked up from Tony Robbins. In his book *Awaken the Giant Within,* he talks a lot about gratitude and said that even if you do not feel grateful, you can always ask yourself, "What *could* I be grateful for?" I've found this to be a great mindset habit that works when you're stuck. A few years ago, when I had Ramit Sethi on my podcast, it struck me in the middle of the interview that I wanted to thank this person whom I looked up to and had learned so much from. (His *New York Times* best-selling book helped me get out of debt from the student loans I had. It was a major game changer in my life when I completed that.)

I don't know why, but saying that was hard. I guess I was worried it might come out weird. People wait their whole life to be acknowledged, and most of the time they only get it when they graduate from school or after it's too late and they are dead (this is the story of at least half of the famous impressionist painters whose priceless works hang in the world's most prestigious galleries). Why wait? I've realized. Every night I recount in my head what I am grateful for. My voice-mail message is about gratitude. And like I did with Ramit, I try to tell people in person how much they've done for me. In fact, you could say that this book is an exercise in gratitude, too!

Have a morning ritual. I learned the importance of a morning ritual from Tim Ferriss. He told me, "I think for entrepreneurs, it's very valuable for a week, for instance, to just figure out what your ritual is going to be in the morning or when you wake up. What is the first 60 minutes going to look like, and then script it out so that you do the same thing every day. I think it's a very freeing experience to allocate more thought power to the things that matter as opposed to trying to decide what you should have for breakfast today. I think ritual and routine are extremely important for people who want to be creative."

It doesn't have to be complicated. Here is my morning ritual on most days when I'm not traveling.

- Wake up and express to myself what I'm grateful for.
- Do a guided meditation for 10 minutes and visualize what I want to create in the world that day.
- Perform light stretching and simple yoga poses.
- Make my bed and brush my teeth.
- Work out for 30 to 60 minutes.
- Shower and get dressed.
- Have a green juice with my vitamins and breakfast.

Only then do I get into what I'm creating for the day with my business and vision.

Let go of reaction. Building a habit to let go, to not take anything personally, is a great way to reduce stress in your body. So when someone cuts you off on the high-way, don't flip them off or curse or react in a negative way; instead, relax your body, take a deep breath, and focus on how safe you are and what you are most grateful for in the moment/day that is bigger than yourself and bigger than someone cutting you off.

Express your wants and needs. So many people shy away from expressing and communicating what they want and need (in life, relationships, business deals, and marriage; with their teammates, etc.). They bottle up their feelings and emotions, and it comes back to make them resentful or frustrated later. Of all the people in my life, my mom taught me this most clearly. She has always been big on open communication and being clear on what you want. Ask questions when you aren't sure about something instead of going along with it, and speak up to discuss what is on your mind even if you don't like confrontation.

Acknowledge others (and yourself). Similar to how I expressed my gratitude to Ramit, getting in the habit of acknowledging others is a powerful tool because our natural tendency is to deflect attention from the crowd. It's a defense mechanism. By acknowledging others—for their contribution, for their assistance, for their existence—you acknowledge their humanity and, in turn, your own. I saw the immediate impact and power of this habit in talking and working with Chris Lee. I watched him help others acknowledge those around them, and the change was almost instantaneous. This is incredibly important in the pursuit of greatness, because you will never get there alone. You need a team that will be your support system. The only way that team works is if you acknowledge each other for all the great things you do and are.

Be vulnerable. I also learned about the importance of being vulnerable and willing to discuss the past from Chris Lee, who showed me how to open up about some of the darkest moments in my childhood. He helped me share things I'd never told anyone before and exposed me to the freedom that resulted from that naked vulnerability. Not only is it a great virtue that helps build self-confidence, but getting in the habit of discussing the past instead of bottling it up is also the only way you will learn from your mistakes and grow as a person. Greatness is about getting better every day—at life, at business, at relationships, at whatever your vision is—and you can't do that if you keep making the same mistakes over and over again.

They say love is about the willingness to be completely vulnerable, but so is success in anything you do. Graham Holmberg doesn't become a CrossFit champion and Shawn Johnson doesn't become an Olympic champion unless they push themselves to the limit of their abilities and the brink of exhaustion—that is physical vulnerability. Angel Martinez doesn't help build Reebok into a footwear juggernaut without taking some serious risks in the early 1980s, just out of a recession, by going all in on an aerobics shoe—that is economic vulnerability.

This was one of the hardest habits for me to learn, because there is a lot from my past that for a long time I was trying to erase or forget or run away from. It's no coincidence that once I turned to face it and allowed myself to be vulnerable enough that I could talk about it openly with people that everything I was working toward started to take off!

I am not going to sit here and tell you that developing and practicing positive habits will be easy or fun all the time. It can be very hard, especially at the beginning. You'll have lapses, and that's okay. You just need to keep your eyes focused on your vision, harness your resolve to persevere against those temporary failures, and bust your butt like the champion you want to become. That is the price of greatness. Like Benjamin Franklin said, "Energy and persistence conquer all things." What I can tell you, however, is that slowly but surely you will begin to make strides and reap the rewards. And when that happens, you will embrace these positive habits with the same energy with which you are pursuing your own greatness.

EXERCISE #1:
The Attitude of Gratitude

As I mentioned in Chapter 2, by expressing gratitude in all areas of your life, you can fight internal and external adversity. If you concentrate on what you have, you'll always have more. If you concentrate on what you don't have, you'll never have enough. Cultivating positivity takes work. I'm not suggesting you can't ever have a bad day, but life is better if you develop an attitude of gratitude. Your homework for the next 2 weeks is simple and straightforward and, if done right, will begin to shift your entire perspective on how you interact with everyone in your life. For the past year, I have made it a habit to tell whomever I'm with at the end of my day the three things I'm grateful for. It's awesome.

By doing this every day, you'll consciously begin looking for things to be grateful for. You'll feel more alive and receptive to the goodness that comes in your life, and you'll increase your joy of simple moments.

Some things that you might want to express gratitude for:

- Catching up with a friend you haven't spoken to in a while
- The great workout you had this morning
- Landing a new client and booking the gig
- Completing any project you were working on
- The love you received today

No matter how bad your day is, there is so much to be appreciated. The fact that you are alive and have been given another day is a huge gift. We have so much to be grateful for, including the essentials and basics—the food we eat, our environment, our health, our friends.

Share your gratitude and give it away. This is something you should do when things are going well in your life *and* when everything seems to be against you.

These small things might feel completely irrelevant and trivial in comparison to your goals or your vision, and I understand that, but what you need to understand is that the effects these small things have on your life bleed into all areas—not just one.

EXERCISE #2:
Write Your Habits Manifesto

This is straight from the Gretchen Rubin playbook of building good habits. She published her own Habits Manifesto in 2014.

HABITS MANIFESTO

What we do *every day* matters more than what we do *once in a while.*

Make it easy to do right and hard to go wrong.

Focus on actions, not outcomes.

By giving something up, we may gain.

Things often get harder before they get easier.

When we give more to ourselves, we can ask more from ourselves.

We're not very different from other people, but those differences are *very* important.

It's easier to change our surroundings than ourselves.

We can't make people change, but when we change, others may change.

We should make sure the things we do to feel *better* don't make us feel *worse.*

We manage what we monitor.

Once we're ready to begin, begin *now.*

Contemplate the dozen statements Gretchen makes. Think about each of them as they relate to your life. How do they apply? What would you add or take away or change? Why?

Now look back to page 162 at the lists of positive habits I compiled for myself and the wealthiest people in the world. Make a checklist to see if you are doing any of them or if you are doing the opposite.

Then look for three things on those lists that you can add to your daily routine for the next 2 weeks, and start applying them right now. It almost doesn't matter which three you choose to start. After the 2 weeks, assess where you are in your life, how you are feeling, and if you see the value in these habits.

After those 2 weeks, add three more habits to your routine and adjust the others to support your vision until you are on track to living a life full of positive habits. I'm not perfect and I don't always have my habits in check, so I don't expect you to either. But when you set a foundation of positive habits, the rewards that manifest down the line are almost always far better than you can imagine. And they get you that much closer to achieving your vision and that much farther down the path toward greatness.

EXERCISE #3:
The 28-Day Morning Routine Challenge

Small changes lead to big shifts. What you do when you wake up sets your pace for the day. And while goal setting, vision casting, and the power of intention are all extremely important, greatness is about taking action toward change.

This month your challenge is a *daily morning* challenge.

This exercise will be like setting the refresh button on how you begin each day. The 28-day challenge is long enough to reset a bad habit and propel you into greatness. Completing this challenge will make you more efficient and focused with your time. Your time is valuable, and I want you to attack this challenge as intentionally as you can with how you spend it.

For the next 4 weeks, you're committing to an action you will be taking on this month to work toward your vision. This challenge is forcing you to break through and commit to the simple (and possibly mundane) tasks that will help you lead a life of greatness.

Choose from one of the following to do every morning before you check your e-mail or phone or do any work.

- Spend 30 minutes writing as soon as you wake up (journaling your goals, free writing from your heart, writing about your vision/struggles/dream).
- Make your bed—this is something I do every morning, as it gives me a sense of completion early in the day.
- Make a to-do list for the day. Create a list of your top priorities or the most important things you need to accomplish that day.
- Work out, stretch, or go on a walk to get up and moving first thing in the morning before distractions get in the way.
- Sit down and eat breakfast. This may seem simple, but instead of grabbing the coffee and bagel to go/ in your car and eating mindlessly, set time before you leave in the morning to prepare and enjoy a healthy, balanced breakfast.

The decision of what to do in the morning is your own, but make it something that, even in a small way, supports your bigger vision. Establishing a morning routine sets the tone for the rest of the day—so select one that can propel you forward in achieving your dreams.

COACHING TIP

It is absolutely critical that you weigh the price and the reward for the decisions you make on a daily basis. And don't kid yourself—everything has a price and a reward. There is a reward for good habits (growth), and there is a reward for bad ones (instant gratification). Unfortunately, the prices for each are way out of whack. And oftentimes, the price can be your ultimate vision. You need to figure out which habits give you the best chance of reaching your goals.

It's time to get connected to your vision, understand its power, and realize that it's not worth the instant gratification that bad habits pay out to you. Because when you put positive habits in place, you set yourself up to win. Period. When you don't have them in place, something almost always falls out of order in your life and you will likely not know why. It's time to step up and get serious with your daily actions, as this is what builds the momentum in your life toward the vision you want to achieve.

GET GROUNDED

Having played sports my entire life, I know the importance of playing with a powerful team and what kind of team to look for when your goal is greatness. With every season in sports and in life, there will always be a different role that we play or that others around us play. Sometimes we'll be the star, and other times we'll need to take a supportive role. We must learn to flow with the changes as we grow and bring on new opportunities and experiences in life. I used to try to do everything on my own when people would "let me down," and I thought I'd go through life solo proving others wrong. That ended up emotionally draining me and was stressful beyond belief (not to mention very lonely). It wasn't until I began allowing others to support my dreams and me that life started to come to me with ease.

If you've been playing solo in your life, I want you to open up to the possibility of what a team could look like moving forward. That might require you to adjust your attitude and mindset or find a whole new team altogether. Let's dive in here and see what comes up for you with my exercises at the end of this chapter.

CHAPTER 7

BUILD A
WINNING TEAM

Justin Bieber has sold millions of records, toured hundreds of cities, performed in front of thousands of people, and personally made hundreds of millions of dollars in a handful of years. If you sat down and asked him how this could have happened, how he could have gone from uploading little videos of himself singing on YouTube to being one of the biggest stars in the history of music, he would give you a single name: Scooter Braun.

That is the hugely successful talent manager who discovered Bieber from a YouTube video when the megastar was only 14 years old and living in Canada. At just 34 years old—still a kid himself by some people's standards—Scooter emerged as one of the music industry's most influential and intelligent people for one reason: He knew how to build a winning team. It's not just about finding talented individuals (creative, management, or otherwise), he realized. The path to platinum status and personal greatness is about turning those people into a team. It's a lesson understood by leading figures across disciplines;

their experience—as well as my own—shows that greatness simply cannot be achieved in a vacuum or through a solitary effort.

Scooter learned this invaluable lesson from an unlikely and unwitting mentor: legendary NBA coach Phil Jackson. As a kid, Scooter wanted to be a basketball player. And like most kids, at some point he realized he wasn't tall enough. It usually happens when you're pretending to be Michael Jordan, down by two, with the clock winding down, and then someone who seems the size of Shaquille O'Neal eats your lunch. When that moment occurs, some kids hang up their kicks while others channel their love of the sport in a different direction. In Scooter's case, he picked up Phil Jackson's classic book, *Sacred Hoops.* By the time he closed the back cover, he had decided he wanted to be a coach. It was there that he fell in love with the idea of creating the perfect winning team.

CULTIVATE STRONG RELATIONSHIPS

Scooter built his first real-life team in college as a nightclub promoter. He learned early on that cultivating strong relationships in business and in life is a basic building block for greatness. Which is why today, if you spent some time in the offices of Scooter's company, SB Projects— considered to be one of the most important music firms in the business—you'd see a team made up of his best friends and contacts, some dating back to high school.

Talking to Scooter about the intersection of his personal and professional relationships made me realize

just how important my own relationships have been
on my journey toward greatness—particularly in
business and sports. With sports, I've been on great
teams and awful ones. I've also been on great teams
that lost and awful teams that won. But it was the ones
that were so toxic and disconnected that I literally
wanted to quit (and sometimes did) that had the greatest impact.

I remember my freshman year at Southwest Minnesota State playing for a coach whose style of leadership
resembled a potent mix of Bobby Knight and the drill
sergeant from *Full Metal Jacket.* If you did something
wrong, he got up and screamed in your face. If you
didn't do something fast enough, he took great pains
(and pleasure) in calling you out in front of everyone—
humiliating you. There is nothing worse than being on
a team with that kind of negative energy. It brings
everyone else down. It's not like we wanted to fail. We
all wanted to win. We all wanted to succeed and do our
best. It was our coach's belief that the best way to do
that wasn't to build relationships with his team and
create unstoppable winning chemistry but instead to
scare us to victory by making us more afraid of losing
than excited about winning.

Needless to say, his leadership style didn't work for
me nor for many of my teammates. Our team never really
gelled. We looked ahead to each game on the schedule not
as an opportunity to get better but as 1 week closer to
the end of this miserable experience. But that team, miserable though it may have been, taught me one of the

most valuable lessons I've learned: You need to get everyone rowing in the same direction, and the only way you
do this effectively is by cultivating the kinds of strong
relationships where heading in the same direction feels
like the only option. And that direction can't be as far
away from you as they can possibly get either: At best,
you will go nowhere. What's more likely is that their
numbers will overwhelm your singular force of will, and
you'll head in the wrong direction.

This phenomenon is especially true in dysfunctional
workplaces and families. Many of us have suffered in jobs
where you are on edge every day, waiting for your boss to
yell at you or call out your mistakes in front of everyone,
never acknowledging you for the hard work you put in
day in and day out. At home, with parents always yelling
at each other (or at you), never feeling like your talents
are being nurtured or cultivated, all you can do is put
your head down and simply do your best to survive without getting punished.

The best companies and families are great teams. The
importance of building winning teams and the principles
that go into them aren't just about sports, they're about
all areas of life, all of the time.

SURROUND YOURSELF WITH GREATNESS

Building a powerful team is obviously important, but how
do you know the difference between a good team and a

bad one? How do you make sure that you have a winning team behind you or, even better, feel like you are just one player on a team that is changing the world together?

These were questions I was not equipped to answer on my own. This was probably the main reason I decided to start (and attend) the School of Greatness, so I could connect a collection of professors and teachers to my own winning team and join them in the great things they were doing.

Don Yaeger is the author of seven best-selling books and is best known for his collaborations with Hall of Fame running back Walter Payton and another famed basketball coach, John Wooden. The most important lesson Coach Wooden ever taught Don was this: You will never outperform your inner circle. If you want to achieve outer success, improve your inner circle.

This is what Don passed on to me in my time with him. Our capacity for success and greatness is embodied by the people we surround ourselves with. If you aspire to greatness, make sure that you have greatness around you. For Don, this was an eye-opening insight that applied not only to basketball and his projects with John and other athletes but also to life in general.

"I find myself, all the time, thinking about my inner circle," Don admitted. "Who's in it? Who should be in it? Whether or not some people maybe need to have a different spot in the circle."

The difficulty lies in the fact that some people who have been in your circle for years, often by default, can't simply be cut off. Don was talking specifically about family members.

"Let's be honest, you can't get rid of a family member, right? So what I realized was rather than the amount of time I was allotting every week to conversation, maybe it's half that. It really is a great challenge, but governing who you put in your circle is one of those places where your decision making will impact you greatly."

Now here's the million-dollar question you need to ask yourself. It's a question Don asked me, and I'm sure Coach Wooden asked him numerous times over their 12 years working together: How is this model for greatness different when we're talking about sports as opposed to business or relationships or life? The answer, of course, is that it's not.

Think about it: A successful book (as I hope this one will be) requires the right editors, the right publisher, the right publicists, the right designers, the right researchers, and the right support staff—all of whom will make you better, none of whom will waste your time. Without excellence in each of those areas, it is impossible to have an excellent and successful book. Don has hit the *New York Times* nonfiction bestseller list seven times. According to him, there are fewer than 50 individuals to ever accomplish that. Don didn't do this alone; he did it with the help of his team.

As transformative as this insight was for Don—after collaborating with Coach Wooden, Don's focus shifted toward mentorship and greatness and the notion of "paying it forward"—it was equally so for me, if only a little

different. I'd heard before how you are the average of the
five people you spend the most time with, for better or
worse. But that advice was related to happiness and
self-improvement. I'd never heard it like this, in relation
to teams and to success and greatness. Then Don hit me
with another John Wooden quote: "You show me your
friends, and I'll show you your future."

That brought it home for me and the entire purpose
behind the School of Greatness. Think about Rich Roll
and his wife, Julie Piatt, who was the one who bought him
the bike that changed his life. She was the catalyst and
inspiration for him to get back to working out and change
his entire health lifestyle. Or Kyle Maynard and Shawn
Johnson, whose parents supported and facilitated their
passions—from football and wrestling to ballet and gymnastics. Or Angel Martinez and the elderly relatives who
took him in and gave him the opportunity to have and
pursue the American dream.

Each of these great men and women had friends and
family who pushed them to be greater, who ensured that
they would have a world-changing future. Beware of people who instead will drag you down or make you feel bad
for having ambition. Sometimes it's hard to be honest
with yourself about relationships like that when you're
focused on achieving your vision and living your dream.
But it's important to take a step back every once in a
while and look at your inner circle. Are they pushing you
to be great? Are they supporting your dream? Because
that's what a winning team does, that's what it looks like,
and that's why you need to have one.

FIND THE RIGHT MENTOR(S)

Let's say you are one of those people who has to rebuild your inner circle, and you're trying to figure out the first person to add to your winning team. Who is it? It's the coach. Your mentor. Your advisor. Your father/mother figure. Their role on your path to greatness is literally invaluable.

The writer Denis Waitley has an apt analogy that I'd like to borrow and paraphrase here, from an article titled "The Champion Within" from his very popular newsletter.

He uses an example relating new military technology to mentors. A missile system that was introduced during the Gulf War in 1991 was revolutionary because it would self-adjust its trajectory to ensure that it kept its target in range. Likewise, as Denis says, "A highly motivated person, when he or she has targeted a worthwhile goal, uses a coach or mentor the same way a missile uses the new guidance system—to assist you in making adjustments and navigating difficult, uncertain, ever-changing terrain."

Without the right mentor, we're like an unguided missile on the path to greatness. If we're lucky, we'll end up exactly where we need to go. But that's only if everything goes precisely as planned. Life never seems to happen that way, though—especially when we're trying to do something different, something more. What we need is someone who can not only help us set our original course but also constantly correct and guide us through the problems and adversity we will inevitably face.

This brings us back to Scooter. His first mentor was Jermaine Dupri, a successful record producer, songwriter, and rapper, whom he met while promoting parties and eventually ended up working for. Dupri taught him the music business and how to work with artists. But Scooter didn't stop there. "Sometimes people say they have one mentor. I've never had one mentor," he told me. "If I had one mentor, it'd be my father, but I have other really great mentors as well: people like Jeffrey Katzenberg and Lucian Grainge, who's the chairman of Universal Music Group. We're very close, and he's been an incredible mentor and friend. David Geffen has become a mentor to me as well. Those kinds of people I'm eternally grateful to because they allow me to draw from them."

When Scooter reached out to Justin Bieber and sketched out a path for the young singer's career, it was these ideas that he founded it on. Without the right friends, without the right guidance, without the right team (along with all the hard work and talent he had), there was no way that Bieber would break through. We are so heavily influenced by the people we spend the most time with that we can't afford to leave it up to chance. Being selective about mentors, friends, and partners is going to be one of the biggest factors in the journey to greatness.

Point being, it's extremely important—I'd even say absolutely necessary—to find the right coaches for you if you want to achieve greatness in any area of your life. Can you be successful without them? Of course. But the greatest athletes in the world all have coaches even when they are at the peak of their game. In fact, they want coaching and feedback on ways to get better and improve more than anyone. Michael Jordan didn't add all those new moves in the off-season or win all those championships in the postseason without Phil Jackson on the bench. It's important to find coaches who inspire you but also give it to you straight. Ones you can look up to and take their guidance seriously. Ones you can commit to and show that you are willing to take action to achieve your own greatness.

THE POWER OF POSITIVE ENERGY

"I've been able to bring some amazing people into my life and surround myself with people, I think, who are skilled in ways that I am not, and we've been able to scale an incredible business because they make things happen," Scooter said. It's something he teaches his artists, too. They can't do it alone. They can't be successful in isolation. But Scooter looks for something else in addition to talent and smarts: positivity.

"I'm a firm believer that it's more important to have positive energy around you than the smartest people. Now, luckily I've been able to have, in my opinion, some of the smartest people around me who are also positive," he told me. I've found this in my own business. I'd rather have someone who has a tremendous amount of heart and hustle over the most talented person who has an energy of entitlement about them and selfish tendencies.

This is the tricky part about talent within a team: It is a delicate balancing act between the positivity of heart and hustle and the negativity that can arise with the natural competitiveness that develops within teams. Smart, talented people want to achieve. They want to realize the potential that so many—including the person who has hired them—have identified in them. The key is to show them, by example, how everyone individually wins when the team wins. If you allow ego to get in the way, the positive energy you could otherwise harness and direct outward at the competition or the marketplace morphs into negative energy and turns inward. You end up with people competing against each other, or worse, against you, and the vision you have built for your business and your life. Defining precisely what success looks like is a big part of turning the natural competitive instincts of smart, talented, ambitious people into positive, supportive energy instead of negative, destructive, selfish energy.

You see this in sports teams as well, where a team of "average" players can beat a team of All-Stars if they work together, are positive, and stick to the game plan. The way they win is by passing the ball and working within the system, not trying to do too much by themselves. Instead, they understand that everyone has their role, and they stick to that role. If everyone does their own job and doesn't try to win the game alone, then they give themselves a chance to win. After all, you can't hit a game-winning grand slam until you have players on base.

"I learned that lesson the hard way," Scooter admitted to me. "I had some negativity in my life before, and you start to question yourself because negativity projects onto you. You start to look in the mirror and say, 'Am I really a good person? Am I doing the right thing?' That isn't you. That's their bullshit feeding on you." You've got to have positive energy to create winning chemistry. It's that simple.

It reminds me of a quote by Edmund Lee, who encouraged people to "surround yourself with the dreamers and the doers, the believers and the thinkers, but most of all, surround yourself with those who seek greatness within you even when you don't see it yourself."

Beyond surrounding yourself with these positive people, it's also important that you build a network of them. Bill Clinton, in his rise from a broken home to the governorship of Arkansas to the presidency, created a network of some 10,000 physical note cards containing the names, addresses, and relationship history of classmates, professors, friends, lawyers, donors, supporters, reporters, and influencers that he could cultivate and call on when needed. He became not just a connector, as Malcolm Gladwell described and I tried to emulate on

LinkedIn, but a *superconnector*—working every room, schmoozing every influencer, charming every guest. Eventually, he digitized this system and continues to use it to this day for his work with the Clinton Foundation. He is living proof that, as my friend and networking expert Porter Gale puts it, "your network is your *net worth*."

PUTTING IT ALL TOGETHER

But not every talented and positive team wins, as we know. There is more to greatness than that. It takes strategy and leadership. This was something I also asked Scooter about. How do you ensure that you get the most out of your team?

"You've got to realize," he told me, "the only way to scale is to delegate and to empower others and to say, 'You know what? They're not going to do it exactly like me, but they're going to do it exactly like them.'" You have to be okay with the fact that some people will be better than you at certain things in the long run. Why should that threaten you? Isn't that why you brought them on in the first place? There is always friction on any team. With a bench player picking up the starting job (which means kicking someone else to the bench), with new hires, as people get raises and increase their "rank" in companies, there will always be competition and egos that come out.

Being transparent in the beginning about the importance of communication and clearing up any misunderstandings with people so no one holds on to frustration is an essential part of a winning team. The "clearing" process, or open communication, will allow the team to have break-throughs in stressful situations instead of breakdowns and implosion.

Scooter brought the analogy home to me after we played a pickup basketball game together: "That's the same idea as when we play basketball. Sometimes you're going to make a great assist and a guy's going to miss that easy shot, and you're going to be frustrated because that was another assist on your stat line. But at the end of the day, it isn't about our individual stat line, it's about winning the game." The key, even if the missed gimme layup was the difference between victory and defeat, is to communicate with your teammate about what happened. Like we talked about in Chapter 6, you need to let go of reaction and get on the same page about what went wrong and what went right, so you can go back out there tomorrow and do it all over again, together. After all, as Scooter reminded me, "you cannot win the game on your own."

Jack Welch, former CEO and chairman of General Electric, who knows a thing or two about building a winning team, has written things on this subject that very much apply to what Scooter was talking about. In an article for *Newsweek* a few years ago, he and his wife, Suzy Welch, wrote, "First, the leaders of winning teams always—always—let their people know where they stand... Second, winning teams know the game plan." It's your job, as you assemble your team, to let them know what's important and create a plan for them to follow. Not a plan that's all about you. Instead, it's about creating a plan in which everyone has a role and everyone's role is designed for them to thrive in. That's what Scooter has done so well.

THE TEAM ISN'T JUST ABOUT THE BUSINESS

There is one final thing I think is worth discussing here, especially as Scooter's most prominent protégé has had no shortage of troubles at various points in his life. Justin Bieber has been arrested for DUI and drag racing in Miami; he's been taken in for egging a neighbor's house in Calabasas, California; he's been charged with hitting a limo driver in Toronto; he tagged a hotel wall in Brazil and ran through customs and passport control in Turkey. Yet Scooter stood by him. Perhaps because he knows that all young people, especially famous young people, do dumb things. But I think there is another reason. Scooter doesn't see what he does as being just business. His clients and his employees are his family. And family is everything.

I realized that when I spotted some writing on Scooter's wrist. It was a tattoo. Just one word: *Family.* When I asked him about his family, he lit up. His grandparents were Holocaust survivors. His brother, Adam, whom you'll meet next chapter, is an amazing person doing incredible things. And his parents? The day I interviewed him for the podcast just happened to be his parents' 35th wedding anniversary.

> To have parents who really, truly love each other and are good to each other, and to witness that growing up and to have that love all the time, I always felt full. I always felt safe.

Yet for a period in his late teens and early twenties, Scooter lost sight of that love. He still appreciated it for what it was but not for its role in guiding his life.

"I was lost, and I was chasing the money because I didn't really understand. I was just going for it. What I realized was all I'm doing it for is this," he said as he pointed to the tattoo. Interestingly, he talked about getting that tattoo for a while before going in to get it inked. What finally pushed him to go in and make it real?

The day before, Jay Williams, the former All-American point guard from Duke and the second overall pick in the 2002 NBA Draft by the Chicago Bulls, had gotten into a motorcycle accident that would ultimately end his professional basketball career. "Jay's one of my closest friends," Scooter said. "I had chickened out about getting this tattoo a couple weeks earlier, and when I found out what happened to him, I realized I couldn't take that for granted anymore."

Add to the mix the fact that his mother had fallen ill during that period—she's fine now, thank goodness—and you can see the power and meaning this tattoo carries for Scooter.

"For the rest of my life, people will ask me about this tattoo," he told me, "and I will have to tell this story of why I got it, which is this simple, and it will remind me for the rest of my life what's really important."

But how can work and family be the same? Much like Don Yaeger talked about, you can't fire someone from being related to you. Okay, so it's not a perfect analogy, but it is important. When I first started my company and I hired people, I used to think that they were there to work *for* me. That almost always ended badly because I set myself and them up to lose. I've since learned that I am actually in service to my team, as well as to everyone else. Just like you are to your family—it's a matter of give and take, mutual respect, and, ultimately, gratitude and love.

What I try to think about after learning about great teams from Scooter and Don Yaeger is this: How can I be of service to every member of my team and set them up to win as best as possible? This doesn't mean I need to hold everyone's hand daily or coddle them; it simply means that I make sure that if anyone ever needs to talk about anything, I'm always there to listen, and that they are set up with what they need to be successful in their position and their role.

Together we win *as a team.* Not just me, not just a paycheck for them, but a winning team, aiming for and achieving greatness.

EXERCISE #1:
Take Inventory of Your Relationships

It's not always easy to find quality people to be on your team. You might go through some disappointing relationships before you find the right people, but don't compromise. If you let a few difficult experiences convince you to go it alone, you'll hamstring yourself. I look back on my career-ending injury, and I had many mentors during that time, but I specifically attribute my transition into business to one man who I am forever grateful to have met— Chris Hawker. Chris was a successful inventor and could have easily brushed me aside when I so eagerly requested to work with him. Instead, I showed him the value I could bring, so he took me under his wing and shared his wisdom and experience with me. Think about the people you most look up to versus the people you spend the most time with. If those lists are drastically different, fix that. Reach out to your role models and mentors and involve them in your journey. Cut out those people you spend a lot of time with who are not helping you on your path to greatness.

To find out if someone is serving you in your life or holding you back, ask yourself these four questions.

1. Do I feel energized or stressed when I'm around or think about this person?
2. Does this person inspire me or have a negative mindset around me?
3. Does this person pursue greatness in their life, or are they often a victim to circumstances?
4. Do they get excited about my success and want to see me succeed, or do they complain about their own life when I achieve my dreams?

If your answers left you on the positive side, then it sounds like this person is still a great team member in your life! If they are on the energy-draining side, however, you may want to have a "clearing conversation" with them and let them know how you feel about your relationship. Come from a loving place when you talk to them about this and don't fault them for anything. Then make your request for how you'd like to be in relationship moving forward and what you can expect from them moving forward.

EXAMPLES OF CLEARING CONVERSATIONS

Hi, (friend/colleague). I appreciate the time we share together. I have created a new vision for my life, and I am making a commitment to being more positive. I feel like the conversations we tend to have are negative and not productive, and I take responsibility for this. Are you open to working on this with me?

Hi, (parent/spouse/friend). I love you and appreciate you. I
have taken a stand in my life to work on my goals and not
fixate on the stress in life. I want to focus my energy on what
I'm grateful for and not complain about what I do not have.
Do you support me and stand to keep me to my word?

Most relationships don't work because people don't
clearly communicate their requests in a loving way; it
usually comes in the form of an attack, which rarely
solves anything. You don't need to tell them where they
are not supporting, but let them choose to support you in
the way you need. This is the path of least confrontation.
If you are like me, you want to get clear with all your
friends, colleagues, and family in the most direct yet least
aggressive way possible.

Hi, (parent/colleague/friend). I want to start by saying I
appreciate you, and I request of you . . .

Hi, (boyfriend/girlfriend/significant other). I care about your
vision, but you seem to be off course and you are also
steering me off course by . . . Let's commit ourselves to . . .

If the relationship doesn't shift over a specific
period of time that you define with the person you are
trying to get clear with, and you continue to need to
make that request, then it's another sign that you may
want to distance yourself from the person and start
surrounding yourself with a more positive inner circle
for your team.

Always try to take action together, but if extreme
measures need to be taken, that is when the power of
no comes into play. It takes strength to remove someone
from your life or take a step back from that person's

energy. Understand that nothing is more important than your emotional well-being. This drain will undoubtedly hold you back from greatness. This exercise is a game changer.

EXERCISE #2:
Join or Create a Mastermind

A mastermind is a group of influential individuals who support you to take your business or life to the next level. With the collective mind of the group, you find support, information, and resources to serve you on your path. And you will get there much faster than trying to do it on your own.

I was just starting out in my business when I joined my first mastermind with an online marketing group. It was essentially a 2-day meeting where we sat at a round table with a group of 15 other online marketing business professionals and shared best practices and ideas and supported each other on our specific goals. The power of the mastermind lies with the people in it and the opportunities you can create from that network. In this first meeting, I ended up sitting next to someone who directly helped me make $250,000 over the next 3 months by selling my products as an affiliate partner and referring me to five others who promoted my product as well. This was a huge boost to everything we were doing at the time, accelerating our profits and success much faster than we ever could have without the mastermind.

Masterminds were the key ingredient for me in taking my business from six figures to seven figures so quickly. There is no other way it would have grown that quickly. It's essential to be a part of at least one mastermind (if not more), and I highly recommend being the creator and leader of one yourself at some point, too.

Napoleon Hill, the legendary author of *Think and Grow Rich*, has a great way to think about masterminds: "the coordination of knowledge and effort of two or more people, who work toward a definite purpose, in the spirit of harmony." This isn't actually his description of mastermind groups—it's really one of his main principles for how to become successful. The fact that those two concepts overlap so fully—masterminds and being successful—is not a coincidence in my mind.

If you're still not sold, or if someone has given you a negative impression of masterminds, let me try to clear things up for you. Here is what masterminds are or can be.

- Teams of influencers in your community connected for a purpose
- A catalyst for business and personal growth
- A space for goals and holding each other accountable
- A peer advisory board
- An education, support, and brainstorming group
- Confidential
- A commitment
- A group of people supporting each other to create the life/business they want

- Supportive of your success
- A group of people who have your best interest in mind

Here is what masterminds are not or should never be.

- Group therapy

Masterminds are meant to help you attain your major purpose in life by borrowing the wisdom and using the education, experience, and influence of other people who are mutually invested in your success. When run right, they allow you to accomplish in the next 6 to 12 months more than you could accomplish without them in your entire life if you depended solely upon yourself.

There are two essential components to every successful mastermind group: the right attitude and the right members. You can have one without the other and get by okay, but we're not interested in that. We're not interested in settling. This book is not called *The School of Average*. It's about greatness, so that's what we're going to strive for: a great mastermind, with a great attitude and great members.

The mastermind attitude looks like this. You are:

- Friendly and cooperative
- Noncompetitive
- Willing to be creative and brainstorm ideas/ solutions for others' businesses
- Supportive of each other with total honesty, respect, and compassion
- Not ever, at any point, indifferent

Think of your mastermind as your basketball dream team. It is a group of differently yet equally talented peers who are there to support your success. Thus, selecting members for your own mastermind group should look like this. They should have:

- A strong commitment to the group
- Similar success and experience
- An agreement about the mastermind attitude
- An agreement on written guidelines created by and for the group
- The ability to give and take equally when it comes to advice, support, and resources

Ultimately, your mastermind group should start with 4 to 6 people (up to 15 max) and a simple (no more than one page) mastermind agreement you're all aligned with that includes:

- The group name
- How you're going to connect (in person or via Skype, GoToMeeting, Google Hangouts, or phone)
- How long your meetings will be (1 to 2 hours minimum is recommended, but some could be 2 or 3 days)
- How often you will meet (weekly, monthly, quarterly, etc.)
- When you will meet
- The agenda for your meetings

Understand all this about masterminds and follow this process with purpose and intentionality, and you are on your way to building a winning team for your business and your life. For more information on this and the different masterminds to join, go to schoolofgreatness.com/resources.

EXERCISE #3:
The Three Lists to Freedom

This exercise I learned from my friend and "Virtual CEO" Chris Ducker. Chris is the author of *Virtual Freedom,* a book that teaches people how to work with virtual staff in order to have more time for themselves while at the same time being more productive. This was specifically designed for businesspeople but is easily adapted to use in your life. It will fundamentally change how you manage both life and business.

Get a piece of paper and a pen. Create three columns with the following headlines:

- Things you don't like doing
- Things you can't do
- Things you shouldn't do

Now fill in all the things that fit in these categories relating to your business or your lifestyle.

The Things You Don't Like Doing

These are the things you procrastinate on all day. Things like replying to social media messages, managing e-mail, doing your bookkeeping, etc. Life and business demand that you get these things done, so it's your job to find someone you can pass them off to or develop a system that allows you to be more efficient.

The Things You Can't Do

Many people, especially entrepreneurs, feel like they have to do a lot of things themselves. The only problem is, there are many things you can't do even if you wanted to. I love design and playing with designs on my computer, but I'm the worst at using design software and designing things myself. After a few hours of intense work, the best I can draw is a bad-looking stick figure of a cat! Just because you have an interest in something or doing it yourself would be cheaper doesn't mean you are qualified to do it at a high level. In fact, your lack of experience and expertise might actually make doing it yourself more costly than hiring a professional, since it would take up more of your valuable time that could otherwise be spent on high-level business and life activities that you're actually good at.

The Things You Shouldn't Do

In my business, I'm very capable of doing a number of different things that I shouldn't be doing even though I like doing some of them. That's just the natural consequence of earning five-figure consulting and speaking fees for a couple hours of my time. It means I shouldn't be spending 15 minutes figuring out what to post on social media or handling customer support. I may be good at those things or like doing them, but they are literally a waste of my time.

Chris Ducker still prepares these lists every 90 days because, he says, we sometimes slip back into bad habits out of necessity or we just get busy with life. I recommend checking in with this as well to see what tasks you can put in these lists and start letting go of them.

DON'T LIKE DOING	CAN'T DO	SHOULDN'T DO
Checking e-mail	Graphic design	Updating social media
Managing my calendar	Developing a Web site	Handling customer support
Handling basic inquiries	Editing podcast episodes	Managing company blog
Researching travel	Bookkeeping and accounts	Collecting dry cleaning

This becomes the road map to working with your team. These lists flag the jobs that aren't the best uses of your time with the skills you have for making a bigger impact and getting closer to your vision. They indicate how to best set up your team or support structure.

When I first started in business, I worked 15-hour days because I did all of these tasks on my own. I wasn't good at a lot of them, which meant they took me even longer. When I switched my mentality and allowed others to support me and join my team, the stress went away, efficiency went up, and I was able to focus on what I loved doing at all times instead of the things I didn't need to do. My life seemed to come together and flow. It's been like living in a dream world ever since, and it's possible for anyone who is committed to making it happen as well!

Keep in mind that this exercise isn't just for entrepreneurs or for businesses generally. It works as well in your personal life. I hate shopping and get tired in about 30 minutes at the mall, I struggle with cooking (I enjoy doing it, but it rarely tastes as good as it should), and I shouldn't be doing yard work or deep cleaning my place. Based on the time I use in my business and toward making money that I charge for speaking, coaching, or consulting, my time is better spent doing what I'm great at and hiring others on my team for support with those lists as well.

Think of all the things in your personal life that you want to add to this. Even if you don't think you can afford to hire or outsource for some of these tasks, put them on the list anyway. There are tools and apps coming online every day designed to solve these problems and offer support on a friendly budget.

EXERCISE # 4:
The Personality Matrix

The Personality Matrix is a process you can follow to discover not only who you are but also to understand whom you are interacting with on a daily basis. Imagine knowing exactly what to say to someone—a teammate, a family member, a business colleague, a customer—because you know their personality type. Imagine being able to immediately connect with them in a way they understand and relate to. There are a number of personality tests online and different ways of examining them, but I learned about this process from Chris Lee, so it has stuck with me to great success. The Personality Matrix divides people into four main personality styles: promoters, analyzers, controllers, and supporters.

The Promoter (Opposite of an Analyzer)

The gift of a promoter is the ability to contribute and grow many ideas. Their primary challenge is with completing projects. They are the life of the party and have a lot of passion but, because of this challenge, tend to break their word and become overwhelmed.

If you find yourself in the position of trying to sell something to a promoter or get them excited about an idea of yours, there's one reliable way to do it: Show up excited. Be enthusiastic. Talk about your experience and how great it will make them feel.

Promoters are relationship driven, all about fun and energy.

The Analyzer (Opposite of a Promoter)

The gift of an analyzer is that they are detail oriented, disciplined, systematic, process driven, structured, and organized.

If you're selling to an analyzer, you must know everything about what you're working with down to the smallest details.

Analyzers are their word. When an analyzer says they will do something, you can take it to the bank. They lack passion and spontaneity, and they can show up as if they are hardly alive. Analyzers are visual and logical. They are formal in their dress and their energy.

The Controller (Opposite of a Supporter)

The gift of a controller is that they can get things done. They are driven, decisive, confident, goal oriented, and focused.

When you're selling to a controller, you better show up powerfully and dressed well. Agree with them and speak in a leading way that implies that they believe your idea was theirs. Stroke their ego. Connect with them at their level.

Controllers appear insensitive, mean, uncaring, and inflexible, and they pay for it in their personal and business relationships. A controller is dominant and formal. You have to present to them in a dominant, formal way.

The Supporter (Opposite of a Controller)

The gift of a supporter is being a giver focused on emotions, love, acknowledgment, and self-respect.

Selling to a supporter is all about emotion. Discuss the benefits not just to those who would be customers or users but also to everyone around who stands to be better off due to the actions or decisions you're proposing.

Supporters often come off like doormats. They don't stand up for themselves immediately, and it may seem like you're taking advantage of them. The way to avoid that is to provide positive feedback, which they respond to overwhelmingly.

So, which one are you? What is your dominant personality and your secondary personality? Being a leader in relationships requires the ability to access and be flexible with each of these personality types at any given time. If you can match or complement the energy of others around you, you can understand them better, and they will in turn feel more appreciated. Most important, being a successful, productive member of a good team demands that you don't tip too far in any one direction.

Are you an analyzer? Be outrageous!

A controller? Be vulnerable.

A promoter? Keep your word.

A supporter? Tell yourself, "I matter."

COACHING TIP

We are all in this together, and it's time to start living in a world where you embrace this concept. Life flows when you find a team you gel with, so why not start finding the All-Star players right now? The way you do this is by first becoming an All-Star player yourself. Do the work, improve your attitude, hustle, and sharpen your skills so that everyone else wants to make you a starter on their team! When you become a valuable asset to the world, then the world starts giving you what you dream of. It's that simple.

People matter. And you can't achieve anything great on your own. Letting people know how much they matter and how much you care about them is equally important (if not more). The saying goes that "people don't care about how much you know until they know how much you care." This is true in family, sports, business, and any other situation in life. Continue to surround yourself with positive people who care about you and always find ways to create a win-win in every relationship in your life. Relationships are the key to success, and it's time to start investing in yours.

GET GROUNDED

For many years, I thought there had to be a winner and a loser in sports, business, and life. I was so attached to the scoreboard and making sure that my team and I had more points than our opponent that I failed for a long time to grasp the meaning of a full life: creating win-win relationships. I never thought about what happens when you do "win." Then what? Are you just supposed to keep winning and gaining momentum and building an empire of success, yet be the loneliest winner in the world? Or is there more to living a great life?

Slowly but surely, moments happened where I witnessed and started to understand the value of giving back and being in service to others. This may be my most important lesson to date. Making money matters, having your needs met matters, achieving your vision matters, and turning your dreams into reality matters. But if you aren't looking for ways to improve the lives of everyone around you—your family, community, environment, and the world—then what's the point of all of it? In this chapter, we dissect the value of giving back. It's not about looking good or doing it because you feel you are supposed to. I want you to really see why giving to others is so important, because it took an army of people to turn you into the person you are today.

CHAPTER 8

LIVE A LIFE OF SERVICE

One family. Two sons. Two different paths toward greatness.

From the first son, Scooter, we learned about how to assemble a winning team. But it was from the second son, Adam, that I learned one of the most important lessons of all.

I met Adam Braun at a Summit Series conference called Summit at Sea, a kind of summer camp for people who want to change the world. When you see Adam for the first time, he seems like just a regular person, not a superhuman athlete or high-rolling entrepreneur like some of the others you've met in this book. He doesn't have the rock star, Hollywood swagger of his brother. He has an Ivy League pedigree, but I don't think anyone would consider him to be an intimidating genius. He's a regular guy with a big heart, whose high-paying job at a major consulting firm left him dissatisfied and unfulfilled. Like Adam, I, too, had made a little money and had what most people would see as the trappings of success. And as I felt after becoming an All-American in the decathlon, he, too, felt he needed to find some greater purpose, some cause or path to follow.

I could deeply relate to his story that day we met, not just the dissatisfaction but also what it was like to have the shadow of a great sibling follow you and shade your decisions. Given how important my own brother has been to my life, it isn't surprising that I have found myself including brothers as champions of these two chapters. So I consider it serendipity that I encountered Adam—at a conference on a boat, no less—embodying the bold decision to make his life all about giving back.

Adam is the founder of Pencils of Promise, a nonprofit group that has built more than 300 schools and changed the lives of hundreds of thousands of children around the world. Actually, wait, he wouldn't like that I said *nonprofit*. He prefers the term *for purpose.* That purpose is helping kids learn and follow their dreams—kids that most of us pretend don't exist. More recently, his *New York Times* best-selling book, *The Promise of a Pencil,* has brought Adam into a much brighter spotlight, but for the past several years he has been building one of the most important charitable education organizations in the world.

There were two seminal events in Adam's life that set him on his unique path. The first occurred when he was 17 years old and a promising basketball player on an AAU team. His parents made the decision to take in two young athletes from Mozambique named Sam and Cornelio. Not unlike what Leigh Anne and Sean Tuohy did for Michael Oher in a story made famous by Michael Lewis in his book *The Blind Side,* Adam's parents wanted to give these kids a chance to fulfill their potential and experience the American dream. For Adam, his parents' choice was a chance to expand his definition of family by adding two incredible people to it.

Sam was a senior when he came to live with the Braun family. He stayed through his senior year, graduated, then went to Brown University. Cornelio was a sophomore and lived in their house for 3 years before getting a full ride to Georgetown and then transferring to American University after freshman year, from where he ultimately graduated. To this day, Adam considers Sam and Cornelio his brothers. One lives in Los Angeles, the other in DC, and they celebrate all their family events together. Their kids are Adam's nieces and nephews.

"Not only did it change the dynamic of our family, but also it entirely changed my personal worldview. I started to realize the path that Sam and Cornelio had taken was the path that people had taken over generations who wanted to strive for a life that was more than the one that they were born into. It opened my eyes up to how many cultures and people exist outside of that small bubble that I had experienced until that point growing up in Fairfield County, Connecticut, really only seeing New England," he told me.

AN UNLIKELY JOURNEY

This was the first step in Adam's path toward greatness. A step that led to aspirations for living a very different life than most people would consider the norm. As a sophomore at Brown University, inspired by his family experience and the powerful 1992 documentary *Baraka,* Adam enrolled to attend Semester at Sea (noticing a boat theme here?), an academic program aboard a large cruise ship that hosts students from all around the country while circumnavigating the globe and visiting numerous countries over the course of about 100 days. Adam had a friend who had been on Semester at Sea, and upon her return, she could not stop raving about her experience. Their stop in India was particularly transformative for her, which in turn was transformative for him, because it just so happened to be a scene in *Baraka* shot in Varanasi, India, that had enthralled Adam with all the potential the world held outside his bubble.

"So I looked at the Semester at Sea itinerary, and they were going to India. I thought, 'This is it. I'm going to go to India, go to Varanasi, and also get to see all these other incredible places around the world,'" Adam told me. As he spoke, I could hear the purpose in his voice. "Sometimes you just have this inner voice that compels you. It's your future self speaking to your present self, saying, 'Follow me. This is who and what you were meant to be.'"

For a moment, however, it appeared that Adam was meant to be at the bottom of the Pacific Ocean. Eight hundred miles offshore, shortly after leaving port, the Semester at Sea ship was hit by a 60-foot rogue wave that could have easily sunk the boat and taken everyone on board with it. His journey around the world nearly ended before it began. This near-death experience put Adam in a particularly vulnerable and introspective place as they continued their travels from country to country. Here they would come, week after week, working with, meeting, and learning from all these people who didn't have much; yet in nearly every case, they were met with unexpected levels of happiness that, to Adam, seemed so scant in the materialistic culture he'd left just months ago.

I imagine that this is what led to the conversation that completely changed Adam's life: "Everyone on Semester at Sea did this thing where they collect one thing per country—a beer bottle or a funny hat, or they got a T-shirt, or they took a photo of a Beanie Baby in front of a landmark. My thing was asking one kid per country what they would want if they could have anything in the world."

When Adam started telling me this story, the implications for my own life hit me right away. For a college kid to have that kind of awareness of others, that kind of empathy, was inspiring. For all my focus and perseverance and hustle when I was playing sports in high school and college, I was also pretty selfish and egotistical. I thought mostly about myself instead of how I could help the other guys around me, and when I look back on it, I'm pretty sure that held me back from achieving the kind of happiness and success I was looking for. As selfless as Adam's "one thing" was, his worldview was still dominated by his life inside the Connecticut bubble, and he wanted to escape it.

"I expected to get answers from these kids that were similar to what I wanted when I was a kid, which was, like, a big house, a fancy car, and the latest technology," Adam admitted. "But the answers were just so different."

The most powerful one came from a little boy begging on the outskirts of the city of Agra in northern India. Adam asked him, "If you could have anything in the world, what would it be?" His answer was simple: "I want a pencil." That's it. Just a stick of wood with some graphite in it. As you can imagine, he probably wasn't too particular about whether it was a number 2 Dixon Ticonderoga pencil or a fancy mechanical one, he was willing to take anything. Why? This precious little boy wanted to *learn,* to go to school, and he believed the pencil was the thing that would get him there.

Even hearing this conversation gives me inspired chills. I know what you're thinking. It shook Adam to his core, motivated him to give up all his worldly possessions and dedicate himself to changing the world, right? Wrong. It did indeed leave an indelible mark on the young man—but he had a bigger vision than becoming a martyr.

MAKING THE VISION A REALITY

After his semester wrapped up, Adam headed back to America, where he did what many in his position would do: get a job in corporate America where he made tons of money. Seriously. It's almost become a cliché to complain about how students from elite universities head to Wall Street, but that's exactly what Adam did.

He found himself with a job offer from Bain, one of the world's most successful (and some say ruthless) consulting firms. And when you hear Adam's explanation of what he learned, you understand why he made this seemingly superficial decision: "I went to work at Bain & Company on the consulting side and just went through this incredible training work with absolutely brilliant people, saw the inner workings of Fortune 500 companies, had exposure to how the best businesses in the world were run and even improved upon."

Are you seeing now? Yes, that moment in the street in India changed Adam, but he knew besides handing the kid a pencil, there was nothing much he could do for him in the way of real change. Adam went to work in corporate America precisely to learn the skills, build the relationships, and earn the money he needed to effect the change he wanted to see. In other words, unlike so many young people who find themselves with good jobs at places with names like Goldman Sachs, Google, and BP, Adam wasn't doing it for himself or for the money.

"I realized about a year, year and a half in, two things. The first was that the nonprofits I was passionate about weren't run with any of the business acumen that I was used to seeing." There's no question most nonprofits have their hearts in the right place, but according to Adam: "When you're actually inside of the organizations, they're incredibly inefficient. It's because they're usually based on passion. So the language that I spoke, the sense that I had around business, it was kind of weird and frustrating to me that these humanitarian issues weren't being approached with the same commitment to results."

There was another benefit from being around sharks in suits. He realized he didn't want to be one, not for very long anyway. "I got really bored of meeting people at a bar and them asking, 'What do you do?' and my answer being, 'Well, I'm a 23-year-old management consultant.' That's a really boring conversation after about the fifth time. In a year and a half of living in New York as a young, 20-something single male, I was living what I thought was this great life. I had this sick apartment and access to awesome parties and dating different girls and had great friends around, but I wasn't connected to anything that wasn't in service of myself."

That's when it hit him: "I didn't want to be a management consultant. I wanted to be somebody who builds something—specifically, schools internationally for children in rural communities. That's who I wanted to become." But now he had the skills and support to be able to do it.

Bain allows their employees to take what they call "social impact externships" that offer hands-on experience working on important educational and development problems out in the world for 6 to 9 months. Essentially, if you make it through the first 2 years of employment at the firm (what amounts to a probationary training period) and they promote you on to a third year, in that third year they let you leave and follow your passion. You don't get paid, at least not by Bain, but you can work for any approved program or company that will bring you on (and potentially pay you). Adam decided he would do one of these externships. Initially, he thought he might work with an organization called the Cambodian Children's Fund that he had been volunteering for since college as a fund-raising coordinator selling T-shirts, throwing parties, and doing pretty much anything that might help these kids.

Then one night shortly thereafter, he went to the New York Philharmonic for the first time. "I'd never been to a symphony before, and this guy walks out onstage to play a piano concerto and just starts crushing these keys. He was exuding so much passion into this instrument. I was just mesmerized by it."

Not only was Adam mesmerized, he was inspired. The same way that pianist felt about his music, Adam wanted to feel about . . . anything, really. "I just wanted to feel that passion, I wanted to feel alive the way that he must when he connected to that piano. And in that moment is when this name literally just popped into my head: Pencils of Promise. It was the perfect name."

It was sort of his Jerry Maguire moment. "I went home, wrote everything that I could on paper—like an original mission statement, a charter, a manifesto, all these stupid fund-raising ideas, all the people I would contact wherever I would travel who I thought could help me try to build the school, the very first one. I was really committed to building the first school and dedicating it to my grandmother, who was turning 80 that year. She is a Holocaust survivor and has just been through so much so that I could be in the position I was in."

He thought, "Let me live in service of her, in particular, honoring her, carrying forward her legacy, and then ultimately educating children in poverty who don't have access to high-quality education."

A few weeks later, he went to the bank to open an

account. He asked the teller what the minimum amount required was—the answer was $25. And with that, he launched Pencils of Promise with a $25 check and never looked back.

THE RIGHT KIND OF ROI

The organization he built meshed Adam's for-profit business acumen with his nonprofit idealism, a model that attracted me. For a few years prior to meeting Adam, I knew I wanted to start giving back and serving others outside of my business, but I didn't know how or what to do. After meeting Adam, I decided this was something I could get behind because even though I never felt like I was a smart kid growing up, I was drawn to learning, I yearned for knowledge, and I valued every type of education on my path to success. I got involved with Adam's organization and donated money to build a school in Guatemala.

Part of the mission of Pencils of Promise is to have the local community take ownership of their school. To do that, the community must build the school themselves. The organization supplies the materials and a contractor with know-how, but the mothers and fathers build the school. The result is an enormous level of pride and stewardship. Investing their own sweat equity, they are determined to keep the school maintained and functioning. I love this mission and follow these principles in my own business with my students. I provide the content, oversight, materials, and tools necessary through my podcast, products, and services, but I don't "do the work for them."

If I did, I'd be enabling them instead of empowering them to use their own genius and talents to learn the skills by executing. This way, they can reap the rewards and have much more ownership and pride in what they create.

Talking to Adam is uplifting and inspiring. "As much as I'm a passion-driven person, my background helped immensely because I'm now an entrepreneur who filters every decision through the question 'Will this provide long-term ROI?'" he said. "I always wanted to build an organization with the head of a great business and the heart of a humanitarian idealist."

Think about that: He's not referring to a return *for him.* He means, how can the organization best be of service and deliver the most value to the people it's meant to serve?

I heard a similar sentiment from Angel about his philosophy as a CEO at Deckers: "Greatness to me is just about being there for other people; living a life that is others oriented is where you achieve greatness." That's how Angel tries to think and act as a leader of more than 2,300 employees with their own stories, dreams, hopes, and needs. "Deckers is about all the people who work here having the kind of opportunity that I had, to live a life that maybe is outside of your expectations or your practical reality or that you dream about but don't have the vehicle. I say, 'Here is the vehicle.'"

That's what a true leader, a really great individual, does, whether they run a for-profit or a for-purpose organization. It's not all about you; it's not all about what you want and need. If you want to achieve those things, I've learned, you have to actively and regularly help other people with their own wants and needs. Only then, when you've moved away from selfishness, can your winning team truly thrive.

In our self-centered world, it's easy to buy into the "me" mentality. We are constantly told that to get ahead, we need to invest in ourselves, and then once we've "made it," we can give back. But as Adam Braun's story shows, giving back can be the vehicle to "making it" if we align our service with our passion. Without service, achievement is empty.

A LONGER, RICHER LIFE

James Clear, the entrepreneur and travel photographer, wrote about this on his blog after reading a 2012 *New York Times* article about the research on longevity:

> The article didn't come out and say it, but what it alluded to was that as people age, they tend to find themselves consuming more and creating less. To put it bluntly: The easiest way to live a short unimportant life is to consume the world around you rather than contribute to it.
>
> Meanwhile, the people who keep on contributing tend to be the ones who keep on living. The message was clear. People who contribute to their community live longer.

If greatness isn't a good enough reason to be of service to others, I think James has given you the biggest reason of all—a longer life. Still, I get why you might be hesitant. *Service* is such a loaded term. Fortunately, being of service also has many definitions and iterations. It doesn't mean you have to work in a soup kitchen or take a vow of poverty or work for a nonprofit.

One of my favorite TED talks is by a guy named Ron Finley, who is known as the "guerilla gardener." For years, he has been planting vegetable gardens across South Central Los Angeles. Why? For fun, for the beauty, for food, and to make a small contribution to a neighborhood that desperately needs it. I love this because he isn't asking for anything in return, nor does he expect someone to pay for these services. He simply does this as a random act of kindness to give back and make his community that much more colorful and fruitful. He takes pride in his community and adds his gifts to it. It makes me think about creative ways I can add to my community as well.

Kyle Maynard is of service to veterans—even though he isn't one himself and his injuries were biological instead of the result of violence. But by connecting with these service members, by seeking out challenges and bigger goals, he provides an inspirational service.

Shawn Johnson speaks on behalf of the Women's Sports Foundation, which was founded by tennis legend Billie Jean King back in 1974 to boost the lives of girls through sports and physical activity. Shawn's taking everything she learned from her Olympic and dancing success and paying it forward to a generation of young girls who might need the same kind of boost that the little boy in India needed from Adam Braun.

The other side of my buddy Aubrey Marcus, the CEO of Onnit who gave us the exercise on what's MISSING in Chapter 5, is essentially one giant quest to serve humanity by exploring the possibilities of human happiness and consciousness. He wants everyone to transcend everything, and he works exhaustingly and selflessly to that end—through his dedication to researching the optimal ways for total human optimization using the success of his fitness and nutrition business to make it possible.

I get the sense from many of the authors whom I've learned so much from that they would have written their books for free if they had to. They not only felt that some sort of muse had struck them and they owed it to their art to get it out, but they genuinely felt the world needed to hear their message and would be better if they read it.

I don't think traditional charity is the only way to act with purpose or be in service of others. Every day, I wake up and feel excited about my podcast not because of the important people *I* get to meet but, rather, because I get to serve as a conduit between them and my audience. I get to learn and help others learn, too. That thought has also helped power me through this book.

That's my point: You can be of service by following your passion. As Adam Smith wrote, "It is not from the benevolence of the butcher, the brewer, or the baker that we expect our dinner, but from their regard to their own interest." Following your passion instead of settling, subsuming yourself as part of a larger goal—that is the first step in being of service to others. But I hope you won't stop there. I hope you'll also see how you can apply your gifts to a big cause and give back without any strings.

Like many successful people, I receive requests for lunch meetings or get asked for advice by people just starting out. They want free coaching, introductions, or a perusal of their business plan. I'm busy, my time is valuable, and the temptation is to say, "Look, I'm sorry, but I don't have the time." And who would fault someone for declining a request for free help? The answer to that question is *you*. You and I, if we are to be great, need to practice empathy and help others. We need to think: "I was once in this person's shoes, and someone helped me out." Like Kyle and Shawn and Aubrey and Angel, we should always be paying it forward.

I'm not saying you need to give an hour of your time to everyone who asks for advice, as you may never get anything done in your own life if you are that popular! However, maybe this means taking a few extra minutes to help a new coworker. Maybe it's pointing out something you noticed in a competitor's game that would help them improve. Maybe it's speaking at your kid's career day. Maybe it's writing an article about a sensitive topic that most people are too ashamed to share their experiences about. Maybe it's smiling at a stranger on the street or helping them pick up something they dropped. For me, it was starting *The School of Greatness* podcast so I could help all those people I couldn't reach or carve out the time for.

It took me a long time to understand how crucial a life of service is to achieving greatness in any discipline. Adam Braun clearly got this early on and parlayed that insight into an amazing career as a social entrepreneur.

Nelson Mandela put it best when he said, "There is no passion to be found playing small and settling for a life that is less than the one you are capable of living."

But Adam realized that thinking about yourself, your bank account, or whatever it happens to be is thinking small. As he puts it, "My definition of greatness would be living a life full of purpose, love, and dignity."

I'll add to that: *for yourself and for others.* I know what you're capable of. I know you can be of service in so many ways.

EXERCISE #1:
Choose Your Avenue of Service

Get involved in giving back, whether it is through your time, talent, or treasure (dollars).

Step 1

Write down something simple you can do *today* to give back to your community, family, and friends or a stranger. Your service can start as a random act of kindness. You could open a door for someone, buy flowers for a stranger, give a compliment, fill someone's expired parking meter, help someone in need, or simply smile. Give back in some way with a positive purpose. You will immediately experience the intrinsic reward whether the act is seen or unseen.

Doing this on a consistent basis, you will quickly find

yourself living a life in service to others that does not feel like it is taking away from some other part of your life. Instead, it will feel additive and necessary—like eating or breathing. As your daily acts of kindness grow, you can research a charity, a nonprofit, or an organization you would like to get involved with. Here is some food for thought.

- Education in your community
- The arts (dance, music, theater)
- Advocating for human rights
- Mentorship programs
- Cancer research
- Fund-raising

The possibilities are endless. Whatever you are inspired by and speaks to you, that is exactly what you should be doing. If an organization is not working for you, start your own! Anything is possible, so get involved and spread the word. There are tons of opportunities out there. Stop thinking about what people will say or how they will look at you and be proud to take a stand for the service you have chosen.

For specific organizations that I believe in and more suggestions, check out schoolofgreatness.com/resources.

Step 2

After deciding on your avenue of service, identify how you can best serve it through your time, talent, or treasure.

Time

Some of us have more time to give and can volunteer directly. Offer your time to volunteer with the organization of your choice. Be consistent, whether it's weekly, monthly, or yearly, in order to create a positive habit.

Talent

You might have a certain talent that organizations need (maybe you're great at graphic design, and an organization needs help with their logo or Web site development). Reach out to these organizations to offer your expertise. Many organizations have a tremendous vision and all the hustle in the world, but they struggle finding a great team. You can be the difference.

Treasure

If you do not feel like you have the time or talent to give directly to an organization, financial donations impact growing organizations disproportionately. Sending $1,000 to the Red Cross is great, but giving $500 to your local veterans group or pediatric cancer charity can change their month. This month, commit to a monthly donation to a campaign or a cause.

Now make a decision about how you intend to get involved and write it down. Make it real. One or all of the three *T*s? Then choose a date that you are going to begin and prepare to take action!

EXERCISE #2:
Do Your First Act

Short and sweet, you've got to put your money (or time or talent) where your mouth is. This month, go do something with and for your organization of choice. This can be actually volunteering at an event, organizing your own event/fund-raiser, or donating money or goods. As in exercise #1, start small with simple daily acts of kindness and build upon them.

Not only will this get you serious about helping, but you'll also get to feel that amazing high of doing good. Of course, this is worth sharing, so once you've committed to your act, post to your social media channels with a photo and an update to let everyone know what you are doing and how it went (#greatnessbook). This is a great way to encourage and inspire others to get involved. The only thing more contagious than giving is the joy and the emotion that come with it!

COACHING TIP

When you fully understand why giving is the key to life, then you make it part of your daily mission to serve others in whatever you do. Don't look at this as an extra task you need to take on. If you do that, you've missed the point entirely. Rather, look at this as a part of who you are, who you become, and your way of being in every moment.

It needs to be in your breath, rushing through your blood. Every aspect of your life should have a component of service. It can be as small as smiling at everyone you come across to as big and broad as you want to take it. There is no right or wrong level of giving; the key is just that you give from a place of love instead of guilt. The way I am sure to do that is a little trick I developed after flying all over the country speaking to and meeting with people just like you. I remind myself of that part of the preflight safety announcement that every flight attendant gives:

Put your own mask on first.

When you make sure your needs are met and you are full, then you'll have even more energy to give to others. Go out and live a life of service!

CONCLUSION

In 2012, I moved from New York to Los Angeles for a girl, arriving with two big bags, a guitar, and a smile on my face. Later that night, she broke up with me. What made it worse was that my life in New York was on fire before leaving for LA! My business was thriving, my relationships were growing, I was doing cool stuff all the time. I felt invincible. This move out to LA for love was just one more thing I was going to conquer. Instead, it put me right on my ass.

We were in our mid- and late twenties at the time, so of course our breakup wasn't actually final. We got back together, dating off and on for a few months. I committed to being the perfect boyfriend, doing everything I could do to make my girlfriend happy and our relationship healthy, but I knew it wasn't right, it wasn't working. Everything about LA wasn't working, really. I was in a bad head space. Everything that was happening left me frustrated, confused, and uncertain about the future. I would soon learn that, as my friend Kyle Maynard says: We are only as good and as strong as our adversity makes us. Sometimes we don't know what is working against us until we make our biggest mistakes, and I was about to discover that on the journey to greatness, you sometimes have to fall.

One afternoon I was playing pickup basketball at the courts down the street from my condo building when everything came to a head. I had been guarding this one guy all game—he was a little older than I was and defi-

nitely a little heavier—and he had been talking trash and
throwing dirty elbows the entire time. Now, I'm a relentless
competitor and have been in all areas of my life for as long
as I can remember. I can take some trash talk and some
hard fouls in the spirit of competition. But this guy was
starting to get personal, and he was trying to assert himself
over me—dominating me, like an alpha dog.

What he didn't know—and neither did I, really—was
that this behavior was one of my major triggers. Being dis-
respected and dehumanized made me see red. We got in
each other's faces. There was a lot of shouting and postur-
ing, literally puffing out and beating our chests like a couple
of gorillas trying to show dominance. I was beside myself
with anger. I couldn't understand why he was doing this to
me. Then he took it a step further and head-butted me right
in the face. This was no warning love tap, like you see sometimes in NBA games when two alpha dogs square up against
each other after a hard foul around the basket. I couldn't
believe how hard he slammed his forehead into mine!

If you've never been head-butted, let me tell you, it
hurts! It makes you see stars, and it makes your eyes
water. And if you're me, it makes you lose your mind a little. I am not proud of what I did next. I pounded on the
guy with every ounce of energy I could muster. Eventually, my best friend, Matt, whom I was playing with,
grabbed the guy, and his teammate pulled me off to break
us up. Unfortunately, it didn't end there. The guy was still
talking trash and insulting me, and I was screaming at
him, asking why he would do that to me. Why would he
head-butt me like that? What was he thinking? Why did
he attack me over a meaningless pickup basketball game?

The questions were rhetorical, mostly. I was basically talking to myself, trying to process what the hell was going on. But this guy decided to answer. I don't remember what he said—it was all kind of a blur—but whatever it was, I responded by running up to him and hitting him one last time as hard as I could.

It was one of those moments like out of a movie. The basketball court went dead quiet except for the sound of my yelling and screaming. I was yelling at everyone, telling them that he hit me first, and I was screaming at him for attacking me. I still couldn't understand it. My friend Matt told me I should get out of there before anything else happened, so I ran. No, I *sprinted* the blocks back to my building, bounded up 11 flights of stairs, burst through my apartment door into my bedroom, and collapsed onto my bed shaking uncontrollably. What the hell just happened? I felt completely out of control and completely terrified of my own behavior.

That's not me. I'm not a fighter. I aspire to come from a place of total love. Why did I react like that?

I repeated those words to myself over and over in my head. The feelings I was being forced to wrestle with were almost totally foreign. I hadn't felt like this in nearly 20 years—since the last time I got into a similar fight as a kid. Lying on my bed looking up at the ceiling, I started thinking about that earlier fight. What I realized very quickly was that this fight was practically a carbon copy of that one.

It happened when I was 12 years old, back in Ohio. Three of us were raking leaves and grass along a path on the golf course where we worked during the summer. Two of us were goofing around and roughhousing. We were playing this game where we'd rake up a little bit of grass, then flip the rake over and flick the grass and leaves at the other person, almost like you'd pick up and throw a lacrosse ball. It was a fun little grass fight. We decided to bring the other kid into the fun. He was older than we were (15), so we decided we couldn't ask him—that probably wouldn't be cool—we would just have to tag-team him a little. The two of us scooped up some grass and leaves at the same time and flicked it at him simultaneously.

At the time, we cracked up, thinking he would join in and playfully fight back. We were half right. As we turned back to keep grass-fighting each other, the 15-year-old kid came up behind me and punched me in the back of the head. I was stunned. Then I was confused. Then I was stark raving furious. All within the span of 2 seconds, I whipped around and hit the kid square across the face with my rake handle. The blow sent him to the ground, and I pounced him. I hit him with everything I had, screaming at him the whole time like in that scene from *A Christmas Story* when Ralphie finally snaps and beats the snot out of Scut Farkus.

Finally, the other kid got behind me and pulled me off in a full nelson. I shook free and sprinted the 500 yards to the clubhouse, where I burst through the employee entrance, ran into the bathroom, and started washing my hands. Like if I washed away the evidence and got home before anyone else saw me, it meant it didn't happen. My knuckles were scraped bloody. Dirt and grass and blood poured into the sink and swirled down the drain. When I finished and stopped shaking, I came out into the office and there was the 15-year-old. He was screaming at me, "Why did you do that, Lewis?! What is wrong with you?!" I barely heard him, because I was sick to my stomach

about what had just happened. Seeing what I was capable
of when I let my emotions get the best of me, I vowed
right then and there to never fight again.

I succeeded in upholding that vow . . . for 17 years.
Lying on my bed staring up at the ceiling, a 29-year-old
man with bruised and bloodied knuckles, connecting the
dots between those two moments and seeing the paral-
lels, scared me to death. I had to do something about this.
I had to figure out what was going on inside of me and
why. What had happened to me? And most important,
why did I allow this to happen?

Two months later, at the suggestion of my friend
Quddus, who'd heard about the fight and the troubles I
was having, I signed up for Chris Lee's leadership workshop. Little did I know, being an effective leader requires
emotional intelligence, and that's a lot of what we covered.
We talked about triggers and being open and vulnerable.
All the stuff we discussed in Chapter 3: Cultivate a Champion's Mindset. Why did being attacked unfairly like that
turn me into the Hulk? Why was perceived disrespect or
feeling taken advantage of such a trigger for me?

Chris helped me trace these emotions back through
my life, teaching me how to be vulnerable and open to my
past. And that's when it clicked. It all went back to the
time when I was 5 years old and I was raped by my
babysitter's teenage son. I won't dive into specifics,
because that is not what this book is about.* What I will
say is that after opening up and sharing this story with

---

*If you want to hear the full story about what I learned about this experience and the
good that has come from it, my dear friend Jonathan Fields interviewed me in episode 61
of my podcast.

listeners of my podcast, I was overwhelmed with love and support from all over the world. I also came to realize just how many people have been affected by sexual abuse in their lives. Listener after listener e-mailed me emotional, heartbreaking stories about their childhood traumas. It pains me to see how many people have experienced their own version of what I went through.**

Before attending this workshop, I had never shared that story with anyone. I'd kept it locked inside for almost 25 years, trying to forget it, trying to deny that it ever happened. But I couldn't anymore. It had planted these triggers in my mind that were starting to sabotage every area of my life—my romantic relationship, my friendships, my business partnerships, my overall confidence and happiness.

With Chris's guidance, I stood up in front of the group at his leadership workshop and shared the story publicly for the first time. And it was a revelation. I had been too scared, too hurt, too superficial to look deep down inside myself and face my own past until that moment. We all have traumas. We all have secret pain. We all make mistakes. It's true. I wish it wasn't so, but it is.

That's the bad news. The good news is that we're all *also* capable of greatness no matter what we've been through. In fact, it's our past that makes us who we are and our adversity has the potential to become our greatest advantage. You see, the breakdown I experienced in my life which exploded on the basketball court earlier that year led to a profound and life-changing breakthrough. I didn't know I was holding onto that kind of

---

**If you are a male who has experienced sexual abuse in your life, check out 1in6.org for more information and guidance. For general support, check out rainn.org.

rage inside nor that I was capable of being so violent. Going back into my memories and becoming aware of the stories I had told myself about the pain I experienced as a child was one of the keys to moving from reacting to responding in my life. I was truly disappointed in myself after that incident, and I committed to discovering what was holding me back from really being the man I said I was and wanted to be. By clearing and coming clean about my past, I was able to align my actions with my values and learn new ways of showing up in the world that were previously counterintuitive: Things like cultivating a win-win environment in everything I do, seeing the power in vulnerability, acknowledging my emotions, and holding myself accountable to my vision every day.

THE SCHOOL OPENS FOR BUSINESS

I began *The School of Greatness* podcast in the months between my big fight on the basketball court and my time with Chris. My first guest was the brilliant *New York Times* best-selling author of *The 48 Laws of Power*, Robert Greene, and we were going to talk about his (then) new book, *Mastery.* Just being in Robert's presence, this man who had not only written several classic, timeless books but had influenced multiplatinum rappers, fashion designers, and world leaders, was inspiring.

As we sat and talked, Robert spoke about how much time and energy and effort it takes to become truly skilled at something. It had taken him decades to get to where he was, and it had taken the greats of history he wrote about just as long, if not longer. He talked about the critical importance of apprenticeship and studying under other masters. That's where I got the idea to craft my own curriculum, to enroll in a new kind of school where I could learn and reach my potential. The title of that first episode with Robert on my newly launched podcast, *The School of Greatness,* was "How to Master Anything and Achieve Greatness." I wanted to do both those things very badly.

Like anything new on the Internet, the podcast had its ups and downs at first. I was learning as I went, trying new things, figuring out most of it all by myself. I had no idea what I was doing. But I also didn't know what I didn't know, so anything was possible. Shortly after Chris's workshop, *The School of Greatness* podcast began to take on a new life and renewed energy. Regular listeners noticed a huge change in the way I connected with guests, how open I was, and how my ego had shifted. I'd learned so much from Chris—and the lessons I learned about myself from his workshop had quite literally changed my life.

The goal now was not just to learn from great, interesting people but to finally get serious about the goals and vision I had for myself as a young man. Yes, I'd accomplished some things in life, but I wasn't fully happy. I knew I could do more. I knew I wanted more. So I availed myself of some of the greatest minds, thinkers, and doers in the world. I put myself at their feet and learned everything I could.

The chapters you've just read are the essence of that education. They are my lecture notes, filtered through the experiences and struggles I've gone through in trying to integrate them into my life.

From Angel Martinez I learned the power and importance of creating a clear vision. He taught me that *you*

become what you envision yourself being. I will never forget those words.

From Kyle Maynard and Nicole Lapin I learned that there is no room in our lives for excuses, especially if greatness is our goal. Greatness is what happens when your talent and your vision face adversity, and you persist in the face of it to learn the language of the new, the scary, and the unfamiliar.

From Shawn Johnson I learned that greatness is not about making it to the top of the medal stand. It is a mindset that is fundamentally about belief in yourself and your ability to accomplish your goals.

From my brother, Christian, I learned that there is no shame in hustle. If you want to be great, you have to work harder and smarter. When something knocks you down—when someone says no—you have to be able to pick yourself up, dust yourself off, and do it all over again.

From Rich Roll, Chalene Johnson, Aubrey Marcus, and Shawn Stevenson to many other wellness masters I've studied with, I learned the importance of physical health to greatness, no matter what the dream or the vision. You have a choice—to move, to eat well, to sleep right—and that choice, if you don't make it soon enough and completely enough, *will* stand in your way on the path to greatness, no matter what else you bring to the table.

From my old buddy Graham Holmberg I learned that it's never too late or too insignificant to develop and practice positive habits, no matter how naturally talented you might be. Those habits are the backbone of the routine that will inch you closer every day to greatness.

From Scooter Braun I learned the critical role of build-

ing and leading a winning team to the pursuit of any kind of great achievement. Strong relationships with great people who have positive energy are fundamental to that team.

From Adam Braun, I learned the power of being in service to others. I learned that you don't have to wait until you make it to serve the world. In fact, being of service, in any number of different ways, can be the path to making it.

And now that we're near the end of the book, I have another thing to say: This isn't the end of the road. This isn't a typical school. There is no graduation ceremony. There is no cessation of classes or summer break. The School of Greatness is sort of like the Hotel California: You can check out anytime you like, but you can never leave. What I mean is, these lessons will stay with you always—and their application should never end.

I also mean this in the sense that you can't get kicked out either. Lord knows I should have been expelled, banned, or written off for my inexcusable violence. Or I should have been placed on academic probation for the times I slacked off and reverted to old bad habits— despite my professors' having taught me better. But that's not how this works. That's not how *life* works.

Greatness is a voluntary degree. Its study is self-administered. That means *it's all on you.* And you get out of life what you put into it. I hope you pursue it with everything you've got. I hope we bump into each other learning from the same master. Actually, I hope one day I might even take a course from you, and you a course from me.

We're in this together. It's time to go out there and do something great!

ACKNOWLEDGMENTS

Thank you to my family. I'm so blessed to have you all in my life and constantly learn from you as your youngest brother and child. To my father, Ralph, who taught me that time was an illusion and that my age and experience level didn't matter in my pursuit of greatness. You supported all of my dreams, taught me they were always possible, and helped me do whatever it took to make them a reality. You are the best dad I could have ever asked for, and I'm so grateful to be your son. To my mother, Diana, I'm the luckiest child in the world, and you've always supported my crazy ideas, even when they scared you. Thanks for letting me finally play football at 15, even when you were scared I would get hurt. I did get some bruises, but I had years of fun and learned many lessons that made me who I am today. To Chris, you are my hero and the brother I've always looked up to. Your hustle taught me how to be the driven human I am now. To Heidi, my spiritual protector and voice of reason, thank you for opening my heart and guiding me toward love. To Katherine, without your support while living on your couch for over a year (rent free), none of this would have been possible. You are the definition of unconditional love.

To every teacher, house parent, and coach I had during my experience at Principia schools, thank you for giving me structure and guidance I needed the most during that time. You exemplified living a life of service. To Brian Morse, Tom Bania, and Ann Pierson—thank you!

Seven years prior to publishing this book, I read the book *The 4-Hour Workweek* by Tim Ferriss that influenced me to start my journey. Thank you, Tim, for opening my mind to what is possible so I could create the life of my dreams.

To my agent, Stephen Hanselman, thanks for believing in me. You supported my vision to write the book that I've always wanted to publish. Your guidance has been legendary, and this book wouldn't be this great without you. To Glenn Rifkin, Ryan Holiday, Nils Parker, and Heidi Howes, thank you for your many months of support in the crafting, massaging, and editing of this book so that the world can receive my vision in a powerful way.

To Marisa Vigilante, Mary Ann Naples, Gail Gonzales, Yelena Nesbit, Aly Mostel (along with Amy Stanton and team), and the entire family at Rodale, along with Jeffrey Capshew, Melissa Miceli, Holly Smith, Elena Guzman, Nora Flaherty, Patti Hughes, Eve Fitzgerald, and the rest of the powerful army! Thanks for your countless hours and support in getting this out to the world!

To my three main mentors, Stuart Jenkins, Frank Agin, and Chris Hawker, who believed in me when I was broke and broken and had nothing but a dream, you all stepped up when I needed support the most early on. I'll always be grateful for your level of service and for giving so much to me when I could do nothing for you at the time.

To my team that supported me for countless hours during the writing of this book, Matt Cesaratto, Sarah

Livingstone, Brittany Rice, Christine Baird, Aja Wiltshire, and Diana Howes—thank you! We are making a powerful impact together!

To Ian Robinson, thank you for guiding me early on with my podcast editing, and to Pat Flynn, Derek Halpern, Ramit Sethi, James Wedmore, and John Lee Dumas, thank you for the inspiration to launch it.

To everyone who has been on *The School of Greatness* podcast, this wouldn't be possible without your incredible wisdom and lessons that you shared with all of us!

Robert Greene, Bob Harper, Tim Ferriss, Bryan Clay, Graham Holmberg, David Anderson, Grant Cardone, Drew Canole, Rich Roll, Jamie Eason, Alex Day, Lissa Rankin, John Romaniello, Adam Bornstein, Adam Grant, Ben Nemtin, Don Yaeger, Kyle Maynard, James Altucher, Pat Flynn, Shawn Johnson, Jon Acuff, Jeff Spencer, Quddus Philippe, Carl Paoli, Leyla Naghizada, Tony Blauer, Ameer Rosic, Chris Hawker, Travis Brewer, Mignon Fogarty, Nick Onken, Aubrey Marcus, Chris Lee, AJ Jacobs, Marc Ecko, Derek Halpern, Danielle LaPorte, Gary Vaynerchuk, Guy Winch, Daniel Negreanu, Sean Stephenson, Christian Howes, Adam In-Q, Josh Shipp, Simon Sinek, Marc Fitt, Charlie Hoehn, Steven Kotler, Liz Wolfe, Adam Braun, Alison Levine, Chris Ducker, Simone de la Rue, Glennon Melton, Jennifer Paige, Alexis Carra, Ryan Holiday, Bryan Bishop, Noah Kagan, John Jantsch, Joe De Sena, Timothy Sykes, Carmine Gallo, Chris Bailey, Jason SurfrApp, Jordan Harbinger, CJ Baran, Ramit Sethi, Bo Eason, Tucker Max, Branden Hampton, Brendan Schaub, AJ Roberts, Brett McKay, Scott Barry Kaufman, Jim Afremow,

Chris Guillebeau, Hunter McIntyre, Chalene Johnson, Dave Asprey, Mike Michalowicz, Tim Larkin, Christine Hassler, Dan Schawbel, Kevin Kelly, Krista Tippett, DJ Irie, Kelly Starrett, Tim Ryan, Daniel Amen, Vanessa Van Edwards, Bill Harris, Ryan Blair, Jairek Robbins, Tony Robbins, Robbie Rogers, Michael Hyatt, Rory Vaden, Jim Kwik, Yuri Elkaim, Scott Harrison, Keith Ferrazzi, Baratunde Thurston, Eric Thomas, Shawn Stevenson, Angel Martinez, Michele Promaulayko, Scooter Braun, Nicole Lapin, Donald Schultz, Mikkel Svane, Vani Hari, Marie Forleo, Peter Bregman, Marc Goodman, Jack Canfield, David Allen, Kabir Sehgal, Julianne Hough, AJ Hawk, Todd Kashdan, Amanda Enayati, Eric Greitens, Abel James, Jeff Goins, Than Merrill, Dorie Clark, Lee Cockerell, Dale Partridge, Amy Wilkinson, Rob Bell, Jay Papasan, Cassey Ho, Sally Hogshead, Arianna Huffington, Kristina Carrillo-Bucaram, Bill Phillips, Jeff Krasno, Gretchen Rubin, Matthew Hussey, Darren Hardy, Kimberly Guilfoyle, Dan Millman, Donovan Green, Suzy Welch, Justine Ezarik, Jacob Lief, Tom Bilyeu, Prince Ea, Nick Symmonds, Rick Hanson, Laird Hamilton, Gabrielle Reece, Jackie Warner, Fabio Viviani, Bryan Johnson, and the future guests that will inspire the world!

To all my friends and supporters, thank you for being there and inspiring me every step of the way!

INDEX

Underscored page references indicate sidebars and tables.